The Fifth Horseman

The

RANDOM HOUSE . New York

NATHAN M. ADAMS

Fifth Horseman

Library of Congress Catalog Card Number: 67-12728

First Printing

The author is grateful for permission to quote from *It Came
to Pass* by Nahman Byalik. Copyright 1938, and renewed
1967, by Hebrew Publishing Company, New York.

*For those who know the difference
between God and Country
and wherein allegiance lies.*

The author wishes to thank the World Jewish Congress and the Institute of Jewish Affairs for their co-operation and assistance.

The Fifth Horseman

"An otter came one day and complained before King Solomon, saying:

"'Alas, my lord and king; was it not thou that didst spread good tidings of peace and truth to all dwellers upon the earth in thy time? Didst thou not likewise ordain peace between one wild creature and another?'

"'And who had broken this peace?' asked Solomon.

"'I went down to the water,' answered the otter, 'to hunt for food, and my whelps I had entrusted into the hand of the weasel. But it rose against them and destroyed them. And now the blood of my innocent children crieth out to me, Death to the Slayer.'

"And the king demanded that the weasel be brought before him, and he inquired of it:

"'Was it thou that slew the otter's children?'

"And the weasel said:

"'It was I, my lord and king, but as the king liveth, it was not with intent or evil purpose. I heard the woodpecker as he thundered with his beak, giving forth the sound of the drum, proclaiming the summons to war. And so it was that as I sped to the battle I trampled on the children, but it was not with evil purpose . . .'"

——HAYYIM NAHMAN BYALIK,
from "Whose Was the Blame"

PROLOGUE

BERLIN

April 30, 1945

Kampass sat on the cobbled stones of the alley like a stuffed panda.

His arms rested by his sides, palms up, in a gesture that was as much hopelessness as it was fatigue. His head, shaggy-haired from the sweatband of his helmet, nodded on his chest.

Now, peeping from under heavy brows, he watched the corpse of the *Wehrmacht* Lance Corporal that lay where he had propped it against the wall. Its uniform had been removed and was piled nearby. The corporal had no face—only a pink scoop of skull ; a ghastly sort of a runcible spoon.

The worst part of it, thought Kampass, was undressing it, forcing himself to touch it. Then he began to weep very softly as though he were afraid he might hear himself.

Kampass could not recall when last he had cried but it had been a long time ago, and he had no idea why it became necessary to do so now except that it was as undeniable a biological function as passing bad food. So he cried, his eyes oysters afloat in tears, the corners of his mouth tugging down, so that his features became at once those of an outraged clown.

After several minutes Kampass rose unsteadily, sniffing, and unbuttoned his tunic. Then he stepped out of his pants. In the field-grey cocoon of his long underwear, he walked with mincing steps to the corporal's discarded uniform.

He shook out the corporal's pants and donned them, and then shrugged into the tunic. The shoulders were soggy with blood and Kampass' thick, hairy forearms protruded from the too-short sleeves. He adjusted the heavy GOTT MIT UNS buckle over his middle, and very tired now, re-dressed the corpse in his own uniform, which bore the insignia of an *Oberscharführer, Allgemeine SS*. Finally he exchanged identification discs, starting as the corporal's ice-cold tag made contact with the bare skin of his chest.

He paused, looking around him uncertainly until he spotted the corporal's Schmeisser. He picked up the machine pistol, and snapping back the lock, sighted along the squat barrel at a point where the corpse's tunic buttons formed a junction with its belt.

Corporal, thought Kampass, Lance Corporal Speirling who sat out his war in the Spandau barracks fornicating with *Abwehr* secretaries and the girls in the air defense center; Speirling, whose first look at war was the last terrible, sputtering seconds he had watched the Russian stick grenade bounce towards him before it exploded and blew his head off. Speirling.

The shots lashed out, ear-splitting in the silence of the alley. Kampass held hard against the climb of the barrel. The corpse bucked and kicked as the bullets tore into and through it, punching it flat onto the cobbles.

A cat, terrified by the noise, shot out of a doorway and cringed against the wall near a mound of rubble.

Kampass changed magazines on the weapon and collected the brown briefcase that lay at his feet. He walked over and picked up the cat.

"It's all right, cat," he said. "I won't hurt you." His ears were ringing. He could hardly hear his own voice.

The cat was grey and stank of cordite. He could feel it warm and trembling against him and he saw one of its hind legs was smashed.

"Swine," he said. "What kind of people make war on cats?"

With the cat secure under his arm, Kampass walked to the end of the alley where a building stood, disemboweled by the Russian shelling. He set the cat on a mound of debris with the briefcase.

"Guard that cat," he said.

He went to his knees, digging at the loose brick and mortar with the wire stock of the Schmeisser. When he had made a pocket, he inserted the briefcase. Before covering it over, he snapped it open. He looked at the neatly stacked packages of pound notes inside.

"Yes," he said.

He covered it with bricks and then rose and stared around him, fixing the place in his mind. He tucked the cat into his tunic so that only its head showed.

At the opening to the alley, he stopped and drew his bayonet. On tiptoes, he scratched the words KAMPASS ALLEE high on the dirty brick wall. He stepped back and regarded the name, which stood out like chalk graffiti, the remains of his identity.

He was going to be all right, he thought. When the occupation came, he would get a job somehow. He would have to survive until he could return to the alley for the money. For a moment he had thought about giving it back. But to whom? You could not return it to dead men. He could not share it with Speirling. Certainly he could not take it back to the safe in the Foreign Section branch of Gestapo Headquarters on Prinz Albrechtstrasse.

The idea that the money might be counterfeit was chilling. After all, he thought, it could be. They were using it to bank agents in the Middle East.

It was the only windfall he ever had and he had decided to take his chances with the money. He was very lucky, he thought. Luckier than Lance Corporal Speirling; luckier too than his former commandant, *Standartenführer* Vogel; Vogel, the bird that had flown the coop.

Three days earlier they had given him orders to destroy files and documents in the Internal Security Section. He came across the *Feldpolizei* circular quite by accident. *"SS Standartenführer* Rudolf Vogel," it said. "Sought for desertion in the face of the enemy, complicity, and cowardice." Then the details. He wondered if the Headhunters had caught him. If so, he would be hanging from a streetlight now with a sign around his neck and the crows picking out his eyes.

"Yes, lucky," he said to the cat.

Well, that was over, Kampass reminded himself. Like the name on the wall, he was rid of it: finished with the business of waging war and all that went with it.

For the last time he looked back at the corporal. It was convincing enough, he thought. They would find him, someone, in the uniform of an *Oberscharführer*. The stitching of bullets across the chest would prove Lance Corporal Speirling died in the uniform he wore. As for the smashed skull, well, Ivan often mutilated SS casualties, Kampass knew. He had seen enough of his own casualties in Russia, their heads bashed in by rifle butts.

Kampass eyed the array of medals and badges pinned to the tunic: the Iron Cross First Class; yes, he remembered how that had been when he and two others held up the Russian advance for nearly a day in the snow at the rail junction outside Moscow; and the Tank Fighter's Badge; yes, he had earned that all right and it had cost him half his stomach; and the hand-to-hand combat clasp, that too.

"No matter now," he said. That was all part of what was behind him.

He resettled the machine pistol around his neck so that it sat over his chest. With his new-found friend, the cat which stank of cordite, Kampass slipped out of the alley and onto Berliner Strasse. At the corner he crouched briefly beside a shattered Panther tank whose turret hung askew on its mountings, the long snout of the seventy-five millimeter Pak gun pointing towards the sky like a twisted finger accusing God for what had befallen it.

Then he moved off, dodging through broken buildings and heading due west towards the flak towers at the Zoo from which still came the distant rapping of machine-gun fire.

The sky was lit on the horizon with the flicker of artillery and somewhere, somehow amidst destruction and the death rattle of the city, a radio was playing. Kampass heard it. A woman was singing in a high, wavering voice.

EXPEDITER

*"In the forests I make believe I am my
shadow and my shadow is me."*
——*Bruno Kampass, age seven*

NEW YORK CITY
December 18, 1964

For a man twenty years on the run, Kampass
lived remarkably close to his clock. Time, he learned, was the
only fact you could trust.

At night Kampass would stare at the ceiling and listen to
the steady tick-tocking of this clock, which was of brass and
stood on his bedside table staring at him through the gloom
like the luminous eye of a great animal. Sometimes he would
count the ticks and sometimes the tocks.

But now, in the morning, Kampass peered over his pillow,
through the window at the rain. There was soot and fly ash
on the glass, and beyond it the world was grey. In the middle
distance the Manhattan skyline jabbed concrete fingers into
low clouds, and as if puncturing them, released a rain which
sprayed over the city, greasing the street below and reducing
the traffic to clogged confusion.

Kampass found difficulty focusing back to the clock. It was
seven-thirty.

"Fifteen minutes," he said. He had beaten the alarm by
fifteen minutes. Still, after twenty years, he was holding his
own. He thrashed his legs against the warmth of the sheets,
rolled, grunted, and reluctantly allowed his feet to fall to the
cold floor. But as he bent down for his bedroom slippers, he
had the distinct and sickening sensation that if he stooped a
quarter of an inch further, he would topple from the edge of
the world.

So he immediately sat bolt upright in his bed and gripped the sheets until his knuckles whitened. Then it went away.

For Kampass it was anything but new. Each day he did battle with vertigo, and lately found himself going to bed at night dreading the arrival of morning.

He put it all down to his drinking, which he found himself unable to stop. The habit began soon after the end of the war and slowly crept up to him, drew even, and then passed him forever. It was now a matter of keeping it in sight; of making a competition of it, if only for the gallery of his own conscience; for the sake of honor.

Rid of his vertigo, Kampass removed his white pajama tops and began his floor exercises, starting first with the push-ups, moving rapidly through fifty sit-ups, and ending with a flourish of running in place; his well-splayed feet going pad-pad-pad on the floor, once tight but now flabby pectoral muscles jouncing, and middle-aged buttocks jig-a-jiggling beneath the pajama bottoms as if they were partners in the throes of a grotesque dance.

Kampass believed floor exercising would offset the softening influence of drink. This rationalization made the burden of alcohol easier to bear. Besides, it was his firm conviction that man, a creature of habit, was most content when regulating himself to a strict regimen. Kampass, although a nonresident member in the family of man, obeyed his own conception of society's rules.

After his workout he carefully entered the elapsed times of the exercises on a chart cellotaped to the wall above his bed. He wrote in "10 min."

"Wizard," he said hoarsely. *"All right."*

Next came a hot and cold shower and shaving in the shower, which he had devised to regain the time he spent exercising.

Stepping from behind the plastic curtain and growling like a bear, he toweled himself briskly. He paused to gingerly dab at a great scar which spread over his lower belly like an obscene grin. Furiously he brushed his teeth, and then blew up into his nostrils to determine if his breath stank.

It was indeed important to take care of oneself, he thought. Personal hygiene was an integral part of the Kampass regimen. So also was vanity. But as his face stared back at him from the mirror, there was a feature he could not accept and that was his nose, which seemed to have been placed by mistake—a smeared hunk of putty lined with tracings of tiny, broken blood vessels. Not a few, because of the nose, took Kampass to be an ex-prize fighter. He did little to dispel the misconception. Once he even went so far as to tell somebody he sparred with Max Schmeling before the war. He considered the white lie little enough compensation for the nose, which was shattered when a drill sergeant slapped his face with a carbine butt for insubordination in basic training.

Curiously enough, Kampass imagined his face attracted women, who perhaps thought his brutal features handsome. Maybe it was the cretinlike nose; possibly his eyes, which were pale blue and set in tight to his nose. A woman once told him they reminded her of a sniper's eyes. He had not understood what this meant, but he took it as a compliment. Really about women he could not care less, for long ago he found himself unable to communicate with them sexually or otherwise.

He sprinkled some talc under his arms, sniffed again, and then whipped his thinning, blond hair back so that it lay like a second skin over his skull.

"Wizard," he chimed again. *"All right."* He congratulated himself on a hard-won victory of time and toilette.

So this then about Kampass; if his honor competed with his drinking excesses, the competition extended to life itself, which had become now finally a contest with trivia.

He finished dressing, and before the cracked mirror over the bureau, adjusted the astrakhan cap that perched on his overlarge head like a party favor. Then he made a final entry on the chart opposite the space reserved for *"Time Out,"* collected the morning paper where it lay damp at his door, and locked up.

At the entrance to the building, he nodded curtly to the doorman, who as usual ignored the greeting, since Kampass had neglected to give him a check for either of the two Christmases he had been in the building.

"Mr. Speirling," the doorman addressed him coldly. "Mr. Cudlipp would like to have a word with you this evening." Then the doorman smiled.

Cudlipp was the building's superintendent and what he wanted to talk with "Mr. Speirling" about was, Kampass knew, the disposition of his garbage. There was a disposal chute across the hall from the apartment, but Kampass never bothered to use it. He would stuff his leftovers in a wax bag and balance it against the wall outside the door. Among other things, he paid a hundred and ninety-five good dollars a month to have it collected. The hell with Cudlipp.

"And there's something else," said the doorman smuggly. "You got a violation."

"What means this, violation?" The rain dripped off the canopy and he unfurled his umbrella.

"You screwed around with the wiring in your apartment. It blew the board in the basement."

"No I didn't," said Kampass.

"Oh, yes," insisted the doorman. "Yes, yes. Con Edison had to send two men yesterday to fix it. They said the wires were all fooey in your apartment. They checked your living-room sockets."

"They were in the apartment, Karl? You let them in?" asked Kampass.

"And you got a violation," replied the doorman, nodding vigorously.

"I do not touch wires," said Kampass. "I do not play with electricity."

"Maybe it was the tenant before you, but you got the violation, okay?"

A passing car threw up a fountain of water from the gutter, splashing Kampass' trousers. He cursed and skipped back. He turned to the doorman. "Two men? Two of them?" he asked. He spoke quietly now. He was beginning to get the old feeling in the pit of his stomach.

The doorman said, "I was with them. They was Con Ed."

He smiled again. "Don't worry, they didn't take nothing."

Maybe, thought Kampass.

"You isn't the only one," added the doorman. "There was two others in the building."

Kampass relaxed. Just a little. But the feeling in his stomach did not go away. He squared off and held the sharp end of the umbrella under the doorman's nose. "You don't let nobody into that apartment, see," he said. "Nobody ever." He shook the umbrella to bring it home.

The doorman took a step backward. He said, "Talk to Mr. Cudlipp about that."

"Your ass," said Kampass. Then he moved out from under the canopy. He tilted his square face to the sky, letting the rain wet his skin. He readjusted the astrakhan, put up the umbrella, and walked down Eighty-sixth Street towards the bus stop on the corner of Second Avenue.

"What's up there, Mr. Speirling?" the doorman called out after him. "You got some girls working?"

Kampass did not rise. He kept walking, passing a Salvation Army Band that was setting up its instruments in the cold rain. He watched the cracks in the pavement disappear beneath his feet. He counted exactly seventy-eight of them between the canopy and the bus stop.

●

The five-story brownstone across the street, number 416, stood empty and sullen in the rain. A large blue and white signboard outside read A.M. CRANE—CANARSIE—DEMOLITIONS. Then there was a brief description of the new apartment building that would soon rise on the site; a scaffold had been hoisted to the second story. Little pools collected on the sidewalk and were dimpling with the rainfall.

From a third-floor window of the semi-gutted building, Jacob Ben-Zvi watched Kampass' retreating figure until it reached the bus stop. Then without looking up from the heavy range-spotter's scope which rested on its tripod by the sill, he said, "Time check, Isaac. He's away."

His partner, who had been dozing on a tattered sofa, stretched, yawned, and sat up. He looked at his watch. "Zero-eight-oh-nine," he said.

Ben-Zvi made a notation on the clipboard in his lap. "Would you please call Dumpling," he asked. "Tell him *Expediter's* off."

Isaac reached down to the foot of the sofa and removed a field telephone from its canvas case. He spun the crank and blew sharply into the receiver twice.

Except for the sofa and two easy chairs the room was bare. Several coffee containers sat in a row on the floor and there was a collapsible Sterno stove near the window.

Isaac talked into the phone. "Good morning, Dumpling. We checked *Expediter* out at zero-eight-oh-nine. Lovely." He replaced the phone and turned to Ben-Zvi. "Tohar is with him," he said.

Ben-Zvi pushed away from the window, rolling his head on his shoulders to loosen the tight muscles there. He wiped at the tears that had formed in his eyes from the cold that sliced over the sill. He looked at the room. "What a dump," he said.

"Beats wiping diplomatic behinds," said Isaac.

"Depends on who the diplomat is," said Ben-Zvi.

•

From the bus Kampass watched the rain become snow: soft and puffy flakes that floated down to melt on the pavement without dignity.

The bus was jammed. Passengers groaned and strained against each other. Individuals frowned at other individuals in early-morning testiness. Kampass took refuge in the folds of his newspaper, which he wrapped closely about his face.

The paper led with story of the Congo massacre, which he had been following dutifully from day to day. The headline read:

STANLEYVILLE FALLS TO PARAS

His eyes flew down the column. By the time he reached the end of the eyewitness account, it was he himself who once again shared rations with front-line troops. It was readable stuff, he thought. But the heat of battle died when he could not shake open the paper to the continuation of the story because of the bodies that pressed against him. Irritated, he lowered the paper to find himself facing a squat Puerto Rican woman. The woman stank of garlic. Kampass gagged, turned his back, and came eyeball to eyeball with an army private who was wearing tinted sunglasses and chewing gum so rapidly that it made little crackling noises between his teeth. Kampass stared into the sunglasses for fully a minute, trying to penetrate through to the eyes of the soldier. Then he became aware he was only looking at his own reflection on the lenses. His head, distorted by the curvature of the glass, looked like some form of hybrid kumquat.

He had no idea whether his stare was being returned. Intimidated, he averted his eyes from the private and looked out the window at the traffic, which was making slow progress against the snow.

He had noticed a patch on the sleeve of the private's green uniform. Underneath the emblem of a black staircase, gold lettering edged with red proclaimed SEVEN STEPS TO HELL. Kampass recognized it as the insignia of a regiment on duty in West Berlin.

The peacetime army, he thought, keeping-the-peace-on-their-ass. The private's arm brushed his and he moved back as if he might contract some strange, communicable disease. There was no doubt of the issue in Kampass' mind. The days of good, honest soldiering were over with, he thought. Now there were only peace demonstrations by people who dressed and smelled badly, and the rank and file of soldiery had deteriorated.

Then, as he often did on the bus, Kampass turned off. His eyes locked on an advertisement for a karate school and he was immediately several thousand miles and twenty-odd years into the past. He was back in Russia and he was remembering how it had been for him and the others that hot and dusty but glorious summer of forty-one:

... in reserve near Lukov, Panzer Group Two including his own unit, the XLVI Panzers, they waited in the cool dawn until the bridges over the Bug were secured. Then they raced across, following the tanks and the scout cars. The rolling plains of the Soviet Union lay open all the way to Kartuska. Everywhere farmhouses were burning, and swelling columns of ragged prisoners passed them on the roads. The stench of burning flesh mingled with the smell of new hay.

Overhead, Stukas snarled and then the snarls changed to moans as they dove on the Russian resistance beyond the Berezina. His outfit fought hard for that bridgehead near Brodets, Christ yes. It was the first time he heard bullets that were aimed personally at himself. Snip-snap they went; like opening and closing the cigarette lighter he carried. He, Kampass, lay in the fields, in the stubble, with the stock of the LMG hammering against his cheek and shoulder. Wizard. God Christ, yes. Then he was up and running, the linked ammunition belts flapping around his neck and the LMG lead-heavy in his arms. Down again, keeping Ivan's head in the grain with short bursts; tap-tap on the trigger like so until one of the others worked around and threw in a grenade from the flanks. Damn Jesus. Then all at once they had broken Ivan's back. There was no more resistance. He took off his mottled battle smock and uniform and plunged into the Berezina, laughing and playing water tag with the others. And afterwards he listened to the tree frogs and tuned in Lala Andersen's songs on the wireless in one of the scout cars.

The others: Willie, the butcher from Hannover with his big butcher's arms; Heinrich, the coaler from the Ruhr and his dirty coaler's jokes; Christian, a history teacher from Coblenz, whose steel-rimmed glasses were always steaming up—all dead. All but he.

The summer had to end. They did not reach Moscow and in the ice and the snow, they died. All but he. But that summer of forty-one, Wizard.

Well, he, Kampass, knew something of a hell that was not

sewn on sleeves and the distance to its gates was considerably
less than seven steps.

"What's that, sport?" The soldier was talking to him.

Kampass blushed. He must have been thinking aloud.

The bus doors hissed open on Seventy-second Street, and
with a blaring of trumpets and a crash of drums in his head,
he descended to the pavement.

The soldier watched him go, noted the martial stiffness of
his gait, and grinned.

●

Ben-Zvi stared hard at the telephone as though he were
tempted to eat it. He said, "Always it's the waiting. It's nearly
two."

"He'll call," said Isaac.

"Yes. I know he will," said Ben-Zvi. He ran a hand over his
unshaven cheeks, making a sound like sandpaper on wood.
He rose from the chair beside the field-phone pack and
walked to the window. He watched the snow falling on the
city, not saying anything and rocking on the balls of his feet.
Below, on Eighty-sixth Street, he could hear the Salvation
Army Band. They were playing "Good King Wenceslaus" and
the instruments belted the brassy notes out happily at the
pedestrians who scuttled past like sand crabs before a breaking wave, faces puckering in the cold and the snow. Absent-
mindedly Ben-Zvi sang the words along with the band under
his breath; ". . . on the Feast of Stephan when the snow lay
round about, deep and crisp and even." He was thinking his
forty-five days and nights of watching and waiting were
nearly over. And he murmured:

> "Hither page and stand by me,
> If thou knowest, telling,
> Yonder peasant, who is he,
> Where and what his dwelling?"

He is Bruno Waldek Kampass thought Ben-Zvi and he lives

across the street and I have gotten to know him so well that I can tell you the brand of toilet paper he prefers. I could tell you about the nights he sits alone at his kitchen table, chewing his food thoughtfully and staring out into the blackness; eating as if only to stay alive. Some people pick their nose and eat it, he thought. But Kampass' habit was infinitely more damning. He must have been cultivating his loneliness for twenty years. Now, after a month and a half, they could see what it had made him. It was not pleasant to watch. It bothered Ben-Zvi and he would ask himself, how is it you are disturbed? Why are you concerned with a man who exterminated seventy thousand human beings?

> "Sire, the night is darker now,
> And the wind blows stronger;
> Fails my heart, I know not how,
> I can go not longer."

Ben-Zvi ran his hand over the fat packet of air tickets in his coat pocket. Shortly, *Expediter* would be Leinhardt's problem, not his. They always left that part of it to somebody like Leinhardt; someone who did not have a bone to pick; somebody who, if things blew out, you could deny. Yes, they would have Leinhardt run Kampass.

What was expeditious about Kampass? Ben-Zvi had wanted to know at the briefing in London nearly two months before. Shoval told him, "Never mind. Deliver him." Shoval ran *Shin Beth*'s apparatus in Western Europe and North America and so Shoval had to be right about Kampass.

> "Mark my footsteps, my good page,
> Tread thou in them boldly:
> Thou shalt find the winter's rage
> Freeze thy blood less coldly."

He did not like Leinhardt. None of them did. Leinhardt was contract labor, a ringer; Leinhardt, who waited in London for them to deliver *Expediter*. As far as Leinhardt was concerned, Ben-Zvi thought, justice and patriotism were financial convertibles, debentures. Conviction for Werner Leinhardt was the name of a crater on the far side of the moon. But Shoval was the boss. Shoval hired and fired and Leinhardt was his property—selected, bought, and paid for.

"Never mind. Just you never mind," Shoval had replied again to his objections. "He was very good once and he's all right now. Besides he's hungry and it might be a dirty job."

Well, if it were up to him to condemn the two of them, thought Ben-Zvi, Kampass for what he had done and Leinhardt for what he was, the choice of punishment would be even.

"The hell with Kampass, anyway," he said aloud. "The hell with Kampass and Leinhardt and Shoval and the hell with Christmas."

"Surely, Uncle, you don't mean that," said his partner. "I say God bless 'em."

Ben-Zvi turned away from the window. He went to the sofa and let his broad wrestler's back relax against the soiled cushions. "I don't know," he said. "After all this it's a little anticlimactic. It's like a good film you've seen too many times. It's not so good after a while."

Isaac said, "I still don't trust Shoval. If something blows, we're the ones on the block."

"There you are, lad," said Ben-Zvi. "That's insight for you."

"He's a gut-fighter, that bastard."

"Yes indeed."

"If there's a flap, I'll bet he told them to drop us in the mire."

"Count on it."

"This isn't Eichmann," said Isaac. "This isn't Argentina. They don't go for political kidnapping. You know what you can get for it here? You know what they give you in New York? They could give you death. That's what they can give you." He started to pace the floor, turning quickly at each end of the small room like a cat in a cage. He went on. "Shoval hasn't informed the State Department. Not even CIA. We can't have immunity. If there's a flap, they're not going to like it. No sir. He's a naturalized citizen and nobody wants a mess like this in their backyard, particularly the Americans." He paused in mid-stride and held up a forefinger as if testing the wind. "Suppose. Suppose Kampass decides to go to the State Department, or even worse, the police. He'll get press attention and we couldn't enter him in a kindergarten much less what Shoval has in mind."

Ben-Zvi shook his head. "He won't," he said. "He wouldn't dare. We can give him his life back and not even God would do that for him." He got up from the sofa and walked to the window. "Why the hell doesn't Tohar call? What's keeping him?"

"Forget it," said his partner.

Ben-Zvi slid his hands into his pockets and worked his fingers around the loose change. He looked at the snow. "How old are you, Isaac?" he asked.

"Me? Twenty-seven. Why?"

"Because you really don't know what it's all about, do you? You weren't even an idea."

"I'm a Jew."

"Not enough," said Ben-Zvi.

"Yes it is."

"Well, I'll tell you . . ." said Ben-Zvi. He paused as if weighing what he would say next, the skin tightening over his high cheekbones. The lines of his face looked as though they had been permanently seared there by the sun. It was a face that might have seen a lot of life, little of it, perhaps, pleasant. "I'm forty," he said. "I remember how it was for us then. And even to me, it's still an anticlimax." Rather distantly, he added, "But I'll tell you what; if there *is* a flap—only a tiny one—I'm going to ticket him."

"There's your anticlimax," said Isaac.

The field phone made a buzzing noise.

"There he is," said Ben-Zvi.

Isaac opened the pack and picked up the phone. "Hello, Dumpling," he said. After a moment he hung up. He made a violent breaststroke in the air.

"We're washed out," said Ben-Zvi, interpreting.

"No sir," said his partner, grinning. "We drew the green light. We're still on for tonight as planned."

"Get the check list. I want to run through it again."

•

Now it was three in the afternoon and Kampass was reeling.

He sat in the office of his one-man, one-room travel agency on the second floor of the brownstone between Third and Lexington on Seventy-second Street, his back to the desk, facing the window.

He examined the pigeon guano caked on the window ledge. He stared at it as though concentration might make it go away. Then, holding himself carefully erect, he turned back to the desk and wrote on a piece of scratch paper "Cleaning woman—shit on window." He impaled this on a spike he kept handy for such memoranda. Briefly he regarded the small plaque which hung on the wall across from him, occupying the place of honor in the dilapidated office:

MANFRED SPEIRLING
GROUP AGENT OF THE MONTH

APRIL 1963

Kampass had been awarded the plaque by an airline for routing a large group of nuns on charter flights to a religious festival in Brussels. The plaque was a kind of stamp of approval in wood and brass and he was very proud of it. Directly below the plaque was a photo of Kampass receiving the award from the airline's agency sales manager. The manager was smiling; Kampass was not.

For the third time that day he looked at his appointment calendar. Little had changed on it since he last checked it. Lines were drawn through scribbled notations and chores covering the morning hours, for Kampass crammed as much of his work as was possible into the morning hours. He knew how things would go in the afternoon.

At the very bottom of the desk calendar he had written a memo to himself: "Eastern Region Travel Agent's Assoc.— Americana Hotel—Travel-o-rama." They were holding the annual travel-agent's ball. It was the one function of the year Kampass looked forward to without some sort of misgiving.

This evening he could "take off the gloves" as he liked to put it. He would savor the delights of—well, nearly—taking part in the human experience. He would relax. He remembered how he passed out in a plate of hors d'oeuvres just a year ago.

Kampass picked up a half-eaten pastrami sandwich from the desk and bit into it; the mustard was bitter on his tongue and crumbs of dry bread fell from the corners of his mouth onto the desk. He wrinkled his nose and tossed the remains of the sandwich into the wastebasket. Then he tried to shake off the quiet desperation that came with his drunkenness. For some people, he thought, a woman might turn the trick: might make the time pass.

Only once in his life had he tasted of the forbidden fruit. The Russians began shelling the farmhouse as he was about to mount the peasant girl. Kampass had been flushed out to seek safety in the fields, pants and dignity rumpled about his ankles. The Russians thought the farm was being used to direct artillery fire. The barn was hit by a Katyusha and all the livestock, the pigs and chickens, were killed. So was the peasant girl. That was the way it had always been with him, thought Kampass; he was a child of circumstance.

And here he was, he meditated, shut away in this office with the world passing him by on every side and only bill collectors and salesmen knowing he was there watching it all. He knew, of course, what really was at the root of it; it was this monstrous lie he had forced himself to live.

Kampass often suspected that Brandt, the immigrant barber on the first floor, somehow saw through it all; Brandt, the ex-*Panzerjager*, a Sudetenlander who fought in the grit and sand of the Mareth line. It was the way Brandt looked at you, he thought. Kampass, coming in for work, would climb the stairs to his office, heavy-footed, and he could sense Brandt's eyes on the back of his neck. Once he paused on the first landing and quickly turned. There it was, Brandt's bald pate, fringed with a rind of monkish hair, looking around the door to his shop. Brandt always wanted to know why Kampass never mentioned the war. Brandt was not Kampass' barber. He talked too much; asked too much.

Then there had been the business of the electricity that morning; his talk with Karl, the doorman; the two men in his apartment. It had given him a bit of a fright. You could be so careful. Security was something he was meticulous about and still he was never sure.

The telephone on the desk rang, cutting through his gin-fogged brain. He considered not picking it up, but the nagging ring would not stop.

"Speirling Traveltours, Speirling speaking," Kampass said. He emphasized his irritation by hoisting himself in the chair, posing on one cheek, and passing wind with a loud croak.

The caller was a Mrs. Bernice Rosen, a rather old customer of some standing in Kampass' good books. She wanted reservations for herself and her daughter aboard the liner *Shalom*. It had to be the last sailing in December, she specified, the Carribbean Cruise—the Bagel Ferry, as they knew it in the trade.

"What's the mean temp. for January, d'you know? The temp. for Jamaica?" she asked.

Kampass fumbled through his top drawer for promotion literature on Jamaica, found it, dropped it on the floor, snatched it up and said, "Seventy-nine degrees."

"And sweaters at night, I suppose?" She had that harsh voice of a middle-aged woman who knows she is on top of things.

"It's suggested," said Kampass. As he gave Mrs. Rosen the details of side tours available on the cruise, he drew two triangles on his note pad, superimposing one upon the other until they formed six points of a star.

"Say, you don't sound so good," observed Mrs. Rosen.

"Cold," said Kampass.

"Well, Merry Christmas, Mr. Speirling. *Enjoy!*"

"Yes," he said and replaced the phone. He jotted down the name of Rosen and adorned it with curlycues under the star, tore off the sheet, and spiked it on top of the message to the cleaning lady. Then he called Zim Lines and made the booking. They wanted to know about the cabin space. He said, "I'll confirm it tomorrow."

Tomorrow, he thought. His life was made up of tomorrows. Well, he consoled himself, at least he performed a service. He was not taking up space and wasn't this the whole point of it, anyway?

He opened his desk drawer and looked at the nine-millimeter Walther pistol that rested there. He removed it and laid it on the desk blotter, studying it thoughtfully. He owned no ammunition for the Walther, which he had purchased out of whimsy on an agent's tour of Mexico City. During working hours he would move it from the safe to his desk. There had been two recent travel-agent robberies and he did not want to be ambushed in his own office. He had no ammunition, but this did not bother Kampass. The pistol gave him a small degree of comfort. It was also a reminder of the ultimate alternative to his masquerade and his misery. Maybe that was why he never bought ammunition. Deep down, Kampass did not quite trust himself.

He pushed himself away from the desk, and collecting the pistol, walked to the center of the room. He was very drunk and now, master of all he surveyed, he raised his arms from his sides, and ever so slowly, began to turn. He shuffled, circling and dipping about the room with outspread arms as though performing a rain dance. Past the chipped desk he soared; past the spike with its two forlorm memos; past the peeling safe. He performed a banking maneuver around the ancient typewriter and alit back in the center of the room like a crippled turkey. Then he stumbled, lost his balance and fell, talking all the time, saying, "Oh God, bless us. Wizard!" He held the pistol aloft as though he had fallen into a gigantic puddle and did not want to get it wet. Finally he pulled himself erect.

Kampass drew a deep breath. He yearned. He wanted to go home. If there was an umbilical cord, if there ever was and it had been cut, he would like to splice it back together. He pictured himself floating off through space like a balloon trailing a never-ending length of string and he laughed. It was a cruel joke. For him, there could never be a home. It was fiction of his own mind. But he thought about it anyway:

Altenau, nestled in the rolling, wooded slopes of the Harz-wald; Little Altenau-near-Torhaus in the shadow of the nine-hundred-meter high Bruchberg; the quiet mountains and the gingerbread *Forsthausen* right out of Hansel and Gretel. There had been stags, fat and lush-coated in the late summer with the velvet still thick on their antlers, and in the winter, the damp-cellar smell of snow—and the forest so quiet under its blanket of white that Kampass, as a child, imagined he heard organ music. He remembered the biting ring of the axes against the cold, hard trees and trying to catch the chips as they flew out from under the bladed—the neat squeak of pried wood and the charcoaly stink of his father's jacket. And Old Metz with tanbark hands, the village *Jager* who had been a sapper in the Great War, thrilling him with stories of the trenches at Verdun; the charges, the orderly attacks, and how they went off against the wire and the British Lewis gunners. But Metz never told him of death or pain or of suffering. Metz did not tell him how to endure; Old Metz, the *Jager* and his boar hounds.

"Balls on rye," said Kampass.

He secured the office for the night, replaced his ticket stock in the safe, and weighted it with the pistol. Back stiff, he negotiated the stairs to the front door. The wind hit him like a hammer. So did the cold. It had stopped snowing. Kampass belched, and walked west.

A mass of humanity flowed and jostled like a turbulent river trying to go back on itself and he allowed himself to be carried along, teetering precariously when he was brushed against, but recovering at the verge of collapse and enduring with wooden-soldier strides.

He crossed Park Avenue, walked a block farther past Madison Avenue, and then turned downtown. Fifth Avenue sloped gently away from him, afire with Christmas decorations. Roars of busses mingled with the ding-dong of bells. Whisps of steam rose from manhole covers in the street as though a subterranean beast lay breathing below. At Sixty-third street he tripped over a collection-kettle tripod and sent the pot crashing to the pavement.

"Hey, Jesus, man," said the Santa Claus attending it. "Chrize, c'mon now. Pick it all up." Kampass could smell the beery stench of the man's breath. He walked away. "Hey, you bastard."

A group of young carolers dressed in red cassocks with broad white collars had gathered at the fountain in front of the Plaza Hotel. They sang in German, their falsetto voices smoking in the cold air. An obese choirmaster in a green loden-coat with staghorn buttons directed them with short jerks of his beefy arms.

Kampass walked to the edge of the crowd surrounding the choir. He waited until the end of the carol, and as the boys thumbed through their sheet music, he moved forward and placed a hand gently on the shoulder of the child nearest him. The boy turned, his blonde hair stirring in the wind.

"Don't be frightened," Kampass said. *"Du bist deutsch?"*

The boy nodded solemnly.

"Woher kommst du?"

"München."

"Ah, München," sighed Kampass. But as he looked at the boy now he read distrust in his face. The child glanced down at the hand which rested on his shoulder. Kampass let his hand fall. The child turned his back. The choirmaster had placed his hands on his hips and was watching Kampass narrowly.

He winced. They take me for a pervert, he thought. They think me one of *those*. How wise they are, children, to such things today. My God, what have *they* done to them.

"Scheiss!" he said vehemently, and he spat on the pavement. Kampass walked on to Fifty-third Street and the Americana Hotel. His head was clearing. He was feeling better.

•

Kampass stopped at the desk by the door to register and picked up his identity card, which he pinned to his lapel. The card bore the words HOWDY, I'M MANFRED SPEIRLING. The

"MANFRED SPEIRLING" was written with grease pencil.

The main ballroom was crowded and the warmth of it made his face burn after the cold of the street. The Association's official greeter who welcomed him at the door did so a bit too politely. He also remembered last year and the disgusting spectacle of Kampass being scraped from the canapé tray. "Keep an eye on Speirling there," he told an aide standing nearby. "Remember last year." It sounded like a sales slogan. Kampass heard it. He couldn't care less.

Kampass threaded his way through the crowd of agents and airline men to the stand-up bar in a corner of the ballroom. He desperately sought a familiar face and found one at last in Walker-Jones of BOAC. In the Englishman, he recognized a potential companion for the evening.

"Harry Speirs," quipped Walker-Jones. "Think Yiddish, dress British."

It went over Kampass' head.

"Hello, Jones," he said seriously, eyeing the thin face.

It took Kampass exactly three pink gins to regain the level of intoxication he had reached that afternoon. But Kampass, like many an alcoholic veteran, was a stoic drunk who seldom showed it until he was at the brink of losing consciousness. Then he became boisterous and aggressive for a short spell— a light bulb blazing before permanent blackout.

Midway through the fourth gin, Walker-Jones became involved with a Slovak travel agent on the subject of Puerto Rican immigration and how to benefit from it.

Kampass, frowning, standing to one side like an obedient Alsatian, listened stonily, trying to find something he might contribute to the conversation.

At last he blurted out: "Me, I came to America with my bare ass, a bad figure, and a tambourine in my stomach." It was simply capital, he thought. Supremely wizard.

The two men stared at him. Kampass looked quickly away and sipped at his drink. The liquid ran down both sides of his mouth and onto his tie.

"There's a slob," said the Slovak agent.

Kampass overheard the remark, but it did not matter, not in the least. His annual metamorphosis had arrived; his once-a-year melding with the world. Ecstasy grew until he could not stand it without shouting for joy. The bulb began to blaze.

"Hey!" he shouted, and without warning vaulted to a chiar and waved his arms for silence.

Agents and airline men looked up, startled.

He began with the Pledge of Allegiance: "I pledge allegiance," he shouted, "to the flag of the United States of America and to the republic for which it stands!"

"Belt up," cried Walker-Jones, who tried to haul him down from the chair.

"Balls," Kampass shouted back gleefully. "You British mouthful of Kleenex."

The official greeter stood on tiptoe, looking over the crowd so that he might determine the nature of this disturbance. When he spotted Kampass atop the chair, he suddenly looked like a man who had swallowed a bee.

By the time he finished the Pledge of Allegiance, Kampass' accent had thickened and sentences were pouring forth in a patois of German and English.

My God, how I love them, he thought as he gazed down at the shocked, upturned faces. *And they do; they love me.*

"Sieg!" someone shouted.

"Sieg Heil," Kampass shot back, grinning.

"Who was the third President of the United States?"

"Jefferson," he barked. "Ha! Ha!"

"Who freed the slaves?"

"The slaves?" asked Kampass loudly. "Why, don't you know? Does no one know? It was me. *Me!*"

This was greeted by a roar of laughter and catcalls of encouragement. He was fabulously alive—fabulously and forever drunk and he hoped it would never end. From out of the sea of faces a waiter's uniformed arm stretched up towards him. It held a brimming glass of champagne. Tottering, but held upright by many arms, Kampass plucked up the glass.

"Mein Herr," he said to the waiter, whose face had grew into many faces, "and my thanks to who?"

The waiter smiled.

"Prosit, anyway," said Kampass. He drained the glass and threw it over his shoulder, where it smashed against the wall.

"Now," he said, turning to face his audience. "Now, I . . ."

He got no further. It was as though an icy hand slipped up his rectum and wrenched at the lower intestines there. He pitched from the chair as if shot.

"That's it," said the greeter.

The group that had gathered about the fallen Kampass suddenly opened like a flower as he came alive, rolling onto his stomach and vomiting into the carpet, his shoulders and back heaving.

There was a muddle among the onlookers as individuals volunteered to help and then retreated as a fresh flow of bile gushed forth. Someone snickered. The greeter said and did nothing. He stared at the stricken Kampass with resignation.

A tall man pushed his way through the knot of spectators. He knelt beside Kampass and gripped the nape of his neck, which was now beet-red.

"I'm the house doctor," he announced. "What's happened?"

"He fell off the chair," said a woman.

"Don't be an ass, he's pissed," said Walker-Jones.

"Drunk?" said the doctor, glancing up. "Yes, he's drunk. He may also be very sick. It could be his liver. He drinks?"

"You might say that," volunteered the Englishman.

The doctor's eyes settled on the waiter, who hovered uncertainly at the fringe of the crowd. "You," he ordered. "Give a hand here. We'll put him upstairs."

"You the hotel doctor?" asked the greeter.

"That's right."

The greeter did not recall anyone summoning a doctor, but his prompt appearance was a godsend.

Together the doctor and the waiter hauled Kampass to his feet. His face was a mask of pain: lips drawn down at the corners and stained with vomit and his eyes rolled back in his head so that only the whites showed.

"Phewy," grunted Walker-Jones and he held his nose.

"It's not funny," said the woman beside him. "He might have had a heart attack or something."

"Not bloody likely," said Walker-Jones.

With Kampass sagging and drooling between them, the two men struggled towards the kitchen annex and the service elevator. Kampass' feet danced on the carpet and there was a smattering of handclaps as they disappeared.

It was all very vague to Kampass, who did not remember falling from the chair. But he was aware of the sour taste of vomit in his mouth and the wet pile of the carpet against his lips. For one ridiculous moment he imagined the morning's sensation had become a reality. He had indeed tumbled off the edge of the world.

He was borne away on a cloud suspended in limbo, and below him earth slowly turned on its axis, and it was true what they said after all, he thought—there was a life hereafter.

What brought him back to reality was the sensation he was having a bowel movement. Voices sounded from somewhere far away, distorted, as though coming from an ancient gramophone that needed winding. Then he was moving again; it did not matter where. He was going home.

"Metz," he called out to a face that swam before him. "Metz."

●

"*Alles in Ordnung?*" asked the face.

Kampass groaned. Gradually life returned, dribbling into his body, beginning at his feet. He raised his head. He saw he way lying on a sofa in a room that might pass as an attic and a stocky man was bending over him. The man had planted one crepe-soled foot on the cushions.

"*Kaffee?*" asked Jacob Ben-Zvi.

Kampass felt a huge void in his stomach and he put a hand down there to make sure nothing was missing. His tongue was dry and rough and it refused to leave the roof of his mouth. Somewhere, he thought, a telephone was ringing. "I'm sorry," he said. He could not think of anything else to say at the moment. He could not think at all. His voice sounded as though he might be talking through a pillow.

Ben-Zvi removed his foot from the couch. "Introductions are in order," he said in German. "My name is Dorn." He pointed across the room. "That's *Herr* Kaufmann."

He could see the man was seated in a lounge chair, reading. As his name was mentioned, Isaac looked up and smiled pleasantly.

Kampass had never seen either of them before. He supposed they were at the party. He guessed they had taken him someplace after his seizure. But they did not look like airline men. They were too much alike, as though they might be partners in a tag-team wrestling act. Their names did not register. The room smelled like old wood. He could see the ceiling was discolored and flaking.

"*Kaffee?*" repeated Ben-Zvi.

Kampass blinked, groggy, and tried to face the back of the sofa to get away from the light. What he wanted was sleep. He felt awful. After a while it would go away: the bright light, this room, these odd people. He would arise in the morning and he would beat the clock at its own game and he would have vertigo. It was as certain as tomorrow itself. He laid his head on the cushions.

Ben-Zvi grasped Kampass under the arms and turned him around, sculpturing him upright. Then he stepped back as if to admire his handiwork, but Kampass slid sideways.

Kampass' eyes flew open like sprung window sashes as a palm smacked against his face with stinging force. And again.

"Hey," he yelped. "Hell." Kampass was awake.

Ben-Zvi said, "I'm sorry, but the doctor gave orders. You can't sleep. He said you might not wake up."

Isaac, still reading the magazine, laughed. There was something about the laugh that was not as pleasant as his smile.

"Alert now?" asked Ben-Zvi, putting his face an inch away from Kampass'.

"Yes," said Kampass. He stared at the man stupidly. His face had a deep tan, but it was pinched as though he had bitten into something sour. There was something else. He realized for the first time the man who called himself Dorn was speaking German. Although Kampass counted in his native tongue when pressed or drunk, he had rarely spoken it conversationally in twenty years. It was like going back to baby talk. He wondered dimly why they insisted on German. So in English he asked, "Where is this?"

"The Garden of Allah." The answer was still in German.

Isaac cackled and flipped a page of his magazine. The noise the turning page made was quite loud in the small room.

Something was terribly wrong.

"You are airline men or what?" asked Kampass in German, feeling a little for the words.

Ben-Zvi flipped open a wallet and handed Kampass a card. It said *Ivan Dorn, Sales Representative, Icelandic Airlines.* The address given on the card was Reykjavík. He went to the window. The shades were drawn and there was a tiny coffeepot resting on a contraption above canned heat. He picked up the pot and came back.

They did not have a kitchen, thought Kampass. It was a room without a kitchen. He did not like it. They had dressed him in a white terry-cloth robe. Beneath the robe he was naked. For one unthinkable moment he fancied himself to have been the victim of some perverted sexual assault.

"You had a bad time of it."

"You weren't at the party," said Kampass, remembering.

Ben-Zvi ignored the remark. "Here," he said. He handed Kampass a steaming mug of coffee. "You should have broth," he added. "Best thing for the bad stomach, broth."

Kampass sipped the coffee. It scorched his tongue. The telephone had stopped ringing, but his scalp felt as though it were shrinking about his skull and his lips tingled. *Jesus God,* he thought. *Jesus Christ, Mother Mary, and Joseph.* He was choking in a landslide of anguish; sick to his stomach over what he now knew was happening to him.

Isaac flipped a page of his magazine.

"Well, how's that little agency of yours coming?" asked Ben-Zvi. "We appreciate all the business you're putting our way."

Kampass had not routed anyone on Icelandic for months. He did not answer. Under the robe he was drenched with perspiration. His upper lip was wet and the backs of his hands slippery. It was over he knew. Over. Over. Over. He sensed it from the very beginning. But he kept hoping it would be all right, willing it, saying to himself they are what they say they are and they are only being nice, and all the while knowing the truth of it. Where had he made his mistake? Where?

"I think it is a most precarious business to be a travel agent in New York," said Ben-Zvi.

"Dicey, indeed," said Isaac, behind his magazine.

Kampass did not listen; he was remembering things he had thought were gone forever—the months of shifting from one DP camp to the next after the war, from bread line to bread line, clearing rubble in Berlin, working with his bare hands and his back, physically breaking himself little by little, the watery soup always the same and the coffee forever ersatz and his underwear sticking in his crotch because they would not let them bathe and barbed wire and misty mornings and dogs barking and questions, always questions. Where did he make his mistake?

"I would like to be a travel agent," announced Ben-Zvi. "Not in Iceland, of course, but in Europe. Portofino would be acceptable. It would be something to retire to. Don't you agree?"

And his joy when the visa came through, Kampass was recalling that too. And in the boat coming over; the cold cabin with condensation on the bulkheads and the two Italians he shared with, who insisted on cooking pasta in the cabin.

"How about that?"

And going past Sandy Hook in the early morning, Kampass standing near the bow so he could be the first to see the Statue of Liberty. It had seemed to mean something. But he never caught sight of it that morning. There was too much fog. Where did he go wrong?

"Well?"

All for nothing, thought Kampass. It was like dying without a cause. It was like buying caviar and getting peanut butter. He said finally, "It isn't necessary to go on with this."

"Beg pardon?"

"It's all finished, isn't it?" Kampass slipped down the cushions, disintegrating, and looking at his hands as though he had only then discovered they were there.

"Yes," said Ben-Zvi. "I'm afraid it is."

•

He sat deep in the couch and squeezed his fingers until the nails turned first white, then crimson. Something was screaming inside him.

"Good," said Ben-Zvi. "Now that's out of the way. Now we speak English. After so long it may be easier for you. We don't wish to be misunderstood."

The younger man moved in the lounge chair. From his lap, and hidden from view by the magazine, Kampass watched him take out a small automatic pistol, which was dwarfed by the silencer screwed to its muzzle. He placed the pistol carefully, almost delicately, at the table by his side, arranging it so that the butt end was towards himself.

Kampass stared at the satin-blue finish of the silencer catching the light. He had never seen one like it before. It looked a bit like the end of a child's squirt gun.

Ben-Zvi walked over to the dresser and picked up a flat metal box. He came back with the box and what looked like an IBM card. Kampass could see the tin was an ink pad. "Give us your right hand," Ben-Zvi said. Gently, as though he were afraid it might break, he took Kampass' hand. He pressed the fingers, one by one, into the pad.

Kampass sat and watched him as though it really were not happening.

Ben-Zvi affixed the prints to spaces provided on the IBM card. Then he gave Kampass a paper towel. "Wipe your hand off," he ordered. Kampass held the towel, rolling it into a sticky little ball between his palms. Ben-Zvi went back to the dresser and compared the IBM card with another. He used a small, pocket magnifying glass. Finally he put the cards together in an envelope and sealed it. Then from out of an attaché case he took two file folders, which were held together by rubber bands. He snapped off the rubber bands and placed the files neatly on the floor before Kampass. He extracted an eight-by-ten glossy photograph from the first file and placed it on the sofa.

Kampass raised his eyes to the photo. It was an enlarged snapshot of an SS sergeant, an *Oberscharführer*, who stood hands on hips, in a black dress uniform, next to the trunk of a large tree. In the background there was some rustic garden furniture. The Iron Cross hung about the sergeant's neck, and pinned below the left breast pocket of the tunic was the oval of the Tank Fighter's Badge.

Ben-Zvi cocked his head in appraisal. "Very Teutonic," he said. "Recognize him?"

The face that smiled proudly back at Kampass from the age-yellowed print, though keener of eye and leaner of jowl, was none other than his own. He remembered the day his father took it in their backyard. It was the day he came back from the Eastern Front. They had sent him home to convalesce.

"You're going to kill me," Kampass mumbled. He tore his eyes from the photo. Surprisingly the idea of dying did not bother him. It was only that here in this shabby place no one would ever know of it. He had walked past the New York City Morgue once—a cold, impersonal building that might have been the headquarters of a life insurance firm. He saw himself, unclaimed, lying in a bin on rollers like so much meat—a bin in the wall like a filing cabinet—and he saw his name inserted in the slot on the cabinet facing. It would not even be his correct name. He said aloud, "No I don't. I don't want to die."

"You're jumping to conclusions," said Ben-Zvi. "You're way ahead of us."

Kampass pressed down on fingers slimy with ink and asked, "There's nothing I can do, is there? I mean, nothing to say." He had an urge to use the bathroom.

"*Schatzi*," said Ben-Zvi not unpleasantly. "You've had your lot."

"*Schatzi*," echoed Isaac. He was back to reading his magazine, but he held it low so he could keep an eye on Kampass.

"Please, may I use the facilities?" asked Kampass. He could feel the pressure building inside him again.

"Absolutely. They've turned off the plumbing, but that's all right. Don't do anything naughty." Ben-Zvi pointed out the bathroom.

Kampass went in and closed the door. Crouching on the toilet seat, he took stock. Was he to be kidnapped or murdered? What? Where would he be tomorrow at this time? Above all, he wondered why it had to be him. He'd made a go of it since, and what about the others; there was that doctor, that Mengele of Auschwitz safe in Argentina; Mussfeld of the crematorium at Majdanek, others. So close he was; a bare six months until they would invoke the Statute of Limitations. Six months away from amnesty and he could reclaim his identity. He would no more have to hide his wartime service than a defense-plant riveter. He was an American citizen now. Things like this did not happen to you in America. Perhaps the *Amis* would understand. He had read once: *We don't generate hate. We are professionals who fight any enemy the President designates.* The Marine Commandant, Shoup, had said it himself. Well, he had been no different. He was a soldier, a weapon, and he exploded in the direction they pointed him. He was not responsible for targets. They would see how it was.

There was a sharp rap on the door.

"Let's go in there," said a voice.

Kampass came out. He saw several sheets of paper had been spread on the table next to the two piles of folders. Each

sheet appeared identical with the next and bore a dotted line
at the bottom, presumably for a signature. He sat down on
the couch, crossed his legs, and summoned every ounce of
bravado left him and said, "I demand to be placed in the
hands of the appropriate American authorities." He pro-
nounced each word carefully and distinctly, but his voice
quavered, and at the word "authorities," cracked altogether.

There was silence in the room. The two men exchanged
glances.

"*I* am a citizen." His voice was a squeak.

They were both staring at him.

"It's true," Kampass went on, if only for the assurance of
listening to his own voice. "I have rights. They are constitu-
tional and it is written in this country. You are on *my* soil
here. Mine."

With one step, cat-quick, Ben-Zvi reached the sofa and
punched Kampass full force on the mouth.

He had not seen the blow coming until it exploded against
his face. His head snapped back and he sagged to the cushions. Blood leaked from his torn lip and gums. There was the
taste of old pennies in his mouth and the telephone started
ringing again.

Ben-Zvi pulled a handkerchief from his hip pocket and
threw it at the sofa. "Here," he said. "You're bleeding."

Kampass righted himself and held the handkerchief to his
battered mouth. His upper lip was throbbing, fattening into
something that felt like a banana.

Ben-Zvi tapped a finger on the sheets of paper. "You're
going to sign these for us," he said. "So listen." He picked up
one sheet and read: " 'I, Bruno Waldek Kampass, declare of
my own free will, that since my true identity has been discovered, I realize it is futile for me to go on evading justice. I
am prepared to travel to Poland to stand trial in that country
before a competent court. I understand that legal aid shall be
provided me and I shall give a true account of my service in
Germany and at Majdanek in Lublin, Poland. This I declare
of my own free will.' " He put down the paper and added,

"Then you sign it. You understand what I've read?"

Kampass said without conviction, "It's an illegal document. I won't sign."

"Don't push me, Kampass," said Ben-Zvi. "You keep this up and it's out of our hands." There was a nasty edge to his voice and Kampass knew he meant it. "It's over with. Don't you see that? Be a soldier; a man. Sign it." He unclipped a pen from his breast pocket and placed it next to the papers. "Sign, and we'll have a chat. You have no choice."

"You are Poles?" asked Kampass, neglecting the papers.

"Sign."

Kampass took the pen, and with one hand holding the handkerchief to his bloated lip, he laboriously added his signature to the three sheets. Ben-Zvi and Isaac exchanged glances again.

Ben-Zvi took the papers and studied them. The signature was all squiggly lines like the results of a lie-detector test. He leaned forward and cuffed Kampass solidly on the ear. "You idiot," he hissed. "You signed Speirling. Cross it out and do it right."

Kampass took the papers back.

While he was re-signing, Isaac rose from the chair and left the room. He returned holding a hypodermic needle and syringe, a ball of cotton wool, and a small vial of clear liquid. Inverting the vial, he pushed home the needle and drew out the plunger of the syringe. Then he squeezed out the excess air from the syringe.

Pen poised, Kampass watched the operation. "What's he doing there?" he asked.

"Never mind about him," ordered Ben-Zvi, as though monitoring a study hall. "Get on with your business."

Kampass finished signing and Ben-Zvi checked the papers again. "All right, take off your bathrobe."

"What?"

"Your bathrobe, take it off."

Kampass stood up and removed the robe. He sat down and crossed his hands over his lap—all pale, loose flesh.

"You're going to make a woman very happy someday," said Isaac.

Kampass blushed.

"Put your hands at your sides," said Ben-Zvi.

Kampass hesitated.

"What do you think I'm going to do, rape you?"

Kampass laid his hands reluctantly on the cushions.

Ben-Zvi lit a cigarette of strong, Turkish tobacco, and going to the nearest folder, opened it, and faced it to Kampass. "Now then," he said. "We are in a position to offer you a compromise of sorts. We might buy you a little time. But before I get to that I want you to look through your dossier. You can see how things are."

"You are Poles," said Kampass. This time he did not ask a question.

"As a matter of fact we're not," said Ben-Zvi.

"Jews," said Kampass. "Israelis?"

"Does it matter?"

"You have no idea what life was like, *Herr* Dorn," said Kampass, neglecting the open folder.

"Don't be a bore," said Ben-Zvi.

"I did what I did as a soldier," Kampass went on, nonplussed. "Have you been a soldier, *Herr* Dorn? Surely so. Have you been ordered to do something you know is incorrect? You do it, that's what. You do it for your country. How can you imagine I was proud of such things? No. It was unsoldierly, this business. You are Jews? You are. I can see it. I never read any of that crap in *Der Stürmer;* that shit Streicher fed us all the time. I was wounded in Russia, you know. With honor. Here. See."—he lifted the folds of flesh and displayed the scar—"There it is. See? Where is my suit? I will show you about it. My suit, please." He twisted on the sofa as if he might see his clothes in a corner.

"This what you're looking for?" said Ben-Zvi, an amused expression on his face. He threw Kampass' wallet on the sofa.

"Yes," said Kampass at once. "Yes. Yes." His fingers scrambled in the pockets of the wallet. He removed a folded news clipping. He opened it, smoothing it out on his bare thigh, patting it neat and flat. "Please, may I show you this, *Herr* Dorn?" he asked.

Ben-Zvi shrugged. "You're wasting time."

"Please," said Kampass. "It will take only a minute. Please." He got up from the sofa and handed the clipping to Ben-Zvi. "There it is," he added. "Now there." He leaned over Ben-Zvi's shoulder.

It was a cutting from *Signal* magazine dated 1942: a dog-eared picture of a young man in a camouflaged smock with a machine pistol slung across his chest. The caption read *One of Many. The Waffen SS*. Ben-Zvi could barely make it out. "That you?" he asked.

"Yes. Me," confirmed Kampass, putting a thumb to his chest. "When I got the *Eisernes Kreuz*." He snatched away the clipping and moved quickly across the room to Isaac. He offered it in his cupped hands, like a drink of water. "Here," he said. "See."

Isaac took the cutting. "Yes," he said. He folded it and tore it twice. The little pieces fell to the floor and scattered like confetti. He smiled at Kampass the whole time.

Kampass went to his knees with a thud, gathering the scraps. He got the pieces together and stood up, naked, fat, swaying. He said, "After I was wounded, after the *Eisernes Kreuz*, they said I was not fit for combat and so I said, 'all right, all right. Let me train soldiers.' But they said no. They said they were short-handed in the camps. I was *Waffen SS*. I was not an executioner. I was meant to fight and I know what it is like out there." He waved a bare, wobbling arm at the window as though a silent battle were taking place on the street below. "It was an obscenity, that's what it was."

"Oh, Christ damn," said Ben-Zvi and he stamped the floor so hard the papers shivered. "Read the bloody dossier, Kampass."

Kampass returned to the sofa. It was true what he'd told them. All of it was the way it happened.

Inside the file there were dozens of photostated documents, all arranged in chronological order. The first was a Xerox reproduction of his *Wehrpass,* which covered his service from 1938 through 1945, and there were sworn statements by people, many of whom he could not remember. Kampass found its completeness amazing. He saw they had included the field-combat records of his wounding outside Moscow and then his transfer from the *Waffen SS, Das Reich* Division, to the *Allgemeine SS.* There was his posting to Majdanek as a *Desinfektor,* and finally, his daily reports—all initialed by himself: *6 October 1943—500 out,* or *12 November 1943—350 out.* Scores upon scores of numbers. How many? He had never bothered to keep track. It would have made you think about it. For the entire year he was at it. He himself recorded it for them, and his job always the same standing in the little green cubicle, the annex to the main chambers, pouring *Zyklon* "B" crystals into the two small tube fixtures. "Don't worry about it," they had told him. "You're a mechanic doing a mechanic's job. You worry about technique." Kampass, the *Desinfektor,* disinfecting. And the screams, they did not tell him about those. As he read on he could almost hear them again; the screams coming through the two tubes and through his own gas mask and the horrid noise of fingernails clawing cement. Reading on, Kampass unconsciously covered his ears, and his lips moved silently, forming each word.

There also was his last fitness report from Majdanek signed by Rudolf Vogel, *Standartenführer,* in a firm scrawl: *Sturdy, reliable, unmotivated,* read the report. The file included with the granting of his request for transfer *due to health.* Kampass always wondered why, after so long, after three similar requests failed, they granted him a transfer. The papers gave no clue.

Kampass moved his hands to his eyes as though shading them from a very strong sun. "I was a soldier," he said. "I swear to you about that. My God, you see what they have done to me? Do you see what they did?"

"Spare the hysterics," said Ben-Zvi. "I've had enough of that."

Kampass rocked on the sofa.

"You came close, Kampass. You nearly made it."

Kampass shook his head. He kept his hand above his eyes.

"I mean, how you ended up as Manfred Speirling. You knew what was in store for death-camp staffers after the Russians found Majdanek. Someday, someone would get around to you. Apparently—and we're pretty sure about this—you absconded with monies kept by the *Sicherheitsdienst* Foreign Section to pay agents-in-play in Turkey and Iran. You must have done this just as the Russians began to enter the city. You did it with the help of Speirling, who was an *Abwehr* orderly attached to the 'Stapo Foreign Section."

"No," said Kampass. "It was his idea, not mine. Speirling blew the safe with some *gelli* he bought from a friend in a pioneer battalion. I do not steal."

Ben-Zvi shrugged. "You don't have the brains to have thought it up, anyway. Did you kill him, Kampass? Did you kill the corporal and take the money? Did you have brains for that?"

Kampass shook his head violently. "He was hit by a *Russ* stick bomb. *Handscheinwerfer*," he said.

"Handy," said Ben-Zvi.

"I tell the truth." Kampass removed his hand from his eyes and squinted.

"It's really very funny," Ben-Zvi continued. "After all this elaboration, after the changing of uniforms, the planning, all this, we have known about it since late forty-five. You forgot Speirling was in the *Wehrmacht* and so he did not have a blood-grouping tattoo on his forearm like the SS. One of your own people turned you in. The Russians used them to clean up their occupation zone, to work in graves registration. One of them found it strange an SS sergeant, once in the *Waffen SS*, carried no tattoo. Then the uniform did not fit, and also, there was a family ring you overlooked. On the inside of the band it was inscribed *M. Speirling*. Well, this man, he was an ex-*Leibstandarte* lieutenant, a certain Berger, buried the corpse as an unknown. He kept the ring, your *Wehrpass*, and the identification disc. One never knew, you see. A few months later he heard about the formation of the War Crimes Documentation Center in Geneva. Fortunately it was one of

our own men we had in play there that Berger eventually
contacted. Our man went to Potsdam to interview him.
Berger was a very poor man. An empty stomach knows no
allegiance, Kampass. He gave us what he had. We filled his
stomach.

"So it seemed logical that we search for Bruno Kampass
using the alias of Speirling. But who was Speirling? We
found out when we checked your last posting to the Gestapo.
You worked together in back-to-back offices in the same
building on Prinz Albrectstrasse. A great deal of money was
unaccounted for in Speirling's office. A listing of the serial
numbers was obtained from the paymaster's files. We took a
chance and waited until the bills began to show up. It was
hard then for a German to cash pounds sterling without
someone remembering it. We followed the trail to New
York. I think it's a flipping howl. All this time you haven't
fooled anyone. We waited, Kampass. Things had to be right.
We were saving you."

So that was it, thought Kampass. He put his hands over his
lap.

"Hands at your sides," said Ben-Zvi. "How did you get the
American visa?"

"There was an *Amis* captain at the Furstenfeldbruck dis-
placed persons camp," said Kampass. "He fixed it."

"What do you mean 'fixed it'?"

"He arranged the visa."

"You bribed him. Is that what you mean?"

"Yes sir," said Kampass.

"And that's how you got your travel agency going? With
the money?"

"Yes sir."

"Name?"

"Speirling Traveltours."

"No, the captain."

"I can't remember."

"Try."

Kampass thought. He said, "Stewart, I think."

"A Captain Stewart?"

"Yes."

"That's simple to check," said Ben-Zvi. He wrote the name down on a note pad. He stubbed out his cigarette and opened the next file. "I want you to look carefully at the photo that appears on the first page here and tell me if you can identify the subject." He reversed the file.

Kampass recognized him at once. "Oh, yes sir," he said. "That's the *Standartenführer*."

"What *Standartenführer*?"

"Vogel. *Standartenführer* Vogel." They were taking their time. Dorn had said they were saving him. For what? Like a man twenty years swimming in the ocean, Kampass felt land, albeit sandy, rise beneath his feet. "That's him, sir," he said. "Yes, it surely is."

"He was a *Gruppenführer*," corrected Ben-Zvi. *"Gruppenführer."*

"I didn't know that."

"You weren't supposed to."

"He commanded the operational facilities at Majdanek," Kampass volunteered. He did not want to say "gassings."

Ben-Zvi scratched his nose thoughtfully. "Your job bring you into close contact with him?" he asked.

"No sir, I saw him only from a distance. He made the selections, then he left."

"But you once worked in his office as a clerk."

"Well . . ."

"Tell the truth."

"Well, yes. Someone got sick and I had to fill in. Two weeks. No more."

"Any personal contact with him?"

"No sir," Kampass answered.

"No dealings, reprimands—nothing like that?" asked Ben-Zvi, diagnosing, probing.

"With *us*? Oh, no. He hardly noticed we were there."

"And you're sure about that photo?"

There was never any doubt about Vogel, Kampass thought. No one could mistake the thin build and the legs, sparrow-skinny in polished boots; his narrow face and dark hair,

which he wore long, and which grew down the back of his
neck the way hair grows on your leg. There were rumors
about Vogel, but that was all. Kampass had heard scuttlebutt
that Vogel was appointed by *Brigadeführer* Globocnik, the
RSHA inspector, and he knew it was true that when Himmler
visited Majdanek in July of '43, the *Reichsführer* spent several hours closeted in Vogel's posh offices. Other gossip, Kampass recalled, hinted Vogel was a homosexual, but this was
contradicted by a cook in the SS noncommissioned officers'
mess who said Vogel lived with a woman somewhere in resi-
dential Lublin. It was all very mysterious and they, members
of the staff, went to great lengths to avoid even passing Vogel.
Everything was hearsay. Nobody really knew about Vogel.

Kampass had resented Vogel in the way most noncommissioned officers resent authority without recourse.
Vogel was the unknown quantity that cast a pall over the
lives of every one of them. Plainly Vogel was no soldier. The
real fighting was left to men like Kampass, to whom National
Socialism and Hitler had meant songfests, parades, beer,
good fellowship, autobahns, and a place in society for the
small man—more precisely himself. Kampass, whatever they
might accuse him of here, considered himself the testicle of
his country.

"Would he recognize you?" asked Ben-Zvi.

"He knew my name."

"Your name?"

"He had to. He countersigned my daily reports. He signed
my fitness chits."

Ben-Zvi pursed his lips and murmured something that
sounded to Kampass like "Technicality." He turned and
stared at Isaac for a moment. Then he said, "You're a lucky
lad, Kampass. You're one in a million we can lay hands on.
You seem to be the only one left who could recognize Vogel."

"Yes sir?"

"Here's the situation. You're going to find him for us, and
then you will make the identification positive."

Kampass opened his mouth.

"Unless, of course," said Ben-Zvi, "you'd rather not."

•

Kampass wrapped his arms about himself. Suddenly it was terribly cold.

"Give him his robe back," said Ben-Zvi.

Isaac tossed the robe over.

"He was a homosexual and a disgrace," said Kampass, struggling into it.

"You can look at it this way," said Ben-Zvi. "It was him, in a way, that got you into this. Now you can do something about it." He tapped the signed copies of the confession against his fingertips. "And depending upon the success of our venture, we might forget about these."

"You could do this?"

"Not me, someone."

Kampass tried to imagine how it might be afterwards. He could not. "The Israelis would do such a thing?" he asked.

"I didn't say Israelis."

"Well . . ."

"Well, forget it, that's all."

Isaac continued to read the magazine. He had put the syringe on the table, next to the pistol.

"I'll do it," said Kampass suddenly.

"That's the stuff," said Ben-Zvi. He reassembled the files and set them aside.

"What do I do?" asked Kampass.

"What you're told," said Ben-Zvi. Then, "If you piss on us just once . . ."—he snapped his fingers—"you'll be turned over to the Polish authorities. If it goes well, you're free. But in case you reconsider and decide to try your chances with the Americans, I want to make clear how it will be. You can't take a crap without us knowing what you had for dinner the night before. The minute you pick up the phone, the minute you attempt to contact anyone verbally or by the post, you're through. Understand? Do you understand that?"

"Yes sir."

"I'm sure. How much are you drinking now?"

"Socially. A little here, a little there." Kampass looked at his hands. They were trembling.

"You're lying. You're on the wagon as of now. But, for the record, you're averaging a fifth of gin a day."

"Yes," Kampass whispered.

"Okay, then," said Ben Zvi. "No more." He reached in his pocket and placed a key on the sofa. The key had a yellow tag. "That fits a locker on the lower level of Grand Central Station. The number is imprinted on the key. In the locker you'll find a suitcase, a pigskin two-suiter. You are to collect that suitcase tomorrow morning. It contains some clothing and your passport, which was borrowed yesterday and altered. You have two days to clear up your affairs."

"Two days?" asked Kampass. "This only?"

"You leave for London night after tomorrow."

"I can't disappear," whined Kampass.

"Why not? You disappeared twenty years ago."

"But my business. The clients."

"Would you rather we forgot the whole thing?"

"No."

Ben-Zvi went over to the sterno stove. He poured some coffee into a waxed cup and added powdered cream. He said, "Outstanding business will be handled in this manner: you phone the client and inform him or her that you are forced to take a vacation because of ill health. Your rent, electricity, and miscellaneous bills will be paid. Incidentally, you're overdrawn at the bank by eight dollars. Bring your balance up tomorrow. Next, you send a wire to airlines which provide you with ticket stock. The body of the telegram has been prepared for you and you'll find it in the suitcase with your documents. You are to return all ticket stock. In short, Kampass, tend to matters as though you are to die in two days. Now repeat this back, all of it."

Kampass repeated it.

"Good," said Ben-Zvi. "You'll be briefed further in London. The name of your next contact will be provided you shortly before boarding the aircraft. You'll get a stipend to defray en-route expenses. At six Wednesday night," Ben-Zvi added, "we'll pick you up outside your apartment."

"About Vogel, he . . ."

"London, Kampass, London," said Ben-Zvi.

Kampass drew the robe more closely about him. His teeth were beginning to chatter.

"No razzmatazz," said Isaac from the chair.

Ben-Zvi stared at Kampass. "Don't you find it strange how roles have switched? Not long ago it was you who owned my life, not I yours."

"*Herr* Dorn . . ."

"Don't give me that '*Herr* Dorn' business. You make me sick, you know Kampass? You didn't have the courage to make decisions of who was to die or why or if anyone died at all. You left that up to the Vogels. All of you did. Seventy thousand people. Shit. How did it feel, you bastard. *Seventy thousand*. Like swatting flies, wasn't it, Kampass? Nothing to it."

Kampass looked at him, his mind going back. No it wasn't, he thought. It wasn't like swatting flies. Not at first, not ever. Seventy thousand was it? Perhaps. He could not remember the figures. And he could not remember the faces save for one: an old man on a cold, fall day who died laughing.

"I, alone, could do nothing," Kampass pleaded. "Don't you see? The swine . . ."

"What swine?" asked Ben-Zvi.

"Vogel," said Kampass. "Vogel and the others."

"I didn't know there was any difference between one pig and another," said Ben-Zvi.

Kampass did not answer.

"I lost two brothers and a father at Majdanek," said Ben-Zvi. "That was in forty-three. You see how it is. You yourself probably gassed them."

"I'm sorry," said Kampass quietly, as though he might be referring to a recent death in the man's family.

"Ahh, Jesus," said Ben-Zvi. "Put on your stinking clothes and get out of here."

Kampass cast about.

"In the closet," said Ben-Zvi. "Quick, I may change my mind."

His clothes still reeked of vomit and excreta. It might have been a bad dream. He began this day as Manfred Speirling, American citizen. That was what they had told him. *Coming to America is like going to confession.* That was what the Italians said, the Italians and their pasta. Now he was quitting the day as bare as he had been forty-five years ago: Bruno Waldek Kampass, bearing the stigma of the crime which dated to Cain.

Kampass put on the rest of his clothes and fled.

The long green building marked BAD UND DESINFEKTION *stood isolated in the center of the sandy yard like a huge community outhouse. Kampass leaned against the small door in the rear, looked up at the woolly sky, and asked, "How many* Himmelkommando *do we get today?"*

A Ukrainian Totenkopf SS *private sat cross-legged on the ground, smoking a cigarette. He said, "Six."*

Kampass shifted his gaze from the sky to the line of trees along the Chelm Road, beyond the double row of barbed-wire fencing that surrounded the camp. On the road, a column of men, women, and children flanked by SS guards moved towards the gate like an incredibly long centipede. Kampass saw an old man was leading them, walking slowly as if he were climbing a high hill. He wore a long beard that blew in the wind.

A rabbi, perhaps, thought Kampass. The elder leading his family.

Some of them, he noticed, carried personal belongings over their shoulders in swag bags, and some were dressed in greatcoats which hung to their ankles. The children wore short pants, exposing their twiglike legs to the cold. Once inside the gates, they gathered in small groups. The younger ones milled about nervously, waiting for something to happen. The aged stared at the ground. None of them spoke.

An SS Politzei Regimente *lieutenant walked up to the old man who had led the Jews down the road. He said something and the old man nodded and turned and spoke to the Jews. Kampass could not hear because of the wind.*

The lieutenant crossed the sand to where Kampass waited with the Ukrainian private.

"All yours, Landser," *he said, holding out a clipboard. "Fifteen hundred of the chosen ones."*

"I don't sign anything here, sir," said Kampass. "You'll find Standartenführer Vogel's *offices at the end of Field Four."*

"You'll do what you're told, Landser."

"I'm an Oberscharführer, *sir, not a Landser."*

The lieutenant frowned. He looked at the combat badges pinned on Kampass' tunic.

"All right, hero," he said mockingly.

Kampass balled up his fist and made an obscene gesture at the back of the departing police lieutenant. Lieutenant, he thought contemptuously. The nearest he had been to combat was in the Lublin Soldatenheim, *and that was sexual.*

The Ukrainian picked his nose and wiped his finger on his trousers. "You're going to get in trouble talking that way," he said.

"Shut up, you," said Kampass. Pigs, they were all pigs, he thought. If he had only known at the beginning how it would turn out. They did not tell him it would end like this— reduced in status from soldier to racial K.P.

In the yard the gypsies were setting up their instruments and sheet music. Vogel's Welcome Band, they were called. They were there to make things easier for the Jews. They were there to soothe.

"If you don't like it," said the Ukrainian, "why don't you go up on the towers?"

"War," said Kampass. "We are at war. I do my job."

THE PATRIOTS

"Jews? What's that?"

——*Bruno Kampass, age ten*

Kampass waited under the canopy. A cold wave had moved into the city in the last two days, and as he watched the people walk past, he could hear the little squeaking noises their shoes made on the packed snow. Where the snow had piled on the curb it was grey with the filth of Manhattan.

Kampass knocked an icicle from the canopy. If he had been asked to give an account of what had happened in the past twenty-four hours, he could not have found words to tell it. It was that confusing. He did not, for instance, know he had slept, although he assumed he must have. He could not recall feeding himself. He could not even remember collecting the suitcase from the lower level of Grand Central Station. But there it was beside him, the pigskin two-suiter. In addition to the suitcase, there was another reality for Kampass as he waited in the cold, doing what he had been told: he was very lucky to be alive. But where it would end he did not know. He did not want to think about that. As for sensations, the only one he could put his finger on at the moment was his sobriety. Kampass had not been sober at this time of the evening for ten years. It took some getting used to.

He pulled the astrakhan lower on his head until it covered the tips of his ears. Israelis, he thought. They had to be Israelis. Had they been Poles, there would have been no bargaining with him. No deals. He knew what happened to the others the Poles caught.

Dorn and Kaufmann, if that's what their names were, he thought; they wouldn't believe him. No one would when he told them how he hated that year at Majdanek; the plains of Poland that went on forever and the dust devils on the roadsides and the turnips and cabbages outside the compound, dusty-white, chalky with human ashes. And the single stack that belched smoke day and night and the stink, my God, the stink of it. You did not know about that unless you were there; Kampass, who was always doing what he was told. Now he was doing it again.

They did not have to threaten him. He would not run. His mind and his legs would not carry him and he knew it. He would do what they asked because he could do nothing else. They showed him how it might be, they told him and that was enough, and even if they had lied to him, it did not matter. They gave him something he could not give himself; hope.

"Hey, Mr. Speirling, you going on a trip there?" It was the doorman, his cap pulled low over his eyes.

"Yes, Karl, I'm going away," said Kampass.

"You talk with Cudlipp?" The doorman beat his hands together to warm them.

Kampass mumbled an obscenity.

"That's all right too," said the doorman.

"I'm sorry about the other day," said Kampass, quickly changing tack.

"What?"

"I didn't mean to shout at you. You only do your job."

The doorman looked at his feet.

"Here," said Kampass. He gave him a folded ten-dollar bill. "I wanted to square things. Merry Christmas."

The doorman took the bill.

"You going south, Mr. Speirling? Puerto Rico, maybe? You look pretty bad."

"No, Karl. Doctor's orders. Just away."

A dark four-door Chevrolet Impala with diplomatic plates swung into the curb. A chauffeur got out and walked around to the canopy. He did not say anything. He picked up the two-

suiter and carried it to the trunk of the car. Kampass saw
there were three men waiting in the car, one in front, two in
the rear. He recognized Dorn and Kaufmann in back. He
had never seen the third man before.

Ben-Zvi opened the door from the inside and leaned out.
"Let's go," he called.

The doorman held out his hand. Kampass shook it.

"When you coming back, sir?"

Kampass noted the 'sir.' "That's up to the doctor," he said.

"Some car," said the doorman. "Diplomatic."

"Yes," said Kampass. "Goodbye." He climbed into the car.

They moved out into the traffic, turning down Second Avenue towards the Queens Midtown Tunnel. The men he knew
as Dorn and Kaufmann flanked him in the back seat. No one
said anything. The stranger in front watched the road. He sat
at attention, and Kampass could see the wrinkles in his thick
neck.

Kampass felt perspiration on his palms and he wiped them
on his knees. A few details filtered back. He *had* left a letter
to the cleaning lady. He *had* left a notice for the mailman. He
had balanced his account. He *had* sent the wire to the airlines, using the copy they had written for him and put in
the suitcase, and he had returned the ticket stock.

They came out of the tunnel, passing on the flyway over
Calvary cemetery; an obscene army of a million monuments
erected to the long forgotten, the just forgotten, and the
never-to-be-forgotten; a city of the dead.

Kampass thought about the pigskin bag and its contents.
He had opened it back in his apartment. There was a suit of
clothes, a pair of shoes, and shirts. They bore the label of a
Vienna men's store and fit him perfectly. His passport had
been on top. He wondered how they had got it and then he
had recalled Karl telling him about the electricians and he
knew they must have taken it then. There was one alteration
on the passport. On the fourth page, an Austrian passport
control stamp declared him to have entered that country on
November twentieth and to have departed three days later.
There was a corresponding entry stamp of US Immigration

below it. Kampass wondered what role it played.

A half-hour later, they slowed and drove into the neon kaleidoscope of Kennedy International Airport.

Ben-Zvi leaned forward and said to the driver, "Parking Lot 'A'."

They bore to the right, passing the International Arrivals Building, and opposite the TWA Terminal, turned into the parking lot. The lot was practically empty and there was ice on the asphalt.

"Get out," said Ben-Zvi.

The driver left the car and opened the trunk. He put the suitcase on the ground and unfastened it. Kampass stood and watched. He felt a lump grow in his throat. There was something else. He had taken the Walther from his safe and put it under the shirts in the bag.

The driver had the bag open and was going through it with the aid of a pencil flashlight. He held the light in his teeth and searched with both hands. His fingers flew lightly over the mound of shirts and socks and probed into the corners. They found two bottles of gin in the side pockets. The chauffeur took them one by one and smashed them on the asphalt. They made solid popping noises like light bulbs being broken, and Kampass watched the gin run into the frozen snow. He licked his lips. They were rough and cracked.

The fingers poked and questioned. Under the shirts they paused. The driver drew out the pistol and held it up delicately, as though it were an inflamed appendix he was removing from a suffering patient.

Ben-Zvi took his arm. "What's the idea?" he asked.

Kampass bit down on his lip until he tasted blood. A jet shrieked overhead, its engines straining on climb. Ben-Zvi studied him quizzically until the shriek subsided to dull thunder.

"How about it?"

"I thought it might help, only that," Kampass explained lamely.

"Now hear this, you son of a pig," said Ben-Zvi. "You try

something like this again, it's all over."

Kampass looked at the ground.

"You look at *me*," said Ben-Zvi. He held Kampass' chin in a viselike grip and wrenched up.

Kampass blinked. "Yes, *Herr* Dorn," he said.

"Louder. I can't hear you."

"Yes, *Herr* Dorn," said Kampass.

He released his chin and took the pistol from the chauffeur. He removed the clip and shot back the ejector, grunting as he saw it was unloaded. He threw the pistol in the front seat. "Pockets inside out," he said, returning. "Lay out your change and stuff."

Kampass placed the contents of his pockets in a neat row on top of the hood: keys, wallet, passport, shot record, and cash.

The driver shone the pencil-light over Ben-Zvi's shoulder as he picked through the bits and pieces. He handed the keys to the driver, but kept the passport. He examined the page carrying the Austrian visa-stamp and said, "Looks fine." He gave it to Kampass. "Okay," was all he said. Kampass put the change and other items back in his pockets.

After going through the suitcase once more, the driver fastened it and replaced it in the trunk.

"Give him money."

The driver peeled off five very crisp twenty-dollar bills and handed them over.

"Let's have your attention," said Ben-Zvi. He held out two cards. "See this?" He took the first card. "This is your London contact, code name: *Uncle Vanya*. The telephone number is on the card. You will call *Uncle Vanya* at nine-thirty tomorrow morning. Your flight arrives at eight, so you have plenty of time. He'll arrange your briefing. Now, this second card, this one here, is where you will be staying: Eden Hotel, off Harrington Gardens. You're booked in for tomorrow, so go directly from the airport. Now, that's not much to remember, is it?"

Kampass took the cards. He nodded.

"I didn't mean it about the pistol," he said.

Ben-Zvi grunted something. He said, "Now there's a simple identification check we're insisting on because anyone could call up and say they were you, right?" He was oversimplifying, as if for a child's benefit.

Kampass nodded again very slowly. He wanted them to know he understood.

"Here it is," said Ben-Zvi. He handed Kampass the torn half of a playing card, the seven of diamonds. "You'll notice your half of the card carries only two diamonds. It's the top half. You'll give it to *Uncle Vanya*. He'll fit the lower half of the card, which he is holding—the five diamonds."

Kampass put the card in his wallet.

All through this, the man who had sat in the front seat said nothing. He stood aside, leaning a little on the fender and watching what was going on. He had his hands deep in his overcoat pockets and his shoulders hunched against the cold.

Ben-Zvi looked at his watch. "So I guess that's all," he said. He looked at the man in the heavy overcoat. The man nodded.

They drove to the terminal in silence.

Once inside the soup dish of the Pan American Building, they saw him through the check-in counter. They walked him as far as the gate. As Kampass prepared to board the ramp to the waiting jet, he glanced back. The three of them were standing next to the manifest desk, watching him without expression, men of clay: Ben-Zvi, Isaac, and the big man in the overcoat who had said nothing. Kampass was tempted to wave. Then he thought better of it.

●

He had selected a window seat next to an emergency exit from the seat-assignment chart posted at the check-in counter. He located his seat and collapsed into it, closing his eyes.

The cabin was warm and he listened to the muffled footsteps on carpeting and the subdued murmur of voices. The

public-address system played Hawaiian music. Then there
was the hiss of the engines starting. Ahead of him the stew-
ardess had stationed herself by the bulkhead and was demon-
strating how to put on a life vest and use the oxygen. Kampass felt the jet move beneath him smoothly, taxiing. He
opened his eyes and watched the blue taxiway lights slide
past. The pilot lined up the nose on the runway and with a
deep rumble, a roar and a jerk, they were moving; slowly at
first, then gathering speed, the lights a blue streak beyond the
tiny window. He felt the cabin tilt, and the jet leap into the
sky. The gear clunked as it was drawn up and they were
climbing, banking tightly.

Kampass, never at ease in the air, gasped, and his feet
scrounged for a hold on the carpet to correct the bank. He
twisted his head and saw the lights of Long Island, a glitter-
ing necklace of expressways, and far to the west, behind them
now, the shimmer of Manhattan against the clouds. Then
there was darkness.

Kampass pressed against the seat and listened to the air
rush over the outer skin of the aircraft. The steward came by,
pushing a small cart festooned with earphones for the piped
music. A couple sat across the aisle from him. He watched
them. After a while, the woman moved her hand over the
man's arm. They sat and drank and looked at each other and
laughed. Kampass shifted his stare back to the window and a
greasy patch made there by some earlier passenger's hair oil.
He felt his aloneness smothering him like a heavy blanket. He
shut his eyes.

*Coming back to Altenau, Altenau in the fall of the year
with the leaves turning; coming back from the purgatory of
Majdanek and the milky Polish sky for his first leave since he
had returned from the Eastern Front.*

There had been no one to meet him, Kampass recalled.
Absolutely no one. It was not like before, when he had returned a hero. There were no heroes anymore; not in the SS.
Gone was the drinking of good dark beer into the small hours
at the *Gasthaus*. Where were the old soldiers and their stories
of the Great War? Where did they go? Did they hide? No.

Most of them were in *Volksturm* forces and their wives, the old women, would look at him as if they blamed him for what was happening; as if he had told their husbands to go and die, to demobilize a Stalin tank at age sixty. Kampass remembered what they used to say; that death was nothing when it was for God and Fatherland. And it was true, they all had said, what Hitler predicted; they would live a thousand years.

There had been no one to meet him at Oker and the train rattled off. The signboards flapped in the wind, bang-bang. The stationmaster sat by the stove and played a harmonica. A *Wehrmacht Feldwebel* sat alone on the wooden benches and listened to the music. The band on the cuff of the soldier's tunic said he had served in the *Afrika Korps*. Kampass knew him. They had been in school together, Konrad something-or-other his name was. But now there seemed nothing to say. He knew it. He felt the hostility. Alone, he hitched the twelve kilometers to Altenau. After the first day home he took off his uniform and he did not wear it on his leave again.

The people, Kampass thought. Yes, there you had it; the people who themselves were the first to soap stars on the windows of kosher shops. The *Dreck*, the *Scheisskerl*. Did they not know what he was forced to do in their name—in the name of Germany? Did they know how it was with the Jews? YOUR FATHERLAND, RIGHT OR WRONG read the sign over the door to the *Desinfektor's* control cubicle.

"*Where is the butcher Schoenstein?*"

"*They took him last night, the SS.*"

"*How fortunate. I owed him for last month's bill.*"

And so that was that and the butcher went up in smoke; maybe at Majdanek, maybe Treblinka or Birkenau. And the butcher's children. And the butcher's parents; all by popular consent.

After the war his own neighbors would be the first to point him out. *Bruno*, they would have said. *Bruno was in the SS. He was in the camps.*

At the old *Gasthaus* where they once gathered for song-fests, they had told him about Metz. Metz was dead. Hadn't he heard? Old Metz dead and his boarhounds auctioned off like sheep.

It was easy for Metz. He went to sleep one night like a baby and he did not wake up. Better that way. Such a fine old man, Metz. He hadn't an enemy in all of the Harzwald. "Do you want to see his grave, Bruno? There's ever such a lonely stone. The Bürgermeister donated it."

No, he had replied. *I don't want to see.*

And so he had left, in the sunshine and in the fall, and he went to Paris to finish his leave. Paris, which was too large for personalities. He did not go back to Altenau.

No more stags.

No more beer.

No more Metz.

●

He had been asleep. Off the tip of the gently flexing wing the sun had risen, and in the thin, high air, it was hard to look at. Far below, the mountains of northern Scotland were white with snow and he could see smoke from individual dwellings. The smoke panned out so that it hung like fog around the hamlets.

Kampass was cold, even though a blanket had been thrown over his lap. The stewardesses passed out small plastic trays with orange juice, a croissant, and coffee that tasted as though it were made yesterday.

Kampass looked out the window and thought about Vogel. Obviously Vogel had made good his desertion. Then how had it gone with him since Majdanek? he wondered. Had it been the same for all of them, officers and enlisted men alike, who had made it out?

Somehow, that was not how he saw Vogel; living in a vacuum as he himself had. Perhaps it was the rank gap between them. An officer was sacrosanct. That was the first thing you learned. You could not imagine him being born or performing his ablutions or loving anyone.

The others had had trades, most of them. Mussfeld, who operated the crematorium, Kampass suspected to have been an engineer before the war. There was that Mengele, the Auschwitz doctor. He could still be practicing somewhere. But Vogel was different. Where does a man go who carried death with him the way others carry pennies in their pockets?

And what did they expect him to do about it? Did they want him to come up and say *See, it is I, Kampass, mein Standartenführer.*

"Find and identify," they had said.

How?

"One in a million," they said.

So close he had come. They admitted it themselves. Twenty years of building torn down, doomed from the first. He was no average immigrant. He had succeeded in the toughest country of the world. He had survived in a survivor's society. No indeed. He did not pass through the bowels of failure to splatter the sidewalks of New York City. He had won at a brutal game. He had persevered. Now because he was that one in a million they had sifted and sifted and they had found him; because of one man, probably a very old man now, who once told him what to do. Vogel made it out, had got away with it and left him, Kampass, twenty years later, holding the shit end of the stick.

Kampass was aware of a dull ache in his jaws and he realized his teeth were fiercely clamped together.

The Boeing began its descent into Heathrow International, bucketing through the low scud and breaking out over the brown smear of suburban London. They skimmed the A-4 highway and settled onto the wet runway. The engines howled in reverse and the gear sent up sheets of water. Kampass looked out the moisture-beaded window at the terminal and at the ground crews in their yellow waterproofs.

One in a million.

Why?

He followed the passengers through the rain to the terminal, kicking out the stiffness in his legs. He took his place in line at passport control. He felt completely naked. They had

stripped him bare. He was not sure how to act and he was, at
once, very frightened. It had not really come home until now;
there was no place to hide.

The customs officer looked at him steadily. Kampass kept
his eyes on the papers by the desk.

"You won't be accepting employment in Great Britain, will
you, sir?"

Kampass swallowed and said no.

"Vacation?"

Kampass focused on the customs badge pinned to the
officer's tunic.

"Vacation?"

"No. I mean, yes."

He heard the validator thump down on his passport.

The confusion at the customs desk so befuddled him that
he took a wrong turn and found himself at the end of a line of
Pakistanis waiting to present their documents at a desk that
said FOR COMMONWEALTH CITIZENS ONLY. It was nearly fifteen
minutes before he realized his mistake. Now the officer was
staring at him again. The officer shook his head and pointed
solemnly at a door to his right. Kampass nodded vigorously,
and turning to comply, stumbled and fell over a flight bag.
The Pakistanis giggled. The passport control officer shook his
head again and went back to stamping passports.

Kampass cleared customs at nine-fifteen, an hour behind
schedule. It was too late to go to the hotel. He would miss his
call to *Uncle Vanya*. He decided to phone from the airport.
He located a phone kiosk and took up station nearby.

•

Second Secretary Mordecai Shoval frowned and stared out
his office window on the top floor of the Israeli embassy. A
squat man, he sat with his back to the desk, and flanked as he
was by the standard flags of Great Britain and Israel, and
framed by the window, he might have been the idol center-
piece on a Buddha altar. He swept his eyes along the length
of Palace Green below, the "Row," with soggy leaves lying

like carpets by the doors of neighboring embassies. Soggy leaves. Soggy weather. Soggy people. Soggy job, thought Shoval. Soggy but pivotal.

It also meant forced courtesy among the diplomatic corps representing ex-colonies or protectorates; all jockeying, squabbling for favors from an empire that was no more; children who refused to admit mother had passed away, shoved into premature obscurity by the sickness called Suez. It was a fixed smile whenever he met a Jordanian official. It was being pleasant to the Egyptian vice-consul over tea at the Dorchester. Even before he accepted the post, they had told him to bear it. After all, they said, peacetime intelligence was merely a form of diplomacy.

Since Israel had joined the family of nations, it seemed that *Shin Beth* case officers were indelibly marked as second secretaries. Now it had become a foregone conclusion, and the whispers preceded him at diplomatic functions: *Here comes Shoval, the intelligence man at their embassy,* or worse yet, *Mordecai Shoval's a spy for the Jews.* Then they made jokes. Well, he wasn't operational. He was a case officer. He was the elbow joint in the arm that reached from Tel Aviv to London.

But for the Americans he would have been alone with his misery. One could count on the CIA undercover case man being the gunnery sergeant of their embassy's Marine detachment. Not so the British who, he reluctantly admitted, were second on the Row only to the Russians when it came to guile. After nearly two years in London, Shoval had yet to discover his British counterpart. It would take a lifetime to get to the bottom of the Foreign Office. Burgess, Fuchs, Vassal, and MacLean had shaken them up. After these fiascos, even F. O. stenos were given covers. Then came Lonsdale, and getting anything from them was like getting talk from a stone.

Somehow, Shoval, at the bottom of it an Anglophile, felt left out. After all, he once spent a year as a Special Branch man in British CID offices at Jaffa, and he had two commendations to prove it. But he never spoke of it. This duty was performed in pre-independence days and there were those who would take a grim view of the details. Somebody always wanted someone else's job. Somewhere, somebody wanted his.

Shoval ran his small section, which included himself, two stenos, a destruction barrel, and an antiquated cipher machine, with painstaking thoroughness. He liked to call it good living habits. All it gained him was a mountain of paperwork.

London, Shoval thought. It was not an intelligence officer's town. Not like Bonn or Prague or Zagreb. One seemed out of place. It was somehow unromantic. Cynically it occurred to him that practicing the trade in London was a little like goosing the hostess of a garden party in Hampstead in front of the company.

He asked the window, "Where was I, Leinhardt?" and turned around to face a slightly built, middle-aged man who sat across the desk.

"Me, not you, Shoval. Me," replied Leinhardt. "I was curious a month ago and I'm still curious. You've got your own people who could run *Expediter*. Plenty of them could. So why me? I asked you then and I ask you now."

Shoval carefully rearranged his desk paraphernalia like a seamstress. "They tend to get overemotional," he said. "This requires a delicate touch. There's a weighty political aspect here. Besides, plenty of them, as you say, don't possess your qualifications."

"Which are?"

"Werner, Werner," said Shoval, sighing. He played with the paper knife. "It's that when I see *Uncle Vanya*, I think of you. Tragic and Chekhov and all that. Nobody else would do."

"That's enough."

"All right," said Shoval. "One, you used to run your own apparatus. You're used to being alone. Two, you're a German national with Gestapo background, so you know the horses that are running. Three, there are certain improprieties in your wartime record of which we are mutually aware."

Leinhardt looked at Shoval's Hitler mustache. "Stern?" he asked. He knew, but he asked anyway.

"Precisely," said Shoval. "Impropriety number one."

"That was one man, Shoval. One man in Warsaw a long time ago. There was a war on, remember?"

"Nonetheless the Poles consider it an atrocity."

The radiator below the window whined and snuffled. There was a loud clank and the noises stopped.

Leinhardt shifted in the chair. "So the game is leverage," he said quietly.

"I needn't explain the rules," Shoval said. He tugged a heavy file from his mail tray. Opening it, he wet a finger and riffled through the first pages. Then he shut the file, removed his glasses, and leaning forward like a politician in a fireside chat said, "I have assigned Vogel the code name *Oryx*."

"Mind if I peek at the file?" asked Leinhardt.

"Yes, I do," Shoval said.

He spun his chair and faced the window again. Clasping his hands before his face, he measured the tree beyond the window over his fingertips. He cleared his throat. "To reiterate," he said, "your concern is simply to insure the machinery operates smoothly. In running *Expediter*, I want you to keep him scared, honest, and safe. But I don't want him disillusioned. Once he's made contact and identification, then . . ." Shoval paused.

"Then?"

"I'll decide that later." Shoval glanced at his watch. *"Expediter*'s due to call in at nine-thirty. A man called Stassen will drop in shortly and give you a quick run-through on his observations. He met Kampass in New York last night. He came by the same plane, different class."

"That Kurt Stassen with Bonn Intelligence?" asked Leinhardt.

Shoval said nothing.

"He used to be number three for Rheinhard Gehlen. Come on, Shoval. How's he involved?"

"My, oh, my," said Shoval, shaking his head.

"I'll give you advice, Shoval. I knew him in the war. He's no good. You need Stassen like you need a tumor. Nothing here." Leinhardt pointed at his concave belly.

"Herr Stassen and I have enjoyed successes."

"I'm sure of it. How's he fit in? I want to know what's going on. I have the right."

"He'll tell you about it when he gets here. Now what do you know about Vogel?" asked Shoval. "What did our people in Geneva give you?"

"Anybody who was anybody knew a little about Vogel. I did homework."

"Just wanted to see," said Shoval.

Leinhardt said, "What surprises me is his deserting like that. He wasn't the type. He finishes in Paris pimping for that woman, Steiner, for room and board. I mean he was so big you used to whisper his name. Now . . ." Leinhardt shrugged.

Shoval took a pipe from the rack at the corner of his desk. He tamped it down with a blunt instrument. He flicked his thumb across a kitchen match. For a moment he regarded the match, turning it with his fingers. "He had reasons," he said. "*Herr* Vogel was a very deep man. Did you get the gen on his part in the Wannsee Conference?" Shoval touched the match to the pipe bowl.

"He sat in."

"More. Much more," explained Shoval, snuffing out the match and waggling his head from side to side. It was so typically Jewish, Leinhardt thought. Despite the veneer of Anglo-Saxon pseudosophistication, it percolated through. What is it about them, he wondered, that they hate themselves so?

Shoval said, "At that meeting there was Wilhelm Stuckart, Josef Buehler, Dr. Meyer and Dr. Leibbrandt, all the *Staatssekretäre*. There was Himmler, Heydrich, and Eichmann. Vogel kept in the background. Only Heydrich knew about him, not even Eichmann. The rest thought he was another SS aide-de-camp to Himmler.

"Heydrich began by explaining that the relocation schemes had failed and everything else—massive sterilization, relocation schemes—everything had failed. Then he presented the *Endlösung* plan, the Final Solution. He told them how he was going to kill eleven million Jews. But,"—Shoval settled back and held the nape of his neck with his hands—"what nobody knew is that it was not Heydrich's idea of how it would be carried out. It was Vogel's."

Shoval moved forward. He relocated his letter knife and inkwell as though they were pieces on a chessboard. "It's ironic," he continued, "how Vogel became involved. At first he didn't want any part of it. He met Heydrich at a cocktail party in Pankow a year earlier and they took to each other. Vogel wasn't even in the SS then. He was an undersecretary of agriculture in Saxony—a minor party official. Anyway, Heydrich courted Vogel because Vogel was the end of old-line Junker aristocracy, and Heydrich was a snob. They liked trappings, Vogel's status. Vogel agreed to give him fencing lessons, imagine that? Heydrich was crazy about fencing. It was Vogel's charm school. In return, Heydrich got him a commission in the SS and took him on the staff. The education continued, but both ways. Then things began to change. Soon it was Vogel who pushed Heydrich, and in turn, it was Heydrich who pushed Himmler. Heydrich was the apple of the SS eye. When he was assassinated in Prague, they made Vogel a *Gruppenführer*. But he continued to wear the uniform of a *Standartenführer* and even his own people thought him responsible only for the Majdanek operation. But in fact it was Vogel who later ran Richard Glücks, Camps Inspector, and in the end, Oswald Pohl, head of the WVHA in Berlin. So he became responsible for the entire killing facilities in the East: Majdanek, Chelmno, Treblinka, Sobibor, all of them. You see how it was? They shaped him and used him as window dressing, and soon he became better at handling the Jewish question than they themselves."

"How did you surface him?" asked Leinhardt. He had never heard the story before.

"Some job to learn he's alive," said Shoval, with a trace of pride. "To prove he was that deeply involved. They destroyed all records. A year ago we got a report from one Franz Janisch that, for a tidy sum, gave us the breakdown of Vogel's responsibilities. Janisch was an executive with DEGESCH, a subsidiary of I. G. Farben, which manufactured gas for the killing centers. He'd had dealings with Vogel, and while the

SS tried to keep their own house clean, they had no control over the files at Farben. Janisch had kept records unknown to Vogel because no one trusted anyone. There was some graft between the SS and the Farben works, payoffs, crazy money, and Janisch was only protecting himself. The rest was paying the right people. We traced Vogel to Paris, where he was posing as an Alsatian by the name of Baldur Kuntz. You know the rest, about the plastic surgery in Vienna and Dr. Herman Wick who performed the operation and now lives here in London. Now, the thing is we have plenty of makes on Vogel then; we don't know what he looks like now. But there are some things you can't change: size—size of hands and height. That's why we have a bird dog, a foolproof locater, *Expediter*."

"What about the woman?"

"There's an old address on her. Doesn't do much good. You know whores. They're nomads. Now for some reason, Vogel bolted Paris in 1956. He crossed over the Spanish frontier and pop, that's it."

"Nothing since?"

"Nothing. That's why we decided to pick up Kampass. We've had him on file ever since the war. We wanted to wait and use him." Shoval sucked hard on the pipe and Leinhardt could see spittle flow. "ODESSA handled his escape route," added Shoval. "They're another interested party in this. That's why the security."

Leinhardt saw it now. He said, "And you want to put Kampass into ODESSA?"

"Perfect credentials," said Shoval. "He's on the run."

Outside the rain began to patter down again from the gunmetal sky. It ticked against the windowpanes.

"They might help him, Shoval," said Leinhardt. "But they wouldn't give him the time of day on security."

"You know their current set-up? They're looking for hands." Shoval leaned back, closed his eyes, and recited from memory: "*Organisation der ehemaligen SS Angehörigen*. It was a clandestine SS cell fronted by legal *Waffen SS* veteran's organizations. They'd siphon funds off to help war criminals.

Then the *Waffen SS* tired of it and shut them off. So they had
to go elsewhere. They sold weapons, old MG-42s and the like,
to the Algerian rebels. Did some business in Syria and with
Nasser's people. In return for guns, they got narcotics. In
return for narcotics, the Corsican crime cartels gave them
cash. The cash went to helping people like Vogel. Now
they've boiled down to hard cases."

"You're right on it," said Leinhardt.

"Job," said Shoval. He opened his eyes and handed Leinhardt another file, with the word *Patriots* written on the
cover in chinograph pencil. "That will update you on
ODESSA," he said.

"Well, they're not all that dead," said Leinhardt. "They
cooled one of your operations this year."

"Feeling patriotic are you, Leinhardt?"

"No. But I heard they earmarked that ex-Latvian Nazi
Party leader, Cukurs, in Montevideo. The word was he
agreed to surface Josef Mengele for you in Buenos Aires. You
had leverage on him. But ODESSA learned about it through
a leak in your Paraguay network. Right?"

"Something like that," Shoval answered.

"Well, this is the same thing," said Leinhardt. "Basically
you're pulling it with Kampass."

"Yes, basically."

"Well, it's your risk," said Leinhardt.

"No," said Shoval. "Not mine. Yours."

Leinhardt looked at Shoval's mustache. "Crafty old
Shoval," he said.

"So-so," Shoval agreed.

The buzzer on the intercom at Shoval's elbow rang. He
reached over and pressed the button. *"Herr* Stassen outside,"
it said.

"Thank you, Julia," said Shoval. "And, oh, Julia, could you
bring tea in about ten minutes." He glanced at Leinhardt.
"Two cups," he added. Shoval rubbed at the lenses of his
tortoise-shell glasses with a bit of tissue, put them in his
mouth, blew on them, and rerubbed them. "How's your family, Leinhardt?" he asked.

"That's none of your Goddamn business."

"No, I suppose not."

The door to the outer office opened and Stassen came in like a strong wind. He was heavier than he appeared at first glance because of the narrow cut to his suit. He was that type of man whose physique resembles a cube: hips and trunk as wide as the shoulders. He was a man whose well-filled pants legs would not flap on March afternoons.

Shoval watched Stassen approach his desk and nod soberly. It was always the same; he got the impression that it was with the utmost difficulty the man restrained himself from clicking his heels. "Kurt," he said, "meet *Uncle Vanya*. *Uncle Vanya*, Kurt Stassen, Bonn's 'Man in Black.'"

"Hello, Werner," said Stassen.

"Break your arms and legs," replied Leinhardt.

Shoval raised a bushy eyebrow. "I wasn't aware you two knew each other that well."

"Sure," said Stassen. "Long time. Werner knows everybody."

"Apparently," said Shoval. "Kurt, want to bring *Uncle Vanya* up to date?"

Stassen sat down and crossed one heavy leg over the other. "How much do you know?"

Leinhardt noted with distaste that Stassen was wearing white athletic socks. He lit a cigarette and blew a smoke ring. "I know *Shin Beth* wants to put a man into ODESSA to try and surface Rudolf Vogel and I'm to insure cover and logistics. I make sure they don't hurt *Expediter*."

"Know why?" asked Stassen.

"I assume Shoval wants to hang Vogel when he's found."

"Not quite," Stassen answered. "We are thinking of something else. Something quite different."

"I wondered why you were involved here," said Leinhardt. "I wouldn't say you and Shoval were natural bed partners."

"The war was over nearly twenty years ago," said Shoval, breaking in. "Go ahead, Kurt."

Stassen looked surprised. "Everything?" he asked.

"What he has to know; need basis."

Stassen shrugged. He turned to Leinhardt. "You know after this May it might not be possible to prosecute war criminals if Bonn passes the Statute of Limitations?"

Leinhardt nodded and blew another smoke ring.

"Well, there is a growing conservative wing in the Bundestag that maintains most important Nazis have been brought in and the administration should drop it entirely. Needless to say, the final decision is going to have an effect on how Bonn conducts relations with Israel. If there's a whitewash, it will sabotage plans now in the formulative stage for an exchange of ambassadors. There are also arms negotiations involved. A number of our people have been assisting the Nasser regime in missile research. We have to counter this by supplying Israel with certain armaments: light-infantry weapons and training."

"Pax Germania," said Leinhardt.

"Don't interrupt," said Shoval. "Continue, Kurt."

"This is strictly an Israeli operation: the penetration of ODESSA, information on the organization, whereabouts of other war criminals, where they get their banking, and finally, the incarceration of Vogel."

Leinhardt looked unimpressed.

Stassen glanced at Shoval again. Shoval nodded.

"Vogel is then to be extradicted to West Germany along with all the information gathered." He waited for it to sink in.

Leinhardt sat up and nodded. He said, "So Vogel is your idea of a pacification nipple."

Shoval leaned forward. "Don't make bad jokes," he said. "*Herr* Vogel is to be the tool with which our two countries will bury the ax. The resulting good will should be incalculable. The Israelis turn over to Bonn a major war criminal for trial and punishment by his own peers."

Leinhardt threw back his head and laughed.

"Funny?" asked Shoval.

"You hypocrites. You bloody hypocrites. You holier-than-thou bastards."

"You have a small mind, Leinhardt," said Shoval with contempt. "You are a small man."

"Big enough to know a cynic when I see one," Leinhardt said. He gasped, catching his breath after the laughter. He said, "What happens if *Expediter* turns up Stassen's name?" More laughter.

"You're a funny man who's going to get his face pushed in someday," said Stassen, his features darkening.

"Yes, that's right," said Shoval. "What's more, accusations aren't relative. It's Kurt's postwar activities that interest me. His record is exemplary."

"At least I didn't quit the Fatherland in a time of need," said Stassen. "I didn't deal with the other side. You don't wear the white jacket, you know."

"You were a pompous ass in forty-three and you're worse now," said Leinhardt. "Pompous ass; *poo, poo.*"

Shoval said, "All right, children."

Stassen exploded out of the chair. He shouted, "I told you!" He pointed a finger at Leinhardt. He turned to Shoval. "Make him stop," he said.

"Sit down, Kurt," said Shoval.

Stassen sat down heavily. Ruffled, he pulled at his shirt as though it were an adjustable bib.

Leinhardt asked, "What did you think of Kampass?"

"Don't throw his name around," Shoval reprimanded. "*Expediter*. Say that."

Stassen, still red, looked at Shoval. He said, "You're going to have a problem. He tried to hide two bottles of gin and a pistol in his suitcase. He's an alcoholic. He'll fold up like a lily."

"That's grand, grand," said Leinhardt. He threw up his hands.

"We can't top him," said Shoval. "You'll have to wring him out, Werner. Dry him and good."

"He's a *Landser*," added Stassen. "He won't win any spelling prizes."

"He's the best we've got," said Shoval. "We went through

the other possibilities. He's the only one around who could positively identify Vogel. You'll have to make do."

"Remember," said Stassen, "I want our name out of this. We have nothing to do with it. I'm only liaising. I can't give you any help."

"Don't worry, Kurt," said Leinhardt. "You won't get your precious little ass in the mud."

A ringing sounded from somewhere within Shoval's desk. He looked at his wristwatch. "That's our bird," Shoval said. He pulled open the lower drawer of his desk and placed a red telephone in front of him. For a moment he looked at it, watching it ring. Then he picked it up. "Imperial Cleaners, good morning," he said. Then, "Who is this? Who? No, this is the right num—wait." He looked up, his face blank.

Leinhardt giggled.

"He hung up," said Shoval, replacing the phone.

"*Landser*," said Leinhardt, nodding.

The phone rang again. Shoval took it up. He said quickly, "This is the right number. . . . What? . . ." He covered the speaker with his hand. "He's calling from a public phone," he said to Stassen. "Isn't he supposed to be at the hotel?" He uncovered the speaker. Then, "Yes he is." Shoval offered the phone to Leinhardt.

Leinhardt took the phone. "Hello," he said. ". . . Yes, this is he. . . . Well, what are you doing there? . . . All right. Now go to the hotel. Do it now. . . . I'll see you in your room at ten-thirty. . . . Ten-thirty. Goodbye. . . . Yes, goodbye. *Goodbye*." He rang off. He looked at Shoval. "Oh, my God," he said.

"Werner," said Shoval. "I think you'd better go. You have a grasp of things. Julia will show you an office where you can study the dossier on ODESSA. She'll give you a contact schedule and security procedure."

"No tea?" asked Leinhardt.

"No tea," confirmed Shoval.

Leinhardt rose. "Break your arms and legs," he said to Stassen.

Stassen glared.

Leinhardt nodded to Shoval and went out the door, leaving

it open for the secretary, who was bringing in tea. The girl, wobbly on incredibly high heels, set the tray in front of Shoval and left.

Shoval saw Stassen watching her. "You like that?" he asked. "She is wearing her come-and-do-it-to-me shoes."

Stassen smiled. It was as though a crack appeared in a rock.

Shoval reached for the pot. "Two lumps with milk, isn't it?" he asked.

•

Kampass reached the hotel, a Victorian pension a block from the Gloucester Road tube station in Kensington, slightly after ten-fifteen.

He was upset over the harsh tone of *Uncle Vanya*'s voice over the phone. What had he done wrong? he wondered. They did not tell him it was a cleaning establishment. He was not looking forward to meeting *Uncle Vanya*.

The reservation awaited him: a single without bath for thirty-seven shillings and sixpence including his breakfast. He signed the registry.

The desk clerk eyed him owlishly over his spectacles. "Six-oh-eight for Mr. Speirling," he said.

The room was at the end of a labyrinth of corridors. It was quite bare, Spartan, with a bed and dresser, and a washbasin in the corner.

The porter put the bags on the bed. Kampass gave him a coin.

For several minutes he sat on the bed and watched the rain falling beyond the window. It slanted down on the slate roofs and chimneys of the adjacent buildings and thin plumes of smoke trailed away horizontally, hammered flat by the rain. Then he began to unpack. He hung his Vienna suit in the closet and put his shirts in the dresser, everything neatly in place, everything where he would find it quickly. Orderly living on the road was as important as orderly living at home.

Because pressure was on was no excuse to lose a grip on things, he reminded himself.

At ten-thirty there was a rap on the door. Kampass answered without opening.

"Yes?"

A piece of paper was slid under the door. Kampass could see it was the lower half of the playing card; the part that carried five diamonds. He picked it up and compared. It matched his half.

"Now push them both back under the door," said a voice.

Kampass put them together and shoved them through.

A moment later, "Open the door."

Kampass turned the knob. He found himself facing a small, dark man several inches shorter than himself. The eyes that searched his seemed flat and disinterested. Above the tiny button of the man's chin stretched a mouth that looked as though it were made to eat plates.

"I'm your Uncle," he said. He let himself in, and pushing past Kampass, went over to the bed and sat down. "I'm told you have butter for brains," he said. "Is that so?"

Kampass said nothing.

"Well?"

"I'm going to do my best." He looked at the surgical eyes watching him. And he knew what it was about *Uncle Vanya*. He had seen them in the camps. He had seen what they had become. The clean, clinical stare; the gauging of competitive abilities; the diagnosis; the relationship between doctor and patient, or was it mortician and corpse?

"Mr. Vanya . . ."

"Call me Leinhardt," said the man. He moved on the bed and the springs squeaked.

Kampass turned his eyes away.

His voice, like his eyes, was dispassionate, bored. Kampass tried to place the accent. He was not at all sure it was German. Perhaps southern. Bavarian maybe. But he could have been any nationality: Slav, Bulgar, or Hungarian. Kampass did not know. He did not want to.

"See I stay happy, and we'll get along," said Leinhardt.

"Remember what I tell you and execute. Execution is nine-tenths of the game. Now we've got a lot of work to do, so I suggest you take off your coat and get some of that hotel stationery and make yourself comfortable. You're going to commit most of what I tell you to memory because I will ask you to destroy all the notes afterwards." He got up from the bed and went to the window. "Filthy day," he said. "How was your trip?"

"I slept," said Kampass. He watched Leinhardt's spare shoulders. His suit did not hang properly. He wondered if Leinhardt carried a gun.

"All right," said Leinhardt, turning. "Let's get started."

•

At noon they had them send up sandwiches of bland ham and pasty bread with a plate of Stilton on the side and a bottle of Chablis. Leinhardt drank the Chablis and dictated. Kampass wrote, the stub of a pencil clutched in his hot hand and his eyes stinging. Leinhardt's voice droned on. Four times they covered the same material, Leinhardt tearing up the papers after each session and flushing them down the toilet.

At three, Leinhardt said, "That's it." He took the final set of notes and shredded them.

Kampass sat back and flexed his fingers. He said, "They won't go back on their word, will they? They meant what they said about returning the confession, yes?"

Leinhardt looked unconcerned. He shrugged. "That's what I'm given to understand," he replied, "depending, naturally, on what kind of a report card you get from *Uncle*."

"I know," said Kampass.

"Splendid."

"I'll prove myself," said Kampass. "Wait and see."

"Stop this probing of me," Leinhardt snapped. "I don't like it. I don't care what you think. Don't come on with me. Not after gassing a few thousand people."

"I didn't mean to upset you," said Kampass humbly.

"Stop it." Leinhardt chopped his hand through the air. "Don't wet on my leg like a dog."

Kampass colored.

Leinhardt lit a cigarette and blew the smoke at the ceiling. He asked, "Were you involved in the November third operations in the Krempecki?—It doesn't matter. I am curious."

"Krempecki?" asked Kampass.

"The forest outside Majdanek. They killed twenty thousand of them there in 1943."

Kampass remembered it all right. Sound trucks playing Viennese waltzes were packed around the camp so that one would not hear the shooting. The Ukrainians had actually done it. He had seen them come out of the forest for lunch. Their faces were pale. They did not like it. It had been a freezing morning and the air carried the crackle of machine-pistol fire despite the sound trucks. All day the Ukrainians had been at it. They said some of them went mad afterwards. Twenty thousand. He could believe it.

"I remember," said Kampass, barely audible. He looked up at Leinhardt. "But I did not go. I had no part of that. It was the Ukrainians, the Georgian guards."

"Some of us did lousy things," said Leinhardt. "Some of us had to. That was the worst."

Kampass did not reply.

Leinhardt stubbed out his cigarette abruptly. Outside the rain continued to fall. It was heavier now. It was driven by a gusting wind. The windows creaked. Leinhardt said, "We'll go through it orally now. The cover. Everything. I'll ask a question or mention a name and you will give me correct responses. Right? First, Herman Wick."

"Viennese," answered Kampass at once. "He operated on Vogel in Vienna. He's a member of the Royal College here. He practices on Cadogan Place in Chelsea. He has a house in Hertfordshire. Ten Lamson's Green. He is in close contact with ODESSA's coordinator in Ireland, Viktor Lodz. Do you want his telephone? Wick's number?"

"No," replied Leinhardt. He stood with his back turned, listening and nodding. He said, "How about Vienna? Give me your cover when they ask how you came by Wick's name."

"Vienna," said Kampass. "I was there on business for my agency from November twentieth to twenty-fourth—"

"No, no," cut in Leinhardt. "Twenty-third. That's important."

"Twenty-third. I met there this Seyss-Dietrich. I told him the Israelis had located me and were only waiting. He suggested Dr. Wick."

"Stop," said Leinhardt. He reached in his coat pocket and took out an envelope. He put it on the bed. "That's a letter of introduction for you to Wick in Seyss-Dietrich's own handwriting," he said. "Do not, repeat, do not open it. How were you introduced?"

"My cousin, Rolf Schneider. He was a policeman in Frankfurt. Before I left Germany I had dinner with him and his family. Seyss-Dietrich was there. He was on the police force with Rolf. Then I met him by accident in Vienna."

Leinhardt nodded his approval.

"I found his political beliefs were as mine."

"*Sympatico*," said Leinhardt.

It was incredible, thought Kampass. They knew so much about him. For instance, his cousin had died of influenza two weeks before he, Kampass, immigrated to America. Rolf's wife went to South Africa with the children soon afterwards. They had gone far back.

"Tell about Vogel's mistress," Leinhardt said. "Tell about that."

"Mistress?"

"Well, companion."

"Ruth Steiner," said Kampass. "Alsatian-German. She was with Vogel in the Paris days. She was a prostitute."

"And still is," Leinhardt added.

"Yes, and still is," said Kampass, nodding.

On it went. On and on. Leinhardt fired a steady stream of questions and Kampass answered, sometimes vague, sometimes sure of himself. They went into Vogel's background, his tastes, his family; Leinhardt prompting, teasing the answers out of him, insulting him, complimenting him. At one moment Kampass would be terribly afraid of Leinhardt; at another he could nearly like him. When they finished, it was dark outside. But it was still raining and the streetlamps threw crooked shadows of bare trees upon the walls. Leinhardt did not turn on the lights. The last part of the questioning had taken place in darkness. Now Leinhardt stood in the gloom, in the corner, so that Kampass could hardly see him, and he asked quietly, "Well, what do you think about it? About Vogel. Personally."

Kampass moved his shoulders. "I don't know. I do my job."

"Come on, Kampass. I want to hear motivation."

"Well, it doesn't seem right, that's all. I was only a sergeant. Yes, I did things. We all did. But Vogel . . ."

"You feel put upon, correct?" asked Leinhardt.

"Well, why did it have to be me?" asked Kampass. "I didn't order it done, the killings." He paused. He should not be talking like this.

"That's all right. Go on," said Leinhardt. "Put me straight."

"Well, it's true," Kampass said. His voice was strained. "Goddamn him, why couldn't he have died? Why didn't they catch him?"

Leinhardt moved away from the shadows. Kampass heard a board groan.

Leinhardt quietly said, "That's funny, Kampass. Because it's exactly how I feel about you. So don't excite me. Don't ever do that." He went to the door. He turned. "Call Wick at nine-thirty tomorrow morning. Nine-thirty exactly. He goes to surgery at ten. Then call me at the same number where you reached me this morning." And he was gone.

Kampass lay down on the bed. He felt drained. He did not turn on the light. He found he liked the darkness and enjoyed watching the shadows move against the walls and the ceiling. If you used your imagination you could make any figure you wanted from them. He tried not to think of the briefing. Leinhardt had told him it would be better if he did not. Once he got it straight, there was no point in overworking it. It would get like a bad painting then, Leinhardt said. There would be mistakes. Cover is like art. You never overwork it. Find the subject, sketch it, and leave it alone. Let it lie deep inside you until you are ready to use it; then utilize a little at a time. Let it go crumb by crumb. Let them nibble, not feast. Whet their appetites. Then they won't know what they are eating. Let them hunger.

A knock at the door brought Kampass out of his stupor. He went rigid. "Yes?" he said.

"Steward here," came the answer.

"What do you want?" Still he did not move.

"Package for Mr. Speirling."

Kampass rose and went softly to the door. "Leave it," he said. "I'm indecent."

He waited until the footsteps receded. Then he opened the door warily, just a crack. The hall was empty. There was a cylindrical parcel tied with Manila cord standing by the doorstep. Kampass nudged it with his foot mistrustfully. It fell over. Nothing happened. He picked it up and shook it. It sounded like liquid. Back in the room, he snapped on a light and carefully unwrapped the package. It was a bottle of Beefeaters and there was a card with it. The card said *Regards from Uncle*. He even had the brand right.

Kampass placed the gin on the bedside table and turned on the reading lamp. For a long time he looked at the bottle, seeing the light catch the clear liquid. He ran his fingers over the label, feeling the smoothness of it. The cellophane wrapped about the bottle crackled.

"No," he said aloud. "Oh, no sir."

It was possible. He *could* do it. For tonight, he could pass it up. And after tonight there would be tomorrow night. But even one night was important. It was a beginning. He would take the dry days one at a time. He knew why Leinhardt sent the bottle. They were testing him.

"Christ," he said. "Wizard!" He smiled and rolled the bottle, seal unbroken, beneath his bed.

Overnight the rain had broken, and it was cold and sunny.
There was the smell of damp leaves in the air. Kampass stood
by the open window and took it in. He raised his head and
sucked in great gulps like a scenting walrus.

Then he went through his floor exercises, the taste of
breakfast still in his mouth.

He had set the alarm on his brass clock, which he had
packed, to nine-thirty, and when it rang, he went directly to
the phone. He gave the number to the switchboard operator
and listened to the hollow burr of the ringing. Do not think,
he reminded himself; let it come out.

"Dr. Wick's office." The voice sounded as though it came
from far away.

Kampass said, "I'd like to speak with the doctor, please."

"The doctor is preparing to go to surgery," replied the receptionist.

"It will take but a minute," said Kampass.

The girl asked him if he wanted an appointment.

"No, well, perhaps," he explained. "It is a personal matter."

"I can put you down for next Friday at four."

"That's impossible," he said. "It's urgent. Only a moment."

"Name please?"

"Ah, Speirling." He spelled it out.

"Just a minute," said the receptionist.

There was a sharp click. Then, "This is Wick."

Kampass spoke in German. *"Grüss Gott,"* he began pleasantly. "Sir, I am wondering if you can help me."

"I'm on my way to surgery," replied Wick. "What's this
about?"

"It's a problem," said Kampass. Leinhardt was right. It was
easy if you let it come out. "A small matter only."

"A clinical problem? For this, my office hours are—"

"This is urgent, *Herr Doktor.*"

"Urgent? How urgent?"

"Very."

"I'm sorry," said Wick. "You're going to have to be more
specific." Irritation crept in.

"I'd rather not discuss this on the phone," countered Kampass.

"You'd rather better," said Wick.

Kampass groped a bit. He said, "Seyss-Dietrich."

"Who?"

"Seyss-Dietrich," he repeated. "He recommended your services. He said to me, 'Kampass, you will see. He is discreet.'" It was lonely, just as Leinhardt said.

"If this is a problem of the young ladies, you have reached the wrong man," Wick said abruptly. "And I thought you said your name was Speirling."

"It is not. Seyss-Dietrich said you would know about the problem."

"So?" Caution replaced the irritation. "He is a patient of mine, this Seyss-Dietrich?"

"He was," said Kampass.

"Of Vienna?"

"Yes, the same." Kampass wiped at his brow.

"The policeman?"

"I believe so, yes."

There was a long and pregnant silence. Then Wick said, "This is an open line, yes?"

Kampass explained about the phone.

"Then we are not being discreet, are we?"

"I need help," said Kampass quickly. "I need it now."

"You consider the affliction to be fatal?"

"Perhaps," said Kampass.

"You are to be in London how long?"

Kampass told him two weeks. That was how it was to be.

"Possibly we can discuss your symptoms. To diagnose is impossible without discussion. Would you permit consultation?"

Wick was talking in riddles now. Kampass was not quick enough to keep up with it. "Whatever is called for," he said.

"You are free for luncheon?" asked Wick.

Kampass tried to identify the flat, metallic voice on the end of the line with a person. He could not. "Yes, of course," he answered.

"Here is what," said Wick. "Do you know the walk, Church Place, behind St. James's off Piccadilly?"

"I don't know London. I arrived only yesterday."

"I see. You best ask a taxi driver. Listen now, there is an accordion player who stands at the foot of Church Place across from the Rumanian Tourist Office. He is blind. Only a beggar, nothing else."

"I have it," said Kampass. He scribbled the streets on the reverse side of the hotel menu.

Wick continued, "At noon, exactly noon, you will ask him to play the piece "Domino." Post yourself nearby. I will be watching. I will contact you. I am careful, you see, because your friend Seyss-Dietrich had some very unpleasant associates."

"I understand," said Kampass.

"By the way, you are staying where?"

Kampass told him.

"It is because there could be a sudden change in our plans."

"Thank you," said Kampass.

"Not yet," said Wick and he hung up.

Kampass rubbed his hands together. He smiled. It was working. It was going to be all right. He called Leinhardt.

•

Kampass left the hotel at a quarter to twelve. A heavy layer of cloud had moved in, but here and there above the grimy buildings, narrow rays of sunlight prismed through. He hailed a passing taxi on the Gloucester Road.

As they turned onto the Bayswater Road and approached Marble Arch, he could see the wide, wooded expanse of Hyde Park. Along the Serpentine nannies pushed perambulators, and a pickup soccer game was in progress on the grass nearby.

Recalling his meager soccer talents as a youth, he watched from the cab as a group of boys darted after the ball, coattails flying. Kampass had a sudden impulse to halt the taxi, to remove his jacket and rush headlong onto the grass to join in the game—if only as referee. He would like to be a part of something again so much so that, seeing them play this way, he felt a dull ache within his chest. If nothing else, they would say that Bruno Waldek Kampass was a fine referee of football. He would not mind referreeing a nonstop soccer game for the rest of his life.

The taxi drove up Piccadilly. The driver stopped and pointed past a bus to a church opposite them.

"Church Place is on the left of the church," said the driver through the glass partition. "It's that small walkway. At the end of it you'll find the tourist office."

Kampass paid the fare and crossed the street, glancing at the bus. Plastered on its panels was FACE THE FUTURE WITH PEARL ASSURANCE.

Now, standing before the walled-in, pigeon-ridden church, he could hear the strains of the accordion over the traffic. He followed the sound, moving down the narrow walk between the buildings. The accordion player stood at the end of the walkway, dressed in an army greatcoat that hung below his knees and a black beret cocked upon his head. He could see that the beggar's face was horribly scarred, the skin spread drum-tight over the cheekbones. The eyes, pupilless, bulged from under his brows like the ends of hard-boiled eggs. The beggar had his face turned to the sky, and as he played, he swayed lightly on his feet. Kampass stared. He remembered again the column on the Chelm Road.

Across the street he saw the blue facings of the Rumanian Tourist Office.

At noon he approached the beggar and requested "Domino." The bald eyes lowered from the sky to Kampass. Involuntarily he recoiled. Then, he put two shillings into the blue bag that hung from the accordion.

Shifting the weight of the instrument on his shoulder, the veteran played, his heavy fingers punching the keys. The notes groaned out sadly while Kampass waited, leaning against the side of the building.

When the beggar had played through one refrain, he

snapped the valves of the accordion shut, and cane tapping, moved off down the street.

No Wick.

Kampass began to feel self-conscious. Something had gone wrong. Maybe Wick had tried to reach him to change the meeting.

He gave up after a half-hour and walked aimlessly down Jermyn Street. Had he said something that alerted Wick? Perhaps he should not have mentioned Seyss-Dietrich so soon. What was he to tell Leinhardt? He retraced his steps back to Church Place. As he drew even with the Rumanian Tourist Office, he saw Dr. Herman Wick. It had to be Wick. He looked like his name.

•

Kampass would have likened the man who watched him from the shadows across the street to a prime Westphalian hog. His chin was tucked into the folds of a mackintosh so that the wrinkles of loose flesh welled up to meet the jaw line. He might have had no neck at all and the side of his face seemed to melt downwards, forming heavy dewlaps. Wick's eyes locked with Kampass' and he smiled a slow smile of recognition.

"My dear Kampass," he called out and walked over.

Kampass grasped the offered palm. It was soft and damp and the back of the hand was hairless. He might have been closing his fingers about a lump of dough. Wick threw a paternal arm around his shoulder and guided him down a street, at the end of which Kampass could see the peek of greenery.

"I told you I was careful," said Wick.

"I understand the need of discretion," said Kampass. "I didn't think you would come."

They walked on in silence, Wick breathing heavily, wheezing. Kampass wrinkled his nose. An odor of stale socks hung about the man.

They walked across the mall to the entrance of St. James's

Park and headed for the pond. In the background, there were the shrill cries of children at play. A pigeon sailed by and landed on the path. It walked stilt-legged to an empty peanut shell.

"I come here every noon," said Wick, breaking the long silence. "It helps me relax. Does it help you, also?"

Kampass said nothing.

In a bed of flowers two pigeons prepared to mate, the male ruffling his neck feathers and making short dashes at the female.

"There's your love," said Wick, pointing. "I don't like people who don't like birds. They lack understanding of freedom."

Wick directed him to an empty bench at the edge of the pond and a short distance from the path. The noises of the children receded. Wick took a packet of birdseed from his pocket and spread some of the seeds on the grass. Several ducks waddled out of the water to investigate. Wick squatted on haunches which swelled outward, great beeves of meat, and began to feed them. "It wasn't very wise, you running like that," he said, returning to the bench and dusting his hands on his coat. "In fact, it was stupid."

Kampass tried to project himself into the personality of the fugitive, running for his life. He tried to forget Leinhardt and the others.

"What do you want of me?" Wick asked presently. He watched the ducks.

"Contacts," said Kampass. "Contacts who are prepared to help."

"They've found you? They've run you down?" Wick turned towards him, his chubby face expressionless, controlled.

"I think so."

"Think so?"

"I cannot afford to guess," said Kampass. "The slightest clue is enough."

Tell it straight, Leinhardt had said. They knew anyway. Wick would have gone to the central locater of SS-camp staffs ODESSA kept in Munich. He would have called this morning. If there had been no confirmation, Wick would never have kept their meeting. *If he meets you,* Leinhardt said. *If he goes this far, you've checked out.*

"I'm not going to swallow you whole, Kampass," Wick said. "How did it happen?"

Kampass said, "Why should I tell you?"

Wick got up. "Well, dear boy," he said, "I don't see that we have much to discuss. We shall forget this meeting."

"No. Wait," said Kampass. Then he let it out; all those things Leinhardt made him repeat so often; about finding the electricians in his New York apartment, electricians when there was no malfunction in his wiring. Then there was the *Wehrpass* left in his mailbox.

Wick sat back on the bench. He watched the ducks squabble over the remains of the seed.

"Here," said Kampass. He used the final weapon they had given him. He gave Wick the letter from Seyss-Dietrich.

Wick opened the envelope, tearing it carefully at one end. He grumbled, making noises inside like a rusty boiler. He scanned the letter, then folded it and put it in his pocket. "Why didn't you show me this first, Kampass?"

"I am also careful," said Kampass.

Wick smiled. "Yes, that's the worst of it," he said. "We don't even dare trust one another any more."

Kampass asked, "How about it?"

"You ever read the newspapers?" asked Wick.

"What does that mean?"

"The amnesty," Wick explained. "Why should I compromise my practice and consultants when Bonn courts declare an amnesty this May?"

"This is December, not May."

Wick shrugged. "Five months. Can't you handle yourself for five months?"

Kampass said, "Wick, my time's out. Don't you understand that?"

"If I do this," said Wick. "If I put you in touch with my colleagues, it will cost money—a great deal of money."

"I can't quibble," said Kampass, groveling. "All I have. You can take it."

"Things have become hard," said Wick.

"Five months," said Kampass. "Put me under for five months." He was begging. *If you have to,* Leinhardt said, *take down your pants.*

"It's very lean," said Wick. "There are those who will not take the risk any more. We are short-handed. Ten thousand in sterling."

Kampass moaned.

Not over five thousand, he was told. Then wait for it. They'll make a counterproposition. They're broke, Leinhardt said. They're bankrupt and short-handed.

Wick reddened. The layers of fat beneath his chin shook with indignation. "So," he said. "It is too much? Ten thousand is too much for me to sacrifice my career? It is nothing. Nothing for the risks I take. You find the nearest rock and when it rains and the rain runs under the rock, you all come to me, me—Wick, and scream help."

"Seyss-Dietrich—"

"Forget about that man," snapped Wick. "The yids murdered him, shot him down on the street in Vienna three weeks ago, and I tell you it's too easy. They said your business card was found in his pocket. He was not one to carry cards like that. It's suspicious. Very foggy. And now he's dead, so we can't check. You must admit we are the ones taking all the chances."

"So this is what I get fighting for my country," said Kampass.

"Look here, dear boy," said Wick. "The time for patriotism is over. That finished in the *Führerbunker.* That was the last *Heil.* Don't come around clicking your heels."

He was like the rest of them, thought Kampass. He was like the people, the trash he defended and killed for; the *Herrenvolk* who would turn him in, point him out. *There, the SS, they were the ones.* And where was Wick during the war? Running a cushy practice? Reconstructing the blown-away faces of soldiers back from the fronts? And after the war? Vogel.

"Cram it," said Kampass. At once he was sorry he said it. It was involuntary.

"That talk won't help," reprimanded Wick, re-establishing pecking order. "And here I was going to suggest an alternative."

"I've come a long ways," said Kampass.

"How much can you pay?"

"Five thousand sterling. No more. It finishes me."

"How would you like to work off the balance? Work it off with expenses? Until May. What would you say to that?"

"Doing what?"

"Courier work. That sort of thing. You'd travel between here and Germany: Munich, Frankfurt. Maybe a trip East."

Kampass said, "I'm wanted in Poland. Anywhere East is out of the question."

"You'll receive adequate cover."

Wick turned to face him. Kampass could see several large pores on the side of the doctor's nose. The pores were filled with dirt. And the way hair grew out of Wick's ears was revolting.

"Well," said Wick. "We shall not go further now. There are others who must approve; someone will call you at your hotel this evening. Don't go out. He'll arrange another meeting. You can have the five thousand by tomorrow?"

Kampass moved his shoulders. "I'll try," he said.

"You'll do better than that," said Wick. Business apparently finished, he slapped his huge thighs.

"Now," he said. "Let's utilize the park. It would be a shame to waste it."

After they circled the lake together, Kampass looked after the departing figure of Herman Wick. From the rear, the doctor gave him the fleeting impression of a pear.

●

Wick made it clear where he stood on National Socialism, the Third Reich, and the SS in general. He was a businessman, a doctor, not a politician. It had been a dreadful mistake about the Jews, he said. Unalienated, they might have aided the war effort. He spoke of Einstein and of what Jewry had done for America and the wealthy families, the Rothschilds and the Petcheks—all gone forever. They had committed national suicide, the Germans. The Final Solution was a catastrophic error. He had no sympathy with Kampass. None whatsoever. His actions soiled the name of all German people including himself, an Austrian, who was after all really a German. They succeeded in bringing the wrath of the world down upon the heads of the innocent majority who sought nothing more than to better their country. For shame.

Kampass picked up a pebble and threw it at a duck. Responsibility was not his concern now, he thought. Vogel was. Kampass had started to think once more as a soldier. He had his orders. He was oriented.

Leaving the lake, he marched purposefully out the entrance to the park up through Green Park to Piccadily and kept walking until he reached the Royal Artillery Monument at Hyde Park Corner.

It was the huge sculptured cannon that attracted his attention. At the base of the monument were larger-than-life bronze figures in various poses. To Kampass, the bronze men sweating over their fieldpieces were grist for the Wagnerian mill. He almost heard the trumpets sound; a sad and distant summons to a soldier's funeral; honor's clarion call. Beside men such as these, he thought, Wick and Leinhardt, and yes, even Vogel were midgets. On one side of the monument, a plaque was set into the stone base:

DEDICATED TO THE 29,924 MEN IN THE ROYAL
FIELD ARTILLERY WHO DIED IN WORLD WAR II.
THEY DIED IN THE FAITH THAT THE FUTURE OF
MANKIND WOULD BENEFIT FROM THEIR SACRIFICE

Rubbish, thought Kampass, rubbish and crap. Of his comrades who were killed that winter outside the gates of Moscow—pulverized into fertilizer by the Russian guns and the huge KV tanks—how many would have said *I am dying for the future of mankind.*

They were dying because they had been told to, Kampass reminded himself. This he saw with his barrack-roomer's

sense of what became reality when the other side began to
shoot at you; he, who liked to think he was the kind of soldier
they said could hear the grass grow.

He walked to the opposite end of the monument. There, an
artilleryman lay under a poncho, a helmet covering his face.
A silence hung about the figure, which was green and
streaked with pigeon droppings. Kampass laid his hand, rev-
erently, on the soldier's face where it disappeared under the
helmet, then drew it back from the touch of the icy bronze.
His eyes swept the length of the corpse, took in the massive
hands, limp, and the calves swathed in puttees that poked
out from the poncho shroud—a monument to the sensibility
of war and death with trumpets and drums and Valhalla ever
after, thought Kampass. Or was it really? He wondered.

He became aware of someone at his side. He turned and
looked into the ball-bearing eyes of Leinhardt.

"Sightseeing?" Leinhardt asked.

Leinhardt was wearing a tyroler hat with a tuft of Hirsch
hair tucked in the band. The hat and the hair above the small
eyes and the wide mouth gave him a comic-opera appearance
—the heavy in a modern Gilbert and Sullivan intrigue oper-
etta.

"I saw Wick," said Kampass.

"So I noticed. It went well?"

Kampass explained. He told Leinhardt about the money,
the five thousand Wick wanted in sterling.

Leinhardt snorted. "Five thousand quid," he said.

Kampass said, "You were right. He wants me to work off
the balance. He wanted ten. I said I could get maybe five. He
said it was courier's work."

"He did, did he? That's fine, Kampass. What about your
cover? How did he take it?"

Kampass explained about giving Wick the letter. He mentioned the doctor's concern over Seyss-Dietrich. "Why didn't
you tell me he was dead?" asked Kampass.

Leinhardt's wide mouth sagged down at the corners as
though the facial muscles had become tired of holding the

weight. Kampass assumed this was supposed to be a smile. He was not sure.

Leinhardt said, "Why should we? How could you know about it?"

"He said someone would call me this evening."

"That would be Lodz," said Leinhardt. "He's the one you'll have to convince. He's the audience you'll play to."

"The one in Ireland?"

Leinhardt nodded. "They'll arrange another interview now. They're not sure. It is Seyss-Dietrich that upsets them. They can't check it. They'll commit though. Little by little they'll commit, all right. We monitored a call Wick made to Munich. It seemed to work."

"What happens if he is suspicious, this Lodz?" asked Kampass. He did not look at Leinhardt, but watched the small cars scoot around the traffic circle.

"Why, he'll kill you," said Leinhardt, grinning. Then he left, a small, narrow man under a lugubrious hat, walking nimbly and dodging around the puddles like a boxer.

●

The first thing Kampass noted about his room was that his passport had been moved. He had left it on his bedside table, he was sure about that, and now it was on the dresser. He froze in the center of the room like a bird dog on point.

His suitcase lay at the foot of the bed and latched, but when he opened it, he found a roll of socks misplaced, his shirts disheveled. In the bathroom, he saw his sponge bag had been tampered with. The toothpaste tube had been rolled flat. They had not worried about hiding anything. It was as though they knew he would understand.

Shaken, Kampass threw himself across the bed. He would rest until five-thirty. That was when they told him the bar opened. He owed it to himself, he figured. He would not touch the gin bottle, but he could allow himself one downstairs. They would never know. One to quiet his nerves. One for the road. It would not matter. Not one.

The bar, a stand-up affair of worn mahogany, opened onto the lobby. It was the smallest bar Kampass ever saw, and he had seen a great many. It was the kind you put up at office parties. He ordered a pink gin.

"Good day for it," said the bartender.

Kampass sipped the drink, nursing it and fixing his eyes on a fox-hunting print over the bar. He held the glass with two hands. He saw the bartender was watching him.

"It's all right," Kampass said. "Good."

"Yes sir," said the bartender.

Kampass licked at the drink, not wanting to rush things. This way he could stop when he wanted.

A middle-aged woman and a small pug entered the bar. She hoisted herself onto a stool, and unleashing the dog, placed it on her lap. The pug investigated Kampass as though he might be a fire hydrant, straining towards his crotch and sniffing loudly. Kampass lowered his elbow and blocked its progress.

"He likes you," said the woman, baring a set of discolored teeth. "Mr. Ming doesn't normally take to people. Dog trusts man; woman can trust man."

Kampass grunted and worked on the drink. He examined the print over the rim of the glass. He did not wish to talk.

In the next room, he could hear voices raised in a minor argument over the selection of a television program. The male voice insisted on ITV wrestling; the female wanted to watch the BBC and a gardening show. Kampass shut out the voices and thought of the call that evening; the confrontation with Lodz and what it might be like. *He'll kill you,* said Leinhardt. Leinhardt ought to know. But he had done all right so far, hadn't he? He'd done all they asked.

"I said he must like you," repeated the woman with the bad teeth.

"Your animal is spitting in my drink," said Kampass. The pug had placed both forelegs on the bar.

The woman said, "Say, you're Hungarian, aren't you?"

"No, I'm not," Kampass replied.

"Do you believe in the stars? When were you born?"

Kampass did not reply. He stirred the drink with his finger. He sucked at his finger. It was all right. He was in charge.

"If you're Pisces, this is a good month," said the woman. She took an astrologer's handbook from her purse. "Here it is," she continued. "You will sign papers. Old acquaintances will reappear unexpectedly from the past. That's what it says here."

"Is that so," said Kampass coldly. "I've already signed papers."

"You see?" said the woman. "Are you a Moon Child?"

Kampass stared at the print and drank. In the next room the argument was over, and droll noises about plant-bed up-keep came through. The bartender busied himself with over-wiping a glass. Kampass sensed the man was watching him. Bartenders always seemed to know, he thought. They smelled you out. That was why he did his drinking at home. Bartenders made him feel like a criminal.

"Well, anyway, you're foreign," said the woman. "I mean anyone could tell that, couldn't they?"

Kampass did not answer.

"I'll bet you had it bad in the war," the woman pressed on. "Do you like it here, then? Oh, it has changed so. About the war . . ."

He turned to her. He said, "Madam, dear lady, fornicate."

The woman showed her bad teeth and said no more. When the pug leaned towards his crotch again, she yanked it back.

At eight, Kampass went up to his room. The phone rang at two minutes past the hour. It was not Wick.

"Have pencil and paper?" asked the caller, who did not identify himself.

Kampass said yes.

He was instructed to take the three-thirty train from King's Cross to Hatfield. Someone would meet him at the station. He was to bring the money. They would talk. That was all.

Kampass conveyed the information to Leinhardt at ten.

Leinhardt said, "Be in your room at seven-thirty tomorrow."

Kampass turned on the electric fire in the corner. Then he reached under the bed and brought out the bottle of Beefeaters. For a moment, he felt it. Then he put it back and went to bed.

Later—he did not know what time it was—he awoke to find his bedclothes twisted and the pillow halfway across the room. Outside the first light was greying the sky, and then Kampass knew he had been dreaming.

He had watched it flow into the room under the door, pulling itself along by its fingernails. Then it was standing at the foot of his bed, smiling at him—the old man, smiling insanely. And it began to howl. He recognized the old man. He could never forget him; out of all the thousands, it was he Kampass remembered. They had shut them into the chambers, the aged, naked and cold. They had slapped the mud on the doors to seal them and he had poured the crystals into the tubes and then watched through the thick glass porthole. The old man saw him through the glass and he smiled. He stood smiling at Kampass until the gas reached his mouth and nostrils, and then he began to howl. His mouth opened and closed, and Kampass knew he was screaming. One old man out of thousands: the old man who had stood at his bed, mocking him.

Somehow, he recalled, Vogel had been in the dream. So had Leinhardt. But Kampass remembered that old man so well he could count the hairs of his beard.

●

When he returned to his room after breakfast, Kampass found Leinhardt lying on the bed reading the morning edition of the *Express*. Beside him was a parcel wrapped in brown paper.

"There's the five thousand quid in the package," said Leinhardt from behind his paper. "You're not going out there at three-thirty," he added. "You're leaving now." All this he said without putting aside the *Express.*

"Why?" asked Kampass. He felt his breakfast move in his stomach.

Leinhardt folded the paper. "Chelsea dropped another. Follow football, Kampass?"

Kampass looked at him. "Why?" he asked again.

Leinhardt swung his legs off the bed. He said, "Up to now, it's been Wick who's done the checking. It wouldn't look right if you just fell in with it, you see. You've got a right to know about them. You'd expect a man running would want to question and suspect. That's why you're going to take an early train and—"

"Look, that's suicide," said Kampass. "You said it yourself about Lodz. If he knew I'd disobeyed, well, he might . . ." Kampass let the sentence trail off.

"Don't lose your head," Leinhardt said. He sat on the edge of the bed, his short legs dangling. "It's all been thought out. I want you to look for a few things out there. If you don't dally, you can be back at the station to meet them in plenty of time. They'll never know you were there."

"And if they come? What then? What if they walk in and find me?"

Leinhardt shrugged. "I told you," he said. "You've got every right to find out if Wick is all he said he was. If Wick can question Seyss-Dietrich's information, so can you. If they don't like it, that's too bad. Be indignant. Tell them that 'it's too bad.' Let them lump it."

Leinhardt reached in his coat and brought out a folded paper. He spread it carefully on the bed. Kampass saw it was a crude floor plan. Leinhardt weighted it down at the ends with ashtrays.

"Come here," Leinhardt ordered. "They keep the key above the front door. On the first floor, you'll find Wick's dispensary. Don't waste time there. And forget the sitting room." He moved his finger on the plan, tapping it. "This is where we think he has his office: second floor, second room. If he keeps anything at home, that's where he'll have it. He must keep files."

Kampass looked at the floor plan. If Leinhardt had the layout, he thought, why couldn't they search it? He said, "I don't know the house. I'd be a risk. You have the plans there."

"Use your head," said Leinhardt. "We can't go in there. These were made from the architect's drawings."

Leinhardt leaned back to the plans. Kampass could see how his hair curled at the back like the pinfeathers of a duck. He said, "Oh, sure."

Leinhardt bounced back from the bed. Kampass flinched.

"You smart ass. You do what I tell you," hissed Leinhardt. "No more smart-ass talk from you. Where the hell do you get off?"

Kampass moved away from him. Leinhardt followed, moving sideways, crabbing, his knees bent a little. Kampass thought he was going to be hit.

Then Leinhardt relaxed. He smiled. "Don't ever talk that way to *Uncle* again. No more cheek," he said. He pulled at his sleeves, smoothing them into place. He went to the window. He stood with his back turned and Kampass waited.

For a while Leinhardt said nothing.

Kampass studied the map on the bed, frowning, concentrating as though he might find the answer to his existence there.

"Visit the USA," said Leinhardt.

"What?" asked Kampass. He did not want to look at Leinhardt. He kept his eyes on the map.

"It's an advert across the street," said Leinhardt, mollified. "How did you like America, Kampass? All right, then?"

Kampass said nothing.

"Europe's garbage can," said Leinhardt.

Kampass detected a note of bitterness.

Leinhardt returned from the window. He looked over Kampass' shoulder at the plans.

"There are only a few items I want you to key on here. Lists. That's very important. Then canceled checks drawn on any West German, Austrian, or Swiss bank. They would be written by individuals, not a company. They would be payable to Wick. Last, but not least, Vogel. Anything about

Vogel or his alias, Kuntz, old addresses, letters, anything. Don't you try and judge what's relative and what's not. We'll do that. And don't disturb anything."

Kampass nodded.

"Ever use a camera before?" asked Leinhardt.

Kampass said yes. He'd had a Leica.

"Ever use one like this?" asked Leinhardt. He took a thin metal box from his pocket, the size of two cigarette lighters put end-to-end.

"It's a Minox," said Kampass.

"That's right," said Leinhardt. "It's all ready to shoot. I pre-set it for you. To advance the spool you do it this way; like you're trying to pull it apart, see." Leinhardt moved the mechanism with a sharp click. "It's focused down to two feet—a special lens. So don't fool with it. Shutter speed is set." He went to his raincoat, which was draped over a chair. He returned to the bed with a small light bulb. He put the bulb on the bed next to the camera. "When you are ready to use the camera," he explained, "screw this into any lamp. The shutter opening and speed is set for this bulb. Put the lamp directly over the subject at a distance of no more than a foot. Shoot from behind and to one side of the light."

Kampass examined the camera and bulb.

"When you finish," Leinhardt continued, "remove the film and throw the camera away. Open a window and throw it as far as you can. Don't have it with you when you meet them. Do the same with the bulb. All right?"

"It will take time," said Kampass. "The photos."

"Then you'll work like hell," said Leinhardt.

Kampass studied the floor plan, memorizing.

"Do you know what EYA means, Kampass?"

Kampass glanced up.

"Eyes in your ass," Leinhardt clarified. "You'd better grow them. When you meet Lodz, you'll know why."

"When do I see you again? What's the next contact?" Kampass was feeling sick.

"Want Papa to wipe you?" Leinhardt sneered.

•

Old, very austere Hatfield, in the county of Hertfordshire, is as much suburbia to London as Greenwich is to New York and its comforts exact an equal toll: an hour's loss of sleep for the commuter and a forty-mile ride home from work at night on British Railways, minus benefit of bar car. Like most of British suburbia, Hatfield has its own line of peerage; the present Lord Salisbury sometimes inhabits Hatfield House and sometimes not, depending on how many intruding tourists pass the gatekeepers on a particular day. Churches are scattered about the countryside like weathered playing blocks on a kindergarten lawn, and the country reminds you of Normandy with its very green fields and sheep lurking behind hedgerows.

Perhaps a dozen miles away sprawls Welwyn-Gardens which, unlike Hatfield, is very new: a monument in concrete and glass to modern cohabitation. But Hatfield keeps alee of its barbarous neighbors and surveys them mistrustfully from a few feet higher like a green and umber nose in the air. Activity at the rail station is limited to a heavy crush of bowler-hatted and pin-striped commuters in the early morning, and again in the evening, but throughout the day the platform remains empty.

The Midday Mail from King's Cross was five minutes late and the Pakistani clerk at the turnstile picked the last rice grain of a curry from between his teeth with a matchstick and watched the train disgorge one solitary figure.

The train vanished to the north into the drizzle, and Kampass stood on the wet platform and watched it go—a last link to sanity—until he lost it among the maze of tracks.

He was no clandestine correlator of information many years musty. More than this, he had convinced himself it would turn out to be a wild-goose chase with a ghastly ending. If Wick did indeed know the whereabouts of Rudolf Vogel, would he be apt to leave proof lying around his house? He began to slip into an abyss of self-pity.

At the gate Kampass handed the Railway's clerk the
clipped stub of his ticket and walked to the taxi stand. He
climbed into the first cab and gave the driver the address.
"Ten Lamson's Green," he directed.

As they drove out of the station and turned left onto the
Hertford Road, a green Humber Snipe which had been parked
across the street eased into the traffic behind them, dropped
back two cars, and took up position fifty yards to the rear.

Kampass saw the Humber as they left. Despite it all, he
wished he had one like it.

The taxi crawled through the narrow streets of Hatfield,
and reaching open countryside, picked up speed. The gorse,
yellow, lay on either side of the road and a thin mist obscured
the tops of the hills. There was the smell of wet hay and cow
dung. It was not unpleasant. Amidst the pastoral idyl, he
nearly forgot caution. He said to the driver, "Leave me three
houses down from number ten."

The driver glanced at him suspiciously in the rear-view
mirror.

Kampass said, "It's kind of a joke."

The road narrowed, snuggled by hedgerows. The houses
seemed larger, isolated upon tracts of land where sheep
grazed peacefully. It was hard to picture Wick in such sur-
roundings, Kampass concluded.

The taxi slowed and stopped next to a small white signboard. The sign read LAMSON'S GREEN and a finger pointed up
a dirt lane.

"Number ten. Last house on the left," said the driver.

Kampass paid him, adding a sixpence tip to the fare. The
driver gave him a sour look.

He stood in the road and listened to the fading sounds of
the taxi as it puttered back towards Hatfield. Then he turned
and trudged up the lane. As Kampass disappeared over the
first rise, the Humber drove past the lane and parked across
the road. The driver turned off the engine and settled lower
on the seat until just the top of his blonde head was visible.

From his first impression of Wick, Kampass half-expected his house to be surrounded by an electrically charged fence and patrolled by a pack of vicious dogs. He was therefore not prepared for the cottage at the end of the cul-de-sac. Two-storied, it squatted delightfully amidst a wide expanse of carefully barbered lawn. A row of shrubs, protected against the winter by plastic bags, ran along both sides of the cottage. The roof was red tile and the walls whitewashed.

At the top of the gravel drive, a sign shaped like an eagle was marked H. WICK ESQ. ROOKERY HOUSE.

As Kampass reached the front door, a bakery truck drove by on the road and he made a frantic dive for the shrubs. He got up, cleaning himself, and now on the porch, ran his fingers above the door ledge. He knocked the key flying.

Inside the house it was cold. The heating was not on and Kampass could see his breath smoke. The carpets were lush and the red walls lined with early prints by Spy framed in gilt. Bookshelves ran about a cozy sitting room which opened off the hall and Kampass could see the books were mainly medical volumes, a majority of which dealt with bone formation, structure, and dermatology.

He set the parcel of money on the hall table. Then, like an overweight husband terrified of awaking his wife following an all-night orgy, Kampass crept through the hall and swung open the doors at the rear of the house. There it was, the way the plan had read: a fully equipped dispensary with powerful overhead lamps and a many-gadgeted examination table. Several plaster masks were fixed to the wall like lost Greek relics and there was a strong smell of ammonia and anaesthetics. He brushed against a tray of instruments. A scalpel clattered to the floor. The sound was deafening. He picked it off the floor and put it back on the tray. He retreated and mounted the stairs, following the drawings in his mind.

Wick's office overlooked the backyard garden, and beyond the garden Kampass could see the fields with sheep grazing slowly. Diplomas hung prominently on the walls. Kampass went directly to the desk and tried the drawers. They were unlocked. He found nothing there but paper clips, stationery emblazoned with "Rookery House," a thin plastic ruler, and a packet of La France prophylactics. Wick on the job, he thought. It approached sheer physical impossibility.

After he closed the drawers, he wiped the knobs clean with a handkerchief. They always did that, he remembered. Then he turned to the file case in the corner, removing each cabinet and going quickly through the various case histories. Nowhere was the name Baldur Kuntz or Rudolf Vogel to be found. Of course it wouldn't be, he reminded himself; nor were there any canceled checks. He had not expected them. He expected to find nothing. He also expected to be caught.

Only the closet remained to be searched. Then he could go. His watch told him it was past one o'clock.

The closet was locked. Kampass considered this odd when it seemed everything else in the room was open. He studied the lock, finding it similar to the one installed in his office door in New York and he recalled how, when once he had lost his key, the janitor managed to slip the lock by inserting a common table knife in the door jamb. He remembered this because he made mental note to have the lock replaced when he saw how easy it was to open.

He sifted through Wick's desk again and located the plastic ruler. Then he knelt down before the door and pushed the ruler into the crack. It buckled.

"Come on," he said under his breath.

He tried again, this time at an angle. He pushed it in to its full length and was rewarded by hearing the latch snick back.

Large, possibly a full ten feet by five feet, the closet was empty. His hands played over the wall, feeling for a light switch but failing to locate it. He struck a match. He nearly missed it—the low doorway at the very back of the closet. Kampass eyed it distrustfully, poised between forgetting it and opening it.

The lock was identical with that of the closet door, but the crack a good deal tighter. He cursed as the match burnt his fingers, lit another, found the opening, and wedged in the ruler. Then he blew out the match, pocketed it, and worked in darkness.

"Hurry up," he told himself.

At last the door swung back, and on his knees he crawled through. It was a tight fit, squeezing his bulk through the doorway. Wick, he concluded, would never make it.

In the blackness he struck another match and it flared, orange and yellow, lighting up the interior of what appeared to him as a kind of attic—a storeroom of sorts. The floor was ribbed with supports, and above, the roof canted down. There was a stifling stench of mold and fine particles of dust hung emulsed in the thick air. Kampass was finding it difficult to breathe and the first pains of a cramp began to shoot along his thigh.

Above him, hanging in three tiers from a crossbeam, were a dozen plaster masks.

Crouching now, pinched down by the roof, he passed a match over the masks. Eyes of stone, they were devoid of any personality. They were faces, that was all, yellowed with age, and he wondered—a little overcome with the mausoleumlike atmosphere of the place—why and for how long they had been hanging there. Trophies, he thought; trophies of Wick. Representative, perhaps, of some shattering new technique in plastic surgery. Why here, hidden from admiring eyes? Maybe they were mistakes. They were like the dead. He did not like it.

Kampass unhooked the mask nearest him. It was repulsively cold, heavy, and smooth. He examined the inside of the mask and saw a name had been scratched into the plaster. By the flickering light of the match, it looked like Voss, Siegfried Voss or Hoess. There was a date next to the name, 1951, and then *Vienna*. Kampass struck another match, and took down the next mask. The eyes gazed up at the match. The lips and features were tight, compressed, as though furious at being disturbed after hanging in peace for so long. He turned the mask over—almost in self-defense.

"Gott!" he breathed.

The name etched inside the mask shell was Rudolf Vogel. Kampass flipped the mask over. There it was, in his hand, the creator of his dilemma, and for one insane moment Kampass felt like smashing the mask against a beam. Instead he spat on it.

The room was a Pandora's box of success for Kampass. He discovered a small, metal file case resting atop a thick beam; it was filled with indexed cards running through the letters of the alphabet.

Behind the letter "V," he found Vogel's name printed neatly on a card. *Ten Rue de la Harpe, Paris, Sixième* was the address given. At the bottom of the card the name *Ruth Steiner* appeared in faded pencil and he could barely decipher it. They knew Vogel had lived in Paris. They knew about the woman.

There were other names in the file, but they meant nothing. In all, there appeared to be nearly two dozen cards. Each card bore a series of dates, and opposite the dates, sums of money had been entered. One, which showed its subject to be a Hans Dimper, San Francisco, California, listed a quarterly sum of four thousand Deutsche marks. The payments ran from May of 1955 through May 1964. Kampass suppressed a low whistle. Over a period of ten years, Dimper had paid out the equivalent of forty thousand US dollars.

Similar entries were made on other cards. The names girdled the globe, at least fifteen of them residing in America. Then, at once, he understood. Herman Wick was not only a leading plastic surgeon, he was also a blackmailer.

Kampass removed the cards. He was not so excited that he could restrain himself from calculating the benefits his find would have brought him under other circumstances. For a moment there in the darkness, he considered withholding some of the names from Leinhardt.

Kampass crawled out of the small room backside first like a hibernating bear in spring. He went to the desk and set the stack of cards down, then took out the Minox and the bulb. He screwed the bulb into a reading lamp and set the lamp a foot from the desk, bending the flexible neck. Then he turned on the light and started to work, moving rapidly from one card to the next, being careful about the distance. His hands slipped on the camera as he opened and shut it, moving the frames of the film. He finished with the cards and then brought out Vogel's mask, shooting it straight on and then at a profile, not thinking, concentrating only on centering the image exactly in the square of the viewfinder.

Kampass snapped off the light and opened the Minox, dumping the film cartridge onto his palm. He tucked the cartridge in his breast pocket, then raised the window and threw the camera far out into the garden. He watched it land in the shrubs behind the wall. He closed the window and went to the closet, replacing the cards in the file box and returning the mask to its hook.

After securing the doors and checking the floor for telltale discarded matches, Kampass brushed the dust from his suit and preened himself in front of the mirror opposite Wick's desk. He took one last look around the office. Everything was in place. Everything the way it was. By God, he'd come through. By Jesus Christ, he'd done it.

He left the office and went down the stairs, turned sharply into the hall, and with a loud *whungh,* collided with the ample belly of Dr. Herman Wick.

"Hey!" screamed Kampass.

•

Kampass thought he was going to faint. He pressed his hands flat on the wall as though trying to hold himself erect. Recovering, he saw Wick retreat behind a lean, blond man who had followed him through the front door. Wick peered anxiously over the man's shoulders with frightened eyes.

There was something almost comical about the situation, he thought; the delirium after the initial shock and Wick standing there, his mouth ajar like a split plum. He could almost laugh—almost. That was until he saw the blond man was holding a pistol, trained on the general area of his navel.

He could not take his eyes off it. "Whew," he wheezed. "You frightened me." He realized how ridiculous it sounded.

"You are doing here, what for?" Wick demanded loudly over the blond's shoulder, hard-won English deserting him in time of crisis.

The blond man seemed to have acute astigmatism and his eyes jinked back and forth over Kampass' pasty face. But the pistol did not waver a centimeter, and Kampass was mesmerized by the rock-steady muzzle. He feebly pawed at the air in front of him, a futile defensive gesture. He intended it to convey *I-know-you-won't-shoot. There's-been-a-mistake-here.* But that was not the way it came off.

"*Nicht scheissen,*" he said. "Don't shoot." And he meant it.

Wick repeated: "Well, you are doing here, what for?"

"I was frightened," he said. "It is safe here."

"Not good enough," said the blond man, speaking for the first time.

Lodz, thought Kampass. "You don't know what it's like," he said. "You are alone and you imagine things. You imagine they are following you."

The pistol moved, pointing to the door of the sitting room. "In there," said the blond.

Kampass obeyed, stumbling in his haste. Oh, please, please, please, he thought. He remembered the film cartridge in his pocket. "I've brought the money," he said.

It fell on deaf ears.

"That's far enough," said the blond. "Put your hands against the wall, spread your legs and lean."

Kampass assumed a brace position. A window was on his right. It opened onto the garden and he could see a bird bath there. "And I had the right to check on you," he said. "I came for that, too."

"Herman, search him please," said the blond.

Kampass stiffened against the wall and concentrated on the bird bath. It was all over. They would find the film. He felt Wick's uneven breath play on his neck, raising goose pimples. Wick ran his hands up the inside and outside of his legs, over his arms and under his armpits, patting, feeling. They hesitated over the breast pocket and moved on. His knees began to buckle. A bird fluttered on the rim of the bath and the hands went away.

"Turn around."

The gun had disappeared.

"I'm Viktor Lodz," said the blond. His eyes flickered in the center of a face shaped like the edge of an ax. And his ears protruded like small banjos.

"You were saying you are frightened," said Lodz.

"Yes," said Kampass. "You don't know what it's like. I wasn't sure about you, not absolutely. One starts to doubt and imagine."

"Did you imagine this address too?" asked Lodz.

Wick was hovering uncertainly to the side. "It was on the Seyss-Dietrich letter," he explained. "He must have copied it before he gave it to me."

"Is that what you did?" asked Lodz.

"Yes," said Kampass.

Lodz told him to sit down. "You could have found yourself in deep trouble breaking in here like this. It's against the law. Besides, it's bad manners."

That sounded like Leinhardt, Kampass thought.

"Drink, please," ordered Lodz. He spoke English with hardly a trace of accent.

Wick said, "Yes Viktor." He went to the cabinet. There was the rush and gurgle of seltzer.

Kampass noted there seemed little doubt who was in charge. Lodz asked; Wick delivered. The relationship was off-key, he thought. You could not put your finger on it; Lodz, a lean husband with a fat wife.

Wick replaced the stopper in the whiskey decanter. He gave Lodz the drink and then positioned himself on the arm of the chair. He said, "Why did you not call, Kampass? If you were frightened, you could have called. If you wanted proof I'd have given it to you."

"It was an open line. You said so."

"But you could have made another appointment, used another phone," Wick persisted.

"I could, yes," Kampass replied. "How do I know you would not have turned me in? The Israelis might pay you."

"That reminds me," said Lodz, interrupting. "Herman, bring the money."

Wick went to the hall and picked up the package. He gave it to Lodz. Lodz counted it like a cashier, whetting his thumb. The bills were all of small denominations, and occasionally he would hold one up to the light and squint at it. When he was finished, he shuffled the bills together and handed them over to Wick. "Good," he said.

Kampass watched Lodz's drink. He heard the neat tinkle of ice in the glass.

"Like one?" asked Lodz.

"No," said Kampass.

"No?"

"It's, well, it's a weakness," Kampass admitted.

"So we're informed," replied Lodz. "You have will power. I like that." He unwrapped and lit a cigar, savoring the tip in his small mouth and letting the smoke trickle up into his nostrils. He held the cigar away from him and examined it, rolling it in his fingers. "Tell me, Kampass," he asked, "how long have you been 'checking' here?"

There was something in the way he said it that turned Kampass' mouth very dry. He said, "Half-hour."

Lodz nodded. "And did you satisfy your curiosities?"

"I believe you are what you say."

"And you put back everything you examined?"

Kampass squirmed. "I did. I satisfied myself."

"And you were here for a half-hour?"

Lodz was giving him a chance to backtrack. Maybe he knew that he had been there longer. Maybe he did not. Kampass guessed he was being bluffed. But it was too late. "That's what I said."

"So you did," said Lodz. "So you did."

Wick turned on the gas jet in the fireplace. He turned his

back and lifted his coat vents to warm himself.

The Squire of Lamson's Green, thought Kampass. Or was it Queen?

"We must be very careful," said Wick. "What with Seyss-Dietrich dead and unable to corroborate."

"He was stupid," said Lodz. "I tell you that now, Herman. Seyss-Dietrich was a fool. It was bound to happen. Anyway, here's Kampass."

Kampass felt Lodz's eyes move on his face like hands.

"Whatever am I to do with you?" asked Lodz.

Kampass stared at him. "Wick said I was to do some courier work. He said I could work off the balance of the ten thousand."

"Herman is more avid than I," said Lodz.

Kampass said, "Then if you won't help, give me my money back." *Be indignant.*

"Spirit," said Lodz. "Herman said you had spirit."

Kampass looked at Lodz's drink again. He ran his tongue around his mouth, trying to salivate. "If you won't help, give me back the money," he repeated, pushing.

Lodz smiled. His eyes flitted. "All right, Kampass," he said quietly. "Come get it. Come try."

It was as though a cold wind had blown through the room.

Lodz smiled again and dumped an ash from the cigar with a birdlike peck of his forefinger. "Herman, would you mind leaving us alone for a while?" he said.

A tint of pink appeared in the doctor's cheeks. He excused himself. A moment later, Kampass could hear him moving about upstairs.

Lodz cleared his throat with a small gurgle. "I would liken this to the nature of an interview," he said. "If we choose, we reject you. Only then will your money be returned. If we find you have been lying, then we will all be in an awkward position."

Kampass fidgeted. "I know all that," he said.

Lodz sucked at the cigar. He said, "Do you know you can tell a man's Jewishness by the way he carries his buttocks, by their very shape? They are soft and dimply. They are disgusting. You have such buttocks, Kampass."

Kampass could not believe it. It was a page from *Der Stürmer*. "What?" he asked, astounded.

Lodz said, "You have Jewish buttocks."

"I assure you . . ."

"Your breeding is on record," said Lodz. "But I do find the resemblance suspicious." Lodz shrugged. "An observation," he said. "Let's hear your story."

"I told Wick."

"Tell me."

So Kampass told him. Detail by detail, he repeated what he told Wick. Lodz made him go back to the war, before the war. He would ask a question and then nod at the answer as if bored. Kampass felt himself on firm ground, but he held back from elaborating. He might have been back at his hotel room in the darkness with Leinhardt talking it all out. It could have been Leinhardt sitting across from him now. They asked the same questions, coaxed the answers. It was as though they had been at the same school; had learned their lessons, their technique, from the same instructor. Kampass even forgot about the small cartridge in his pocket. He was playing to an audience, and now he felt he had got over stage fright.

"And that's how it was," he ended. "That's when I called Wick."

Lodz said, "I see." He walked over to the cabinet and made another drink. Over his shoulder he asked, "If we take you on—I say *if*—what will you do afterwards?" He came back and sat down.

Kampass shrugged. "South America. Middle East." He wished Lodz had stopped at one drink. It was unbearable. He watched the fizz rise to the surface of the drink and dance there.

"It's killing you, isn't it, Kampass?" Lodz asked.

"It is?"

"Yes, my drink."

"I'll live."

Lodz brought his cigar back to life. "What do you think I'm drinking, Kampass?"

"Stop it," he said. He wiped his mouth.

"Scotch? Or is it American bourbon?" He held out the drink. "Here. Test the bouquet."

Kampass turned his head away.

Lodz laughed a little tinkle of a laugh. "Well, you put out a good line."

"Line?"

"Your story. I like the way you told it. I like your candor."

Lodz blew smoke. "I'm going to tell you why you're in this mess," he said. "You're the kernel of a political power play."

"I don't follow you," said Kampass.

"Forget it," said Lodz. "History is running out for the Kikes." He rolled the word on his tongue as though it were a gumdrop. "There's all this chatter about an amnesty in May, so Israel is grabbing everybody they can lay hands on. Well, we're seeing to it they don't make it. Want to know why we bother with insignificants like you?"

"I want help, Lodz."

"You don't want to know?"

"I'll be thankful for whatever help you can give."

Lodz puffed dreamily at the cigar. "The time is at hand when the West needs a strong Germany. We are the natural buffer against Russia. We don't mind being buffers. On the contrary, the Soviet Union is our mortal foe. Our alliance with the West is necessity. But Germany belongs to no one, East or West.

"The *Führer* recognized the Jewish-Bolshevik menace. The Americans will rue the day they didn't heed him."

Lodz went on, "If we are to be relied on, this new Germany, the first step is to reassert the dignity of the German soldier; of yourself, for instance."

It made sense, thought Kampass. Whatever he thought about Lodz, that part of it made sense. Dignity.

"Every so-called war criminal brought to trial and incarcerated is a blow to morale. It is self-intimidating. Can you follow that?"

"I certainly can," said Kampass.

Lodz leaned closer, and his voice took on a biting edge. His cigar lay smoking in the ashtray, forgotten. His quick eyes gleamed.

"They label our organizations neo-Nazi, desecraters of graveyards, baiters of Jews. Well, I'll tell you this: who's going to lead us tomorrow? Erhard? Ridiculous. He's a stooge for the *Amis*. We live from the military doles of the Americans.

"There is a wave of re-entrenchment sweeping Germany. Look at the recent pollings in the south, in Munich. At best we can't count on the American. He has been consumed by greed. He's fallen victim to the international Jewish conspiracy. The British are skeletons in history's closet. When De Gaulle is gone, the French return to the government-of-the-month club. Who will lead in the West? Where is the nucleus? In Germany, I tell you. My God, look what we have done: reduced the debt from three billion dollars, a half million men under arms, a productivity the envy of Europe. My God."

Kampass listened. Lodz sounded more like a politician than a coordinator for ODESSA. He did not sound like a killer, he thought. But that was only when you were not looking at his eyes.

"We are damned tired of having our noses rubbed in it. There are no criminals in war—only losers. Our sons are not aware of the Jewish problem. Mention Treblinka and there are some of them who will tell you it's a town in Turkey. We don't wish to remind them. They are tomorrow's leaders. They must mature with love of country, with pride in the Fatherland."

Kampass said, "About the courier's position."

"Is that all that worries you?" asked Lodz quietly. "Have you not been listening to me?"

"I was listening," said Kampass.

Lodz said, "You are to go back to the hotel and await our decision. A day possibly. Very little longer. Keep out of sight."

Lodz turned his head. "Herman!" he shouted.

There was a scurrying of feet overhead and Wick came down the staircase a little too quickly, Kampass thought. As he entered the sitting room, Wick's face was the color of pie crust. The tiny cartridge in Kampass' breast pocket seemed to feel as heavy as pig iron.

"You're upset, Herman," observed Lodz. "Your fat is quivering."

Wick stood in the center of the room. His tuberlike arms flailed once. He had the appearance of an obese ten-year-old lost in a fun fair.

Kampass could see something had gone wrong. What? He was careful. He had put everything back. He had . . . *Oh God,* he thought. He had forgot the bulb. He had not removed the *bloody bulb*. That was it. Wick had turned on the reading light. Kampass looked quickly at the door, measuring it, evaluating his chances of making it out of the house alive. The odds were against him. But it was better than waiting for it. He gathered himself together, tensing on the chair for what he was sure would end in an ounce of nickeled death ripping through his insides.

"Herman, call a taxi for *Herr* Kampass," said Lodz.

Kampass looked at him, unbelieving.

Wick's mouth worked.

"Call the taxi, Herman," Lodz repeated quietly but firmly.

Wick left the room. Kampass could hear him dialing from the hall.

Kampass felt sweat trickle down his sides under his clothing.

Lodz crossed his legs. He began to talk amiably. He had been in the Gestapo, he explained. He had worked for Heydrich in Prague before his assassination. He spoke of Prague as an "enjoyable interlude": the bridges, the cold, clean Pilsner. How unfortunate, he commented, that Kampass was bottled up in Poland, "which, as we all know, is the whorehouse of Europe, and Lublin was the whorehouse of Poland."

Kampass had heard the expression before. Only he heard it after the war and it referred to Germany, not Poland: Germany and Hamburg.

Lodz droned on. Now talking of how things might have
been; now talking of how they were.

Yes, Kampass could see Lodz would have been all Gestapo: cadaverous, tough, little men who wore leather over-
coats with the party pin in the lapel and looked at you as if
you had committed treason.

Lodz had stopped talking. There was an awkward silence.
Once Lodz caught his eyes. Kampass smiled nervously,
quickly.

At last the horn of the taxi bleated from the drive.

"Tomorrow or the next day," Lodz assured him at the
door.

Kampass grabbed at Lodz's offered hand. The palm was
surprisingly horny. Then he bounded to the cab, past the
Humber parked in the yard.

●

Viktor Lodz watched the taxi turn out of the drive and then
he burst out laughing. He shook his head and closed the
door.

"Herman," he said. *"Herr Doktor."*

Wick appeared at the top of the stairs. "What he says to be,
he is not," he said.

"Of course not," replied Lodz. He eased another cigar from
his breast pocket. He moved the cigar around his mouth with
his tongue. Above the cigar his eyes zigzagged up the stairs
to Wick.

"You let him go," said Wick.

"That's right," said Lodz. "I told him to wait. I put him at
ease. He will wait until I am ready to use him. He can be
handled."

Wick screamed, "You let him *go!*"

"Come down here, Herman."

Wick came down the stairs as though he expected to be
spanked.

"You know something I don't," said Lodz evenly. "I don't
like that. I followed him out here. There's nothing that would

involve us, is there? You have been discreet, haven't you, Herman?"

Wick's mouth opened and closed like a fresh-caught bass.

"I asked you a question," said Lodz.

Wick's fingers fluttered at his sides.

"Poor, sweet Herman. Answer me."

Wick took a deep breath and expelled it, a tire going flat with a slow leak.

"He found the masks and the cards. He was photographing. He left a high-wattage bulb in the lamp. We nearly caught him."

"What masks, Herman?" asked Lodz.

"The masks I made of the others. The lists he has seen also. He took pictures of them. *All of them!*"

Lodz looked at Wick as though the doctor were something he had stepped in. "Are you telling me you kept those masks here, Herman? Right here?"

Wick nodded at the floor.

"You should not have let him go, not like that. Not just free," he said.

"All these years?" asked Lodz. "All that time and they were sitting upstairs and you telling me, lying to me, telling me you destroyed them?"

"Why did you let him go, Viktor?"

Lodz did not answer. He returned to the sitting room, thinking, and made another drink. Wick padded after him expectantly, wringing his hands. Lodz stood at the window and looked out at the dusk. In the west the overcast was breaking with sunset and the sky was turning a pearl grey. A Trident jet with BEA markings rose from behind a hill in the distance like a frightened swallow, heading east from the de Havilland aircraft works. Lodz followed the path of the jet until he lost it in the sun. "They've assigned a passing acquaintance of mine to him, Werner Leinhardt," he said.

"What do you mean?" asked Wick.

"The Israelis are using him to find someone through us. *Someone.*"

Wick said, "I knew it. I knew it right along. I warned you. I said the Seyss-Dietrich thing was too neat."

"And I knew it too, Herman. I wanted to feel him out; to find out what they are after. It could be anyone. Anything. But there's something up. There's been a rumor about an exchange of diplomatic niceties with the Jews. When Kurt Stassen came to London yesterday, I knew it. He's Bonn's man. He and Leinhardt together and this Kampass. Then Shoval made two trips last month to Tel Aviv. That's frequency I can't dismiss. And last week he went to Bonn. So I smell a rat. It's a political ploy. But using who? That's what we have to know; who? What do we have that they could use politically?"

Lodz put his hands behind his back and paced the room, leaning forward like a speed skater. He paused and looked at Wick. "Don't you see," he said. "They've blackmailed Kampass. That would fit the pattern. They must have told him, threatened him, that they'd send him East, turn him over. If he co-operates they tell him he can go free. That's the scheme of it. The Sammies tried it with Cukurs when they were working on the Mengele thing in Montevideo. Now they're doing it with Kampass. I get the feeling they're looking for one man. They'll take what they can get, mind you—like your lists. Oh, that was silly, Herman. So very silly."

"I was going to destroy them."

"No you weren't," said Lodz. "I am sick with you."

"I was."

Lodz paced on. "Well, we're going to have to turn Kampass back on them," he said. "We'll make their own weapon work against them. We must deal for him. Alter his allegiance. His pride. Maybe his pride."

"He hasn't any pride," said Wick. "After Majdanek? That broke his spine."

Lodz turned and watched the gas fire.

Wick looked around at the sitting room. "I'm going to hate having to leave this," he said.

"They're not going to let him go, you know," said Lodz to the fire. "They'll use him and then destroy him. If we could show him this he might be turned. But talk's no good. There must be proof. Somewhere, they've put it down. If we can turn Kampass we can stay ahead of them. We could use him as a conduit."

"How to propose getting proof," said Wick. "They're going to give it to you, are they?"

"What's the bank now, Herman?"

Wick shrugged. "Eight thousand in Dublin plus Kampass' five."

"We're going to need all that and more," said Lodz. "What I want to buy is expensive."

Wick smiled. "It's going to be all right, isn't it? I mean, you'll handle it?"

"Yes, Herman, I'll protect you," said Lodz. "What would I ever do on cold nights?"

"I knew you'd handle it, Viktor."

"Yes," said Lodz. "But your greed is a problem."

"Greed?"

"Some of us are parasites and earn livings from misfortunes. You are a parasite, Herman. That's all right. I can forgive parasites, but not indiscretions. How many names on the list?"

"Thirty or so," said Wick. "He got them all."

"International?"

"Yes."

"That's too bad. These people have been running for years. Now they're only a few months away from amnesty and you collapse them."

"Listen here," said Wick. "I am due remuneration. I take risks, I never consider this blackmail. How dare you? My protection is on a continuing basis. Who else can do what I do, or as well? Who can give them a new face, a new personality? I am like a long-term investment."

Lodz stared at him. "As of now," he said "you're devalued."

"Then you can just get out of here. Just get out," shrilled Wick. He was on the verge of tears. "How dare you?"

"Tut-tut, Grandmother," said Lodz.

"You filthy bastard!"

"Doesn't it ever bother you, Herman? Don't you ever think about what you are?"

"Me? *Me?*"

"You're priceless," said Lodz, smiling. He went to the telephone. "I'll be busy with this idea for a day or so. I'm going to ask Speiss to come over and help out." He picked up the phone. Suddenly he covered the receiver and looked back at Wick. "You've really done it, Herman," he added. "You're making me earn my keep."

●

So they both, he and Leinhardt, sat together in the sun at the sidewalk table in Charco's on Coulson Street, off the King's Road, where the next day's meeting had been arranged. And it was then that Kampass read about it.

Leinhardt, eyes squinting into the sun above the pastel yellow and white houses across the narrow street, shoved the noon edition of the *Evening Standard* at him and said: "You'll be interested in this."

The item did not rate front-page space, but neither was it buried on page nine in the middle of the obituary column.

Noted London Surgeon Victim of Hit and Run, said the bold type. *At Eight-fifteen o'clock last night,* the item continued, *Mr. Herman Wexler Wick, member of the Royal College of Surgeons, was struck down and killed by an auto on the B-158 between Essendon and Brayfordbury.*

The second paragraph informed Kampass that the Hatfield Police were questioning witnesses, one of whom had seen the auto involved. The story concluded by giving a brief description of the car, a green Humber Snipe.

Across the table, Leinhardt ate his antipasto noisily. "No British reported among the injured," he said sardonically, through a slab of peperoni. Then, "Um, it's so good. Delicious."

Kampass thought of Wick lying in the road like a squashed toad. Then he remembered the Humber; the Humber he had seen outside Hatfield Station, the same Humber in the driveway in front of Wick's house. "Lodz," he said.

"Yes," agreed Leinhardt. "Lodz." He wiped at his mouth. "All right," he asked. "What went wrong?"

They had not talked about it. Kampass had come back from Hatfield to find a note waiting for him at the hotel: *Charco's, Coulson St. Chelsea at noon tomorrow.* It was signed *Uncle.*

"Let's have it, Kampass," said Leinhardt.

Kampass twisted on the hard chair.

"You haven't been doing the job for us, have you?" said Leinhardt. "You haven't been coming through. Why did they kill Wick?"

Kampass did not know about that. He said, "I did it." I got the pictures. There was a list with thirty names. I took shots of that and a mask, Vogel's mask. He'd hidden it in his office. He was blackmailing them."

Kampass took out the film cartridge. He pounded it down on the white enameled table like a bridge player trumping an ace. "There," he said. "It's all on there."

Leinhardt took it up and examined it carefully as though Kampass might have been cheating. "You haven't answered me," he said. He put the cartridge in his pocket. "I asked you what went wrong out there."

Kampass shrugged. "I got what you wanted," he said again. Nothing else seemed relevant. He had got the photos and he had returned.

"You're stalling me," said Leinhardt.

The waiter came over and cleared away the antipasto. Leinhardt ordered the turbot. He looked at Kampass, who shook his head. He was not hungry. The waiter went away with the order.

"Well?"

Kampass looked across the street. A boy in knee pants was playing on the pavement with a toy pistol. "It was the bulb," he said, hesitating. "I forgot to unscrew it from the lamp. Wick went upstairs. He must have found it."

Leinhardt made a face as though he had a stomach pain. "You were there? When they found the bulb?" he asked.

"I was downstairs with Lodz."

"And they let you off like that? You walked out of there?"

Kampass shrugged. "Yes," he said. "I didn't have time to get back to the station. I was finished, see. I was coming downstairs and there they were."

"Then what?"

"Well, Lodz had a gun and they searched me. At first they were upset, but then we talked, Lodz and I, and Wick went upstairs. That's when he must have found the bulb."

"And Lodz never mentioned it?"

Kampass said no. He told Leinhardt about the conversation.

"I don't understand it," said Leinhardt, shaking his head.

The waiter came with the turbot. Leinhardt tucked the end of his napkin in his shirt and cut a sliver from the fish. Using his knife as a pusher, he impaled this and several peas on the tines of his fork. The wide mouth yawned and closed over the forkful, working slowly. His Adam's apple rippled.

"It's all there on the film," said Kampass. "Everything. When do I get the papers back, the confession?"

Leinhardt looked up. "When do you *what?*" he asked.

"The papers I signed in New York. That was the bargain. They said I'd get it back. You said so yourself."

"You're joking," said Leinhardt.

"Joking?" asked Kampass, who had followed orders, who had fulfilled his responsibility. He could not believe it.

"Identify and confirm, Kampass," said Leinhardt. "That was the arrangement."

"I told you, his mask is on the film: what he looks like now."

Leinhardt shook his head. "Masks are plaster," he said. "People are flesh. You can't tell a thing from a mask."

"Well, I took a picture of his card, his address."

"What was the address, Kampass?" asked Leinhardt.

Kampass thought. "Rue de la Harpe," he said quickly. "In Paris."

Leinhardt nodded. "And when did I tell you Vogel left Paris?"

Kampass said nothing.

Leinhardt attacked a roll and buttered it. "Let me lay it out for you," he said. "What you've given me here is small change, pennies. You've taken yourself out of play, so we'll never get the escape routes they use. We'll never know who does the forgery work on their travel documents. We won't know who banks them. Finally, you haven't learned anything about Vogel we don't know now. Bits and pieces, Kampass. You've given us scraps."

"The names," said Kampass. "I photographed the other names."

"They'll relocate."

"It's worth nothing?"

Leinhardt's great mouth enveloped the hunk of bread. "Hmmm," he grunted, spewing out a wet flake that pasted itself on Kampass' forehead. "To the right people, it might be worth something," he said. "If they didn't know about it."

He finished chewing the bread and swallowed. He said: "Sloppiness. You've been sloppy. All you had to do was use your head. You have no idea what you've destroyed. All the pieces were trimmed to fit; Seyss-Dietrich, your cover, it was hand tailored. But we're going to play you out, Kampass. Right to the bloody end. You haven't even begun."

The boy in the knee pants darted across the street. He skipped over and began firing his toy pistol at the patrons in the restaurant. *"Bang-bang,"* he shouted. *"Bang-bang-bang!"*

"Let's have a look at that, son," Leinhardt called out, extending his hand.

The boy walked over to the table and quietly handed the toy to Leinhardt. He thought he was about to be scolded. Leinhardt turned the little silver pistol in his palm. He said quietly, "That's not the way you do it. Here, watch."

He placed his elbows on the table and aimed the pistol in his right hand. With his left, he cupped the butt for stability. "Like this," he said. He pointed the pistol between Kampass' eyes and pulled the trigger three times rapidly, the gun making snapping sounds. Kampass stared back impassively, a Gibraltar of silence. Leinhardt gave the pistol back. "Always use two hands," he said.

"*Bang-bang!*" mimed the child. "*Bang-bang-bang!*" He used two hands to hold the pistol.

Leinhardt waved at him and went back to eating. When he finished, he snapped his fingers for the waiter. He asked for Port-Salut and biscuits. When the cheese arrived, Leinhardt put a chunk on a cracker and offered it over the table to Kampass. Kampass declined, shying back from the evil-smelling biscuit. Leinhardt popped it into his mouth with gusto.

"We're very angry about Wick," he said through the crumbs. "As long as we could watch him, we knew what they were up to. Now he's gone. Lodz eliminated him because he was a risk and a blackmailer, but Viktor could never have found out if you'd not left that bulb. What I'd like to know is why they let you go. Possibly they think keeping an eye on you will tip them off. Ever box, Kampass?"

Kampass said nothing.

"You watch the shoulders. The shoulders tell you what the hands are going to do."

A beatnik walked by the café, his hair down to his shoulders.

"*Weich,*" accused Leinhardt. "Poof." He craned his neck, looking after the swaying figure. "The thin, queer line," he said. He took a thin metal flask from his coat and poured some liquid into his glass. Kampass watched. Brandy, he thought. It was odd Leinhardt would not purchase a drink but brought his own.

"It looks as though we're left with the Steiner woman," said Leinhardt. "Are you good with women?"

"What do you mean?" asked Kampass.

"Biology," said Leinhardt. "This," he illustrated, wrapping his forefinger in his fist.

Kampass looked away.

"You a poof, Bruno?"

Kampass said nothing. He stared over the street.

"You know," said Leinhardt, "everybody in the trade's a poof these days. It's kinky. Vogel was a poof and so was Wick; Viktor is queer too. They both were living in sin. We've got pictures of them together. If you ever want to . . ."

"No thank you," said Kampass. The subject was like opening the refrigerator door on mildewed cabbage.

"Bother you then?"

Kampass adjusted his tie knot.

Leinhardt said, "I'm not one if that's worrying you." He called for the bill.

"What's going to happen now?" asked Kampass.

"Many things," said Leinhardt mystically. "We've had a tap on Wick's phone for ten days. Viktor made a call on it last night, probably after you left. There's a man called Speiss who's ODESSA's muscle in Munich. Viktor has asked Speiss to come over. Now Lodz and Speiss have been together in the past. They were a killing team before Lodz worked his way up in the organization. I'm not saying that's why he's coming, but it's a consideration we must keep in mind. I think it best we get you out of the country."

Leinhardt paid the bill. He said, "You've restricted us to Ruth Steiner. Her last reported address was the same as Vogel's, the one you say you got. It's a brothel and it's out of the country and it's got to be looked into. It's your last gasp, Kampass. If you let us down again, you're dead; you go East, *Landser*."

Kampass looked at the brandy in Leinhardt's glass. Leinhardt picked it up and drained it. Over Leinhardt's shoulder Kampass could see a big man in a fawn-colored sheepskin coat. The man was watching them, not steadily, but that was what he was doing, Kampass noted. He leaned across the table. He said to Leinhardt, "The man behind you, he's been looking at us."

"That's his job," said Leinhardt abruptly.

Kampass relaxed.

"We thought something might go wrong. It is a contingency we considered," said Leinhardt. "So we have a secondary cover for you. The big job is to locate the woman and you'll have to start with that address, the one on the Rue de la Harpe. They may not know where she is now, but someone is bound to remember where she went immediately after she moved. Somebody there will know. We don't think she left Paris. Now nothing brings them out like money, Kampass. That's the tonic. You shall be representing a firm, Gettling and Koll. They're bona-fide solicitors in Strassbourg. You're looking for Baldur Kuntz, who inherited a large sum of money. Time is short and you've got to find him, or the money will go to the state, you say. You have been given to understand Steiner was an acquaintance. Find Steiner. Find Kuntz. Ask if they will help locate her and offer them a finder's fee—say two hundred francs; that ought to talk."

"And if I find her?" asked Kampass. "You'll take over?"

"No," replied Leinhardt. "Give her the same stuff we went through; what you gave to Lodz and Wick. Tell her ODESSA turned you down because you were too hot, too dangerous. Tell her Vogel's your last play. And suffer, Kampass, suffer for her. They spent nearly ten years together. But a man doesn't completely walk out. Not like that. He doesn't take a decade from life and erase it. And she won't either. She'll know something. She has to. So suffer for her and then strip her down."

Kampass looked worried. He said, "What's stopping her from betraying me?"

"I don't think she'd do that," said Leinhardt. "There's some sympathy there. After all, she's German." He produced a small memo pad. He printed a number on a page. He ripped it out and gave it to Kampass. Then he removed the impressed leaf beneath and burned it, turning it slowly over his lighter and dropping in in the ashtray.

"Odeon five-six-two-four," said Kampass, reading from the paper.

"That's where you can reach me in Paris," said Leinhardt. "I'm getting you out tonight on the boat train. It leaves Victoria at nine o'clock for Gare du Nord. I'll have the ticket sent round to the hotel along with your Gettling and Koll identity card."

"And Speiss," said Kampass. "You're going to stop him?"

"I'm going to *try*," said Leinhardt. "He attempted to enter the country illegally two months ago. So we have something on him. If he comes through any legal gateways, we can hold him at passport control and turn him back. By then, it will be too late for them. I think it's better that way until I know their next step."

Kampass nodded.

"You know this is your last move, don't you?"

Kampass started to say something and then changed his mind. "Yes," he said.

"You're going to find her, Kampass, if you have to copulate your way through every whorehouse in Paris." Leinhardt turned and beckoned to the big man in the sheepskin coat. "This is Emil Laski," he said, introducing him.

Laski nodded at Kampass. Kampass saw there was heavy scar tissue around his brows. He had a hard, knuckled face and his hair was clipped as though a barber had put a bowl on his head and trimmed around it.

Leinhardt said, "Take a good look. He'll keep an eye on you. I may not be able to make the train, but if I can't, Emil will be aboard," He got up from the table. He collected his tyroler hat from an empty chair. "Got it all?" he asked.

Kampass said yes.

"See you in Paris," said Leinhardt.

He watched Leinhardt and the heavy-set man turn the corner onto the King's Road: Leinhardt, springing easily on the balls of his feet; Laski, trudging, head down.

There was more that concerned him than his own fear of Leinhardt. The utter detachment of the man. In Leinhardt's sarcasm there was no humor. When he smiled, that obscene mouth would go through the motions, but his eyes remained flat. Kampass read somewhere that people with mental problems could have an operation that severed the emotional lobe of the brain: no love, no hate, no fear. He would not mind that, no fear. Maybe Leinhardt had the operation. It was strange also that Leinhardt should call Lodz by his first name. Very strange, Kampass thought.

He left Coulson Street and set off towards Knightsbridge, walking nowhere in particular; killing time. From over near the Chelsea barracks came the sound of band music, the authoritative crump-thump of a bass drum punctuating the notes. He walked past parks, dapplings of green sprinkled here and there in unexpected places. Babies, like little old men, frowned at him from prams. He walked up Sloane Street as far as Harrod's, and then Kampass did not think he could stand being alone any more, and so he went in and mingled with the crowd. He bought a glass of sauerkraut juice in the health bar and rode the escalators, pinching fabrics with his fingers and smelling their clean, woolly odor. Eventually he found himself at the entrance to the toy department. He liked toy soldiers. He liked to pick them up to get the feel of them and arrange them in mock formations when no one was looking. In New York he had spent hours at it in F. A. O. Schwarz.

A slim man stood at one of the counters, a tyroler hat snuggled on his head. From the rear, Kampass could have sworn it was Leinhardt. But he dismissed it as a case of Leinhardt-on-the-brain.

Then the man turned, presenting his profile. It was Leinhardt. Leinhardt was buying a crying doll.

"You do your job," the Ukrainian repeated, nodding.

Kampass looked at the private squatting and finishing his cigarette. "Get off your ass," he ordered.

The private got up, slowly, defiantly.

Pigs, thought Kampass. He watched as the slim figure in black came towards the group of Jews in the yard. Kampass saw him coming from a long ways away, his boots raising small puffs of dust. A lean Doberman trotted at the man's heels.

"Vogel," Kampass said, not taking his eyes from the approaching figure.

The mention of the name itself seemed enough to propel the Ukrainian through the door into the cubicle. He returned carrying a cardboard case. He set the case on the sand and tore away the cover. Inside were two dozen grey cannisters.

"What do you make it?" asked the Ukrainian.

"Four grams per kilo body weight," answered Kampass automatically. "We rate each body at seventy-five kilos."

The gypsy band had tuned up. They had begun to play.

Vogel and the Doberman walked directly through the Jews, who moved back forming a sort of an aisle. The dog lagged behind, sniffing at the bundles of belongings on the ground. Vogel paused. As if by a silent command, the Doberman loped towards him.

They did not know, thought Kampass. Vogel was so small among them. If they only knew, they could tear him to pieces. *They would die then, but they would not die like animals.*

They were not wasting time now, he saw. Once Vogel arrived things began happening. An officer with a bull horn was talking to them, telling them to line up against the fence, informing them that those not selected for duties would be deloused.

They set up an old school desk at the head of the line. The SS medical officer sat at the desk and Vogel stood, as if bored by it all, at his side. The old man took up his position at the head of the line. Vogel made a limp gesture with his gloved hand. The old man went to the left. The medical officer made a mark on a paper. The old man was a reject, and he walked over to the door of the green building and turned, waiting, watching as the selections continued.

Whenever a child passed the desk, Vogel would pat its head and hand it a sweet. The children always went to the left. They joined the old man. They did not like leaving their mothers, who were judged fit for work, and some of them began to cry. The old man went here and there. He would pick one up and point to something beyond the double row of barbed wire. The child would laugh then and it would be all right. And the old man would laugh too.

The old man had authority. Maybe he had been the head of a Judenrat in some far-away ghetto, maybe Greece, maybe Hungary. They saw so many. It was hard to tell nationalities any more, thought Kampass.

Kampass could hear the Ukrainian arranging the cannisters inside. The band picked up the tempo.

Don't think about it, Kampass reminded himself. It was like Father Radl of the Altenau parish had said, "It's the same as church. If you do not agree with a few of the rules, you don't resign. Your country is your religion too." And Father Radl was always right.

THE BOAT TRAIN

"For Führer, God, and Fatherland!"
———*Bruno Kampass, age sixteen*

The fog came with the sunset and settled upon the city like a damp bath mat, rolling out from the Chelsea Embankment.

The nearer the taxi brought Kampass to Victoria Station, the more congested became the traffic; a mechanical conga line which jerked to the rhythm of the stop-and-go lights. The streetlamps tried, unsuccessfully, to burn holes through the fog and equally unsuccessful policemen in fog suits fought against the tide of autos.

Kampass turned on the dome light and studied the ticket that had arrived later that afternoon with his new identity card. He flipped open the red jacket of British Railways. The ticket assigned him to compartment 13, *wagon-lit* 206. Kampass saw they had given him a double compartment to himself. He put away the ticket and tried to read a copy of *Der Spiegel* which he had bought near the cab stand outside the hotel.

They reached the station at half past eight; the great iron-girdled mausoleum of Victoria. The station was jammed. The only trains not behind schedule, the boat-train clerk informed him, were those which originated at the terminal. He was lucky to be going to France and not arriving from Rugby or Crewe, the clerk said. They were running two hours late. The clerk told him the boat train would be a half-hour behind schedule. They were coupling on a diner to accommodate connecting passengers from the North who, because of de-

layed arrivals, had not had time to eat. He took Kampass'
ticket and tore the foil. "Fifth car in, when they call it," he
said.

Kampass awaited the announcement nervously, and when
it came he went through the gate and walked past the green
sleepers marked with the seal *Compagnie Internationale des
Wagons-Lits*. He paused at the fifth car and matched its
number with the ticket.

The steward took the pigskin bag.

"Thirteen," said Kampass. He said it with authority. This
at least was something he knew about; trains and planes and
how to assert yourself with the staff.

Kampass followed the steward, mounting the steps to the
wagon-lit and entering the hushed, red-carpeted, quiet of the
car. The steward led him down the aisle and stepped aside
to let several passengers through. He slid back the door
marked "13." Inside, he hoisted the bag onto the shelves,
opened the cabinet for inspection, and turned the taps over
the steel basin on and off.

When the steward left, Kampass settled himself firmly onto
the seat and began to read *Der Spiegel*.

The steward returned with his seating card for dinner.

"It is at what time?" he asked.

"They'll beat for it," the steward replied.

Condensation lay heavy on the window and Kampass
leaned forward and drew a little man in the moisture; a little
man with stick arms and legs and nappy hair, and then he
fingered in the name KAMPASS below it. Finally he wiped it
clean so it would allow him a narrow vista of the outside
world. In the cubbyhole of the compartment, he felt warm
and secure. He put aside the magazine and opened one of his
suitcases. He arranged his toilet articles in the cabinet: lo-
tions, razor, and toothbrush. He puttered. It was pleasing
to have his things about him so. He wanted them where he
could see them. He could look at them and imagine he was
home.

The illusion was shattered by a loud hammering on the
window.

Kampass jumped. He looked up and saw a lumpy, carbuncular face pressed against the glass. The mouth worked violently and two spade-size hands gestured. Kampass pulled down the shade. The hammering continued, growing in intensity. Then there was a sharp rap on the door paneling and the steward said, "Please to open the window so the man can place his valise."

"Valise?" Kampass said. "What valise?" he demanded.

"Please to open. Allow me."

Kampass lunged forward, blocking the astonished steward. "No," he said shrilly. "This is my compartment. Mine. I was to be alone."

"It is a double. You must share."

The insane pounding continued.

"Please." The stewart said the "please" very softly.

"No." Kampass stood fast. "It is paid for. It is for me alone."

"Please to wait here."

The steward returned carrying a clipboard. "It is here," he said. He stabbed a finger against the space opposite number 13. It was the berth-arrangement chart and there was another name alongside Kampass'.

"But it *was*," wailed Kampass, holding his hands together beseechingly. "It was for me only. There's been an error."

"Error?" He pointed at the space again. The name there read *Thomas*.

Kampass cursed.

The steward said, "The gentleman must have insisted on this compartment. It is the only double available so placed. He insisted, and well . . ."—the steward made a gesture with his hands—"I tried," he said. "You'll get a refund."

"What do you mean he insisted?" asked Kampass warily. He was remembering what Leinhardt had said about the man, Speiss. Leinhardt said he would *try* and intercept him. What if they were on the train, both of them, Speiss and Lodz?

"It is the only compartment available; I must comply."

Kampass fished out a wad of notes, but the steward placed

a restraining hand on his arm.

"Please believe this, it is impossible. It is the rules. I will let you know if there is an empty compartment on another car when we enter Dover."

The steward unlatched the window and pulled it down. The station noises poured in: announcements, the jumbled cries of the porters, the metallic grumblings of the engines. A tattered, many-stickered suitcase crashed to the floor. There was a gruff *Danke* outside the window, and a moment later the man appeared at the compartment door. Kampass shot him a sullen, suspicious glare.

"Why did you not open the window, huh?" the man asked.

The man spoke in *Schweizerdeutsch*. Kampass could barely understand him. He was dressed in ill-fitting, badly rumpled tweeds, and even from where he stood four feet away, Kampass could smell eau de cologne. He picked up the copy of *Der Spiegel* and pretended to read. Dear Christ, he thought. A Swiss. What was it they said about the Swiss? A Swiss is a person who would enter a revolving door behind you, and somehow, emerge in front. That, and they were always two beers behind everyone else and then again, he thought, maybe he wasn't Swiss at all. Kampass pressed himself as close as possible to the window, allowing the maximum space between them. Where was Leinhardt's man, Laski? Why wasn't he here? Kampass wondered.

The Swiss sat down, his sirloin features crimson. "Hey you there," he said.

Kampass continued to look holes through his magazine.

"Hey you there," said the Swiss again and he poked at Kampass' arm.

Kampass moved out of range.

"We travel as one, we should be friends." He held a card in his heavy hand.

Kampass stole a quick look. The gothic print said *Anton Thomas, Interiors, Zurich*. Maybe, he thought. Damn Leinhardt. Damn him for this.

"I decorate," said the Swiss.

"Good," said Kampass. He checked his wristwatch. It was

another half-hour before the first dinner sitting. He went back to the magazine, building a wall between himself and Thomas.

Thomas reached in his inside coat pocket. Kampass caught the movement and tensed. The Swiss held out a photo.

"We have some common interests? She is only eighteen."

The edges of the snapshot were worn from handling. The girl was on her back, legs raised and looking between her knees with the frozen, knowing smile of a whore.

"Scrutinize the plane of the stomach and the breast positionings. Is she not superb? She is eighteen."

Kampass went back to *Der Spiegel*.

"You want, I give." The Swiss wiggled the photo.

Kampass shook his head.

"It is not dirty," said the Swiss. "It is erotica. I collect. It is only, how to say, *divertissement*."

Kampass said nothing.

The Swiss, rebuffed, propped his feet over his bag. He shrugged and replaced the photo. Then he began to clean his nails with the leaf of a match packet.

Kampass tried to keep his eyes on the magazine and on the Swiss at the same time. Where was Laski, anyway? He felt abandoned.

The train moved so smoothly out of the station that it seemed the platform was passing and he was stationary. They passed a maze of sidings and knelling signals and toy-train boxcars parked in ghostly rows in the fog. Then they were crossing over the Thames, click-clack-clunk over the switches with barges hooting blindly below, picking up speed until the noises of the wheels merged to form one continuous rattle. He wiped clean the hole he had made on the sweating window and watched while the stations of Clapham, Brixton, Denmark Hill, and Peckham Rye—misty halos—bulleted by. Then, at last, there was nothing more to see—only darkness.

The steward walked past beating the gong for the dinner sitting.

"Do you mind?" asked Kampass.

The Swiss removed his legs from the suitcase and allowed

him to pass. Kampass made his way to the rear of the rocking car. He stopped outside the steward's small compartment. The curtains were fastened back and he could see the steward was studying a newspaper. Kampass cleared his throat.

The steward slowly folded the paper. "Yes?" he asked.

"Is there a *Herr* Laski on this car?" asked Kampass. They wouldn't leave him like this, he thought; leave him alone in a compartment with a man they did not know.

The steward consulted the berth chart. "How to spell it?" he asked.

"L-A-S-K-I."

"No. No *Herr* Laski."

"You are positive?"

"Absolutely. It would be carried on the plan."

"He is big," said Kampass. "Like so,"—he diagramed with his hands.

"There is no such Laski on the car, this one or the one ahead or behind us."

"Try Leinhardt," said Kampass. "A small man, very small and thin."

The steward went back to the chart. He shook his head.

It was hopeless. Kampass felt the beginnings of panic. He rummaged in his pocket and found a pound note. He gave it to the steward. "Look," he said, "it is important. Can you look in the other cars to be sure? Will you do that and then tell them I am here. Say that I am in the dining car and I want to see them. It is very urgent."

The steward put the note in his pocket. He shrugged. He said, "I know there are no such men on this car or the other two."

"Try," said Kampass. "Look anyway." He left, lurching his way back through the cars to the diner, thinking the steward had to be wrong; that they would not leave him like this, not alone and vulnerable.

He seated himself at a table in the corner and studied the menu.

Somewhere, after all this, there would be a crack for him in an unknown corner of the world where he could make a fresh

start; a truly realistic fresh start; and there would be no
nightmares of old men with beards who laughed at him,
mocking him while he gassed them. There would be a place,
there would have to be, that would not remind him of the
plains of Poland and the nights that struck like a clock; where
no one pointed fingers; but where he would not be anony-
mous; where he might participate; where there were no
Vogels.

Maybe New Zealand: green, pastoral, with afternoon-tea-
and-biscuits happiness. He had read about it in his own
travel brochures. Ireland, with warm whiskey and wattle-
roofed comfort. And why not? He might. He could. He might
even marry and reproduce. The Kampass *Kinder*. He would
make the ground grow things again as his father had. *Why
not?* And he could put his medals on display above the fireplace. He did deeds he was proud of. They were approved: his
assault-badges, his campaign shields, and his Iron Cross. He
would get them back. The government would replace them.
Somebody had them somewhere. They owed it to him after
what he did for his country. He was a hero. That was a fact.

"Hey you. Ho-ho-ho, you eat!"

Thomas, the Swiss, loomed over him.

Kampass jumped. He thought he was going to be ill.

"I found you," said the Swiss.

"Leave me alone," replied Kampass miserably. He looked
out the window into the passing darkness.

"You are rude," said Thomas.

"No I'm not," he contradicted. "I want to be alone."

"Well, I must sit with you," the Swiss insisted. "See, no
more tables."

The seats in the dining car were occupied. Thomas sat
down and folded his arms, resting them on the white tablecloth. "What's good for the eating?" he asked.

The train clattered and swayed over a switching and Kampass watched the water slop around the inside of the carafe.

"Please. I do not speak much," said the Swiss. "We shall be
friendly. The steward explains to me the matter of the berth.
This I am regretting."

Kampass looked at him. "I have no choice," he said.

The Swiss jabbered incessantly through the meal. He was a compendium of vulgarity, it seemed to Kampass. And the worst of it was this:

Thomas asked him to join hands so that their palms were flush, their fingertips lightly touching. Then he said: "I am a Martian. Yes, that is what I am from space, but I am nearly same all over as you: same head, same arms and legs and the eyes, and I eat with the mouth and it goes out the other end like you. You know what it is that makes difference? I explain." The Swiss leaned closer. "It is that my sex things are in my fingertips."

Kampass snatched his hand back as though he had laid it on a hot griddle.

"Ho-ho-ho," Thomas guffawed. "You know now the difference." His heavy body heaved with mirth. *"Vive la différence,"* he gasped and broke anew into peals of dirty laughter. He wiped his eyes and turned to the window, giggling.

They passed Ravensbourne, Shortlands, and Chatham. The fog thinned and a quarter moon had risen, dusting the heath with silver. Kampass could see pockets of fog in the hollows, and suddenly, he saw something else that made the hairs of his neck stand up like dry grass. Instead of staring through Thomas' reflection in the window, he looked directly at it.

Thomas was using the thick glass as a mirror, watching him. His expressive face had gone slack.

How long the Swiss had been observing him, Kampass did not know, but there was no mistaking that look. He saw it once before when he met Leinhardt. The wolf and the sheep. A wolf in Swiss clothing.

It became frighteningly lucid. There had been no mistake about his compartment. That was the way they planned it. And who had made the reservations? Who spoke of Lodz on a first-name basis? *Leinhardt.* That was how it was and this man, this Swiss Thomas of Zurich, was none other than Speiss himself. Speiss and Lodz and Leinhardt, the killing team. They had made a deal and if Leinhardt was in it, so too was Laski.

Thomas turned and smiled broadly. He had one gold tooth, an incisor, and it gleamed like a beacon.

The accumulation of seventy-two hours of stress had taken its toll. Kampass tried to hold onto himself, but found he was slipping, fast losing control.

The gold incisor blinked.

"Go ahead," Kampass said. "Do it."

An expression of puzzlement crossed the red face.

"Go ahead," he barked. "Do it. Do it. Do it."

Passengers eating at nearby tables twisted in their seats.

"Do what?" asked the Swiss. He smiled and shrugged.

"Yes, Speiss or whatever your name," Kampass continued. "Do it under the table then if you are afraid. *Kill* me!"

An embarrassed hush swept through the car. Forks and spoons hung in mid-air. The clink and scrape of cutlery on crockery died and there was only the noise of the wheels on the tracks. The chief steward bustled down the aisle. "Something not adequate, sir?" he asked.

"Nothing wrong," said Kampass, near hysterics. "Except this person means to do me. But it doesn't make any difference. There's nothing you can do, so go away and wash dishes."

The gold beacon flashed and Thomas shrugged again. "I do nothing," he said. "I don't provoke."

"You lying swine," said Kampass. "*Schmutzfink!*"

Thomas burst into a loud stream of *Schweizerdeutsch.*

The chief steward attempted to keep track of the dialogue, his head turning from Kampass to Thomas and back again like a spectator at a ping-pong match.

Kampass regained a modicum of self-control. He pulled his napkin out and folded it up. Then he methodically checked the bill. He deposited ten shillings on the plate and said, "It doesn't matter, you see. I'm sorry."

Ears burning, he got up from the table. He marched out of the car, looking neither to the right nor the left. Once clear of the diner, he dogtrotted through the train. He burst through the door to his own car. The steward made a grab at his arm. Kampass tore free.

"No luck," the steward called out. "You wait, please."

But Kampass kept going, staggering now, panting, until he could go no farther. Then he locked himself in the toilet of the last car. He leaned against the door, trying to catch his wind, feeling the muscles flutter in his legs. He breathed in long sobs.

People, he thought. He needed people. They wouldn't do anything with witnesses. He decided to wait in the toilet until they loaded the car on the ferry. Then he would go on deck. He would go to the saloon and he would stay there. He could buy himself some time. He did not want to think of what he would do when they docked at Dunkirk.

Kampass lowered the lid of the toilet and sat down. Nervously, he shredded a roll of Bronco toilet paper to pass the time.

•

The train pulled into the siding at the Dover Marine Terminal at eleven-thirty. Kampass felt the jerk as the cars were uncoupled and shunted into the bowels of the night ferry. Outside, chains rattled and crashed. Orders were shouted. A half-hour later the noises ceased. Kampass allowed another forty-five minutes before unlatching the door.

The car was empty, a curtain-lined bowling alley, and the silence was such that his ears rang with it. He moved forward, leapfrogging from toilet to toilet. If he made the deck he would be all right.

In the final car of the row, the third *wagon-lit*, he found a door open to the platform that ran the length of the ferry's hold. He slipped out, avoiding some chains and tackle. A sign posted on the side of the hold above a flight of iron steps pointed the direction to the deck and the lifeboats. *Canats 1-3-5-7*, it said. Next to it was the word *saloon*.

He clambered up the steps and emerged on deck. A freezing wind moaned across the ferry. The lights of the Dover Terminal faded to starboard.

A lifesaver attached to the rail said *Twinckenham Ferry*
and above him, amidships, the twin funnels towered into the
night.

Kampass shivered uncontrollably in the cold and the wind;
wretched. He crossed the pitching deck to the main cabin
and the saloon. A miasma of noise greeted him as he opened
the door. The room was packed with young men and women,
some of them dressed in leather jackets and trousers, and
most, apparently drunk. In the corner, on a leatherette settee,
a young man, his head nodding in semiconsciousness, was
trying to slip his hand under the sweater of a girl who sat and
watched the hand's progress with a disinterest that approached boredom.

He edged his way to the bar as though he were stalking it,
and pushing aside a pile of cyclist's safety helmets, ordered a
brandy.

"Hey, you old fart," said a voice behind him. "That's my
kag you're doing."

"Excuse me," said Kampass. He faced an aggressive-jawed
young man whose neck swelled out like the base of an oak
tree from somewhere directly below his ear lobes. The boy
took his gear and went over to the settee. Kampass sipped the
brandy, feeling very much out of place and completely out of
date. He finished the brandy and called over the bartender.
"I'd like a bottle of this," he said. "Can I buy a bottle here?"

"Duty-free prices," said the bartender.

"Yes, good," said Kampass. "Same as this,"—he indicated
his drink.

He paid for the bottle and took it over to a small formica
table in the corner. He drank three very quickly, snapping
them down with his wrist, feeling it burn in his gullet and
finally his stomach. He did not think, and after a while he felt
his face grow hot. He would stay here all night. He would
stay with these people and he would be all right.

On the settee the boy had given up trying to force entrance
under the front of the girl's sweater. He was hard at work at
the back, his fingers searching out the brassiere catch. Good
luck, thought Kampass, warming to it. Good luck to you. He

was relaxing now. The brandy was going to work.

Someone switched on the radio behind the bar and pop music slammed out concussive, twanging and thumping, banging. The music stopped and an announcer said in a static-stuttered voice, "This is Radio Caroline." It was as though he were announcing the return of Christ, Kampass compared. He had little rapport with the music. Another drink. Another. He left the table, bottle dangling from his hand, and squeezed into the companionway. He edged past an embracing couple and went to the stoop where the companionway was open to the deck. He drank deeply from the bottle and examined the night beyond and wondered what he could do next; where he might go; what would happen when the ferry docked at Dunkirk. They would watch the gangways, and when he did not appear they would come after him. They would find him like a rat. They would find him and then they would kill him like that.

Old fart. The old soldier gone to seed. If they only knew; he, who had dispensed more death than they in the course of their lives would read in obituary columns. Someone who mattered should know about it, he felt. He desperately needed someone to pity the ordeal of Bruno Kampass. But nobody cared. They didn't care one crap: not the boy with his cycle helmets, not the girl with her breast being fondled, not Thomas-Speiss, not Lodz, not Leinhardt or Laski. He had no one.

Look, I could tell you a thing or two, he could begin.

Yes. Do you know what a man thinks of when he is dying? What would *he* think?

Well, I tell you this, they don't often pray, and I've seen a lot of them go. Would *he?*

They talk about what they should have been and what they should have done and they talk about their mothers. What mother? He could barely remember what she looked like.

That's the way of it and they scream and they cry and they kick and they wish they were young again. And he would too, he knew.

But some of them say nothing.
Do you want to know how I know this?
Do you?
So thinking, Kampass watched Anton Thomas walk by.

●

It was Thomas—Thomas walking, leaning into the wind;
Thomas heading for the fantail, red face lowered into a fur
collar.

Kampass was now cut off from the train. They had missed
him below and they sent Thomas to deck to ferret him out, he
concluded: to flush him from cover, to drive him back to the
hold. Or maybe it was Thomas who would do the killing, and
some shell collector or fisherman would find him a day later
washed up on a beach in the bleak dawn; that was unless the
ferry's screws had chewed him to pieces, and then no one
would ever find him.

Kampass grappled with terror, fighting it, willing it back,
and panic ebbing, was surprised to discover anger took its
place: anger against all of them and anger against Vogel who
was responsibile for it; the controlled anger of the animal
pursued to exhaustion and brought to bay who turns on its
pursuers, crafty, and at last, unafraid. So—cornered, goaded
—Kampass blindly struck out.

His eyes searched the companionway and settled on a fire
ax attached to the bulkhead near the saloon door. He se-
creted the brandy bottle behind a door and working quickly
now, freed the ax from its restraining brackets. He slipped
out the opposite end of the companionway to the deck; holding the ax loosely across his chest in a position he might parry
or strike from, and avoiding pools of light case by the portholes, he moved towards the stern.

It was an emotional enema, this ridding himself of fear, he
thought. You got the juice flowing; that's what they used to
say.

In the dark, he pressed against the cold side of the cabin
and waited. Minutes passed, but the decks remained de-

serted. No Thomas. Ten yards from the cabin, in the direction of the stern, the black mass of a steam winch rose from the deck like a museum skeleton. Kampass weighed it as cover. The thinking, the movements, they came back quickly now, spanning the years—nearly a quarter of a century. How strange, he thought, one never really forgets.

Crouching, he moved away from the skeleton of the cabin, and reaching the winch, dropped to his knees. He hugged the lee of the machinery against the wind, the smell of grease heavy in his nostrils. There were the noises of the sea and he could hear lifeboats creaking on their davits. The canvas tarpaulin covering the nearest boat struggled in the wind. It tautened and flapped back, sounding like a pistol shot. From somewhere forward came the clang of the ship's engine telegraph. Kampass' eyes bugged, focusing and adjusting to the night. By degrees he made out the lines of the stern bridge and wheelhouse twenty yards away and above him. Then it began to rain. It fell lightly at first and on the canvas boat covers and then, with a roar, it whipped over the deck with a fine mist. Beyond the gutters to port, he could see the tops of the waves rising in the squall, hissing, and shredded creamy at the crests.

His fingers began to numb and whiten about the ax handle and he beat them upon his thighs and blew on them. He held his hand out, palm down. It was rock-steady. He amazed himself. Was it all that long ago? He recalled another night in another land and it had been raining then too. Pouring. The factory of Bryansk. They had fought there by their senses and they cleaned out one workshop after another, cleared a thousand-and-one passages and shafts that night, going from floor to floor with rain roaring on the tin roofs, the rip of Schmeisser bursts and the whiplash crack-wham of concussion grenades and the slow, answering phut-phut-phut of the Russiam Maxims. Not so long ago, really, he thought.

Then at once the squall subsided, and in the half-light, he saw the Swiss. Thomas stood on the stern bridge, looking out to sea, his back turned. Kampass might have missed him, so closely did the man's bulk merge with the outline of the tiny wheelhouse. A solitary figure watching the sea.

Kampass crawled the twenty yards to the bridge gangway, making a face as the axhead nicked the railing. Thomas was standing slightly to port. That would put him about six yards from the Swiss when he reached the top of the gangway, he estimated. With some luck he would cover it before Thomas turned to meet his rush. Kampass climbed, feeling with his feet for the steps. At the last rung he cuddled behind the iron grating. Inside, he was tightening up, freezing himself and destroying all his emotions. Living, Kampass reminded himself, was for those who wanted it more than their opponent. Living was for the predator.

So, as he had done twenty years before, Kampass entered the jungle.

The wind tore the subhuman scream of a bayonet charge from his lips and flung it to the sea. He lumbered up from the gangway, the ax swinging in a vicious arc.

Thomas half-turned, his face registering surprise and his mouth forming a perfect circle. Then the flat of the axhead crashed against his temple, buckling the skull with a wet sound. Closing in behind the swing, Kampass dropped the ax and hurtled into the sagging Swiss. He gripped fistfuls of the heavy fur-lined coat, and using his hip for leverage, heaved upward. Thomas hung over the railing, his distorted head above the boiling wake of the screws. Then, turning over slowly in the air, he somersaulted into the Channel.

•

Kampass sat down solidly on the wet deck, the adrenalin trickling away, feeling light and giddy, a little sick. The memory of Thomas turning as though someone had called his name stayed with him; Thomas, who now rolled in the sea behind him. With his mouth open and the incisor gleaming in the murk, Thomas was going to say something. What was he going to say? Or had the axhead cut short what was only the intake of breath before a scream? What would the others have said if they'd been asked? But truly, Kampass thought, it

was not as it was then; the emptiness that one feels upon
leaving a cinema.

He remained sitting on the deck with the wet soaking
through to his skin, feeling as though he could go to sleep. He
sucked in great gulps of air, turning his face to the wind.
Then he saw the ax lying a few feet from him and he crawled
over to it. A grey gummy substance stuck to the blade and
congealed in the cold. Kampass picked up the ax and threw it
overboard. Up forward, the decks glistened under a mast
light and they were as empty as the sea itself.

Kampass walked slowly back to midship, feeling as though
he were wading through beach sand. He went to the railing
and leaned over it. A lugger was passing to port, bucking
heavily into the swells, its superstructure lights and portholes
twinkling merrily on the choppy water. As it vanished to
stern, its horn gave off a mournful grunt. What had he
gained, he asked himself. Another hour? He looked at his
watch. Soon they would raise Dunkirk. Then it would be
over. He might avoid them for a while by hiding. But they
would find him. He would be running in circles and the circles would get tighter and tighter. The fight was going out of
him. Little by little it was leaving him.

He looked at the sea, watching the phosphorescence boil
past beneath him. "Why?" he asked aloud. "Oh, God Christ
why?"

Kampass stiffened and gripped the rail. Someone stood behind him. He could see the shadow next to his own in the
light from the open companionway. He looked out into the
darkness and the sea.

"Get below."

Kampass slowly turned. Laski stood a yard or so away
watching him, moving easily, swaying with the roll of the
ferry. The lapels of the sheepskin coat were pulled up on the
sides of his face. "They want you below," he said.

Funny, Kampass thought. It wasn't so bad. You made up
your mind about it you know; you faced it and admitted it
and accepted it as something that was going to happen. That
was how come the Jews were so good at it, dying. He often

wondered why so many of them didn't kick up a fuss. Now Kampass knew why.

Laski pointed at the companionway. Kampass saw he didn't have a gun. Laski did not need one, he thought. He walked to the companionway. They went down the iron stairs to the hold, Laski keeping behind him, pushing him along firmly.

They walked on the platform beside the rows of sleeping cars in their berths, steam drifting up from the pipes beneath them. Inside there was the faint whirr of the ventilation, and at the rear of the car someone was snoring. When they reached his compartment, Laski knocked on the door. Leinhardt's voice said, "Come."

Lodz sat on the unmade lower bunk, his ears looking very large. He was smiling. Leinhardt was standing behind the door. He wore seaman's oilskins and greasy Wellingtons with rolled-over socks. He held a heavy automatic pistol at his side.

"All right, Emil," said Leinhardt.

Laski nodded and left, securing the door.

"Just keep quiet," Leinhardt told Kampass. Then he began to converse with Lodz, speaking in a tongue Kampass could not understand. As they talked, Lodz would glance at him from time to time. Once, Leinhardt laughed and shook his head. But when Lodz reached for a cigar, the pistol in Leinhardt's hand jumped. Plainly the gun was there for Lodz's benefit, not his, thought Kampass. He could not understand it. What was the relationship?

"No one is questioning that, Viktor," said Leinhardt, switching to German.

"Then it is settled," Lodz replied. "I am free to go?"

Leinhardt said, "Surely."

Lodz seemed to relax. "There was no need to be childish," he said. "I told them we could reason with you. I know Werner, I told them."

"Do you remember the old days?" Leinhardt asked. "Do you remember that time in Rome we all had dinner on the Aventine Hill? Then we went to the Hassler, and later

Helmut stole that *carabinieri*'s hat, Cipriani was his name, and we bought him a drink on the Via Sistina. They forgot we were people. Because we wore uniforms they forgot about that. Even we forgot."

"Yes," Lodz said gravely. "Yes, I do. I remember."

"Break your arms and legs," said Leinhardt.

"Yes," said Lodz. He turned to leave. Leinhardt stepped aside, moving towards the bunk.

What happened next was so sudden Kampass was left in a state of shock, blitzed by the rapid change of events. There was a loud thud from the lower bunk and the compartment turned snowy with feathers. Lodz surged past with a grunt, slammed into the door, and toppled backward onto the floor. The astigmatic eyes moved once, and then stared fixedly at the washbasin. A pink bubble grew out of one nostril and popped.

Leinhardt stood by the bunk holding a pillow over the automatic. The gaping hole in the pillowcase was still smoking from the powder burns. He put the pillow aside and slid the pistol under his oilskins. "Don't touch anything," he said. "I'll be right back."

Just like that, thought Kampass; it was as though a valuable vase had fallen and shattered.

Leinhardt grasped Lodz's ankles and pulled him back from the door as though he were handling a wheelbarrow. Then he stepped over the body and left.

Kampass stared stupidly at Lodz. One trouser leg was disarranged, revealing a shiny, hairless calf above a bright maroon sock. A tear welled up in Lodz's left eye, brimmed, and squeezed out. At the corner of his mouth, a small nerve moved. Kampass felt his stomach grumble and constrict. It was different seeing it this way.

There was a movement in the corridor and Leinhardt reentered the compartment with Laski. They shoved him aside, and going to their hands and knees, cleaned the floor. They worked silently and quickly as though they had rehearsed it many times; scooping up feathers and dumping them on a tarpaulin they had brought. They rolled Lodz on top of the feathers. Laski produced a ball of heavy cord and cut it into three lengths with a silver penknife. He bound the tarp-wrapped figure securely, tying it off at each end and adding one length about the middle.

Leinhardt retrieved the pillow from the bunk, and then, together, they hefted Lodz like an old rug. As they left the compartment, Kampass could smell the pungent odor of Laski's wet sheepskin.

The only clue to what had happened were two wet spots on the floor. Kampass rubbed at them with the toe of his shoe, but this seemed to smear them; so he gave up and sat back on the bunk.

Leinhardt returned alone. He came smiling through the door and said, "I'll wager you'd like to know what this is all about, wouldn't you?" He seated himself on the bunk next to Kampass and brought his hand down heavily on his knee with a loud smack. "Well, I'll tell you," he said.

Kampass saw his teeth behind the smile as large as piano keys.

"Viktor was wanting to strike a bargain," explained Leinhardt. "He asked to know what we are looking for. I told him. Vogel, I said to him. Then he said if I would return the photos you took in Wick's office, he could produce Vogel. He wanted to set a date in Paris for the exchange. You were to go with the cards."

Kampass moved on the bunk. He felt very uncomfortable.

Leinhardt continued: "The idea was credible. But we know now ODESSA hasn't the foggiest where Vogel is. He isn't in Paris. You see, they were doubling up on us. They would have produced someone who would pass for Vogel. By the time you checked, it would be too late. But Viktor was going to cross me, and once you allow that, the word circulates. They'd be saying that old Werner Leinhardt could be had. *Uncle Vanya* would be out of business—*zerschlagen*."

Leinhardt lit a cigarette. The mouth yawned and out came a perfect smoke ring. Kampass watched it float towards the basin, revolving slowly until it hit the cabinet. He continued: "Kampass, you're not half the man Viktor was, even if he was acee-deesy. He and I used to be on the same side once, but he never got used to the idea Germany lost the war. He wasn't adaptable. He was an idealist. God put his finger in a navel somewhere and Viktor was born a pure Aryan. If he'd been Jewish and in the right place he might even have died in bed."

"You weren't going to kill me?" asked Kampass, who only minutes before was waiting to die. "Then you hadn't planned it with that man in Munich and Lodz?"

"What the hell are you talking about? What do you mean, kill you?"

"The man in this compartment with me," Kampass explained. "He wanted to kill me. He got on at the last minute in London. You made the reservations and so I thought you planned it." His hands were shaking.

Leinhardt's eyes had fixed on the stickered valise of the Swiss which rested on one of the overhead racks. "What man?" he asked quietly.

"A fat man. He said his name was Thomas, a Swiss from Zurich. But he wasn't. I knew it from the start that he wasn't. He was watching me all through dinner. I know that look."

"What look?" asked Leinhardt.

"He was looking at me *that* way."

"Which way?"

"You know."

"No, I'm afraid I don't," said Leinhardt. "Where is he then?"

"He was the man from Munich. That Speiss fellow."

"Where is he, Kampass?"

Kampass explained. He told Leinhardt how careful he had been, throwing away the ax and all. "No one saw," he said. "I'm sure of that."

Leinhardt kept watching the suitcase. "My God, Kampass. You killed him?"

"Well, where were you?" Kampass simpered. "I asked the steward and he said you weren't on the train. What else could I do? He came up on deck after me. I tried to avoid him, but he followed."

Leinhardt said nothing.

"That's why I thought you were in it with him."

"The steward didn't give you my compartment number?" asked Leinhardt. "He didn't tell you that I was in the next car back?"

"He said he hadn't seen you or Laski. I even asked him to look to make sure. I tipped him."

Leinhardt bit on his lower lip.

"I assure—"

"Keep quiet," said Leinhardt. "I want to think." After a moment he butted his cigarette in a receptacle attached to the wall. Then he said, "Speiss was detained at Heathrow passport control nearly three hours before the train left. He didn't even make it through customs. You've bunged the wrong man, Kampass."

Kampass did not believe what he was hearing.

Leinhardt looked at him. "You stay here," he said. "Just stay put. Don't do anything. I don't think I could stand it." He slid back the door and left.

The Swiss *had* followed him on deck, Kampass thought. He *had* watched him in the window. Then he remembered Thomas standing on the stern bridge, standing and looking out to sea and turning with surprise at the last moment.

Leinhardt returned with the steward, who was rubbing both fists in his eyes. He had been asleep.

"Who do you show occupying this compartment?" Leinhardt asked him.

The steward looked at the small man in his oilskins. "What's going on?" he asked.

"Never mind," Leinhardt said. "Who had the compartment?"

"A Mr. Speirling. Mr. Speirling and Mr. Thomas." The steward buttoned up his tunic, mumbling.

"That's not him. That's not the one I spoke with," said Kampass.

"Of course he isn't, you stupid bastard," snapped Leinhardt. "They put the other one off at Dover."

"That's right," said the steward. "We change at Dover. He

was a new man and he confused the berthing charts. This was supposed to be a single, but he overbooked. He wasn't English. Most of them are English on that run. His first day, he said it was. The delays have confused everything—even staff scheduling."

Leinhardt pursed his lips. "Yes," he said. "Maybe."

"Is something wrong?" asked the steward. He was beginning to look alarmed. He was wide-awake now. "What's the matter?"

Leinhardt looked at him. "There may have been an accident," he said.

"Accident?" asked the steward. "Accident?"

"Yes, perhaps a suicide." Leinhardt pointed at Kampass. "This man Speirling said he saw the passenger, Thomas, go on deck. He was very distraught. It was an hour ago. He went up. This man was worried for him. He told us he couldn't find this Thomas."

"Who are you?" asked the steward. He was looking at Leinhardt's oilskins suspiciously.

"Seaman Rapp," said Leinhardt. "I was working on the fantail. This man came to see me about it."

"*Mon Dieu*," said the steward. "A suicide? He jumped?"

Leinhardt shrugged.

"Well, do something," said the steward. "Stop the ferry!" He turned quickly in the compartment as though he might find the engine telegraph mounted on the wall. His face was ashen.

"We've done what we could," said Leinhardt. "The captain said it is too late to come around in this sea. We're still searching the ship. He may yet turn up. He sent me down to look in the cars."

"Oh, *merde*," said the steward.

"There's nothing to be done," said Leinhardt. "This man reported it an hour too late."

"This is the first time," said the steward. "It's never happened before."

"Don't talk about it to the other passengers," said Leinhardt. "Go back to your quarters. The captain said he might want a statement from you when we dock."

"This is terrible," said the steward. "Oh, *merde*." He left, talking to himself.

Leinhardt waited and then secured the door. His eyes bored into Kampass'.

"But Lodz," said Kampass.

"I was watching Lodz," Leinhardt said, his eyes snapping. "Lodz boarded the train at Dover. I think the steward was their man and Lodz replaced him. Like us, they were keeping an eye on you."

"They weren't trying to kill me?"

"No. Lodz was waiting here for you. I think he wanted to talk. He wanted to bargain. Instead, I came. Then he had to deal with me."

Kampass lit a cigarette. It took three matches.

"You got jumpy," said Leinhardt.

"I could have sworn," said Kampass.

"And you've been drinking." Leinhardt walked over to the bunk. He grabbed a fistful lof Kampass' hair and wrenched back hard. Kampass shrieked, his eyes rolling, watering from the pain.

"That's what you've been doing, isn't it, Kampass? You've been getting stinko-pissed." He put his face an inch away from Kampass'. Then, so softly it was nearly a whisper, he said, "Never, never again." Then he let him go. Kampass held his head.

Leinhardt stood back. "You were drinking, you were scared, and you took your courage from the bottle and killed him." He hauled down Thomas' suitcase and set it on the bidet and opened it. Piece by piece he removed the contents. There were three bolts of cheap silk, a soiled shirt, two rolled-up pairs of socks, a set of underwear, a stack of pornographic photos, and a plastic bag that held toilet articles. Leinhardt opened the bag and removed a tortoise-shell comb. He wiped the comb on the bunk and put it under his oilskins. He glanced through the photos and shoved them in the outside pocket of the oilskin jacket. Kampass sat silently and watched.

"What did he say he did?" asked Leinhardt.

"Interior decorator."

"Bloody bad taste," said Leinhardt. He held up a grey paper folder. He tossed it onto the bunk. Kampass picked it up, looked at it, and dropped it back on the blanket. It was an international driver's license issued by the Automobile Club of Switzerland and made out to Anton Thomas.

Leinhardt repacked the articles that argued Anton Thomas, Interior Decorator of Zurich, had been alive. As he picked up the bolts of silk, a small black skullcap fell onto the floor.

Leinhardt picked it up. "Did you know Thomas was a Jew?" he asked.

Kampass looked at the cap, at the suitcase, and then at the carpet. The two small stains were still there. "I don't want to talk about it."

"Oh, come on," Leinhardt said. "You're going to make me cry. I'm surprised—an old campaigner like yourself." He put the cap on the back of his head. He held the skirts of his oilskin up and out from his sides, robelike. He said in a deepened voice, "Therefore, I, Levi—Yitzchok Ben Sara, say: *lo azus mimkom!* I shall not stir from here. An end must come to all of this. Israel's suffering must end. *Isgadal viskadash shmay rahbo. Oivez! Oivez! Oivez!*"

"Don't," said Kampass.

"Don't what?"

"I don't want to think about it."

•

Werner Leinhardt took off the cap and studied Kampass as he sat on the bunk massaging his sad, doggy features. He examined him as though Kampass were some weird species of virus.

Here was a man, thought Leinhardt, who had killed seventy thousand human beings. Now he worried over one; a case of mistaken identity; a casualty of little consequence.

Kampass, he decided, still had a maidenhead. For him,

killing in war was one thing; in peace quite another. At Majdanek there was an authority he could have looked to: a Vogel. With the Swiss, Kampass was not capable of making the ends meet. He could not resolve it.

Leinhardt required no authority for murder. The need of that had been trained out of him.

He knew well the gutters of the western world and he knew the castles too, and like bad water, he moved through both with equal ease.

Four years in the Gestapo trained off the baby fat, what little of it had been left on him. He had become hard and lean and opportunistic. And in '44, it was all too plain to him how the war would end. He had been in northern Italy then, in counterpartisan warfare. The British and Americans pounded away at them to the south in the Gustav line. He had decided to contact British Intelligence and serve out his time as a counteragent. He wanted the proper credentials when it ended.

None of the nuances of his trait escaped him, from the correct use of electrodes as physical and tongue-loosening stimuli, or the application of a nail clipper on female nipples, to the subtle art of microdot reduction and high-speed radio transmission.

Immediately after the war, in a topsy-turvy Berlin, he formed his own network. He worked a payroll of fifty agents and two false flags in play on both sides of the Curtain. But Gehlen fixed that. Gehlen underbid him on three successive American contracts and the CIA rolled him up. They operated on the theory of what you can't use, no one else would use: you disarm the weapon.

Gehlen had been nice about it, all right. He had offered him a job. But there was such a thing as pride, and since then Leinhardt's star had fallen. He was reduced to free-lancing: picking up leftovers. He was on retainer to the Egyptians and even the CIA did not want to alienate him. They kept him alive in the Pool. But the luster had worn off. Only the tarnish showed.

But he stayed outside. He could have quit long ago, he told

himself. He could have hung it up. The truth of the matter
was he could not. The business of intrigue was like a narcotic
to him. He could not cope with the withdrawal symptoms.

Then two months ago he became the target of the tool he
used so well: blackmail.

Two *Shin Beth* men came to his house in Berne inquiring
after property he held in Malaga. Right away, he knew. It
was the way they carried themselves; that self-assurance. He
could pick them out like they were hash-marked. They sat
together on his terrace overlooking the river Aare and the
green hills and leas and they were very polite. They told him
about *Oryx*. Then they turned the screw. They brought up
the Stern affair, the torture-killing of the Jewish underground
leader during the Warsaw uprising.

Stern was an incident Leinhardt had regretted. It had
lacked polish. It was something a Kampass would do. Stern
knew the locations of three arms caches the British para-
dropped; the Gestapo did not. There was no time and so they
threw the book away. They went to work on Stern with a
blowtorch. He died silently. Afterwards they dumped the
charred body in a sewer and filed a report with the *Wehrmacht* that he had resisted arrest and they and the SS were
forced to burn him out with *Flammenwerfer*.

These things had ways of getting out, Leinhardt knew. The
truth does in time. The wise man, he knew, manipulates
truth. He fibs.

Vogel. Who the hell cares any more? Leinhardt thought to
himself. Eichmann gone, hanged and cremated, with his
ashes scattered upon the sea. If they decided to release Speer
and Hess from Spandau tomorrow, it would raise few eye-
brows, if any. God knows how many vanished into the rank
and file of the Vienna police or were driving taxis in New
York or selling beer in Munich. Germany was filled with face-
less men who looked at the ceiling when you stared too long
at them.

The shifting values of modern society never ceased to
amaze him. So six million Jews were liquidated. Death was
bloody death and it did not matter if you wore a prisoner's

uniform or a flying suit. It was the equalizer. The patriots are wrong. There is no dignity in any form of it. It is merely a state of ceasing to be.

But to get a Kampass to do what he had done, one had to apply the elixir, the heady wine of God and Country.

Leinhardt watched Kampass. If he only knew, Leinhardt thought, that there was no way out of this for him. Kampass was practically on a plane to Poland right now. The papers were signed and the Poles had granted Shoval a stay of a month. Kampass was on loan as it were. If the operation leaked, then Leinhardt had orders to eliminate Kampass and the hell with the Poles. Deal. Double deal. Triple deal. In the meantime, despite the fact he and Kampass orbited at different ends of the human cosmos, their fates remained linked. Leinhardt likened himself to an unwilling passenger on a plane to nowhere with a complete idiot at the controls. A *Kamposity*, that's what it was, he thought.

Kampass was a somebody who would follow you into the men's room and insist on piddling in the very next urinal even though there were several others open right down the line.

Leave him alone for a minute and look what happens, he thought. Like a drunk driver, you never knew what he would do next. One had to anticipate. This, Leinhardt knew, was when good men were lost; when you were dealing with someone like Kampass who didn't follow the rules.

He was forced to think quickly about the Swiss. The suicide explanation would get them as far as Dunkirk, and after that he did not care. The steward would not ask questions until they docked. There would be an investigation. Finis. Exit Anton Thomas, panderer, *Kamposity*.

Leinhardt followed his thoughts ahead to Paris and the Steiner woman. If Kampass could not learn Vogel's whereabouts from her—if indeed he found her—then he would be forced to employ his own techniques. Applied to a common prostitute who had nothing to gain by silence and everything to lose, mere threats would be sufficient. The thing was to locate her. While Kampass worked through the old address, he would check the local gendarme files. Whores have records, he knew. They have records, and records carry addresses. He only hoped that if Kampass found her first, he would not botch it; not frighten her off. He would have to be sincere. He would have to suffer and she would have to know it.

ODESSA would try for Kampass again, Leinhardt knew. They would not quit, not after Lodz. They would send someone else in. The steward was still unaccounted for. And what, he wondered, would they have offered Kampass? What deal could they possibly have made? He would have to keep the wolves from the door.

You never knew who you would meet on a run like this, Leinhardt thought. Shoval was right. He knew the horses. There was Viktor, for one. He had not seen Lodz since they were staffers together in Rome. He remembered how nationalistic Lodz had been. When things went badly, Viktor was still convinced the Allies would somehow be pushed back into the Channel and the Russians, by some miracle, evaporate. It was funny. Now Viktor was on the bottom of the Channel weighted down with tackle and feeding crabs. That was the biggest joke of all.

Fleetingly he thought of his wife and their daughter in Switzerland.

Leinhardt looked forward to playing house from time to time. It was a kind of busman's holiday and he could temporarily forget what he was.

He went to the cabinet and lowered the washbasin. Filling it with hot water, he carefully scrubbed his hands. "Give us a towel, will you, Bruno?" he asked, holding his hands aloft surgeon-fashion.

Kampass handed him the green-striped towel and Leinhardt asked him: "Say, what are you going to do with yourself after all this?"

"All set in here," the Ukrainian called out from the control cubicle.

Kampass joined him inside and shut the door. He put on field-grey coveralls and zipped them up to his chin. In front of him were the two tubes, capped now, which led to the series of cement chambers on the other side of the glass porthole. Two gas masks hung from their pegs above the tubes.

Beyond the chambers he knew what would be happening. They would be undressing. They would have closed the doors and they would not hear the gypsy music now. They were undressing in silence and hanging their clothes on the hooks, arranging them carefully so they could locate them when they returned—only they would not be coming back. The males would be on one side of the room and the females on the other. He had seen how it worked. That was the first thing that they had shown him. The men and women would keep their private parts turned away from each other. The children, too young to care, would cavort in the center of the room. A SONDERKOMMANDO would be handing out bars of ersatz soap. One bar per six people. They would be handing out the soap now.

The Ukrainian uncapped the two tubes, readying them. The cannisters, in prescribed numbers, were on the floor beneath the tubes.

Through the porthole, Kampass could see the entire length of the chambers, from one through to the next.

The door to the farthest chamber swung open. Then they came, buttock to belly, looking at the neck of the person in front of them and their feet doing small, shuffling dance steps on the floor.

The old man led. The chamber filled.

Suddenly the old man's face appeared before the porthole. Kampass looked at him. Their eyes held. The old man smiled. He knows about it, thought Kampass. He has it figured out.

They were all in now. The door would be closing. Kampass knew they would be plastering mud around the jambs to seal them.

"Start the blowers," he told the Ukrainian private; he looked at the sea of heads behind the glass.

There was a distant hum as the switch was thrown and warm, moist air was pumped into the chambers. The air whined through the big ducts over Kampass' head. The whine built to a whistle.

Kampass tried not to look at the porthole where he knew the old man was. But his eyes were drawn to it.

"Floodlights," he ordered.

The Ukrainian threw another switch and the chambers were bathed in a harsh glare.

They knew something was up now, he saw. Their eyes rolled with alarm. They could hear the air too.

The old man's eyes did not waver and his smile held as though it were permanently stamped to his face. The lips moved. The old man was talking to him through the glass.

The Ukrainian picked up the nearest cannister. Kampass took it away. "That's my responsibility," he said.

He shook the crystals, innocent-looking like pebble candy, into the funnels on the tubes. They rattled through. The Ukrainian gripped his arm. He put his hard Slavic face close to Kampass'. "Don't you ever think about this?" he asked. "You never say."

RUTH

———

"A soldier has no time for women."
——*Bruno Kampass, age twenty*

The madam of the bordella on Rue de la Harpe had cheeks the texture of Gorgonzola cheese. She wore a heavy perfume that reminded Kampass of the inside of a lavatory and she stood in the doorway wearing a quilted bathrobe, studying Kampass' Gettling & Koll identity card skeptically.

"Please to come in," she said in English, handing back the card.

She ushered Kampass into the building, past a small cloakroom, and asked him to take a seat in the drawing room.

"I'll see if any one of the girls knows where she lives now," she said and went upstairs.

The room was cold and the walls were hung with imitation red velvet tapestry. Two women were seated across from him. They appeared in their early thirties, their faces tough and chiseled and hair lacquer-stiff. One wore a shawl thrown about her shoulders over a nightgown. She was doing her fingernails, dipping the lacquer brush into a messy line of bottles arrayed next to her on a table. The other stared at Kampass, who twisted uncomfortably on the settee and tried not to look back at her. There was a discarded copy of *Paris-Match* lying on the floor at his feet and he picked it up and thumbed through it, but he was conscious of the prostitute's continuing stare. He looked up and flushed brightly when he saw she had undone her robe and was cradling her right

breast, smiling and offering it to him as though it were a loaf
of bread. Quickly he went back to the magazine. He wished
he could cover his nose with a handkerchief. The smells in
the room were a cross between a manicurist's salon and a
zoo.

The madam returned shaking her head. She sat down next
to him and said, "No one knows about her."

"But you recall *Herr* Kuntz," he said.

"Yes," she replied, "they had an arrangement."

"And they left here together?"

"It was after the trouble of the police. They closed us, you
see."

"The police?" Kampass tightened.

"It was a matter of uncleanliness. It was simply corrected."

"They did not return?"

"No. I heard they argued. Really, it is true that Baldur is to
get all this money?"

"If he can be found," Kampass answered.

"I would like to claim the reward, *m'sieur*, but I would be
lying if I told you I knew where he was."

The prostitute who was lacquering her nails set aside the
brush and said from across the room, "Baldur was very *sym-
pathique.*"

"Yes, that is so," said the madam, nodding seriously. "Baldur was a good man."

"You knew him, then?" Kampass asked the prostitute.

"Oh, yes," she said. "He was forever here with Ruth, but it
was long ago you know. Many of the girls have left."

The madam said, "That is Corinne. Corinne, *M'sieur* is of a
solicitor's firm in Alsace. He is trying to locate Baldur or
Ruth. Baldur has inherited money."

"Good for Baldur," said Corinne.

"There is a reward," said Kampass hopefully, eagerly.

"Baldur left Paris," she said.

"We know," said Kampass. "We hope to find him through
Ruth Steiner."

"They had hard times during the war," said the madam.
"Ruth had been to Ravensbrück and Baldur was a deserter.

He was Alsatian and the *boches* conscripted him. They were very frightened and careful about their friends, those two. If you know bad times, you are like that."

Yes, Kampass thought. You certainly are.

"They did not like to talk about it much," said Corinne.

"There's a reward," said Kampass.

"There's always a reward," she said with a shrug. "I do not believe Ruth's papers are in order. A *m'sieur* like you came before with questions. He wanted to take her back to Germany for the DP camps."

"What *m'sieur?*" asked Kampass, alert. "When?"

"He was from the UN. We said nothing because it would make her insane, *tout fou*, to go back to a camp—any camp. She could not even stand being in too small a room."

"When did he come?" he repeated.

"Last year."

Kampass relaxed.

"How do I know you are what you claim to be?" Corinne asked. "Maybe you are from the UN too, yes?"

He crossed the room and showed her the identity card. She took the card and turned it around. She made a vulgar noise with her lips and gave it back.

"It is so," said Kampass.

"We'll see," she said. "You return this evening after six. I will have spoken with her. She herself can decide if she will see you."

"Really, it's only to speak with her," said Kampass.

"It is not for the reward," she said. "I do not want your money. It is that they should get what is theirs."

Absolutely, Kampass thought.

He left the house, glad to be breathing fresh air again. He found a phone kiosk and called Leinhardt. He listened to the purring of the ring and surveyed the narrow street while he waited.

Somebody picked up the phone. This time it was a bookshop. Leinhardt seemed mildly surprised to learn he had located an acquaintance of Ruth Steiner's. Immediately he asked for her address. When Kampass told him he had not yet obtained it, he went back to being Leinhardt.

"Go to a cinema and stay there," he said. "Go until six. As soon as you've heard more about Steiner, call me. No. Call me anyway. Call at eight."

"Is something wrong?" asked Kampass.

"Just call," said Leinhardt and he hung up.

Kampass left the kiosk. He saw an *agent* on the corner and he approached him and asked directions to the Boulevard des Capucines. He remembered the Café de la Paix where he frittered away the end of his leave. Paris had looked sad with the streets full of the wood-burning gazogenes and the field grey of the *Wehrmacht*. The armed forces information booklet called it the capital of the world: *Here are some helpful suggestions if you find yourself posted to this charming city,* and it gave the addresses of the *Soldatenkinos* and the visiting hours to the Louvre and other Parisian points of interest. *Remember always,* it concluded, *that you represent the Third Reich. Conduct yourself accordingly.*

Kampass had stayed out of uniform, but even in civilian dress he was as Germanic as strudel and the Parisians were coldly hostile. After Majdanek he needed to be in touch with the living again. He failed miserably. Nothing was alive then anywhere in Europe. The people were dead. The leaves on the trees were dead. It was the season for death. To dispel it, he allowed himself to be talked into going to a filthy film by two *Rottenführers* of the SS. Kampass sat through it, unstimulated. It was of a doctor and a patient. The doctor was examining the patient. Then he made love to her on the examination table. The audience clapped and whistled, keeping time with the movements of the doctor and his patient. Kampass lost interest. Then he went to a newsreel; flickering images of victorious German soldiery in Russia, in North Africa, in the skies and under the seas. But nowhere did it mention the soldiery of Majdanek. Later he had gone to George Carpentier's to try and wash it away.

Kampass walked down the Rue des Martyrs to the Boulevard Haussmann and the Opéra. No. He would not go to any more cinemas. Not this time.

Finding a seat at the Café de la Paix, he ordered coffee and a croissant. He envied the men who sat at the tables sipping pernod and he envied their women for being there with them. And such women, he thought; strong-legged with fine breasts and skin and eyes that hinted at affairs on silk sheets. The nearest he would ever come to it would be in the audience of one of those films. He had never given it much thought before, women or the having of them. But he wanted one now. Perhaps only one to be like everyone else. Perhaps because it was the thing to do.

He remembered the first time the opposite sex occurred to him; back in school, in puberty, when he looked up Gretchen Frick's dress to see how girls were different. She told on him, screaming and running to his teacher. He was punished and they sent him to see Father Radl who smelled of incense and told him such activities would place him beyond the eyes of God. *You are a good and decent boy, Bruno,* he had said. *Do not soil your mind.*

Some things you never forgot, Kampass thought.

A German couple and their two children sat down at the next table. The husband was festooned with cameras and his wife, blond and laughing, wore an expensive-looking fur babushka. The new Germany, thought Kampass. He was the old Germany; as old as the cement of the autobahns over which they drove their Volkswagens. They had erased him from their history, he thought, in the same way a teacher wipes a four-letter word from a slateboard.

He called over the waiter and paid for the coffee and the croissant. There was a newsstand just outside the café selling a variety of European newspapers and typically French drawings of dogs urinating. He bought a copy of the Paris *Tribune.* Stanleyville was off the front page and as he stood scanning the paper, a grey Citroën pulled into the curb beside him. The driver reached out from the window and tugged on the tail of Kampass' mackintosh. *"M'sieur,"* he said in bad French, *"est-ce que la Rue de la Harpe presqu'ici, s'il vous plaît?"*

Kampass heard him, and yet, he did not hear him. At first

he thought the question was meant for someone else. Then the name Rue de la Harpe registered and he whirled. The driver of the Citroën was the steward who had been replaced at Dover: Lodz's man.

"I think you want to talk with me," said the steward, looking up from the window.

Kampass felt an itching between his shoulder blades.

The steward crooked a finger at him. "To negotiate," he said.

The itch grew to a nagging ache.

Kampass threw the newspaper in the direction of the Citroën's window, spun, and sprinted towards the corner of the Rue Scribe, sending an elderly woman and her net-bag of groceries spinning to the pavement. As he pounded around the corner, he shot a glance over his shoulder. The Citroën had gone, disappearing into the line of cars converging on the Opéra.

•

Kampass could hear the telephone jangling even as he unlocked his door in the Hôtel Vignon. He propelled himself across the room, and snatched up the phone.

"Leinhardt," he said. "Listen . . ."

"*You* listen," said the voice on the other end. "You don't know friends from enemies."

He held the receiver away from his ear as though the caller, whoever it was, might press a button and cause it to explode.

"Now, hear me out," purred the voice. "The Israelis promised you clemency for co-operation. But you are going to get the noose. They're going to turn you over, Kampass. You're going East."

"Liar," Kampass said.

"If you go to the desk, there will be a letter in your box. It contains duplicates of extradition orders. You see, it's all arranged."

"It's a trick. They're forged," said Kampass. "I'm not a

fool. You're not dealing with an idiot here, you know." Leinhardt was right, he thought. He should have gone to a film and remained there.

"No trick," said the voice.

"I'll go downstairs and that will be the end of me. I'm not going to make it easy. No."

"Fine," replied the voice quietly. "Don't go. You can be tried in France for murder as easily as Warsaw."

"What?" asked Kampass.

"France," said the voice. "Thomas came ashore this morning. Dunkirk authorities think it was suicide. They assume the skull damage to be caused by the ship's propellers. But there's some confusion about who reported it; a sailor called Rapp who was not a sailor; a passenger called Speirling who has vanished."

"There's not a shred of evidence," he said.

"Oh, but there is," the voice contradicted. "There was that unpleasant scene in the dining car. It was most inappropriate and in bad taste. I recall that you both argued in the compartment. I remember how you both went on deck and Thomas did not return. I am sickened by the whole affair. I don't feel I can keep it to myself any longer."

Kampass did not answer.

"Coming downstairs?"

"There is nothing else," said Kampass. He failed to add the questioning "is there?"

"Bad situation all around," the voice agreed.

"What do you want?"

"Collect the letter, read it carefully, verify it. I'll ring back in ten minutes." The phone clicked.

●

Kampass thought of calling Leinhardt, but then he realized he had to know; to know for sure.

The envelope stood out plainly in the bank of pigeonholes behind the desk. He crossed the narrow lobby, and for a moment, contemplated the letter as though it were his obituary. The concierge handed it over the desk to him. He balanced it in his hand. It felt officially heavy. He did not open it until he returned to his room.

There were five slick, stapled, orange-colored sheets of paper of the type run off by photocopying machines. The first page bore the words *Restricted* at the top and the bottom, and between, in the center, *Order 29255.* This was followed by a single sentence: *Bruno Waldek Kampass, son of Siegfried Kampass and Emma Brunner Waldek of Altenau.*

The second page was headed: *For Crimes Against Humanity and the Polish Peoples, 1943.*

All told, there were six pages. Three listed crimes being preferred by the state against *Bruno Waldek Kampass.* The final page was a signed and sealed agreement of extradition: *Wherefore the states of Israel and Poland hereby make agreement . . .* He did not need to read further. Two signatures appeared. One he could not make out. One, he could: *Mordecai Shoval.*

He was stunned. They had promised, hadn't they, his freedom and his confession? For crimes against humanity. My God, they had promised him. Right from Leinhardt's mouth it had come. He hadn't loafed. He had worked at it, hadn't he? What were they doing to him?

They had never meant him to go free. They would let him find Vogel, and when he did, they would send him back. He would hang. Or he would end as Wick and Lodz had. He would play out his string and the scissors would close.

Kampass squeezed his head. It felt as though it were full of worms.

The phone rang at the bedside.

"Read it?" asked the voice.

"Yes," Kampass whispered.

"You believe its authenticity?"

"It looks to be so," said Kampass. He was a cake of soap in a hot, turbulent bath—slowly eroding, melting away to nothing. He looked at the papers on the bed.

"I apologize," the voice went on, "for this unorthodox contact, but I did try to reach you on the train. Somehow the seating arrangements became mixed. We didn't count on *Herr* Thomas but it was, how to say, providential. There is no need the authorities know any more than they do now. You see the position?"

Kampass said nothing.

"Kampass? You there?"

"Yes."

"How would you like to return to Germany? Would you like to go home with a different passport? It's only paper, Kampass. It can be arranged. They would never find you again. Never."

"I can't go home," said Kampass. "I can't go anywhere. They'd find me. You don't know them."

"Do you want to go East then?"

Kampass looked out the window at a room across the way. It was very near. There was a man and a woman in it and they were eating by candlelight. The man was laughing.

"We want two pieces of information, two only. You can accomplish this intelligence in a day, perhaps this evening. Simple. Easy."

The man in the room was looking past the woman's shoulder; looking directly at him, Kampass. The man left the table, and going to the window, closed the louvered shutters.

"The film you took in Herman Wick's office, where is it? Can you get it back?"

"I gave it to Leinhardt," said Kampass. He was suddenly tired. He could hardly keep his eyes open.

"Then the Jews have it."

"I suppose, yes."

"Can you get it back?"

His eyelids felt like bedclothing.

"Kampass."

"Impossible."

"Number two," said the voice. "We know what they want now. We know all about *Oryx*. They want Vogel. What is Ruth Steiner's address? She is the only one who could tell them."

"Go away," said Kampass.

"Don't be stupid. Listen, get her address. Leave it written on a piece of paper in your mailbox downstairs. We'll replace it with a new passport and money enough to get home."

"Leinhardt," Kampass mumbled.

"Don't worry about him, that double-dealing bastard. We're going to fix his hash."

"I can't get the film," said Kampass. "I can't."

"You have twenty-four hours. Find out who has it or you'll go East. The Poles and the French can battle it out for custody."

The caller rang off.

Kampass went to the high windows. He looked out at Paris, smouldering with streetlamps in the dusk. Somewhere he could hear the lonely hoot of a saxophone, and in the room next to his there was the sound of a typewriter going hard. The beacon atop the Eiffel Tower revolved in the sky, searching out the bottoms of clouds.

So he looked at the city. And he was altogether alone in it. There was nowhere to turn. But would it have been any different in New York? Indeed, would it have been other than this in Altenau, his home? No one is completely without friends, he reminded himself, but try as he might, Kampass could not think of one.

The string *was* out.

Lodz's men, ODESSA, they considered him a traitor. No, he would go East anyway. France? A murder charge would be brought against him. And he had barely forty pounds in his pocket and twenty-four hours in which to do something about it.

It began to sleet, the crystals rattling against the glass. He threw open the windows. The cold poured in. He squinted as the icy particles peppered his face and it all came back again: the alley and dead Speirling and the throaty rumble of the Russian artillery; the thin figure walking in the Majdanek dust in polished boots. Was his name still scratched there in the alley? Was there something, somewhere he could return to? Then he saw the Swiss, Thomas, with his golden incisor and Lodz with a tear in his eye and bloody pap on his lips and Leinhardt sitting on the bunk in the train and grinning and asking, *What are you going to do with yourself after all this?* And he saw fat Wick feeding the pigeons and then he saw him on the road, and at the end of that road, he saw himself. He was turning slowly on a hook like a sausage displayed in a butcher's window.

He shut his eyes, hoping to blot it all out. Then he decided to do the last thing left him. Consciousness ended. Reaction prevailed. Kampass ran.

•

"It's not six," the prostitute told him. "I said six." She looked up from her knitting at the figure crouched on a chair in the corner of the room. She took in the way his heavy hands perched on his thighs; how his eyes fixed themselves on the floor as though trying to see the cellar. Lawyer's investigator or not, she thought, this one was a very odd man. She regretted having called Ruth. Now it was too late. She could not stop her. She would come.

"There's tea in the back," she said. "Would you like some?"

"Tea?" asked Kampass vacuously. His eyes, bloodshot, were like red punctuation marks alongside his thick nose. So much did he look like a beaten dog, that she had the urge to cross the room and stroke the back of his head.

"Sugar and milk?" she asked.

"What?"

"Never mind," she answered.

She brought back the tea and he accepted the cup, holding it with both hands. "I am not well," he said. "It's my stomach. I have gas."

"I have something upstairs," she said.

"No," he answered. "It is nothing."

Whatever is amiss with you, *monsieur*, she thought, it is not gastric.

The tea was sweet with sugar and mud brown, and Kampass rallied. He had come to this place because there was nowhere else for him. What he would say to Ruth Steiner, what he would ask of her, he was not sure. But she had known Vogel. And Vogel was free. It was barely possible she knew someone who might help. It was a small chance. But by now Leinhardt would be looking for him and so too would ODESSA, and small chances were all Kampass had.

The prostitute, Corinne, sat across from him with the shawl over her shoulders and she knitted, the needles clacking and darting. Every time he glanced at the clock on the mantelpiece, the hands seemed not to have moved. Kampass drank the tea and waited and hoped. When six o'clock came and went, he said, "She's not coming, is she?"

"She's coming," said Corinne. She did not look up from her knitting.

He did not think anyone had followed him. He was too panicky to be certain, but he tried to be careful. He tried to recall what one should do. He took the Metro to the Concorde and doubled back, waiting until the last minute when the doors slid closed. From the Bastille, he walked over the Pont Sully. He had taken a bus on the Boulevard Saint Germain, crossed the Seine again at the Pont Alexandre, and then hailed a taxi.

He did not hear her come in. He looked up and saw her standing in the doorway to the sitting room, dressed in a belted raincoat with a red kerchief bound about her head. She was staring at him. The light picked out the drops of rain which clung to the fringe of dark hair above her forehead.

Corinne set aside the knitting and rose from the sofa, smoothing out the folds in her housecoat. She held a palm upward to Kampass. "This is the one I spoke of," she said. "He has come about Baldur and money from Alsace."

Kampass rose nervously. "Ruth Steiner?" he asked.

She did not answer. She removed the kerchief, shook out her hair, and hung her raincoat on the back of a chair.

Vogel's woman, thought Kampass. She must be middle-aged, he judged. But she had kept herself well. There was something about her that reminded him of a flower pressed between the pages of an album, preserved from some long-forgotten dance. The flower wrinkles and fades, but it never loses a hint of better times. She was small. She held her body straight, as though she were afraid it might collapse without warning. Seeing her that way, watching her movements slow as though she doled out each one, there was something of the aristocrat in her. There was breeding, he thought. You could never miss it. Kampass could tell real class when he saw it and he thought of a rose growing in a lettuce patch.

"You have news of Baldur?" she asked. She seemed to choose her words like her movements, carefully. Her eyes were very large and dark.

"Could we speak confidentially?" he asked. His voice came out as though something were caught in his throat.

Corinne looked at Ruth. Kampass saw her give a small shake of her head.

"It's all right," said Ruth. "We will go across the street. There is a small *chi-chi tabac.*"

She collected her kerchief and raincoat, and in the hallway, spoke quietly to Corinne for a moment.

She turned to Kampass. "You are ill?" she asked.

Kampass said, "I'm not well." Next to her, he was at once aware of his clumsy bulk; of his nose and wrinkled suit.

"They have something good at this place," she said. "Negroni. It is good for bad stomachs."

Together they crossed the street and entered the *tabac*. It was warm. The windows sweated. There were two pinball machines and a jukebox by the door. The jukebox was braying a cha-cha-cha. Ruth led him to a table in the rear. The waiter came over and placed his hands on the plastic table-top. She seemed to know him. She reached up and patted him on the cheek. "Marcel," she said. She asked him for two negronis. The waiter flicked the dishrag at the table. He looked at Kampass. Ruth laughed. She said, *"Pas affaires."*

The waiter returned with the drinks. Kampass took the small glass and turned it in his fingers. How to say it? he wondered.

"What's this about money?" she asked.

"I'm not from Gettling and Koll," he said. "The card I

showed to the others, it is not me. Kampass is the name. I must be frank."

"Oh?" She did not seem at all surprised.

"I know no one and I am in some trouble—much trouble."

"*Vraiment?*" Ruth sipped her drink, her eyes huge over the glass.

"Yes," said Kampass. "I can't handle it."

She ran her finger around the rim of the glass, watching him, not saying anything.

Kampass swallowed. "I must go to the south," he said, "to Spain."

Ruth smiled and rubbed a thumb and forefinger together rapidly.

"I have no money," said Kampass.

Ruth shrugged. "Too bad," she said.

"You knew a friend of mine," said Kampass, leaning closer. "You see, it is about the war, and, well, they say I did things —committed crimes. They are going to send me East, to Poland."

Ruth nodded, "And our common acquaintance is Baldur Kuntz."

"Yes," said Kampass. "That's it." She understood, he thought. He brightened. "That's my friend."

"Well, stop lying," she said. "You mean Rudolf Vogel." Her face drew down. "You're too late," she said. "For me he is dead. He never was."

"Dead?" Kampass looked at his tie.

"For me he is dead and his friends, they are dead too. You want to find him don't you? You think I know and will tell you. Help? Really?"

Kampass sipped the drink. It tasted like medicine. "You are mistaken," he said. "Believe me, please."

Ruth set down the negroni. "You or another was certain to come one day," she said. "But he is gone. You see, you can't hurt him now. You can only hurt me and if you want that, go ahead. I have been hurt by experts and I don't think you are an expert. You are a liar, but not an expert. It is like death. It may happen today or tomorrow or next week or in a year and two months. But I have died a little every day of my life. You are like death itself, *Herr* Kampass; you are inevitable, but a curiosity. That's why I agreed to meet you."

"Listen to me," said Kampass. "Hear me out." He placed a hand on her arm. She shook it off. "You can determine yourself," he added. He explained to her. He told her how they were using him and what was going to happen afterwards. He took the thermofax copies of the extradition papers and laid them on the table in front of her. "They are looking for you as well," he said. "It will not be nice. Three have been killed. Another will be nothing for them."

Ruth did not look at the papers. She opened her purse and took out a packet of cigarettes and a small gold lighter. She lit one and handed it across the table to Kampass. He dragged at the cigarette and blew the smoke onto his shirt.

Ruth said, "So you were at Majdanek with the General?"

Kampass nodded.

"He warned me this would happen, you know. You're not the latest news. I told him the same as I tell you. *I-just-don't-care.*"

"Then they will kill you," Kampass said. "They will kill you finding out about him."

"I should have been dead in your camps twenty years ago," she said.

"Ravensbrück? They said you were there. Political?"

Ruth snorted. "Politics?" She threw back her head and laughed. It was a crude, biting laugh. Her eyes watered. "Do you know to whom you have come for help? A *Jew.* Yes, a *Jew.* My name is Stein. *Stein.*"

Kampass blinked.

"You're not a proud man, are you?" she asked, a smile playing at her mouth.

"No," said Kampass. "I am nothing." For the first time, he was ready to believe it.

She asked him, "What did you do for Rudi? Did you work for him?"

Her voice was getting louder. Kampass looked apprehensively over his shoulder.

"I asked you what you did."

"I was a sergeant," said Kampass. "Please speak lower."

"A sergeant? Sergeant? Do you have a sense of humor, Sergeant?"

There were people looking over at the table. Kampass mopped his brow with a napkin. He looked at the customers and attempted a smile.

"Don't you see it?" she went on.

"Please," said Kampass. "You are being loud."

She laughed again. "You're all the same. Generals and sergeants. All in the same boat at the same oar now. How terribly amusing."

The waiter, attracted by the noise, had come over and was standing at the next table. He was not sure if he should do something.

Ruth stopped laughing. She wiped her eyes. Her mouth grimaced. Kampass saw she was crying, really crying.

"Damn you," she hissed, shaking her head. "Goddamn you. Why did you come? I'm not your Goddamn mother." She calmed a little. She leaned forward. "I don't care," she whispered to him. "I-really-don't-care."

The waiter came and stood behind her. "Do you want something?" he asked her. He kept his eyes on Kampass.

"Yes, I do, Marcel," she said. "I want you to throw this pig out."

The waiter walked around the table to Kampass. He flicked his finger against Kampass' ear. "All right, pig," he said. "Out."

Kampass pushed back his chair. He looked at Ruth. Her mouth was trembling. She was twisting the handerchief, wringing it. "You bastard," she said.

Kampass left. He walked out onto the pavement and stood there limply. Then his hands moved, clenching at his sides. A slow, animal moan built in his throat and his teeth clenched. His lips pulled back into a snarl. He looked up at the sky, the clouds, and raised his fists.

"*Verdammter Gott!*" he shouted. "*Du verdammter Gott!*"

So he stood like a breakwater against the people passing by

on either side. Some paused and followed his stare to the sky as though a would-be suicide were perched on the ledge of a building above. Then they shrugged and moved on.

A bar-café was on the corner opposite him. Kampass put his hands deep in his pockets and shuffled towards it. He did not notice the small, raincoated figure standing in the window of the *tabac* watching him.

•

Shoval said something indelicate and bit off the end of his pencil eraser.

Leinhardt sat uncomfortably in the frame chair and tried to avoid Shoval's eyes. In the corner, the flags of Israel and France stood side by side. Shoval seemed to have prepared offices in half of Europe, Leinhardt thought. He saw Shoval was wearing a Légion d'honneur button in his lapel.

Shoval drew a new pencil from the cup and began to nibble it. "So he's gone to ground," he said. "Your man lost him on the Boulevard Saint Germain."

"When he got on the bus," Leinhardt contributed. He hefted weight from one buttock to the other. "May I smoke?" he asked.

Shoval grunted and pushed an ashtray, the sawed-off base of an eighty-eight millimeter shellcase, over the table as though he were dealing with a butler.

Leinhardt lit his cigarette and said, "You read the report. If we could get assistance from the *Sûreté*, it would help. Pick him up on a vagrancy charge and release him into our custody. We'd triple our manpower."

"Stick that on the wall," said Shoval abruptly. "We might as well put an advert in 'lost and found' for him." He leaned back in his chair and aimed at Leinhardt over the gnawed pencil eraser, using it as a gunsight. He said, "When we contracted you for the operational run on *Oryx*, I assumed you could provide your own answers. You conduct everything like a child."

"He hasn't much money," Leinhardt countered. "He's got to come up for air soon."

"Soon is not enough," snapped Shoval. "The timing here is essential. The Poles want Kampass. They want to know about the delay. Stassen's getting nervous."

"Tell Stassen to stuff it."

Shoval said, "We must have our parcel gift-wrapped for delivery in two weeks. They've moved the debate on the amnesty question ahead. Stassen said they want him now."

"Kampass has got to come up for air," Leinhardt emphasized.

"You know how long a whale can stay under water?"

"Sorry?"

"If you knew," said Shoval, "you wouldn't make a silly-ass statement like that."

"We'll go back to the beginning," said Leinhardt, "where we know he went first, the Rue de la Harpe."

"I don't mind," said Shoval. "But I want him found.

"Incidentally, Werner, there's another matter of some delicacy. I got a call today from the CIA liaison officer. They've caught wind of something. He was only fishing in a friendly sort of way, but he wanted an even break if we turned up the names of naturalized American citizens. You see, the Soviets have accused them of harboring war criminals and now they've put it on the agenda at the UN. It's embarrassing for the Americans. *Expediter* is living proof. The Russians discovered some of Vlasov's Army immigrated to the States from DP camps. They hold annual meetings in New Jersey or someplace. They call themselves the Sixteenth SS Cossack Cavalry. The Russians are upset about it and I don't blame them. Langley uses them as spotters and sometimes operationally this side of the Curtain. Very few of them are German. Most are Rumanians who were with Antonescu; Rumanians and those Vlasovites. So, if one is exposed, it would set a precedent. The Americans might have to give them all up. It might cripple many of their illegals in the East; uncover and jeopardize the whole *Apparat*. But we can't have the

Yanks in on this. You wouldn't know who tipped them off about the *Oryx* exercise would you?"

"There are leaks everywhere," said Leinhardt. "How did ODESSA find out about *Oryx*? How about that?"

Shoval said, "They reached a Pole in the embassy in London. The copies of Kampass' extradition papers are missing from their safe."

So, thought Leinhardt, that was what ODESSA was going to bargain with. That was why they were trying to reach Kampass on the train. They were going to show him the document, show him how Shoval acted in bad faith. Shrewd, thought Leinhardt. Very good indeed. Then they would use Kampass to pipe out information.

"Anything come out of Kampass' visit to Hatfield?" asked Shoval.

"How do you mean?" asked Leinhardt.

"Any data?"

Leinhardt looked at him steadily. "No," he said.

"You still in the Pool at Langley, Werner?"

"What's that supposed to mean?"

"That."

"Well, it's none of your Goddamn business what I do when I'm off this job."

Shoval looked deadly serious. "My friend," he said. "If you cross me you'll go East with Kampass, and that's gospel."

Leinhardt changed the subject. He said, "I'm having a check on all the police substations here. You never know; he might have jaywalked, anything. He's that kind."

Shoval signed a paper, leaving the conversation in mid-air. He belonged on a stage, thought Leinhardt. There was that much ham in him.

The telephone jangled. Without looking, Shoval languidly reached out and brought it in. He cuddled it between his neck and shoulder. He put down the pen. "What's that? Repeat that again," he said.

Leinhardt sat up in the chair.

"When?" Shoval asked. ". . . I see." Then, "Who did?" He

put up the phone. "Well," he said. "You were right about the jails."

Leinhardt jumped up. "There you are," he said.

"Kampass was arrested at seven-thirty this evening."

"They've got him then."

"He was arrested for vandalism; he was making water on the steps of Sacré Coeur."

"How's that?" asked Leinhardt.

"A slash. He was taking a slash on the church steps."

Leinhardt smiled. He nodded. He said, *"Kamposity."*

Shoval looked at him gravely. He said, "Very funny."

"What's wrong, Shoval? Relax. They have him."

Shoval's expression did not alter. Slowly, he shook his head. "He was bailed out an hour ago."

"Bailed out? By whom?"

"Ruth Steiner."

Shoval went back to signing papers, his pen scratching loudly. He seemed totally absorbed in his signature. Then, without looking up, he said, "Get going."

•

The desert was yellow-hot under a broiling sun and copper sky and Kampass felt the sand gritty in his socks and underpants. He wiped away the perspiration from his brow, and lifting his head above the lip of the wadi, looked through the binoculars at the Oryx, which stood peacefully eight hundred yards away.

He put down the glasses and picked up the scoped rifle that lay beside him. The heat bounced off the sand dunes and shimmered in the lens of the sight. He dug his toes into the soft bank of the wadi and aimed carefully, holding the cross hairs on a point slightly above the animal's spine. He expelled his breath and squeezed the trigger. The rifle jumped against him and the shot punched out in echoes over the dunes. Fifty feet beyond the Oryx, a fountain of sand erupted and drifted slowly in the searing wind. The Oryx tossed its head and moved out of range, grazing.

He cursed and ejected the spent cartridge. Then he slung the bandoleer of ammunition over his shoulder and set out after the animal, which was by now only a speck against the side of the farthest dune.

All day it had been going like this for him and the Oryx. He cringed under the burning wafer of the sun.

Then the sun went out and Kampass was plunged into darkness. He woke up, sweating.

"You're wasting electricity."

The light coming through the high windows made the room look grey, and he turned his head on the pillow and saw Ruth standing at the door, her hand on the light switch. Beneath his head the pillow was damp.

His eyes followed her as she crossed the room and set the bag of groceries on the small table next to the two-burner stove. She filled an aluminum kettle with water, and placing it upon the stove, struck a match and lit the burner. It made a soft *whoof*.

"Do you know what day it is?" she asked.

"I've lost track," he answered, getting off the bed, his mouth feeling dry and unclean.

"It's Christmas."

Kampass thought back. He had been here how long? Two days? Yes, that was right, Christmas. Most of the time he slept, feeling as though it were a perpetual night. He vaguely remembered how it had been; her coming to the substation tank to bail him out. She had followed him, she had said. No one told him why he had been arrested. He remembered none of that except an *agent* who had beaten him with the lead-lined skirts of his cape and kept calling him a filthy pig, swatting him, hitting him there on the streets. Then he must have passed out.

Ruth had disturbed him once only, when she brought back a client and Kampass lay there on the cot she had put up behind the curtain for him and listened to the sounds of their lovemaking.

He did not know why she had taken him in; why, after denying him, she had relented. They had not discussed that since he arrived in her flat. Nor had they spoken of Rudolf Vogel. Ruth would bring in the groceries: a long loaf of granite-hard bread, a few eggs, and sometimes a slab of Danish bacon. She would go through his pants pockets and subtract from his change whatever was owed her. She would tell him what she had taken. When she went out, she cautioned him to stay off the streets. He never asked her where she went nor did she mention it. He trusted her somehow.

The teapot on the stove shrieked and Ruth poured the hot water into two cups over tea bags and set the cups on the table in the center of the room. Next she poured the water, fresh from the tap, into a bowl for the small mongrel dog which occupied a cushion in the corner of her side of the room. Every time Kampass saw the dog, he was surprised. It was so quiet you never knew it was there. It would eat and silently return to its cushion. The dog, like himself, seemed to do nothing but sleep.

He splashed some cold water on his face. In the warped toothpaste-dotted mirror above the basin, he saw himself, distorted. The skin beneath his eyes was purple as though it thinly covered two reservoirs of ink, and a dark stubble had formed on his lower jaw. Kampass shaved carefully, using the razor and mug she had bought him. Then he patted his face dry, came to the table, and said, "I need air. I have to go out."

"You can't do that," she said, sugaring the tea and putting a little milk in her cup. "Anyway, I've found someone who may be able to help. It won't be much, but he can get you to the frontier below Oloron-Sainte Marie. You'll have to cross the mountains at Laruns. You'll have to hire a guide of some sort. You could die up there and they'd never find you until the spring." She drank some of the tea and set down the cup as though it were made of bone china. "Merry Christmas," she said.

"Not very merry for you," said Kampass.

"I've known worse," she said, and he knew she spoke the truth. He loaded a slice of the bread with marmalade and wolfed it down. "You're going out again?" he asked.

"On Christmas it would be profane," she replied.

191

They ate and finished the tea in silence, and then he said, "I dreamt about Vogel. I was hunting him on the desert, but I could never catch up with him."

Ruth reached across the table and laid her hand on his arm. When she touched him, his arm jerked. "That is because he doesn't exist," she said. "Forget about him. He is dead. If you keep on with this, you'll be dead too."

Her eyes lifted from the fly-spotted tablecloth and Kampass felt something inside him move as though it were alive. He saw her high cheekbones shining in the half-light and he was conscious of the pull of the jersey over her breasts. Her neck was long and incredibly white, he thought. He stared at her lap.

She saw him looking at her and said, *"Herr* Kampass, do you want to make love to me?"

He lowered his eyes to the empty teacup.

"If you do," she said, "it's all right."

Kampass felt a little sick thinking about it. "You and Vogel," he said, his throat constricting, "how did it begin?"

She shrugged. She said, "It was survival. I was at Ravensbrück and he saw me on an inspection tour and I went away with him. I should be dead. Many left on the trains for Auschwitz the next day and I was to go with them."

•

She looked at him leaning across the table. He was trying to understand, she knew. He was trying to understand something even she herself was not sure of. And he had been on the other side of the barbed wire. How could anyone know when they were on the right side of the wire? Now he knew though; now he did.

He was one of them, she thought. Any of them. With orders all of them became as mindless and insensitive as rock slides. He was different only in name from the one she remembered who used to peer down at her from the guard tower by the south gate, leaning over the barrel of his machine gun and studying her in the exercise yard as though she were an insect performing in an entomology experiment: one of those glass-encased ant communities you bought in toy stores. And here he was, leaning towards her with simian brows wrinkling with concentration; a superman trapped on the wrong side of the wire. Had she helped him because he was just a curiosity, a curio? Or did she help him because she had to? She did not know. She had seen him go, standing outside the *tabac* screaming insults at the sky, and suddenly she felt an immense sorrow. She followed him.

What did he want her to tell him? About the dikey SS matrons with chests like wine casks. Did he want that? About the Renaissance Brunhildes in field grey? Or did he want to know about the *Kapos* who took what they wanted when they wanted. Maybe he would like to know about her own feces steaming in the cold and the *Appells* and the dogs and the lice and the urine-stiff blankets covering evil-smelling straw. She could certainly tell him about all that. She could make Ravensbrück live for him; the way station on the road to death.

But he would never understand about Rudolf, about how it happened between them. He had been so small and thin, undernourished. She could hardly see him as he drove by in the mist that morning and they were all standing out for *Appell*. Just the top of his cap she had seen in the back of the Mercedes, the cap with the eagle and the skull and crossbones stud above the visor.

Later a *Kapo* came and took her from the barracks. They deloused her and brought her to the infirmary for a medical and inoculations. Then the dentist cleaned her teeth. She did not know what it was about, but that night they let her sleep in the infirmary between clean sheets and they gave her real sanitary pads—not old socks filled with older socks. Sheets; a clean-smelling pillowcase. The next morning they told her. She was to accompany the *Standartenführer* who had seen and admired her on *Appell*. She would be his baggage and she would live. How could one refuse?

She went back to the barracks to collect the few articles she still possessed before leaving and the others spat at her and called her names. *Go ahead, you whore, you pig, you gar-*

bage, they had screamed. And the *Kapos* had to restrain them or they would have torn her apart—all of them except Judith, who understood and said: *Go. Don't pay any mind. The important thing is to live; to survive.* Judith with rickets, who later died when she volunteered for typhoid injections so that she could sleep between clean sheets as well. She had asked Rudolf to help her and he had tried. He had done that. But it was too late. Judith, who was always saying, *Somebody is forever being beastly to somebody else.* Judith, who accepted the inevitability of injustice. *We are scapegoats,* she had said. *It is all one wretched joke. It's on us and even we are forced to laugh at it.*

That was what Judith had said before she, Ruth, left with Vogel. And the others who wanted to kill her, they went to Auschwitz the next morning. She, Ruth, lived. She went with Vogel, and she found in time she could live with it. Although they had nothing in common, they did have a need for each other.

Hope. That was all.

> *When all hope has gone*
> *When it ceases to exist*
> *There is nothing to fear.*
> *There is nothing to death.*

This she had read on the walls at Ravensbrück. It had been written by someone who understood. She had read it and immediately knew how six million of them met death without a whimper.

She looked at Kampass and decided to tell him. She would answer his question even though he could not ever know about it; the superman now caught on the wrong side of the stockade.

●

Ruth brought more tea to the table. She refilled the cups. She sipped the tea and said nothing for a moment. Then she stared at the table and told him:

"They took away everything you loved. You had nothing, you see. Nothing. So the idea of dying was not terrifying. One wanted something to love. Desperately you wanted this. For a woman it is hope, and when you have hope you care about living. Rudolf came to Ravensbrück and took me away. He was something to love, like a rag doll. He was someone to care about and it was not important what he was. I knew what I was doing, but it never got to where I could not live with myself. But it was true, he gave me something." She moved in her chair, adjusting herself, and then went on:

"At first I was only an alternative for him, a kind of coat-tree where he could hang his conscience, but then . . ."—she shrugged and made a gesture with her hand. "He believed in what he was doing, he told me. There was nothing he would not do for Germany, he used to say."

"But we all said that," interrupted Kampass. "It was part of the oath."

"No," she continued. "For Rudolf, it was more. It was a way of life. He was descended from a Junker family in East Prussia and his father was a major general in the Great War. Rudolf is not a cruel man, not naturally. He could be quite tender. The Nazis knew his background, his patriotism. They convinced him the Jew was the Babu of Europe: that we had doomed all their *Kultur* and Germany would become a nation of shopkeepers. The Nazis used him as an example they could hold up to others. They needed aristocracy and Rudolf was an aristocrat. He gave them a little dignity."

Kampass went from the table to the bed. He recalled the rumor about Vogel having a woman in Lublin. He looked up through the grilled skylight at the somber clouds. He said, "He deserted. Why did he desert?"

"He discovered what was greater than his country, and in some ways, it destroyed him. His world went upside-down. He had to make a new code of living for himself."

"And he changed like that?" Kampass asked, unconvinced. He was trying, unsuccessfully, to equate it to his own experience.

"He fell in love," Ruth explained. "He fell in love with a Jew."

"No," replied Kampass adamantly. "He was a queer. He fooled you, you see. Because of him I am here. He was a bastard. Look at me." He held his arms out from his sides.

"You have never loved other men? Not the other way—just loved them?" she asked. "Is that as you say, queer?"

Kampass remembered Willi Haas, the butcher, and of how Haas died in his arms; lying on the snow before Moscow, Willi holding his severed leg, cuddling it to him as a mother nurses a child and he, Kampass, crying and watching him die; yes, he had loved Willi Haas.

"I don't understand," he lied. "I'm sorry."

He looked at her, and in the murk she suddenly became an old woman. Her hair fell across her face and she put the teacups in the sink and ran water over them.

"If he loves you," Kampass asked, "why then did the bastard leave you like this? Tell me that."

"It was the doctor, that beast Wick, who was trying to blackmail us," she explained over the noise of the faucet. "Besides, Rudolf did not need loving any more. He found his own way and I knew that we were with each other because of need and the need was then over with. Need is not sufficient. I was no longer the alternative for him and he stopped being a rag doll for me. He left and I have not heard from him."

"And you don't know where he is now?"

"I don't want to know," she answered.

And they did not speak of Vogel again.

They spent the afternoon quietly, Kampass helping her with the washing, hanging her stockings and underwear—which he noticed was holed and laddered in places—on a rope clothesline slung across the middle of the room, feeling inadequate, and somehow, unmanly about it all.

She cooked a chicken for dinner, preparing it with an almost intense care and then she sat watching him while he ate it. She ate only half of her own plate which she divided equally between herself and the dog.

They prepared for bed quietly. She put an electric fire in the center of the room, and before switching off the light, she said, "Tomorrow I will go out and bring some clothes for you."

Later, he could hear her turning in bed across the room. Then he heard the sheets rustle as she got up and saw her vague outline as she took down the blanket that hid his cot. Kampass drew the bedclothing taut to his chin.

"Are you sleeping?" she asked.

Kampass lay stiff as a board in the bed, his feet pressed together and cold beneath the quilt.

"Do I wake you?" she said.

"No," said Kampass. He looked at the pale square of the skylight above.

Ruth got in beside him, saying nothing. Kampass moved in the bed, pressing hard against the wall. Her foot brushed against his. It felt warm.

"You're cold," she said. "The heat is so bad."

"I'm all right," Kampass replied. He moved his feet away, not wanting to touch her.

"What's wrong?" she asked.

"Nothing. Nothing is wrong," he said.

Together, they stared up at the skylight, and near them, the coils of the electric fire pricked, bright red.

"Why did you come back?" he asked. "I mean at the police station."

"Don't talk," she said.

The bed became very warm now with their bodies and Kampass felt himself begin to perspire. Still he did not move. Somewhere in the room he heard a creak as a board settled. There was a movement on the pillow and he knew Ruth had turned her head and was watching him in the darkness. After a while she asked, "Don't you want me? It's all right, you know."

Kampass did not reply. He kept to his side of the bed.

"It's silly lying here," she said. "People would not believe it, a man and woman in bed together like this. I will go."

She moved in the bed.

"Don't," said Kampass. He did not mean to say it. It just came out. Then he felt the length of her body press to his, and at once he turned towards her, losing himself in the musty swarm of her hair as though he could hide himself from all the world there. He allowed himself to be led, not wanting to be aware or to disappoint or to hurt, oblivious.

"You don't know about it, do you," she said. "You really don't."

He awoke in the dawn and saw that she had left, and only the still-warm depression of her body on the cot reminded him they had been together. There was a deep stillness in the room, made more profound by the faint creaks of the tin reflector in the electric fire. The skylight glowed, paled, and then a single ray of sunshine cut the darkness, falling on the table. It lit a half-empty bottle of milk on the table like a spotlight. Then it was gone. He curled into a tight ball in the bed and waited.

He heard her coming from some distance away, her feet plodding on the stairs and then pausing as she caught her breath on the landing. The key sounded in the lock and she came in. Kampass peeked at her from over the pillow. She dumped a heavy brown parcel on the table, and walking to the bed, stood over him. She touched his leg.

"It's time," she said.

He sat up in the bed and yawned, pretending to have only just awakened. Ruth went to a corner of the room and began to change her clothes. She undressed as though he were not there. He could see her bra was soiled grey and there was an ugly bruise on her upper thigh that was beginning to turn yellow. She came back to the bed. "You must go now," she said. "I have brought your clothes."

He reached for her, but she pulled away and turned her back.

She said, "They took Corinne last night and questioned her. A small man came. They could be here any minute. Get out, and I don't want to hear of you again."

Kampass raised himself on an elbow. "Leinhardt," he said. "You can't stay then. You've got to go with me. Come with me. Will you?" He was begging now.

"I am going nowhere," she said.

He left the bed and opened the parcel. It contained a back-pack, a well-worn pin-stripe suit and a soft-brim hat. There were leather patches on the sleeves of the jacket and around the edges of the pockets.

"You'll need the pack in the mountains. The suit was the best I could get," she said, watching him dress. "When you leave, go to the *tabac* on the corner. A man called Dierks will meet you in fifteen minutes. He will see you to the frontier. He thinks you to be Hungarian. I told him if they catch you, they will send you back."

Kampass stood in the suit, looking like a scarecrow. "I can't leave," he said. He was thinking of Leinhardt and of what Leinhardt might do to her.

Ruth turned and he saw her eyes were wet. "Get out," she snapped. "Get out. *Get out!*" Then she seemed to wilt, to bend, and she looked at him through her tears and said, "I'm sorry. Leave me with something."

Kampass fumbled in his pocket.

"Not that," she said.

Then he understood. For so long they had taken from her and no one had given, and like the others, he had nothing to give in return. Suddenly he felt terribly helpless faced with the inevitability of it: that there was nothing he could do for her. For Kampass, standing there avoiding her eyes, the situation brought to mind a similar experience. There had been a young woman he had seen near the Zoo after leaving the alleyway that April afternoon in Berlin. She was walking down the middle of Berliner Strasse carrying a loaf of bread under one arm and pulling a perambulator filled with bloody slabs of recently butchered horsemeat. Bullets snapped about her, but she did not seem to mind. She kept walking towards the Zoo and the German lines. Kampass had stood in a door-way and watched it all; as she reached the corner, three Russians, Mongols, sprinted out from behind a building and caught her. They dragged her back, shrieking, into the rubble and there raped her; one after another while a fourth soldier sat on her head. He had seen it, standing there in the doorway with a machine pistol, and he did nothing. Nothing. He was fascinated by it. Then the fourth Russian got up from her head and took his turn. When he finished, he unholstered his pistol and shot her twice. The woman's body bounced on the debris. She lay, white on the red brick, like a broken doll.

Kampass looked at Ruth. "I can't," he said, wanting to scream. He turned at the door. Ruth had not moved. She watched the floor, her thin hands clasped before her.

He went down the dark stairway to the street. On the pavement, he blinked in the sun and his skin moved under the cold. He must not think about it, he told himself. He mustn't.

•

The *tabac* smelled of coffee and cheap, raw cigarettes, like burning manure, and the espresso machines, polished to a high silver, sighed and steamed behind the bar. Kampass shouldered through the customers and found an opening at the very end of the room. He set the pack down and asked for a coffee. He had just sugared the coffee when a young, spidery man squeezed in beside him and said, "I'm Pieter Dierks." He had a huge pituitary jaw that sprang forward when he talked and he looked Kampass up and down critically. He said, "You have no time to finish that coffee. *Pas de temps.* We must reach Laruns before midnight. It will be difficult as it is."

Kampass put down a franc for the coffee and followed Dierks through the customers and out to the street.

"No bags?" Dierks asked. "No sweetycase?"

"No," Kampass replied. "Only the knapsack."

Dierks showed him to a small Citroën panel truck parked nearby. The lettering on the truck read *Dierks—Boucherie.*

"You are Hungarian?" asked Dierks as he pulled the truck out into the traffic.

Kampass nodded.

"Communist shit," said Dierks. "*Merde.* You understand?"

Kampass said, "Yes, *Scheiss*."

"You speak German?" asked Dierks. "So also I." He drove like a wild man, with no regard for auto or pedestrian, lying hard onto the horn at intersections and weaving down the cobbled streets. Kampass sucked in his breath and stamped at the floor for an imaginary brake whenever they careened about a corner. Dierks looked at him and giggled. He hunched over the wheel, fiercely intent.

"I am going to be a *para*," announced Dierks suddenly. "I report to Pau for the training courses tomorrow. That is why I take you. Laruns is only a little farther." He spun the wheel to avoid a vegetable cart. "You like De Gaulle?"

"He's fine," said Kampass.

"That is good," said Dierks. "If we are to get along together, it is important that you like De Gaulle. He is the best for France since Napoleon. I tell you, he hates the Communists. France is the only thing that stands between Europe and Communism. So I am Dutch, but I adopted France. No, better to say France adopted me. I must do my part. I am enlisting in the *paras*."

Kampass wished Dierks would keep his eyes on the road when he talked. The conversation reminded him of Lodz. He tried to think ahead to the mountains and Spain. But it was no good. He kept returning to Ruth Stein. She remained behind, he thought, waiting for Leinhardt. Maybe she would have sense enough to run. But she had said she would not leave. She meant it. Dierks said something, but Kampass was not listening. How could he have done it? How could he have left her there waiting?

"Stop!" he shouted.

Dierks stepped on the brakes, narrowly avoiding an onion peddler who was about to step down from the pavement. Dierks pulled into the curb. He whined, "I might have hit him."

"I'm getting out here," said Kampass. "I'm not going."

Dierks looked at him, stupefied. "What are you saying?" he said. "You're crazy!"

Kampass pulled fifty francs from his pocket and threw

them on the seat. "I can't go," he said.

"They'll send you back. Do you want to go back to Hungary?"

Kampass got out of the truck. He leaned through the window and said, "I've got to go back for her."

Dierks laid a hand on his arm. "Look," he said. "Get in and let it alone. Forget her. She will be all right, I say. She is looked after. They will not bother her."

Kampass looked at him. Now there seemed nothing ludicrous about Dierks.

"I know," added Dierks kindly. "But let it alone."

"No," said Kampass. He pulled his arm free and ran, dodging cars until he found a taxi. He gave the driver Ruth's address. As they left they passed the panel truck and he saw that Dierks had not moved. He sat staring ahead of him, holding the wheel at arm's length.

After the ride with Dierks, the taxi seemed to crawl.

When he recognized the *tabac* on the corner, he told the driver to let him out. He burst into the building and pounded up the stairs, two at a time. He reached the final landing below Ruth's door. Suddenly he found himself on his knees without knowing how he got there. He must have tripped, he thought. When he made the effort to rise, he fell back on the landing. He could not seem to coordinate and there was the sound of running water in his ears. Looking back down the stairs, he saw a frightened face peering from a doorway and was conscious of the smell of cooking. Then words were spoken and the face quickly withdrew. Someone was lifting him under the armpits and pulling him along the landing into the shadows and there was nothing he could do. He felt the soft rub of suede and sheepskin against his face, and one flight of stairs above him he heard noises that were only remotely human. Then he fainted.

●

Kampass swam up from the bottom of a lake of undulating patches of sunlight. His tongue was fat in his mouth and he

clawed his way to the surface. He was lying on his face and
the coarse boards under his cheek stank of excrement. Hands
roughly hauled him to his feet and shoved him towards the
last flight of stairs.

"Up. Up," said Laski over his shoulder. "Up the stairs.
Move."

Kampass tumbled over the first step and a foot landed
painfully against the base of his spine. He scrambled upward,
reaching the top on his hands and knees. He was kicked again
and went down on his stomach. Laski grabbed a fistful of his
hair and slammed his head against the floor. Bright rockets
streaked and exploded and he felt himself sink back into the
shadows. He shook his head.

"Move it," Laski ordered. "Double-quick, fast."

Kampass got to his feet, caromed off the wall, and stag-
gered into the door which gave under his weight. He stumbled into the room.

Another blow to the side of his head spun him around. He
fell forward against the unyielding bulk of the sheepskin
coat. He buried his face in the soft lapels, and with his arms
encircling the waist of his antagonist, slipped to the floor. He
sank back on his haunches and cupped his hands over his
face. His hands seemed warm and slippery and his face felt
like rubber. Kampass knew he was bleeding.

Two suede shoes planted themselves in front of him. They
shifted slightly and made a neat, squeaking sound on the
floor. Then there was only one shoe. The other crashed into
the pit of his stomach and his breath shot out of his lungs.

He rolled onto his side and tucked his knees up under his
chin to protect his groin. He gasped for air that would not
come and the waters began to close about him again.

Unexpectedly the pummeling ceased, and gradually his
lungs filled. Above him the bare light bulb swung like a pen-
dulum on its thin cord; first putting the room in light, then
into darkness, like an auditorium during an old film. He
watched the light bulb and waited for the next blow. When it
did not come, he ventured a look about him, peeping through
his arms.

Leinhardt was washing his hands in the sink. He turned and said, "You had balls coming back here." He dried his hands on a dishtowel, his fingers leaving red smudges. Leinhardt rolled down his sleeves, stroking them over his forearms and buttoning his cuffs. "Why?" he asked. "Just you tell me why?" His mouth was a thin scar across his face—tight and unsmiling.

In a corner of the room Ruth's dog lay on the calico cushion, its eyes moving back and forth between Kampass and Leinhardt.

"What did you do with her? Where is she?" Kampass demanded from the floor.

Leinhart nodded at the bed.

Kampass sat up. He did not have to look twice. Only a bare foot and a tacky tangle of hair showed at either end of the sheet they had thrown over her. Two crimson stains spread, soaking through the sheet where it rose over her breasts.

"She didn't know!" Kampass shouted. "Damn you. I could have told you she didn't!"

"You're wrong, Kampass," said Leinhardt. "She did know. She knew and she told us."

They didn't have to do this, he thought. Not to her. Him, he could understand.

"Oh no," said Leinhardt. "Don't tell me you had it off with her." He half turned and moved his shoulders. "Who cares about whores? Was she good, then?"

"I care about whores!" Kampass roared.

"Excuse me," said Leinhardt. "I fail to appreciate these sentiments after a review of your record." He waved his hands like an orator. "Bruno, oh Bruno. I doubt the honor of thy intents." Then he balled up the towel and threw it at Kampass. It landed on the floor, soggy. Kampass saw the stains and the room reeled.

Leinhardt lit a cigarette and walked over to where the dog lay, its head on its paws. The dog jumped as he approached, drawing back against the wall. Leinhardt cooed at it and stroked its ears. The dog began to lick at his fingers and its tail stirred on the cushion. Leinhardt straightened up and said, "You've been so bad, Bruno. You've put *Uncle* to a great deal of bother. Do you know what *Uncle* has to do now?"

Kampass stared at Leinhardt. He decided that if he ever left the room alive, he would kill Werner Leinhardt. It would not be a case of mistaken identity.

Leinhardt turned away from the dog and squinted at him. "*Uncle* must punish you even though it will hurt him as much as it will hurt you."

Kampass reared back and spat. The saliva succeeded only in running down his shirt front.

"Good," said Leinhardt. "Fine."

Kampass heard the shoes scrape behind him on the floor and Leinhardt raised his eyes slightly. "Emil," he said softly. "Beat upon Bruno. Make him hurt. Hurt him like he's never been hurt before."

Leinhardt pulled over a chair and sat down. He crossed his legs. "Emil?" he said.

Kampass hurled himself forward, but Laski's legs became entangled with his own and he skidded to the floor. A punch to the back of his neck paralyzed him. Then there was a sharp jab in his arm. He tried to lift it, to move his legs, but there was no feeling in them. He could not breathe properly. Laski was sitting on his head and chest and hands were moving on his belt buckle, tugging his pants below his knees. He screamed, babbling curses at Leinhardt. Then he screamed again; this time not from hate but pain. It came, flowing up his torso from his groin, ripping through his insides, drawing the breath from him. A red film descended over his eyes, his ears roared, and his body bucked. Amidst waves of agony he sensed what they were doing to him, and he felt the indignity of it nearly as much as the pain.

"Please," he whimpered. "Don't."

It was very hot now in the cubicle; hot and humid.

"No, I don't think about it," Kampass answered the Ukrainian. "You know we're not suppose to."

You must believe it, he told himself. You must believe we are right. Gott mit uns.

The old man was shading his eyes against the floodlights. Kampass could see the whitened tip of his nose where it pressed against the glass. The smile widened. Kampass could see he had no front teeth. Kampass drew back into the darkness of the cubicle, but it was as though the old man could see him no matter where he went.

It was like watching a film without a sound track. The crystals were dissolving. The entire chamber was moving, pulsing, like a beating heart. Some of them punched with their bony fists against the wall. In a corner a woman was beating her head on the cement.

Gott mit uns.

Some tried to climb upon the shoulders of others to reach what they thought was the safety of the ventilation ducts. Screams began to filter through like waves breaking on a distant beach.

The porthole was misting over but the old man's nose, now a white dot, pressed hard upon the glass.

Gott mit uns.

They were dying now, Kampass saw. They were dying upright. Why didn't the old man die?

Here and there a body would move, an arm lift, a fist clench in reflex. The dead stared into one another's eyes as if surprised at what had happened to them.

The old man threw back his head and howled. Kampass could see right back to the fillings in his rear teeth. The face vanished from the porthole.

The Ukrainian threw a switch to reverse the ventilation system: to pump the poisoned air from the chambers. He removed his gas mask and wiped at his face. He lit a cigarette. "Long way from Russia," he said.

Kampass did not reply.

"Those medals you got. How did you get them?"

Kampass did not want to talk about it. That old man, Christ.

"I was with Vlasov's people," said the Ukrainian. "I didn't get any medals."

Kampass knew the private was pushing him.

The Ukrainian's piggy, little eyes narrowed. "Maybe they'll give you one for this. Not me. I do it for free; I don't like Jews. Will they give you a medal, Oberscharführer?"

Kampass unzipped his coveralls. No medals for this, he thought. No medals period. He remembered the training they had given him after he left the hospital. A Desinfektor. A lousy Desinfektor trained on rats and mice to use the gas, like he was not good enough for anything else.

"You haven't got the belly," said the Ukrainian. "I saw you looking at that old bastard. I saw your face."

"I'm a soldier," said Kampass. Gott mit uns, he thought.

ORYX

"I love my country. Everyone does."
———*Bruno Kampass, age twenty-two*

Thirty thousand feet beneath them, the baked, parchmentlike wastes of the southern Sudan lay sweltering in the desert night, and widely scattered clusters of lights pricked the darkness like dew upon a lawn of black grass.

Kampass pressed his forehead against the Perspex and looked down at the lights. It was almost impossible to separate them from the stars on the rim of the earth. He thought of the people below; half-naked savages, he guessed, scratching a living from the wrinkled land and here he was, above it all, like God. He rubbed at the mark his forehead had left on the glass and then straightened his legs. He winced at the pain in his groin. He ached from it. He ached all over.

" . . . and, oh, I don't know," Leinhardt was saying in the next seat, "all these touches are unnecessary. Take me, for instance; now all I'm interested in is getting there." He was talking to a pretty hostess who perched upon the arm of the seat, hanging on his every word.

"And I'm sure it is the same with my friend, huh, Bruno?" Leinhardt dug his elbow into his ribs. Kampass gasped.

"Your friend looks ill," said the hostess, mildly concerned.

"He is indeed," agreed Leinhardt, nodding seriously.

"I'll bring some aspro," said the hostess, lifting herself from the arm of the seat.

"That would be sweet," Leinhardt said. "Isn't she sweet, Bruno?"

Kampass nodded.

"You see, my friend here also contracted food poisoning in

Paris," Leinhardt elaborated. "Nothing worse. In short, he is a wreck."

"Napoleon's revenge," quipped the hostess and Leinhardt laughed. The hostess went back to the galley.

Kampass watched her go and he remembered Ruth. He could only see their two-day relationship as though it was a bad reel passed too rapidly through a home-movie projector. He kept wanting to stop the action, to say: Stop it there. Stop it where I awoke and could still smell her next to me. Stop it where she comes back and I am in bed pretending to be asleep like a little boy surprised in the act of abusing himself. Stop it where the ray of sunlight comes through the skylight.

But the reel spun faster and faster and the projector whirred on, and then at once the film snapped.

The hostess held a Dixie Cup full of water and a pill under his nose. He washed the pill down and looked back out the window. He could distinguish the earth from the sky now. A faint belt of pink, a growing corona, to the east. The hard, pimpled land became more distinct until, at last, he saw the seams of dried riverbeds stitched amongst the scrubby quilting of the hills: the Great Rift which ran the length of Africa like an open fly.

Kampass felt as though it were the day before yesterday. Somehow the two days seemed to vanish from the calendar of his life. It had been the day after Christmas when they found him at Ruth's flat. From then until he revived to find himself in a wheelchair at Orly, things were missing. Leinhardt was pushing the wheelchair, his face grim under the unavoidable tyroler and its ridiculous tuft of hair. Seeing Leinhardt and remembering, he had automatically shied back. Leinhardt asked, "How's the invalid?"

That was when he had noticed the copy of *Le Monde* lying on his lap. The paper was dated December 28. Leinhardt saw him examining it and removed the newspaper.

But it was what Leinhardt said at the Air France ticket counter that helped bring back a small part of the missing two days. He had said, *Flight eight-seven-six, for Nairobi.* It

211

was the sequence of the numbers that did it. Where had he heard them before? Then the dispensary and the man in the grey suit with a toothbrush mustache came back. He remembered it like he was looking through the wrong end of a telescope—the man with the mustache bending over him saying, *"Count from ten, backward: ten, nine, eight, seven, six . . ."* And he had counted.

White and wooly, the dispensary closed over him. There was the clink of instruments in enamel trays and he was certain there were several people in the dispensary with him besides the man with the mustache.

Somewhere a band was playing. He had tried to move his feet in time to the music, but weights held down his legs. Then, as if he were in an echo chamber, conversation drifted to him through the strains of the music, the voices gargled as if they were shouting under water.

The mist rolled and the band played and they were telling him, "I am the only friend you have and you must trust me when I say I will not betray you. Do you believe me?" . .

He attempted to answer, but when he mouthed the words, nothing came; no sound at all.

"Certainly you believe me because I am your only friend."

No, he had no friends. He had no one.

The mists parted and the mustached man was doing something to his eyes, prying open the lids. A harsh beam of light seared his eyeballs.

"Do you hear the music?" he was asked. *"Then march to that music."*

Kampass moved his feet. They were so heavy.

"It's marvelous music!"

The beat picked up.

"You feel splendid. Tip-top."

"Yes."

"March, march, march, links . . . links . . . links."

The weights left his feet. There were springs in his boots and the pack, bread bag, and rifle of the man ahead of him swayed in time with the cadence of the drum, the regimental drum. The crowds lined the streets. They were wav-

ing small flags and the line of march was carrying them to the foot of the Brandenburg Gate. They were marching on flowers. The band broke out with "Ich hatt' einen Kameraden."

Then at once the music ceased, and he could see tall trees and hear the thwack of axes and feel pine needles. There was old Metz. Now snow lay on the ground and he and Metz were hunting boar again and he could hear the braying of the dogs; feel the whip of saplings as he followed their calls. He came upon a clearing. The boar stood in the middle of it, all hoary, its head low and the jaws, the muzzle extending out. The dogs were on it, worrying it, and suddenly it spun out towards him, sending up chunks of snow. Metz was beside him and he looked at the old man, waiting to be told to do something. "Shoot!" Metz said. "Shoot quick!" He lifted the old Mauser. The boar was nearly on them now and he could see the slime on its lips, the short, evil tusks. "Shoot!" And Kampass tried to comply. He tried, but the trigger froze. He screamed.

Someone was slapping his face. He opened his eyes. The room swayed.

"Where did you get this?" asked the man with the mustache. He held the extradition orders.

Kampass laughed. There was something funny about the man's mustache.

"Who gave it to you? It was in your pocket."

"They gave it," said Kampass.

"Who's they?"

"They."

Leinhardt was there. He saw Leinhardt and his wide mouth. Leinhardt whispered into the man's ear. The man nodded.

That mustache, thought Kampass.

"Look," said the man. He tore up the papers. He ripped them to little bits. "There," he said. He threw away the scraps. "So. It is a lie. These are forged."

Kampass looked at the scattered papers on the floor.

"Your salvation is your faith in us," said the garbled voice. "You will have faith. We keep our word here. Identify Vogel

*and you are free, free as wind. One last trip, Kampass. One
more run and you are free."*

Kampass jerked forward in the seat, his head splitting.

He looked over at Leinhardt who had dozed off, his head
nodding onto his chest.

As though Leinhardt had heard his thoughts, he opened
his eyes. For several seconds they stared at each other. Then
Leinhardt closed his eyes again.

The land slowly changed to the open green of the veld,
heaving gently and dotted with acacia. It was like flying over
a golf course that went to the horizon.

The cone of Mount Kenya poked through the clouds on the
horizon, dented slightly.

•

Leinhardt told him nothing of where they were going.

"You'll find out. Follow instructions," he said.

They drove east from Nairobi, sitting in the rear of the
Peugeot, the African driver holding the wheel loosely in his
thin hands. They crossed the khaki plains, leaving the dust
boiling behind them and passing the scattered shacks of
Kajiado, and Leinhardt sat with arms akimbo and stared out
at the hills, which rose like petrified primitive animals. When
they saw game, he would point and say: "Look at that. Wilde-
beest," or "gerenuk." He identified each animal. He had
taken off his coat and opened his shirt. A Browning automatic
pistol rested in a spring holster under his armpit and sweat
had stained his shirt where the supporting straps crossed his
back and circled his shoulders.

A giraffe loped across the road in front of them with its
outlandish rocking-horse gait.

Leinhardt pointed a finger at it and said, "Powy!"

"No bwana," said the driver. "Royal game."

"Fooling around," explained Leinhardt.

Kampass watched the road stoically. Since they left Paris,
Leinhardt had not let him out of his sight. They had driven
from Embakasi into the city and hired the car and the driver.

Leinhardt rented them for three days. "After that," he had said, "we part and may never the twain meet."

Why, Kampass speculated, did Ruth lie about Vogel? She claimed she did not know his whereabouts. Why would she protect him? He wondered if it was from some distorted sense of loyalty, or perhaps she was still in touch with Vogel. It was all beyond Kampass, but it hurt him that she had withheld this from him; this one thing over all else—her trust.

They turned south, entering a series of rocky hills, grim and parched under a sky like burnished copper; a place where it might always be midday. Great heaps of elephant dung dotted the shoulders of the road and sparsely leafed baobabs stood nearby like gnarled and tired sentinels. It was like a lunar landscape, thought Kampass.

The driver, a Kikuyu provided by the car-rental company in Nairobi, lounged behind the wheel. The smell of him settled to the rear seat of the Peugeot, spicy, like a smoked ham. The Kikuyu twisted on the seat and one scrawny arm disappeared from the wheel. The car began to weave on the road. Leinhardt leaned forward and slapped at the man's arm. "Filthy habit," he commented, sitting back.

A little after noon, Leinhardt instructed the driver to pull over to a group of galvanized tin-roofed buildings standing to one side of the road. The signpost identified the settlement as Namanga.

Leinhardt ordered the Kikuyu to fill the Peugeot with petrol and stand by, and they left the car and walked towards the main building, passing a group of Masai *moran* who squatted in the shade of an acacia, their ropey hair tinted with ochre. One left the group and trotted out in front of them. He carried a long-bladed spear and a short club. He planted the spike end of the spear in the ground and posed, smiling.

"Pic-a-cha," he said, his teeth showing clean and very white in his inky face, making a gesture of holding a camera.

"No pic-a-cha," said Leinhardt, pushing past. "No baksheesh."

The *moran* shook his head sadly and returned to the group.

Near the group an African peddler sat on the ground on a rug behind a row of carved curios; miniature shields and wooden hippopotami. His eyes were shut tight and he breathed shallowly against the heat like a man awaiting death on a mountaintop.

There were a dozen tables and a lunch counter in the rear of the building.

"Not exactly Claridges," said Leinhardt. They sat down at a table against the wall and an Indian waiter came over and gave them a greasy menu card, his sleepy eyes immediately alert as he saw the Browning under Leinhardt's armpit.

Leinhardt grinned up at him. "That's correct," he said. "I've come to kill you."

The waiter stepped back and wiped his hands on a soiled apron. An African eating at the next table stopped waving his fly whisk and turned to watch.

"It's about money you owe in Nairobi," Leinhardt clarified.

"I am not having bills in Nairobi, please," said the waiter, thoroughly terrified. "I am not wanting trouble."

The African at the next table broke into squeals of high-pitched laughter.

"Good. Good," cried the African, and slapped his fly whisk sharply on the table.

"Never mind," said Leinhardt. "Give me tea and eggs turned and toast. That will be safe."

The waiter rushed off with the order.

"Where we going?" asked Kampass again.

"We're there," said Leinhardt, squinting out into the sunlight.

"Vogel's here? He's here?" Kampass pointed a finger at the table as though he might expect to lift the tablecloth and find him.

"Not far," replied Leinhardt. He shifted the shoulder holster, grimacing. Then, to relieve its weight, he took out the pistol and jammed it into his belt. Kampass saw that the hammer was at half-cock, which meant Leinhardt kept a cartridge in the chamber.

The waiter returned with the eggs.

Leinhardt broke the yolk and mopped at it with a slice of toast. He pointed the eggy toast at the window. "We think he's on a farm twenty kilometers from here," he said. "That is Steiner information. He is calling himself Janek Baldur. He manages a farm in West Kilimanjaro, *Kilitanga*." Leinhardt munched at the toast. "Been there ten years," he added. "Snug as a bug."

So, Kampass thought, a quarter of a century of waiting and here it was. He did not feel any differently. Outside the heat was shimmering over the road. Nothing stirred. The sun came straight down. "She could have lied," he said. She lied to him, she could lie to them. They killed her, but she could have lied. She was not afraid of them. When you are not afraid of it, you can lie.

"That's why you're here," said Leinhardt. "We're sending you in tomorrow. You have to remember there are certain physical traits that are unchangeable. First is size. Bones of the basic structure are unalterable. So you disregard his face. He won't look at all as you remember him. But he may act like it. And his hands, watch his hands."

Kampass tried to recall Vogel's hands. It was like asking someone to remember the color shoelaces an acquaintance wore a decade ago. Hands were something you did not normally make note of.

"And his eyes," said Leinhardt. "You can change those with contacts, but after ten years out there, he'll be careless. Time plus security equals carelessness."

What if it was Vogel? thought Kampass. What then? Did they tell him the truth in Paris? The man with the mustache in the dispensary, he said they would destroy the confession. They would give him "logistical" help to make a new start, whatever that meant; the man with the mustache and his very soft, brown eyes.

"You'll be using your Gettling and Koll cover," Leinhardt continued. "You stay with it until you've made up your mind one way or the other about it. He'll deny being Kuntz. That's all right, you'll say. People change their names, you'll add. It's none of your business. You've got a job to do about the inheritance. Your information comes from *Fräulein* Steiner. That ought to bring out something right there. Watch his face for expression."

Kampass wondered if Leinhardt knew the story about her. Did he know she was a Jew? Did she tell him that before she died? No, of course, she wouldn't.

"If you have a reasonable doubt about it," said Leinhardt, "if you are at all unsure, then try revealing yourself. Dole it out. It's the same technique you used before, so there's nothing new about it. In the end, you will tell him you're desperate. Tell him he was the last contact you had. Say you want a safe house until May and then it doesn't make any difference, anyway. That ought to bring a reaction."

The African paid his chit. He looked at the Indian and then at Leinhardt and he tittered. Leinhardt waved. The African swished his fly whisk.

Leinhardt said: "You know, we thought Baldur Kuntz was an alias. But it seems there was an Alsatian of that name. The French told us the Gestapo arrested him for terrorism and intimidation. He was with the Resistance. They questioned him and later sent him to Majdanek. Vogel must have picked out the name when he deserted. The similarity in name, location, time chronology—it all fits in perfectly. Tanganyika *was* a German colony. He may even have friends here."

"What if it is Vogel?" asked Kampass.

"I'll make a check call to you tomorrow night. The cover will be East African Airways reservations. They're calling because you haven't confirmed your space on the Fokker to Dar es Salaam. If it's Vogel, all you say is 'I can confirm that space now.' If you need more time, say you wish to extend your reservation to the following day. If it's not Vogel, 'Cancel the space.' Understand?"

"Cancel the space," Kampass repeated.

"We'll start you off tomorrow at noon. Between now and then I want you to be thinking about Vogel. I want you to be remembering. Think of detail and correlate. It all depends on you."

"The confession," said Kampass. "My confession."

Leinhardt reached in his pocket and placed a sheaf of papers on the table. He folded his hands and looked at Kampass. "All right?" he asked.

Kampass picked up the sheets and scanned them. They were the sheets he had signed. Yes, they were. He remembered signing them as though it were ten years ago; the crummy apartment and the man, Ben-Zvi, saying: *You didn't have the guts to make the decisions. You left that up to Vogel.* He had come a long way since then. He gave the papers back.

Leinhardt said, "If the space is confirmed, you will say, 'My baggage is at the Namanga Inn.' That is all. I'll have the boy come and collect you. You'll wait here at the Inn until we have him. Then you can witness the destruction of the confession and verify it."

The waiter came over to collect for the lunch. Leinhardt stuck a ten-shilling note in the Indian's apron pocket. They left the dining room and walked down the steps to the yard. A dhoti-clad African saw them coming and pulled out into their path. His legs were twisted and he moved along the ground like a lobster. There was a growth the size of a cantaloupe in the middle of his forehead and flies clustered about his eyes. He sat in the dust and extended his open palm.

Leinhardt gave him a shilling. The coin fell in the dust and they watched the beggar scramble after it.

But Kampass thought of Viktor Lodz and Ruth. He saw the pink stains on the towel. He remembered Leinhardt sitting in the chair savoring his agony while big Laski worked him over. Suddenly Leinhardt's concern for the beggar seemed extremely droll.

An olive-drab short-wheelbase Land Rover turned in from the road and came to a shuddering halt in front of the red gas pump. The driver got out and smacked the dust from his clothes. Laski had discarded his sheepskin in favor of a sleeveless bush jacket from which his powerful arms dangled like short, muscular legs. A red bandana and a pair of dust goggles hung around his neck. Kampass watched him warily.

Leinhardt walked over to the Land Rover and stood chatting with the big man for a moment. Kampass hung back. He heard Laski say: "I had two flats. Filthy roads."

Three Masai sauntered around the rear of the Land Rover. One of them started poking under the open canvas flap. "Get out of there!" Laski shouted, and ran back to the truck. The Masai stood their ground and Laski came back. Leinhardt laughed. "I'd watch it if I were you. You'll get skewered."

Laski looked back at the Masai, his eyes taking in the tall spears. He grunted something. Then they both walked back to Kampass.

"Well," said Leinhardt, drawing designs in the dust with the toe of his shoe. "I think we'll send Kampass in tomorrow. That suit you?"

Laski grinned and nodded. His eyes gave Kampass a thorough going-over.

"All right," said Leinhardt. "Let's all take a nap."

●

They came to the Namanga Inn that afternoon about tea time, two of them—a Negro and a European—with twelve tourists in a zebra-striped Volkswagen minibus. They stood apart from the group, frowning in the sun and looking as much like tourists as milkmen.

Kampass, sitting on the veranda, drowsy like a grandfather in the mid-afternoon heat after his nap, failed to notice them. Leinhardt, sitting with his feet up on the railing said, "See, the competition cometh." He did not seem surprised.

"The *Amis* are here. CIA."

Laski, seated next to Leinhardt, moved uneasily on his chair.

Leinhardt said without moving his lips, "Forget it." Then, "you too Kampass. You won't get a foot."

The Negro was short and stocky, built close to the ground like a dark pumpkin. The white man was stocky but not as short.

Leinhardt said: "The European is CIA. American. Black's name is Moi, I think. A local. He's their resident in Dar es Salaam."

The American was dressed in khaki shorts and high socks, his knees pale, clenched fists below the shorts. As they watched, he unslung a Rolex and started shooting pictures of a Masai *moran* who lay beneath a nearby tree in a state of unshakeable torpor. The toga had fallen away from the *moran*'s groin and the CIA man moved in closer, aiming the camera. After he had snapped the picture, he shut the camera case and returned to where the Negro waited, laughing. Two other Masai sitting at the foot of the veranda saw what was going on and they laughed as well.

"Good," said Leinhardt, playing the audience.

The CIA man put up his camera, got his suitcase, a heavy, blue B-4 bag, down from the rack atop the minibus and lugged it over to the steps. He crossed the veranda without giving them a glance.

"Marvelous," said Leinhardt.

The agent reappeared and joined the Negro. Together they began to stroll along the road in the bright afternoon sun, matching steps like a color guard. When they disappeared behind the trees, Leinhardt rose and said, "Come on."

They followed Leinhardt to the desk. The Indian clerk was working on the ledger with a dip pen under an advertisement that said *Cigara yaku, cigara yangu, Crown Bird*. Leinhardt tapped the counter. He asked, "Who was that?"

The clerk glanced up. "Who was what?"

Leinhardt said, "The American."

The clerk turned the register around for his inspection. Then he started to thread coins on a length of twine.

Leinhardt held the ledger out and squinted. He read aloud, "William Brayboy, Skokie, Illinois." Then below, "Kipsang Moi, Dar es Salaam."

He put the ledger back on the desk.

Laski looked concerned. "We do nothing?" he asked.

"Right," Leinhardt confirmed. "I'll talk with them. We can work this out like gentlemen."

At dinner, Leinhardt, Kampass, and Laski picked through the first course. Laski said he could not eat; swill for pigs, he said. Kampass ate. He was hungry, the hunger born of emotional strain.

The dining room filled. The twelve tourists were seated in the center of the room under a four-bladed fan, and the CIA man and his Negro companion from Dar es Salaam ate next to them, their backs turned.

Leinhardt pushed aside his plate and said to Laski, "Notice all that stuff on the roadside on the way up?"

"What stuff?" replied Laski.

"It's the main course," said Leinhardt.

The big man grimaced, the scar tissue over his eyes looking very white.

"Really," added Leinhardt. "Delicacy of sorts."

Outside the dining room night had arrived and bugs tried to get at the light inside, throwing themselves against the screens that surrounded the room with sharp, punging noises.

The CIA man ate quietly, looking at the cars passing on the road and pretending not to notice them. He finished his coffee and stood up. The Negro remained seated.

"Oh, oh," said Leinhardt.

The agent turned around to face them. Leinhardt swiveled in his chair.

"All right," said the CIA man. "Let's cut the crap."

"Sure," replied Leinhardt. He motioned to the chair. "Sit down," he invited.

The man sat down and indicated Kampass. "That Mr. Kampass?"

"Yes it is," said Leinhardt. "And this is Emil Laski," he added. Laski sat motionless.

The CIA agent turned and called, "Oh Kip, want to join us for a minute?"

The Negro rose and pulled over a chair.

"My name's Brayboy," said the CIA man. He shook hands cautiously.

"Skokie, Illinois," said Leinhardt, bobbing his head with exaggerated effort.

The American grinned. Kampass put him in his mid-thirties and imagined the bright, well-washed astronaut's face behind a soda fountain.

"What's he doing here?" asked Laski, looking at the Negro.

"Shut up," said Leinhardt.

Kampass sat and listened. He felt like merchandise.

Brayboy said: "We're not after the same things, you know. We're not competitors."

"Everyone's a competitor," said Leinhardt, being indefinite.

Brayboy shrugged. "I don't care about *Oryx*," he said. "We're not interested in names residing beyond our jurisdiction. I don't care if you've got Vogel packaged in the next room. I came to deal."

"Fine," said Leinhardt. "Deal."

Brayboy rubbed his wrist. He wore an identification bracelet and Kampass had a quick look at the name etched there. It was not Brayboy.

"I'm sure we can arrive at a mutually satisfactory arrangement," said the American. He ran his eyes about the table, looking for signs of approval.

"Parsimoniously, of course," said Leinhardt. His mouth was back to that thin line.

"Generously," contradicted Brayboy.

"Offer," said Leinhardt.

Brayboy cocked his head. "We could suggest something in the range of twenty-five thousand," he said. He looked at Laski and Kampass.

"Don't worry about them," said Leinhardt.

"All right, twenty-five thousand."

Moi nodded. "I think that's fair," he said.

Leinhardt again said, "Parsimonious."

"I started with the top figure," said Brayboy. "That's all I'm authorized."

"Consider the nature of the goods," said Leinhardt.

"Not enough," said Laski, leaning in.

"I said shut your mouth," said Leinhardt.

Kampass listened. They were talking about the film he'd taken. Leinhardt seemed to be selling out. Right in front of him, Leinhardt was selling out. He was doing business like a rug dealer, bargaining.

"This is sophomoric," said Brayboy. "Let's go somewhere."

Leinhardt shook his head. "I'm not leaving this table, he said.

The Negro had been playing with a beer coaster. He put one of his hands in his lap.

"Get your hands back on the table, Moi," snapped Leinhardt.

The Negro put his hands where Leinhardt could see them. "It itches," he said.

"All right, Kip," said Brayboy.

A car went by in the darkness with a crunching roar. They could hear pebbles from the road shower against the side of the building. The twelve tourists began to file out of the room.

"I didn't want it to come to this," said Brayboy.

"It hasn't come to anything yet," said Leinhardt. "But it's certain to come to more than twenty-five thousand." He leaned back and held out his hands like a priest in the midst of consecration. "It's a lobbying fee," he added. "My principals—"

"Principals, hell. Jews," said Brayboy. "For Christ sake, cut out the crap, Mr. Leinhardt. Jews."

"All right," said Leinhardt. "The Jews. Sooner or later they'll know I sold the list. I need run money," Leinhardt added. "I've a family to think of. I'll have to relocate."

"You want the deal or don't you?" asked Brayboy.

"Look here," said Kampass, intruding.

Leinhardt gave him a steely glare. He said, "If you were involved I wouldn't be talking about it here, would I?"

"Well?" prompted Brayboy.

Leinhardt was silent. He picked at the label on the Tusker

Lager bottle in front of him. He shook his head. "No," he said. "It's not worth it. If that's the final offer, tell them no. I'll turn it over for forty thousand."

Brayboy got up. He said, "We'll be in touch, old buddy."

"I'm not your *old buddy*," said Leinhardt.

Moi rose. He looked at Brayboy. Brayboy nodded and bent down. "Oh, by the way," he said to Leinhardt, "I'd take what you can get from us, Mr. Leinhardt, and I shit you not. There's unfinished business in Warsaw. Stern. A tip."

Leinhardt's features froze.

Brayboy and Moi left the table.

Leinhardt followed them with his eyes. Kampass saw he was moving his fingers nervously, twitching. Leinhardt began to talk as though he and Laski were not at the table.

"Ten whole years," he said, his voice edged with venom, spitting out the words. "Ten years for those bastards, washing their dirty laundry, cleaning up their mistakes. Ten years of it and they roll up the best network in the East. Roll it up and throw it away. Obsolete, they said. Leinhardt is obsolete."

Laski looked out the window, keeping his face turned away from the onslaught.

It was a little frightening, thought Kampass, who had seen Leinhardt this way before—at the hotel in London. You never knew which way he would turn.

"Do they think I have no *pride?*" asked Leinhardt. He continued jabbering, swearing, threatening like a domestic servant who, after years of faithful service, finds himself left out of the family will. Then he brought himself under control. "Drop it," he said.

They finished their coffee and left the dining room. Brayboy and Moi were not in the lobby. Leinhardt went to the phone. It was an old crank phone and he worked the handle savagely. "I want Criminal Investigation Division in Arusha," he told the operator. He waited. Kampass saw his fingers were still working against each other.

"CID?" asked Leinhardt. "Well, Sergeant, is it? Sergeant, I want to report two neo-colonialists. CIA . . . Yes, that's it, CIA. There's an American, Brayboy, and one of your own,

Moi. M-O-I. . . . At the Namanga Inn, room twenty-three. You'll find armaments. . . . Me? I'm a friend of *Uhuru*. *Uhuru na Kazi*." He hung up. Leinhardt came away from the phone, smiling. His old self, thought Kampass.

"Bruno," announced Leinhardt. "Seeing as this may be our last night together, let your *Uncle* buy you a drink."

●

Kampass could not sleep. He thought about Vogel and he thought about Ruth and he thought about what she had given both of them. He turned and tossed on the wet sheets. If it was Vogel, he wondered, would it make things any different for him? Would it make the faces and the old man and the scratching fingers go away? Would it rub away the past? And the future? He did not dare think about that. It was like having your hand on the doorknob to a room you'd never seen before. And Vogel was the key that would open it, the door he'd battered at all his life: the rules, the circumstances that stood between him and what might have been ahead, the person he might have been. Skinny Vogel and his chocolates and his big black dog.

Leinhardt and Laski had taken the next room. Kampass could hear voices. They were arguing. He went to the sink and wet the rim of the tooth glass. He pressed the glass against the wall and listened through it. Laski was telling Leinhardt to accept the deal. Leinhardt was refusing. The squabbling continued. Finally Kampass became bored with it and went to bed.

Much later, he heard the police come for Moi and Brayboy. Through the window screen, he saw Brayboy brought out to the yard from their room in the wing opposite. Brayboy was trying to explain something to the *askaris*. He kept pointing in th direction of Kampass' room. Kampass could distinguish the shrill voice of the CID constable and the lower, calmer tones of Brayboy. The policeman was brandishing a small revolver as though it were evidence. Two *askaris* disappeared into the room and dragged out Moi, who was holding his head and bleeding badly. They threw him over the tailgate of their Land Rover. When they started to pull him into the interior of the truck, a tug of war developed: the *askaris* in the Land Rover at Moi's head and Brayboy pulling at his feet. The constable tired of it. He walked around behind Brayboy and hit him twice, quickly in the kidneys. From twenty yards away Kampass heard him say *"Ah, ah,"* softly as though he were tasting good food. Then he sank to the ground. The *askaris* put him in the back of the Land Rover with Moi and drove off. Kampass kept his head down until the taillights disappeared around the corner.

Back in bed, he lay quietly and listened to the night insects, the cicadas and the almost human screams of the tree hyrax. Then it was getting light. He was able to distinguish the washbasin. In the dawn, on the road, heavy trucks began rolling by. They were loaded with laborers singing in the clear morning air. There was a sudden noise of breaking crockery nearby. Then at once sun filled the room, streaming in the windows.

They dawdled through the morning; Leinhardt and Laski playing liar's dice on the veranda, Kampass racking his brains for long-forgotten details of Vogel. How had he carried himself? How had he spoken? He could only remember the sharp face indelibly burned upon his brain; the face under the visor cap, the eyes hidden by the shadows there; a sharp but smooth face and quick lips. Neat. He was neat as a pin. Vogel was always precise. When he had been a clerk in the outer office, the ADC had once given him Vogel's pistol to clean. A little Sauer, it was. Kampass had scrubbed it with oil and dope. But the ADC brought the weapon back. Not clean enough, he had said. Can you change the picayune? He was numb from thinking about it.

A little before noon the Indian clerk called Leinhardt inside. He was absent for only a moment and then returned carrying a radiogram. He folded it and put it in his wallet. For a while he said nothing. He looked across the road, thinking.

The heat waves bounced off the crushed rock and murram

of the highway. A secretary bird darted across the road and vanished into the thick brush on the other side. Kampass watched it and then asked Leinhardt: "What if it isn't him. You didn't say about that. What about the confession?"

"Then my astute advice," said Leinhardt, "is not to come back."

"I'll be back," said Kampass. It was odd about Leinhardt, he thought; the way he broke down last night. There was something very small about it.

After lunch they took him outside. In the yard in front of the Inn, Leinhardt told him, "You're on your way." He kicked at a rock in the road. "It's been a bad run," he added. "Stinky."

Kampass said nothing.

"Yes," said Leinhardt, scrubbing at the ground again with his toe. "It's been a porridge of shit."

They then all looked at the sky, Kampass and Laski and Leinhardt, as if there were nothing left to say. A hawk wheeled there in ever-widening circles, dipping, holding firm in the wind, searching the ground below.

"That's it," said Leinhardt. "The boy had orders to drop you a mile from the farm. You walk the rest of the way." He turned on his heel and walked back to the veranda.

•

It simply was not possible, thought Kampass.

Potbellied and bent in many places, Janek Baldur stood on the grass edge of the driveway, his baggy corduroy pants and while hair moving in the wind.

"Speirling, is it," he said.

He looked a living replica of photographs Kampass had seen of the Egyptian, Ramses. His face was weathered and wrinkled like a dried prune, but the eyes were strong, a deep blue. He must be at least eighty, Kampass judged.

"Would you like to converse in English, French, or German?" he asked in English. "I am fluent in French and German, but I speak the English as well."

"English," said Kampass.

Baldur handed back the identity card. "The name Baldur is only coincidence," he said. "You have come all this way for this? For coincidence?"

"Yes," said Kampass. "From Strassbourg. The money involved in the will is considerable."

"I hate to disappoint, young man, and there is much that could be done with it here."

Kampass found the old man's voice had a strange ring to it.

"But the woman in Paris confirmed it," said Kampass. "I have no wish to know why you changed your name. If you do not accept it, the money will go to the government."

"Ah, the woman," said Baldur in his clear, tenor voice. "But I told you, I can't remember the name of a Kuntz and I know the European community very well. Moshi is not far. Perhaps she meant Moshi."

"She was sure about it being Arusha," Kampass insisted.

"To think of all that money is sinful," said Baldur.

They walked to the rear of the house, which looked out on yellow fields of hay. A combine was moving in the farthest field, throwing up a cloud of chaff. Beyond the combine there was only the wide valley running to Mount Meru, which stood like a giant purple shanker against the sky.

Baldur stooped painfully and plucked a handful of bougainvillaea from a hedge. "What would you do with the money if it were yours?" he asked.

"I don't know," Kampass answered, looking about him; looking at the mountain and the fields. "I might buy a place like this and forget about everything else."

Baldur shook a bony finger at him and clucked. "That is the great danger. One loses one's soul to the country and reality ceases to exist."

"I enjoy that," said Kampass.

"It is what we all enjoy," replied Baldur. "It is delightful nonexistence."

Kampass studied Baldur's profile outlined against the bursting sunset. Vogel had a sharp nose like a Roman senator.

Baldur's was sunken, almost like a pug's. It was not a nose. It was a snout. Noses can be changed, he thought, but not a man's height. Baldur and Vogel's height would be identical if you allowed for the stoop of age.

"If you are quiet," said Baldur, "you may hear elephant. They call from the forests each night. It is a pity you can't see the mountain from here."

Kampass remembered it as he drove up from Namanga after leaving Leinhardt. It filled the entire sky, towering like a wedding cake: Mount Kilimanjaro.

"There," said Baldur.

He heard it: a thin shriek carried on the wind which was cold and brought a damp hint of ice and snow from the mountain.

"So I have come for nothing," said Kampass "They will be disappointed. We were all so sure."

"We?" asked Baldur.

"The firm," Kampass stipulated.

Baldur's eyes betrayed nothing. But there had been something about the old man and he just realized what it was. Baldur had a habit of shredding his cigarettes after he had smoked them down to practically nothing; field-stripping them, they had called it in the army. It was not an old man's habit. Kampass found himself thinking of Leinhardt destroying the impressioned page of notebook paper at the restaurant on Coulson Street.

Baldur took his arm. "I can't turn you out after this. I'll try and make it worth more to you than nothing. Come, and I will show you something of Africa. After dinner we can see the labor line."

They drank tea and ate honeyed toast on the porch, watching the last of the sun against the clouds before it sank behind the hills to the west of them. An African dressed in a white robe and a green fez with a tassel padded noiselessly on bare feet as he served them. Baldur spoke of Africa. He elaborated on the sleepy, honest life and of how he came there out of the chaos of Europe and of how he knew he could never return. He spoke of forced labor in Germany at the Krupp mills in Essen, and the DP camps after the war, and listening to him, Kampass could hardly see how one might suspect Baldur. He had met few gentle men. Baldur, he had decided, was one of them.

". . . but Africa," Baldur was saying. "Now Africa is the key to the soul." He swept his arm, taking in the dark expanses before them. "Do you not find it soulful?" he asked.

"It's stirring," said Kampass.

"Our roots are in Africa," said Baldur. "Yes, that is so," he added when he saw doubt register on Kampass' brow. We came from near here: the Olduvai Gorge. Anyway, some of us went to the south to the great velds and some of us stayed behind and remained vegetarians. The others became meat-eaters to survive. There was no suitable vegetation on the veld so they invented means to kill. They used the shoulder bone of an antelope. Anyway, those who remained behind were no more than apes, you see, and things were hard for them. But their brothers to the south, the killers, flourished. They survived and reproduced. They did this like crazy, as killers will, and soon they began to come back—just by twos and threes, mark you, and more later. But they remained meat-eaters, killers, and do you know what came to pass?"

"No," said Kampass. He did not.

"Well, they met their brothers, the ones who had not left and were dying anyway, because they had chosen to remain vegetarians. He was an unsuccessful experiment and he died by his brother's hand, by the shoulder bone of the antelope. So there is your Cain and Abel and we are their children. Do you see how Africa is the key to our soul?"

Not exactly, thought Kampass, for whom a soul might be a wart on the end of one's nose, or perhaps, the bottom of his shoe. He had never stopped to think it out. But he listened to the old man because he sensed Baldur had a deep and desperate need to talk about it; Baldur living here like a hermit; Baldur who was as much like Rudolf Vogel as cheese is like asparagus; Baldur who was, of course, mad. You had to be certified to talk that way. "But what happened afterwards?" he asked, feigning interest.

"Afterwards, you became you and I became me, and in a sense, nothing changed. The world is inhabited by vegetarian animals and there are many carnivora to feed from them. Some of us are one, some another. Naturally we no longer use a shoulder bone. We have become refined. We have sophisticated the missile and the gas chamber."

Baldur leaned back in his chair and unhooked a pair of ancient field glasses which hung in their case from a nail in the stucco. He adjusted the binoculars and scanned the fields below. For a moment he said nothing. Then his lips moved below the glasses. "So it's the one group against the other, Speirling. To survive, one allies with the tribe. It is a matter of allegiance and this cancer of the mind is called patriotism. They say fascism is the bane of man, but really fascism is only extreme patriotism. The Bible told of us Four Horsemen, Speirling. They were war, famine, conquest, and death. But there is yet another; there is one more." The binoculars shifted slightly, covering the valley to the east and Baldur continued: "All the tragedies; the Jews, and what has come to pass in Europe. The Jews were wandering vegetarians. They were born to be preyed upon. And those who do the preying, they know the evil of it. But they are told, you see, My Country Right or Wrong. That was, and is, the excuse. That is what happened to your Jew. And so genocide becomes as natural for us as a hiccup."

Baldur put down the glasses and lit a cigarette, letting the smoke out of his mouth and inhaling it through his nostrils. Kampass could see the tiny crinkles forming at the corners of his eyes and mouth. It gave him the impression that Baldur was wearing some kind of rubberized mask, as if he could reach out and pull the flesh and it would snap back in place.

Baldur said: "Here I am trying to eradicate tribalism, for nowhere is it as strong as in Africa. I have created a controlled environment."

He was mad, thought Kampass. Really mad.

"I employ no patriots on this farm. They are dangerous to others. Here,"—he handed the field glasses to Kampass—

"they are bringing the stock in for the night."

Kampass focused the binoculars on the fields. In the farthest pasture, drovers were herding boran cattle towards a kraal some five hundred yards' distant. Kampass watched the herd move, stringing out across the lush green of the field. The herders were dressed in animal-skin togas and moved through the knee-high grass with bouncing strides as though walking on mattresses. They carried long switches, applying them vigorously to the flanks of any animals that lagged. Their shadows lengthened on the grass.

Kampass put aside the glasses. He began to feel the chill of the evening air.

"Here is the only patriotism," Baldur said, whacking his chest with his knuckles. His breastbone gave out a hollow rap. "Here, the soul, the id,—man himself."

Kampass remained silent, thinking.

"You are carnivorous," said Baldur, looking at him through half-shut eyes. "I think you are a killer."

Kampass twisted on the chair.

"I, on the other hand," Baldur continued, shrugging, "am a vegetarian."

Kampass said, "During the war, I was in camps."

"How horrible for you," said Baldur. He leaned forward in his chair. "Go on."

"Yes," said Kampass. "I was at Majdanek. Do you know of that, Majdanek?"

Baldur watched him. If anything, his face portrayed pity. "Yes," he said. "I know this place. It was in eastern Poland."

Kampass nodded.

"We never learn," said Baldur. "It is not in us to change—only the potential is there. The potential keeps us going. The potential is the sugar and we are horses."

"I was in Majdanek as a guard," Kampass elaborated.

Baldur said again, "How horrible for you."

"Yes it was," Kampass agreed. "More horrible later."

"I can imagine."

"No one can imagine unless you have done it and been through it yourself."

"I should bear you animosity," said Baldur. "The SS took me from Alsace to work for Krupps. Yet, that is over—at least until the next war."

For the first time he looked closely at Baldur's hands. They were blotched as an old man's skin should be, but their size surprised him. They were small, adolescent. He saw also that Baldur wore an open-neck shirt and he could detect the gleam of a religious medal. The medal was a small golden star, the six-pointed Star of David. Baldur was a Jew.

●

"You will stay for dinner, of course," said Baldur, breaking the momentary silence, "and perhaps the night if you wish. We see few strangers here. You update me on the outside world." He emphasized the word "outside." "For example," he went on, "the reports of the Congo disasters were most inadequate. One gets little reliable news from the African services."

"Yes," said Kampass. "I read about the Congo before I left . . ."—he caught himself before he said New York—"Strassbourg."

Where the sun had vanished, it left a wake of pink cloud which gradually changed to purple, pink on the bottoms and then purple, and finally the clouds disintegrated into small, dark pus that Kampass identified with drifting flak bursts.

As it grew colder they went inside, passing under the massive, bleached skull of a buffalo which hung above the door and stared down at them from empty sockets. The drawing room was long and there was a zebra skin spread before a deep-set fireplace. Next to the fire screen there was kindling, which had been put into a tub made from an elephant's foot.

"I'll be a minute," said Baldur. "I want to get the boy started on the fire and tell him about dinner. You like leeks, Mr. Speirling?"

Kampass nodded. "Leeks would be fine." he said.

Baldur hobbled from the room and Kampass saw that he dragged a foot slightly behind him. He could hear him talking with the boy in the next room in Swahili, and through the screen doors to the porch, which were ajar, came the chirp of tree frogs. Kampass moved around the room, inspecting the stuffed heads mounted on the walls. A spiral-horned kudu watched him from dead, dusty eyes above the fireplace, and beneath this, there was a rifle balanced on wooden brackets. He ran his finger along the barrel. It came away oily. Baldur was not quite the vegetarian he claimed to be.

The boy came in and knelt before the fireplace. He folded up some newspapers and stuck them under the tepee he had made of the kindling wood. He lit the paper carefully and blew on it for draft until it caught. He stood up, wiping his hands. He said, *"Saa n'gapi, bwana?"*

Kampass shook his head. The boy pointed to his own bare wrist. Kampass showed him his wristwatch and the boy said, *"Asante."*

There was an archway in the far end of the room and through it he could see Baldur's office, so he walked over and ducked under the archway. He kept his hands in his pockets.

There was a work desk, an old one, with a roll top and pigeonholes, and on the wall behind the desk, an oil portrait of a young woman. The painting was abstract. Paintings should look like things really do, Kampass thought, and he moved on to a display of photographs. They depicted Baldur among Africans; here, holding up a child; there, posing with an African in a Colobus-monkey headdress or a Masai and showing off a boran steer. Kampass assumed the Africans to be prospective buyers or politicians. About the desk were scattered odd bits of memorabilia; an ashtray made from a buffalo's hoof, a brass paperweight which celebrated Tanganyika's independence from Britain, and an oversized clothesline pin with a decal that said *Unpaid*. Baldur came back into the room, carrying a silver tray with two glasses and a cutglass decanter. "Come," he said, "schnapps."

Baldur sat in the easy chair and painfully propped his leg

on a hassock. He poured the liquor from the decanter, holding it tightly in his baby fist.

"Now," he said, settling back, "bring me up to date. I crave details, Mr. Speirling, absolutely *crave* them."

●

Baldur ate his food like a dietician might, sampling a little from each plate in bird-size mouthfuls. There were two candles, one at each end, and they cast weird shadows over his mummified features, not unlike a gypsy peering into an illuminated crystal ball, Kampass compared. Baldur had put on a tie and a corduroy jacket for dinner, and when he chewed his food the tie knot jumped up and down. Kampass wondered if the old man did this every evening: putting on his coat and tie and insisting that candles be placed.

The two of them sitting and eating there as though they were dining at the Trocadero was somehow ill-placed, Kampass thought. It was like two Africans sitting on the pavement outside Bonwit Teller's in New York, eating posho. He was a little fuzzy from the schnapps.

"Have you decided when you'll leave?" asked Baldur, spearing a roast potato with a quick jab of his fork.

Kampass shrugged. "Tomorrow. There is nothing now to stay for." He poured himself another drink from the cutglass decanter.

"East African Airways or what?" Baldur watched him drink.

He remembered the forthcoming call from Leinhardt. "They may call me here about my seat." He fingered the glass self-consciously.

"Only airline that makes money," said Baldur. "Fokkers. Who would believe it, Fokkers out here?" He pushed his plate aside, leaned back, and slid a finger between the buttons of his shirt. Kampass thought he was scratching his chest, but when the finger stayed there, he knew Baldur was toying with the medal.

Baldur said, "What did you *really* come here for?"

A shred of string bean fell from Kampass' lips to his plate. "What do you mean?" he asked, sobering slightly.

"Well," said Baldur. "Surely your people have contacts in Dar or Moshi or Arusha. Why the expense of sending you all the way?"

"I don't follow you," said Kampass nervously.

"Couldn't they have managed it locally?"

"It's an important case," hedged Kampass. He watched Baldur's finger move under the shirt, massaging.

"I think you wangled the trip. I think you a fraud."

Kampass stopped chewing and watched Baldur across the candlelight.

"Come now, Speirling. You wanted to see Africa, admit it."

Kampass laughed dryly. "I'm a bad liar," he said. "It's true. Somebody here could have done it."

"Where are your offices in East Africa, Mr. Speirling?"

"Arusha." Kampass thought quickly.

"Gettling and Koll in Arusha?" Baldur shook head. "It must be new."

"Yes, new," Kampass explained at once.

"Very new?"

"Yes. Quite lately."

"Who acts for you here?"

Kampass hesitated. "You know," he said with a choked laugh, "I don't really know. I have their address here somewhere." He searched through his pockets, patting for a mythical piece of paper.

Baldur said: "I sometimes find myself in need of legal advice. If they are good, that is."

"Oh, they're good," Kampass volunteered. He finished the drink and poured another.

"You must give me the address before you go."

The boy came in and whispered something into Baldur's ear. Baldur got up, hauling himself forward with his hands on the table. "You're in for a treat," he said. "Have you seen a baby delivered?"

"Baby?" said Kampass, startled. His face was heating up with the schnapps.

"Yes, that's right," said Baldur. "There's a woman on the labor line. I thought it might happen tomorrow or the next day, but she's early. In Africa, Speirling, one is jack-of-all the trades. I run the farm, I teach the school, I tend to simple stomach aches, and I deliver babies. I'm the midwife."

"A doctor?"

"No," explained Baldur. "One needn't be. If it were not for this, they would give birth in the forest. A mother can have it alone. She chews through the cord herself."

Baldur said something to the boy, who left the room and returned with a black bag, a doctor's bag.

"We'd better hurry," said Baldur. "He says the pains are coming every few minutes."

•

The huts crouched against the side of a heavily forested hill and Kampass could see the cooking fires outside the shacks from a long way away. There was no wind and the smoke rose straight into the air. Baldur led him along the rows of shambas, no more than lean-tos most of them, and they stopped outside one at the end. Kampass could hear a woman crying inside. The smell that came from the shack reminded him of the Kikuyu driver and Baldur told him: "You'd better not go in. I'll be back in twenty minutes or so."

Baldur pulled aside the jute sacking that served as a door and Kampass glimpsed a pile of glowing coals on a dirt floor and black shiny faces. A roaring gas lantern hung outside the shack. As he waited he could hear the babble of voices. Then it was quiet except for the sobbing of the woman. The sobbing built up and ended abruptly in a shriek. Then he heard the thin wailing of a baby. Baldur came out of the shack, carrying his coat and the black bag. He turned and looked back at the shack. He said, "It's a fine baby, a girl."

Kampass was thinking how to tell Leinhardt what a boner they pulled.

They walked back up the path to the farmhouse in the moonlight, climbing over the clumps of grass.

"Any snakes here?" asked Kampass anxiously. He was not that drunk.

"Walk heavily," said Baldur. "They feel you coming."

Kampass put his feet down a trifle harder. He fell once and rolled back down the hill a few yards. Baldur helped him to his feet. "Careful here," he said.

In the moonlight he could almost count the blades of grass. It was as light as day. They reached the farmhouse and the boy came out to greet them, smiling and pounding Baldur on the back. Every time the boy slapped his back, Kampass saw the old man's knees buckle. At the doorstep Baldur doubled up with a fit of coughing. It was a racking cough, and afterwards he spat something into his handerchief and held it up to the light. Then he pulled himself erect and walked into the house. Inside, Kampass could see the old man's eyes were watering. Baldur would keep humping forward as though he wanted to cough, but could not.

"You all right?" asked Kampass, concerned.

"It passes," gasped Baldur. The boy brought him a glass of water and a piece of paper. Baldur drained the glass and looked at the paper. "You've had a telephone call," he said. "You're to call this number. It was East African Airways."

Kampass thanked him and took the note.

"The telephone is in the study. Close the door if you want."

The phone was the old crank type and it took some time to reach the West Kilimanjaro exchange. Kampass gave the operator the number. Leinhardt finally answered the phone and said, "Where have you been?"

"Cancel it," said Kampass, cupping the receiver. "I've been with him all evening and I tell you he's not Vogel." His voice was thick with the brandy.

"You've had a drink," said Leinhardt.

"Yes, I have," said Kampass. "I've had several drinks. Why not? It's finished. He is a doctor of some sort. He delivered a baby."

"Did he?" replied Leinhardt.

"He's sick. He's a sick old hermit. Somebody pulled a boner."

Leinhardt said, "Listen, I'm coming up myself. You wait there. I'll pick you up."

"I don't care," said Kampass. "It's not him. It's finished."

"Fine," said Leinhardt. "I'll be up in three hours or so."

"What about me?" asked Kampass.

"I'll think about it," said Leinhardt. "Can he hear you?"

Kampass told him about the door being closed.

"Fine. Repeat 'flight six-oh-one' and hang up."

"I tell you, it doesn't make any difference. It's finished. Now what about me?"

"Do it anyway," ordered Leinhardt.

Kampass repeated the flight number loudly and hung up.

●

Kampass reviewed his situation. Yes, it was over. He could run again, but by last counting he had only five pounds in his pockets with few prospects or replenishment. Five pounds would see him to Dar es Salaam but not much farther, maybe Lorenco Marques if he conserved it carefully. Why had Leinhardt decided to come up to the farm? Was it only because Leinhardt did not trust his judgment? Or was it for some other reason—something Leinhardt knew and he did not? The radiogram—did that have anything to do with it? Kampass suspected treachery. As he thought he stared at the abstract portrait behind Baldur's roll-top desk; all orange, purple, and red it was. The woman's eyes had the unnerving habit of following him about the office wherever he moved. He frowned at them. It was not the zigzag handling of the brush strokes or the obnoxious color motif that held his attention; it was the eyes. They would not let him go. Maybe it was because he was a little drunk. He shifted position to the far side of the small office. Still the eyes tracked him. They were soft and sad and they were the only feature of the painting that held meaning for Kampass. He could never forget those eyes. You could put them in the sockets of an elephant

and know that, beneath it somewhere, you would find Ruth
Stein. He squinted at the portrait, trying to mold the confused tangle of color and perspective into legible features.
But it came down to the eyes. He moved closer to the painting and ran his finger over the crusty ridges of the brush
strokes. At the lower right-hand corner of the canvas there
were three initials and a date. The initials were R.H.V. and
the date 1944. R.H.V.—Rudolf Something Vogel?

Kampass stepped back and squinted again. He tried to
shed years from the woman he had known in Paris. If it was
Ruth in the painting, she was doing something he never saw
her do before: she was smiling. He was drunk, Kampass
thought. It was only a pair of eyes, and the initials could
stand for Reinhard Verbeck for that matter.

He remembered Baldur's habit of shredding his cigarettes
and how Baldur questioned him closely on the subject of
Gettling and Koll's nonexistent contacts in Arusha. He was
the same height as Vogel, and who knew what Wick's surgery
accomplished. But Vogel amongst the Africans like a long-
lost brother? A man might change his face but not his heart,
Kampass concluded. And this man, this Baldur, was a Jew. It
was too far-fetched. Ruth had died. She had fooled them and
then she died, taking the truth with her.

He came out of the office into the living room and saw
Baldur sitting by the fire watching the leaping flames. He had
wrapped his small hands about a steaming mug of coffee as if
to warm them and he did not turn around when Kampass
opened the door. He said, "You've fixed it with them?"

Kampass sat down in the easy chair on the other side of the
fire. "There was a confusion about the reservations tomorrow," he explained.

Baldur had closed his eyes. He looked tired. The fire sput-
tered and sneezed sparks onto the stone hearth. One ember
arched onto the zebra skin and Kampass pushed it back with
the toe of his shoe. "That painting in your office," he said. He
had to know about it. He had to know for sure. "Did you do
it?" he asked.

Baldur looked at him, the flesh loose and heavy on his

face as though his facial bones had collapsed. Ignoring the question, he said: "It's not every day you see life brought into the world, is it? It's a miracle. Do you know that?" Then he closed his eyes again and said very slowly: "*Oberscharführer* Bruno Kampass; *Desinfektor* in charge of gassing bath two. I think I even called you 'sturdy and unmotivated' in a report once. I might be able to give you your old serial number. I might make a mistake because it has been a long time. Want me to try?" Baldur looked as impassive as a sphinx.

Instantly Kampass was sober. His head cleared so quickly the effect dizzied him.

Baldur said, "You can't fool an old dog, Kampass." A series of coughs racked his body and he wiped at his lips with the handkerchief and cleared his throat. "I knew the moment you came here. All those clumsy traps about Majdanek . . ."—he shook his head and Kampass thought he saw him smile. "But you see," he went on slowly, "it makes no difference. You're too late."

Kampass stared at him, bewildered. This was not the man who handed candy to children before they took the ticket. This was not the man who kept the black Doberman they said was trained to go for the throat. This was an old man, a few months shy of death.

"So what are you here for, Kampass? What do you want? Were you calling them on the phone there? They're coming tonight, aren't they?"

He could think of nothing to say.

"It's me, all right," said Baldur. "What did they do, force you to work for them? Did they blackmail you into it? Is that why you're here?"

Kampass felt cheated. Vogel, an old man. All this time, all his life and it came to this.

"Or do you want to avenge yourself? Did you come here to kill me, Kampass?"

Kampass became acutely aware of the night noises and the popping of the fire. He finally got it out, "You made me a killer."

Baldur shook his head like an ancient sage. "Oh, no I

didn't," he said. "I only accept responsibility for giving you the opportunity. I remember you. You were the one with the medals. And do you know how you were transferred to Berlin? I—I Rudolf Vogel—signed your transfer. Weiss would have none of it. He wanted a permanent staff. They let nobody go then. They didn't want too many people knowing."

Kampass looked at the wizened face. He thought about the years he spent living from one bowel movement to another because of this man before him. He thought about the children singing carols in front of the Plaza Hotel and the blond boy with his hair blowing in the wind, a young Kampass, looking at him and thinking him a pervert.

Baldur went on. "I have made a bargain. I have struck an understanding with myself. You see, I'll be dead in eight months. It is terminal cancer. It is eroding me inside." As if the thought of it triggered a reaction, Baldur hunched forward, his shoulders moving. He looked up, his eyes moist. The tenor was gone from his voice. It was strained, rasping. "If you are to kill me, go ahead. Use the rifle on the wall. You'll find ammunition in my desk. But if you came to take me back, if that is what the call was about, I am not going. I will not be held up in a glass case like Eichmann—like some odd animal; like a sort of bloody memorandum. I assume you will grant me the honor of an officer, of your former commander, who once did you a favor, and let me hurry the process in my own way."

The children singing carols, that was what Kampass was thinking about. That and his filthy little office and festering nights filled with empty gin bottles.

"Or did you come to make a Pontius Pilate out of me?" Baldur went on. "Did you want to see me wash my hands of your guilt? Was that it? Did you expect to see me grovel? You are going to be disappointed. You, you coward. *Du Feigling!*"

Kampass jumped as if he were slapped. Baldur's voice lost its haziness. This was the commander speaking, the whippet-lean figure in polished boots with the cap visor low on his nose.

"Yes, you are a coward. You obeyed. You did not cope, you obeyed. I know your ilk, Kampass. Only too well I know you. You want me to write it off for you. You want me to say, 'Don't worry, little boy, you were only doing what you were told.' Then, so as not to be reminded of it, you would destroy me. You imagine me as the cause of your inadequacies. I am right, aren't I?"

Kampass got up from the chair. He looked down at Baldur who stared back, now smiling.

"I think I was wrong about you," said Baldur. "I don't think you are carnivorous at all."

Kampass reached for the rifle.

●

Werner Leinhardt smacked the mosquito on his cheek, mashing it to juice. Then he drew the Browning from its place under his armpit, and working the action, shucked the cartridges one by one onto the bedspread. They landed there and clicked into small clusters. Next to the cartridges, the radiogram lay open. The typed, pasted strips read:

CORRESPONDENCE LOCATED STEINER DOMICILE STOP
REVEAL ORYX RESIDING KILITANGA STOP REPEAT ORYX
KILITANGA CONFIRMED STOP EXPEDITER UNACCEPTABLE
NOW AS FIRST HUNTER.

The woman had told him the truth, thought Leinhardt. At first he suspected she had said it to avoid the pain. She had died before he could be sure, before he could use the trap questions to double-check her.

Shoval must have had her place gone over. He himself had searched, but before he could finish, Kampass returned to the apartment, cutting him short.

"What a break," said Laski. He was sitting, flowing over a camp chair by the writing desk. He clapped his hands together. "It's too much."

Yes, thought Leinhardt, the timing was perfect. It couldn't

be better, not even if he had set it himself. He would not take chances with Kampass. Kampass knew he still had the film, knew he had made contact with the Americans. Kampass could not survive to tell Shoval, and now the radiogram was his excuse. He would tell Shoval afterwards that the wire had arrived too late. He would say they followed Kampass to the farm and there had been unpleasantness. He had tried to run. There was a scrap. Kampass had not made it.

Shoval had told him: *If it is Vogel and Kampass overreacts, ice him. We can't carry him any further.*

He did not need Laski for the job. It would be that easy. A shot of Nembutal for Vogel and a shot of something else for Kampass. They would have Vogel on the plane out of Embakasi tomorrow night and no one the wiser. Shoval promised to have a chartered El Al DC-7 air freighter standing by. He would schedule it into Nairobi eight hours after he got word they had Vogel. They would keep him in the cooler at the embassy until the crew called in.

It was going to work out splendidly, thought Leinhardt. Shoval would get what he wanted and he, Leinhardt, would retain the film.

But it had been a near thing in Shoval's office with Kampass, he thought. Very near. He thought Shoval was going to question him about what he might have found at Wick's house. Shoval would try and learn if he, Leinhardt, was holding out. Under drugs, Kampass would have told him that he had the cartridge. So it had been a bad half-hour. Instead, Shoval used the drug to plant the idea that the extradition papers were forged. And it worked. Kampass had not mentioned them since. No. Shoval could never see Kampass again.

Laski said, "You'll take the offer then?"

"I'll give them three days," replied Leinhardt, wiping the pistol free of oil. "If they don't up the twenty-five thousand, we'll accept."

"They're not going to like your turning in two of their men," said Laski. "I've been thinking. Maybe you shouldn't have done it. You were angry."

"I want them to know they're not doing business with anybody's fool, that's all."

"Well," said Laski, "the story was in the *East African Standard* this morning. The government in Dar is very hot about it. They're going to send an official protest."

Leinhardt coughed. He said: "The film is more important to them than two red faces. They'll still offer. They'll send in another man. You wait and see."

"What about Shoval?"

"Oh, he'll add two and two and get four, but not right away. He still thinks it was a leak in his own setup that tipped off the *Amis*. By the time he comes up with an answer, we'll have relocated. I mean, what can he do? He knows I'll expose him if he pushes too hard. If you were Shoval, how would you like everybody knowing about the operation, the arrangement he made with Bonn, dealing with an ex-Gestapo type like Stassen? It's supposed to look like a good-will gesture, not a plot."

Laski nodded and smiled. "Poor Kampass," he said.

"Yes," said Leinhardt. "Poor Kampass."

"Everybody's fool," said Laski.

Leinhardt said, "That fool, as you call him, got me the most important piece of merchandise I've ever had. Give him that."

Leinhardt went to the window and lit a cigarette. He looked out through the small screen at a group of Masai that had gathered about a fire behind the inn. Shrill giggles came through the night. He watched them for a moment and then said, "That's a life I envy."

"Most of them have clap," said Laski.

"That would be all right too," said Leinhardt. "I wonder what they'd say if they knew what was going on? They'd probably think we were crazy."

"Yes," said Laski. "On the other hand, they're broke and we're not. They have no films," he laughed.

Leinhardt stared at the Masai thoughtfully. "Emil," he said, "you have to go through a lot of shit to earn a living, don't you?"

"You're getting old," said Laski.

"Yes, old," said Leinhardt. "I look at them out there. All they do is drink blood and milk and shag the odd *bibi*."

"They've got their problems," said Laski.

"Not like ours, they don't," answered Leinhardt. "Not like that Steiner business."

He recalled how they had dropped her body over the embankment into the Seine by the Île de la Cité. He pinned a note on the back of her dress with the words *Vive l'Algerie,* and she had floated off with the slow current, turning, rolling on her back with her hair fanning out. They would find a whore in the river. That was all.

"She was a looker for her age," said Laski. "She held out a long time."

Leinhardt said nothing.

Then they had returned to the embassy, he and Laski, and Shoval wanted to work on Kampass under the drug; Shoval, who did not want to hear about what they had done with the Steiner woman; Shoval, sitting in his office with invitations to diplomatic teas like a dowager while he, Leinhardt, wiped the blood off his hands; Shoval, who was as bad as they were; Shoval, who lost his family at Sobibor and had become the same as the people who put them there. You had to be in the audience, thought Leinhardt, to appreciate the low comedy.

He said finally, "Vogel will hang. They can't afford to let him off."

"Jesus," sighed Laski. "They never let it alone."

"You're forgetting," Leinhardt admonished. "We killed six million of them. It wasn't long ago, either. You don't remember what it was about. You were getting your diapers changed."

"I remember the bombing," said Laski, slighted. "I remember when the Frogs let Senegalese niggers take the town. The only virgins were three years old and ran like hell."

"And you'd like to get back at them, wouldn't you?" asked Leinhardt.

Laski answered, a bit puzzled, "I'm German."

"German," Leinhardt confirmed, nodding.

"Same as you."

Leinhardt opened a small flight bag with BOAC stenciled onto the canvas. He took out an oily rag and unfolded it to reveal a long silencer, a tube of blue-black metal with a nine-millimeter hole in each end. He dropped the silencer into his pocket.

Laski rose from where he was sitting.

"No," said Leinhardt, motioning him back. "You're staying here."

Laski shrugged, holding his heavy arms out from his sides.

"Where'd you hide the gear?" Leinhardt asked.

"Glove compartment."

Leinhardt turned at the door and said, "You know, Kampass wouldn't understand it. He said Vogel was some kind of a doctor."

"Don't get any traffic tickets," said Laski.

"Break your arms and legs," returned Leinhardt. He went out through the screen door, which was dotted with very large moths, and walked to where the car was parked. The Peugeot was in the shadows at the side of the old petrol pump and he could see that the Kikuyu driver was asleep behind the wheel. He reached through the window and shook him awake. He told him that he wouldn't need him for the rest of the night. The Kikuyu got out and held the door open.

Leinhardt carefully fitted the silencer to the muzzle of the Browning. He put the pistol into the glove compartment, next to the blue box which contained a hypodermic needle and the vial of Nembutal. Then he turned the key in the ignition and pulled onto the rutted road. Ahead, in the lights, he could see the glowing eyes of animals winking at him. Leinhardt began to sing to himself.

●

Janek Baldur smiled at Kampass and he asked, "What are you waiting for?" His hidelike face was calm and he pointed a forefinger between his eyes and added, "There."

Kampass stood before him, holding the rifle as though it were too heavy.

"Would you rather we went outside?" asked Baldur. He sized up Kampass, Kampass of *Bad und Desinfektion II:* Kampass, the head *Desinfektor,* who stood outside the green building in his field-grey coveralls like a garbage man. And in peacetime he would have made a good garbage collector. But his country made him a not-so-fictional Himmelstoss, a single vertebra in the rigid spine of a machine that led him to perdition in dress uniform. Poor, mundane, malleable Kampass. Baldur said, "You can't do it, can you? You can't even do this without being told."

Kampass allowed the rifle to slide through his hands until the butt rested on the floor.

Kampass looked down at the muzzle of the rifle. No, he was not going to kill him. He was dying already. Baldur related the whole story: his desertion from Majdanek and assuming the identity of an Alsatian who had died in the chambers and how they, he and Ruth, lived together in Paris until Wick tried to blackmail him. Then he had to go. He had to make it by himself, somehow. He could no longer involve Ruth. Passports were easy then, Baldur said. There was nothing to it, providing one had the cash. He crossed the frontier and booked passage on a boat from Algeciras through the Suez to Mombasa, and there answered an advert for a farm manager. As a boy he had known something about it. His father had a farm in East Prussia, but it was the machines, the balers and combines, that had taken getting used to. But he managed. He settled in and began what he came to do. He subtracted from life, he said; now he would add to it. It was restitution, he explained. There was nothing else that would do; certainly not a noose. The irony, he had said, was unbelievable. Hanging a man for killing a million people was lunacy. He would set his own penalties. He would be his own judge and God; and now, with death working away inside him, he knew he had been correct.

He had become a Jew, he explained. He had to know about it, and what he did now he did as the Jew of West Kilimanjaro. The Jew, the midwife: not the Alsatian. "And I am," he said, pointing a finger at his caved-in chest, "I *am* a Jew. I. I. I."

And how was Ruth, he wanted to know, and when he asked this, Kampass knew he held the weapon in his hands that could destroy him. He could tell the truth about what happened. He could tell him she was tortured to death by Leinhardt, who wasn't a Jew. She had protected him all the way and she gave the last thing she had to give. What she had done, what she had sacrificed, made Kampass feel unclean for having taken her. He did not use the weapon. Instead, he had said, "They spoke with her and they let her go. They only talked with her." And Baldur had nodded and had said, yes, that was all right and that it was too much of a secret for her anyway and that it had been their agreement from the start that she was to tell what she knew when she had to. She had suffered enough as it was.

Baldur said: "You see, Kampass, you were a soldier. I was a politician. Politicians change. That is their cause célèbre. Soldiers can't. They are what they are for that reason. Politics are a matter of the mind and an approach to living; soldiering, good soldiering, is doing what you are told. So, Kampass, for you there is no up or down. Now there is no one to tell you what to do. Finally, you must commit to yourself, not to your country or its order. No marching bands now, eh, Kampass?"

"I can't go back," said Kampass. He thought about the office and the chore of living. He could not go back to being Manfred Speirling even if they let him, even if he somehow made it back. He could not, that was all.

"No, of course you can't," said Baldur. "But, my friend, I am not going back either, so make up your mind."

Kampass felt himself strangely paternalistic towards Baldur because he had the means to shatter him at tongue-tip. "She wanted to help me, do you know that?"

"She would do that," said Baldur. "That was how she helped herself."

Kampass said, "She arranged for a Dutchman to help me over the frontier."

"Why didn't you go?"

"I would have," he lied. "They found me."

Baldur nodded. "And the Dutchman's name was Dierks."

"Yes, that's right," said Kampass, startled.

"Our son," said Baldur. "He was born at Majdanek. I arranged it so he was listed as a child born to one of the prisoners in Field Four. The woman had perished. Then we sent him to a friend's home in Coblenz. Later we took him to Paris where Ruth and I were married. He never knew."

Kampass remembered the spidery young man who bragged about how he was to join the *paras* the following week. He wondered what Baldur would say if he knew.

But, most of all, it was Ruth who Kampass now thought of: the pale skylight and the electric fire, the dog that always slept, and the smell of Ruth on the bed after she had left him. And he recalled the bruise on her thigh. He never asked her where she had got it.

"You better decide," said Baldur. "Time is growing short. Your friends will be here and I am not going back with you or anybody else."

Kampass lifted the rifle.

Baldur waited on the chair, his hands neatly on his kneecaps while Kampass found the box of ammunition. He shook three cartridges onto his palm. They looked the size of cheroots. He opened the bolt on the rifle and pressed them into the magazine. He closed the bolt.

Baldur looked at him like a horse with a broken leg. He knew what was coming. He said again, "I'm not going back."

Kampass slung the rifle over his shoulder and walked to the door. "You won't have to," he said. "I am."

"Don't be a fool," said Baldur. He rose awkwardly from the chair.

Kampass paused at the door. Baldur, he thought. It was not possible. A sick old man. He said, "Yes, perhaps. But don't tell me what to do. Not any more."

●

Looking back from the track that led from the farm, he could see Baldur outlined in the doorway, steadying himself there with two hands like a sad marionette. But Kampass looked back only this one time and then he forgot about Rudolf Vogel. He shifted the rifle on his shoulder and went down the track. His shadow followed him in the moonlight and he left the track, cutting through the fields towards the road below him where he could see the infrequent lights of passing cars. He walked easily, feeling the dew-heavy grass sweep by him, and once something jumped up ahead of him and scampered away. It seemed that he walked for hours. Finally he found himself at the front gate and its cattle guard, and here he slid into a drainage ditch. He remembered Baldur's advice about snakes and poked around in the weeds of the ditch with the barrel of the rifle, using it in the way a golfer searches for his lost ball with a iron. Satisfied, he rested the rifle against the culvert, within easy reach. He took off his coat and spread it on the weeds and sat down, leaning back on the side of the ditch; and for a while he played with dirt clods, crumbling them between his fingers, and then he looked up at the night sky.

So he waited, watching the moon inch across the sky. How big the stars were, he thought. He had never seen them that large before, even in Russia, and they had been very clear there on winter nights. As big as oranges they looked. A thunderstorm was building up across the valley and behind Mount Meru and he could see the lightning throwing shadows in the canyons and hammerheads of clouds. The storm growled and grew closer. Then the rain came, beating the grass flat and partly filling the drainage ditch. The storm swept past and the smell of wet trees and ferns came across the fields from the forest above. The rain water gurgled from the culvert, and from somewhere behind him, there sounded the absurd cackle of a hyena. He listened to this and the other noises of the bush that only live at night, and somehow, he was no longer afraid. The key had turned in the lock and the door was open. It was only what was ahead of him that mattered.

It was past midnight when he heard the cattleguard rattle beyond the front gate and saw the headlights of an auto cut like a scythe through the darkness over his head. He heard the car door open and the sound of a radio playing African music. The gate clanked and groaned and feet sloshed in the puddles. Kampass eased up the side of the ditch from his hiding place until the top of his head showed above the rim. He grasped the rifle by its barrel, feeling moisture on the steel, and drew it up beside him and laid it across his arm. The wood of the stock slipped over his cheek and he sighted on a point midway between the two headlights. When the figure was outlined between them, he fired. The rifle went off with a busting roar and the muzzle flash blinded him for an instant. There was a tinkle of broken glass and the figure reeled against the hood and pitched forward onto the road. One of the headlights glowed brightly, smoked, and went out.

Briefly Kampass bent over the figure, turning its pockets out. Then he found what he was looking for. He broke open the cartridge, grinding it beneath his foot. Then he stripped out the film and threw it into the fields.

The Ukrainian recapped the tubes and put away the funnel and the gas masks.

They finished cleaning up and went outside. Rain was beginning to spit from the clouds.

The Himmelkommando had backed trucks up to the door of the chambers. When they opened the doors, the bodies just toppled out onto the sand.

Kampass watched while they threw them, one by one, like sides of beef, into the open backs of the trucks. When one truck filled, they backed up another, walking now on the bodies, packing them in. When they stepped on a corpse, it would fart or belch. Nearly five hundred of them, there were.

You could not think about them as being people any more, Kampass knew. They were nothing. Dead weight. Big weights and little weights.

They brought out a very fat woman.

"That one didn't come from any ghetto," said the Ukrainian.

Her body landed on the truck with a wet thump. Kampass flinched.

The Ukrainian went on making comments, speculating as to what each corpse did in life. His language became coarse. He said lewd things about the women. . .

Kampass could not take it any longer. He faced the private. He drove his fist into the wide face. The private skidded onto the sand. Kampass unbuttoned the flap of his pistol holster.

"Go ahead and do something," he said.

The Ukrainian got up, brushing himself off.

"I'll kill you someday, you peasant trash," said Kampass. "You're not fit to wear the uniform."

The Himmelkommando *brought out the old man last. His chest was wrinkled and falled like a crone's.*

Kampass saw that his features had softened in death. They had become those of a child. And he was still smiling. His eyes, open, seemed to probe him yet. They put the old man on the truck. His white hair and beard moved in the wind. There were varicose veins bulging on his calves. He had done a lot of walking, thought Kampass. He must have been on his feet most of his life. Perhaps he hadn't been a rabbi. Perhaps he'd been a beggar. Maybe a farmer in a field in the Ukraine or Yugoslavia. And Kampass knew he would remember that old man for a long time.

Kampass looked to the corner of the building. Vogel was standing there and watching them load the last truck.

Kampass drew back. He kept his head turned and looked from the corner of his eye.

Vogel's gloved fingers moving slightly, his face pinched and dark below the low visor of his cap, his legs bowed in the breeches. Only his fingers moved. He was very still, like a small statue.

The truck drove off. Kampass watched it disappear towards the crematorium. When he looked back at the corner of the building Vogel was gone, almost as if he had never been there.

The clouds opened and the rain came.

Down the Chelm Road another column was moving, inching its way towards the gates. Kampass squinted through the rain. There was no old man this time. A small boy was leading them. He was holding a staff, moving it, prancing like a major-domo.

EXPEDITER

"God is on our side, isn't he?"

——*Bruno Kampass, age twenty-four*

The dawn of the new year broke upon Jerusalem. It splashed color on the slopes of Mount Scopus and pinked the crest of King David's Tomb. There was no wind in the dawn.

Behind the walls of the Old City, the Arab Quarter, pyedogs fought over yesterday's garbage, and from the minarets of the Aqsa and Omar mosques, muezzins caterwauled the call to morning prayer. One-eyed beggars, tattered cyclopes with hashish-stained beards of white goaty hair, rolled upon stone floors and grumbled in the cold. In the far distance, deep into Jordan, hills rose like icebergs on a hazy sea.

The duty officer at police headquarters in the Russian Compound coughed and spread the papers out with one forefinger on the desk before him as though sifting through buttons. He took the passport and opened it, weighing both leaves with a penholder so it would stay open. He looked at the man standing before the desk. Seedy, the duty officer thought. The man looked as though he had come through a hedge backward. He cleared his throat. "Kampass, is it," he said. It was not a question.

Kampass shifted weight.

"Doesn't mean anything to me," said the duty officer. He studied the passport again, studied the photo, and then looked back at Kampass. He turned his head. "Zagagi," he called. "Zagagi, wake up."

There was a long bench behind the desk. A pile of old

clothing arranged there stirred. An old man sat up. He was wearing an army greatcoat against the chill. He scratched in the beard that flowed halfway down his chest.

"Zagagi, it's time," said the duty officer.

The old man bent down and fastened on his sandals. He straightened up, holding himself erect with a hand at the small of his back.

"Atara is open now," said the duty officer.

"He looks like a wife-beater," said the old man, watching Kampass.

"Go on," said the duty officer.

The old man moved to the door, which was open to the dawn, his sandals scraping on the dirty tile. At the door he stopped and turned. He said: "Death. The sentence is death." He cackled and left.

The duty officer pointed a finger at his temple and wiggled it. He smiled. "Fruity," he said.

Kampass said nothing. There was something disturbingly familiar about the old man.

The duty officer put aside the passport. He shook his head. "Kampass," he said again.

"Call your Foreign Office then, they'll confirm it."

"And you said you took last night's flight up from Dar es Salaam?"

"Yes sir."

"And who's this Leinhardt?"

Kampass put both hands on the desk and leaned forward. "I told you already. Don't you understand? Call them. They'll tell you."

The duty officer shrugged. He picked up the telephone. He spoke, reading off the information on the sheets before him, asking. Then he listened, his eyes widening. They shifted from the papers to Kampass, then back again. "Yes sir," he said.

●

Kampass was watching the spider. He had been studying it for three days now and was beginning to fancy himself an

authority on the subject. In the beginning the insect hung by
a tenuous thread in a corner of the cell, directly over his
head. That was three days before—after they had driven him
from Jerusalem to Maasiahu Prison in the suburbs of Ramla.
He was fortunate to be in the new wing of the jail, they told
him; that, and the fact that the cell adjacent to his had been
occupied by Adolf Eichmann.

So he lay on the cot under the ersatz blanket and examined
the spider's web above his head. The spider crawled into the
corner and waited. The web was ready to trap a fly.

He rolled over on the cot and stared at the tile wall. The
cell reminded him of an apiary he once visited in the Berlin
Zoo. Kampass was on display and he knew it; every so often
the panel on the heavy door would slide back silently to
reveal an eyeball. But it was not this—this knowing he had
become an exhibit—that disturbed him so much as the boredom between interviews. One after another they had come,
at all hours of the day and night since he had walked into
police headquarters. He was no longer a nonentity. They kept
asking him if everything was all right. Did he have com-
plaints? Did he require medical attention? Kampass felt the
anonymity of a wounded soldier home from war. They examined him as though he were some rare fungus growth, shining
pencil flashlights up his rectum and other orifices, listening to
and recording his pulse and heartbeat, thumping his back
and testing his reflexes. These indignities he had patiently
borne. He complained mildly when they took away his belt
and shoelaces, pointing out that he had no intention of hanging himself.

Then, as if intent on making a record for posterity, they
gave him an IQ examination on which he tried very hard, but
succeeded in scoring a mediocre 105.

During his first interrogation they asked him how he obtained the funds to travel from East Africa to Lod Airport,
and without hesitation, he told them; he had taken the money
from Leinhardt. He drove Leinhardt's Peugeot back to
Nairobi and left the keys with East African Airways at
Embakasi Field. He had made a careful accounting of how

much cash he spent for meals and air fare. He had sealed the unused bills in an envelope with a complete expense sheet and turned them over to the duty officer at headquarters. It was all exact. He had not spent a penny more than was necessary.

An inspector and a plainclothesman interrogated him. They were very courteous. They said they could not believe it, about the money, but he said yes, it was all there. He was many things, but not a thief. They let it drop. Not once did they mention Leinhardt. He assumed then that by now they had checked the story he gave the duty officer. Kampass wondered who had found him at the bottom of the road by the cattle guard. Vogel? Laski, who would have followed when he did not return?

Kampass looked forward to his interrogations like a hospital patient anticipates visitors' hours. They made him feel important somehow. He never knew when they were coming. The electronically controlled door panel to his cell would hum back and there would be somebody new, someone he had not seen before. He and the visitor would talk. Kampass would usher him to a leatherette chair they put in the cell as though he were showing the man into his living room. It was going very well. Yes indeed. Wizard.

The Americans sent their vice-consul, Savory.

Savory walked into the cell, looking about him, bewildered, as though he had stumbled by mistake into the ladies' powder room. He had a closely shaved head that gave it the appearance of a cue ball. He said, "Mr. Kampass?" asking as though it might have been someone else.

Kampass noted he spoke with a slight lisp.

Savory opened his briefcase and arranged papers on the writing desk in the corner. Next to the papers he placed a transistor tape recorder. He opened the machine and threaded in a spool. Then he took a parcel from the briefcase and gave it to Kampass. "Our compliments," he lisped. "It's kind of a survival kit. After all, you're still technically one of us."

Kampass thanked him. He saw that the parcel had been opened at one end.

"There was some chewing gum and a tube of toothpaste," informed Savory. "But they're holding it for inspection."

Kampass shook out the contents. There was a Bible, courtesy of the Gideon's, a sheaf of writing paper bearing the seal of the United States of America, a five-cent packet of Kleenex, a Tek toothbrush in a plastic container, and a copy of John F. Kennedy's *Profiles in Courage*.

"Thank you," Kampass repeated.

Savory shrugged and said, "Forget it."

Savory returned to the tape recorder and made an adjustment. He unraveled a microphone and plugged it into the machine. Then he brought over the recorder and a sheet of the paper which Kampass saw was a question-and-answer script.

"This is a formality," said Savory. "I have to take your statement and ask you a few questions about your immigration. You answer the questions in your own words into the mike, okay?" He pressed a switch and the tape recorder made a whirring noise. Then, reading from the prepared script, he said: "The following statement was made this date, January third, nineteen sixty-five, by Bruno Waldek Kampass at detention quarters in Ramla, Israel. Now you read on from there, Mr. Kampass."

Kampass read the statement. His statement. He swore that the American government was unaware of his wartime service or of the alias he used to obtain the entry visa. He absolved the United States of guilt, knowledge, or complicity.

When he had finished, Savory spun the tape ahead. "Fine," he said. "Excellent. Now, in your own words, please explain the details of your immigration. Don't leave out the part about the visa and the DP camp at Fürstenfeldbruck."

Kampass told the microphone what he could remember, including the name of the captain whom he had bribed, Stewart.

Savory asked him: "What do you know about ODESSA's

activities within the United States and Canada? What do you
know of the membership?"

Kampass held the man's eyes. "Nothing," he said. "Zero."

"You deny the existence of such an organization with affili-
ations to, ah, certain conservative groups in the United
States?"

"I didn't say that," reminded Kampass. "I don't know about
it, personally."

"Personally?"

"Yes."

Savory made an adjustment on the machine. "What do you
know about the existence of two dozen photos concerning a
list of names of men implicated in wartime atrocities and
currently naturalized Americans?"

Kampass looked at the small window.

"A Mr. Leinhardt had the list. Our information is that you
killed him. Did you take the film? Where is it? Did you take
it?"

"I found it, yes. I threw it away."

"You *what?*"

"I threw it away."

"Speak into the mike."

Kampass repeated himself for the tape recorder.

"Why did you do that, Mr. Kampass?"

Kampass said nothing.

Savory blinked twice, very rapidly. "Were the films developed?"

"No," said Kampass.

The man sighed and switched off the machine. He un-
plugged the microphone and replaced the machine in his
briefcase. "It would be best all round if we had a candid
discussion here. For some time we have known certain ele-
ments immigrated to the United States, such as yourself.
They were sought by eastern European countries which were
under Nazi domination during the war. Some of these men
hold rather high positions in industry. We wish, of course, to
co-operate with our friends in bringing them to justice. We
suspect some of these men's names were on the film."

"I took the photos," said Kampass. "I don't remember the names."

"Try."

"I was in a hurry," said Kampass. "I was thinking about the camera, the right light, and exposure."

Savory cleared his throat.

"You are with the FBI?" asked Kampass. It seemed logical.

Savory shook his head in annoyance. "I'm a consular official and I'm trying to do the job as best I can. You're not helping, are you? We can still offer you our good offices. It's not too late to claim jurisdiction. I don't think you appreciate the gravity of the position you are in. You're in deep trouble, Mr. Kampass. Deep trouble. And we can help."

"I threw it into the fields," said Kampass. "It's the truth."

Savory leaned closer. "We'll be pleased to arrange protective custody, a protective residence for you in any country of your choice. Yes, even Germany."

Kampass thought about the proposal ODESSA had made him in Paris.

Savory went on: "There might be some form of pension arrangement we could qualify you for. It would be a stipend, but you would not be neglected."

"I'm sorry," said Kampass.

"All right," said Savory. "I'm going to go the limit with you. What would you say to full, bona-fide American citizenship—full rights, the past forgotten?"

They did not understand, Kampass thought to himself. They refused to see how it was. Ruth said it. *I really don't care.* She was right.

Savory stood up. He drew back his shoulders. "Mr. Kampass," he said, "it is my duty to inform you that you have been stripped of your citizenship. Do you know what it means to be a man without a country, Kampass?"

Kampass played with the bristles of his toothbrush.

"You are nobody. You do not have an identity. Stateless. You are less than an animal."

"Yes," replied Kampass. "I know."

"You're pretty smug too," said Savory, turning nasty. "You baby-murdering son of a bitch."

Kampass looked up quickly. "Yes, Mr. Savory," he said. "I have killed babies, many of them."

Savory collected the papers from the desk and stuffed them into the briefcase. Then he banged on the door and called for the guard.

It seemed that the only people who had not visited him were the Germans themselves. It was like coming home again and not having your family there to greet you. What was delaying them? he wondered. The Jews were turning him over to Bonn. That was the rumor, his guard had said. He would be sent to Braunschweig, pending trial. If so, where were his own people? The family does not disown its children. He threw back the blanket and stood on the bottom of the bed so that he might see out the small window high in the cell. The view was not much. Suburban Ramla served as a collection point for Jewish immigrants and refugees from North Africa; from Algeria, Tunisia, and Morocco. Some of them walked by beneath his window, wrapped in grey cloth, unable to discard the heritage of the Arab world even though they could never be a part of it. In a vacant lot next to the grimy walls of a factory, boys with dirty legs, short pants, and suspenders played football. Suburban Ramla.

•

Kampass was finishing a breakfast of sausage and pumpernickel, served him on a stainless-steel tray, when the cell door made a sibilant sound and in walked a swarthy man dressed like a mourner, in a dark, vicuna coat and black bowler. Kampass recognized him at once. The toothbrush mustache seemed glued to his lip, as though it might have been hastily applied from a child's disguise kit.

"I'm Shoval," he said. "Don't let me disturb you. Finish your meal."

He removed his vicuna and laid it carefully across the end

of the bed. He placed his bowler on top of the coat, and arranging the seams of his trousers, sat down slowly on an imitation-leather easy chair they had put in the cell, as though he were worried he might break it. Through the thick lenses of his tortoise-shell spectacles, his eyes looked like agates. He watched Kampass eat. "Good?" he asked at length. "The food is all right?"

Kampass put his knife and fork into the napkin and rolled them up together. He put the napkin on the tray and set it on the floor, below the cot.

Shoval removed his spectacles and rubbed at the red marks they made on either side of his nose. He looked around his fingers and said, "The Americans interviewed you yesterday, yes?"

Kampass nodded. "A man called Savory from the embassy."

"And he brought you things, yes?"

"He called it a survival kit." Kampass smiled. "He brought me books."

"Some survival kit," said Shoval. "A chemical analysis on the toothpaste we confiscated showed it contained enough strychnine to clean out the entire prison. That is some survival kit."

Kampass felt his scalp move. "But why?" he asked. "They wished to make an arrangement with me."

"In the end, they would make nothing," Shoval said. "They wanted you dead. You would not be here to embarrass them. American quality control. Savory was all right. He didn't know. They made up the package and gave it to him. There's going to be a stink about this. But that's all right, you keep the books."

Kampass put his hands on his knees carefully as though cupping coins.

"Vogel's gone, you know," said Shoval.

"Is he?" asked Kampass.

"He beat Leinhardt's man to Arusha. He crossed into Portuguese East Africa. He's in Lorenco Marques. So he's on the run again. He won't last. He's too old now."

Kampass nodded. "Yes, he was very old," he said. He did not really care about Vogel any more. There was just an old man called Janek Baldur and Janek Baldur did not matter.

"You're going to take the rap for him," Shoval went on. "You could have done your job and we'd have let it go."

Kampass smiled. He'd taken stock. Of course, they would not have let it go. He knew too much about the operation. From the time he met the two agents in New York, his fate was a foregone conclusion. No. It was foregone long before that. He was facing it now, that was all.

"He let you take the rap for him," repeated Shoval.

"You won't believe this," said Kampass. "I told myself that once." He kept his hands on his knees, sitting on the edge of the cot.

"You could have gone with him. You didn't have to come back, Kampass," said Shoval.

"Yes I did," said Kampass. "You wouldn't know, but I did."

Shoval stared at him and pulled at his mustache thoughtfully. He said, "He converted you, didn't he? He told you to kill Leinhardt. He twisted and turned you, Vogel did."

"You said he was Vogel, I didn't," said Kampass.

"He was Vogel, all right," said Shoval.

Kampass said, "He will be dead soon."

"He'll be dead, yes," said Shoval. "He played a trick on you. That's the trick, you see. He got away with it, with everything he did. He's laughing at you because you're in his place."

"How do you hang a man?" asked Kampass. "How does the punishment fit the crime?"

"Let's not be moral," said Shoval. "You're out of your depth. You moralizing is like a cook running an army."

Kampass nodded slowly. "I have thought it out," he said.

"Well," said Shoval. "I've just finished breakfast and I don't want indigestion. We'll move to something more immediate. Let's talk about the film. Now Leinhardt's man got frightened and told us all about it; about how he and Leinhardt planned to sell the cartridge to the Americans and keep us out. Leinhardt was on his way to eliminate you when you shot him. You were the only one who knew what he planned, outside of Laski and the *Amis*. So he couldn't let you come back. There was too much risk you'd tell me about it and ruin the negotiations. Our guess is he received the wire I sent earlier and the idea of sending you up to the farm needlessly and faking a jam occurred to him."

Kampass said nothing. He studied the dandruff that lay heavy on the shoulders of Shoval's suit.

"I don't care about Leinhardt," said Shoval. "He was a whore."

Kampass nodded in agreement; the small, unpleasant man with the mouth that was made to eat plates. The noises of children playing in the early morning came through the cell window.

"Emil Laski said Leinhardt was carrying the cartridge," said Shoval. "They hadn't time to develop it. Laski said he found the body the next morning and there was no film."

"I've been through this a million times," said Kampass.

"Go through it again."

Kampass explained.

"Don't be a martyr, Kampass," said Shoval. "They wouldn't do the same for you. The war's over twenty years. The forces have scattered. It's everyone for himself."

Kampass said, "Survivors." He was remembering.

Shoval looked at him strangely. He said, "You know something? You might have done it. You might be telling the truth." He began to chuckle. It built up in his throat like a deep burp. "It's priceless," he said. "We deal for a general and we get a sergeant. What was it? My kingdom for a horse? As Leinhardt said, we got a *Kamposity*. He had a sense of humor, Leinhardt did," added Shoval. He shook his head. "He was a very funny man." He walked across the cell and offered Kampass a cigarette and lit it for him with a gas lighter. Kampass saw he had hairy arms that for some reason reminded him of a barber.

Shoval touched the lighter to his own cigarette. He said, "You're very lucky." The words came out with the smoke. "You're our little olive branch, Kampass. You're a poor substitute, but you're the only thing we have to offer now and you are the dregs."

"I don't understand," said Kampass.

"You're going home. You're going back to Germany. We're giving you to Bonn."

So the rumor was true, thought Kampass. He had not really allowed himself to believe it. When no representative of Bonn had come to see him, he had been sure it was just that—a rumor. Exhilaration surged through him. It built to his face and he smiled broadly. The expression felt unnatural.

"You are to be exposed in front of your own people," said Shoval. "They will see you for what you are—a rabid dog— and they will put you in a cage for the rest of your life. But they will see we are forgiving. We do not wish revenge. Let them punish their own. Let them spit up the past. You are phlegm, Kampass. You get stuck in craws every twenty-five years or so. We must clear our throats. Get it out in the open so all may see what it is."

There was a buzzing noise in the corner of the cell and Kampass saw a fly struggling in the web. The sound of its wings came like Morse code. The spider left its hiding place and drifted down the web towards the fly.

"You'll like going back, won't you, Kampass," said Shoval. He was not laughing now. "You don't like it out there, do you?"—he motioned to the small window.

There was a mechanical purr and Shoval pulled up his sleeve and looked at his heavy wristwatch. He touched a button and the noise stopped. He looked at Kampass. "It's been, well, it's been an education, Kampass, hasn't it?"

Kampass did not answer. He was looking at Shoval's watch. "Is that an alarm watch?" he asked.

Shoval stared in astonishment at Kampass for several seconds. Then he slid the watch from his wrist and tossed it on the cot. "If it matters that much," he said, "you keep it."

Kampass said, "I couldn't." But he picked it up and examined the mechanism, anyway.

Shoval said, "You need it more than I do." They were all the same, thought Shoval. There were more lists; more names; all of them poured from the same mold—sergeants, generals, privates. In the end, they had to quit the obscurity of the shadow world they lived in. It would consume them until they became shadows themselves. And Kampass, he even measured minutes of reality.

So it ended, thought Shoval. The guests had eaten and left. The packages were small. It had been a lean Christmas.

"You'll be leaving in an hour," Shoval said. "There's a photographer outside, but you are not to speak with him. We will allow photos, but no interviews. He hesitated at the door and turned. "I knew an *Oberscharführer* once, Kampass," he said. "During the war they collected me in Warsaw and sent me to a factory of the bombs in Radom. My people went to Sobibor, but as I was strong, I went to Radom. While there I worked as a clerk in one of the offices, under an *Oberscharführer* called Erik, and one day I asked, 'Erik, why do you want to kill me? Why do you want to kill us Jews?' And Erik said he did not want to kill us, but it had been ordered by the *Führer* and Himmler so, in a sense, we were already dead. So in Erik's mind it didn't make any difference if he did it or if the *Rottenführer* down the hall took his pistol one day and shot me. So, anyway, Erik and I got along splendidly. He even told me he had been a horse thief in Bavaria before the war. Then one day, the *Totenkopf* came to take me to Treblinka. That was the end, I thought. But good old Erik. He said, 'Mordecai, I'm sending you to a work battalion to dig tank traps on the Bug because if I don't you'll end up as fertilizer.' And so I dug tank traps and I survived. Then I asked myself this: if Erik, this *Oberscharführer*, said I was already dead and it did not matter who carried out sentence, why did he send me to dig tank traps? Kampass?"

But Kampass was lost in studying the watch.

Shoval left edging past the guard and a photographer from United Press who stood holding his camera and strobe as though he were afraid someone might confiscate it.

Kampass took his eyes from the watch. He was aware that the buzzing from the corner had ceased. He saw the spider had settled itself upon the fly.

●

The duty officer spoke into the phone. He said, "They've asked us for four motorcyclists. They're bringing him in this morning and they asked us for an escort." For a moment, he was silent. "I don't care which four," he added. He put up the phone. "Nobody ever fills out a proper requisition here. I never know what's going on," he mumbled.

"I do," said Zagagi. The old man was sitting on the bench again. He was drinking coffee from a plastic cup and some of the liquid ran from his lips into his beard.

"Would you like to sit at this desk, Zagagi?" asked the duty officer. Then he remembered how it was with the old man and added, "I'm sorry." Then, condescendingly, happily, "Just what *is* going on, Zagagi?"

"They're letting him go," said Zagagi. "They're letting the Germans have him back."

"There are wheels within the wheels," said the duty officer.

"You think I'm crazy, don't you?"

"No, Moses, that's not true."

"Yes it is," said Zagagi. "I don't mind. I get your coffee and your sandwiches, you and the others, and I don't mind that you think I'm crazy. The children, yesterday they threw rocks at me in the Jaffa Road. They also think I'm crazy."

"It is because you are old," said the duty officer. "Children don't understand age." He was watching the old man drink his coffee. He was not the Moses Zagagi of yesterday. There was a queer light in his eyes.

"All those people," said Zagagi. "*Our* people, and they're letting him go, sending him back as though all he did was rob a bank, this Kampass, this sergeant." He folded his hands. He had not thought this clearly in twenty years. The confusion had disappeared and he was remembering days that destroyed him; days when he did not wear a beard and when children did not throw rocks at him; long before he was reduced to mending bric-a-brac and taking orders for coffee and newspapers from duty officers. He was recalling Poland and Treblinka, where he worked as a *Himmelkommando* for a man who was the same as this German. No, the fog had gone, rolled back as if by a fresh breeze. This morning, Moses Zagagi could smell ashes in the air again.

"You were here," the duty officer was saying. "You saw him walk right in here."

"That doesn't make it all right," said the old man.

"Put it out of your mind," said the duty officer. "It doesn't concern us."

The old man shook his head.

The duty officer was growing impatient. "I'll give it to you, Zagagi. Go out on the streets and talk with the youngsters. Ask them if they care. Ask them if they remember. That's why you are stoned. You are one big memory."

"You don't have that, you have nothing," said Zagagi. "I do not turn the other cheek and you see what they have done to me."

The duty officer drummed his fingers on the desk. "You don't understand. Can't you see we don't want to remember? We have our own country here, our Israel. We have come back. We are no longer part of another's tragedy. We master our own destiny. We are home. You have forgotten the Arabs?" The duty officer swept a hand around. "Only yesterday, there was a sniping. There lies the threat. Concern yourself with the present, old man of a million hairs, not the past."

Zagagi nodded. "And fetch the papers and the coffee," he said.

"I didn't mean that."

"I know what you meant."

"Zagagi, look," said the duty officer. "You know Yad Vashem, the memorial to the Martyred of Europe? Well, more of us visit the old fort of Masada where we stood against Rome than go to Yad Vashem. Three times as many. Why? Because we wish to remember with pride, our national pride, that's why."

The old man looked out the open door. The sun was falling on the streets and a parade of autos was filing past. But the noises of the traffic were faint in the station. "Justice will be done because thus it is written," he said.

"Well, *I* think of Israel," said the duty officer. "Soon we shall have an ambassador in Germany. Even our former enemies, our exterminators, recognize us. They defer to us. Our past is catastrophe, Zagagi. Do not dwell there. Me, I want a natural death. I want to go to sleep and never wake up."

"To hell with Israel," said Zagagi.

The duty officer opened his mouth.

"Yes, I say to hell with it and to hell with you."

The duty officer smiled.

"There you are," said Zagagi. "You think me crazy."

"You know that's not true, Moses," said the duty officer. He started to sign some papers on the desk. His relief was only a half-hour off. Imagine that, he thought, arguing with Zagagi; rising to the bait and arguing with an old man who should have been certified years before. He smiled to himself. He was tired.

Zagagi went to the small bathroom behind the orderly room and removed the parcel he had kept hidden beneath his coat since early that morning. He knelt down on the tile and unwrapped it, folding back the oil-stained brown paper.

He had not touched the pistol since he buried it behind his brother's house during the Arab war. Now, after twenty years, he was not sure that it would operate. He put the greasy paper in a receptacle and set the Mauser on a nearby toilet seat. In a pocket of his greatcoat he located the magazine. He wiped away the cosmoline and inserted it. The rough butt of the Mauser felt good against his palm. He did not know if he could hit anything with it. It was so small. He would have to be very close. He stood in front of the washbasin, and holding the weapon in both hands, sighted on his reflection. The barrel and sights quivered uncontrollably. He drew a deep breath and held it. That seemed to help. Damn this palsy, he thought. It so angered him, that undignified disease of old men, that he often punished his hands by beating them against a rough wall.

He studied the movements of the pistol. How to load it? At last he found out how to operate the slide action so that a cartridge would feed from the clip. The slide snapped back with a satisfying *clack*. He was ready. He would show them. Crazy, indeed.

●

The countryside along the Jerusalem Road, in its final stages, winds between steep hills that are hackled with pygmy pine and cluttered with slides of white chalky boulders. But nowhere is it as unkempt as where it runs from Ramla to Jerusalem before giving itself up to the respectability of the Jaffa Road. The shoulders of the road where it passes through the hills are strewn with the burnt-out shells of armored vehicles, many of them on their backs like helpless, singed turtles; victims of Arab ambushes while running food through the blockade to the beleaguered defenders of the city during the Arab war. They lay there in the sun and the rain, and sometimes the snow, and although the roasted bodies of their occupants have long since been removed, they are not totally forgotten.

As they drove by, Kampass watched one of the relics with detached interest and inquired of the guard seated to his left, "What's the wreath for?"

"Memory," the guard, an Israeli, answered. "The fallen of Israel."

"*Judensoldaten?*" asked Kampass. He could not understand what the wrecks were doing in such a place. Why didn't they remove them?

"Yes, soldiers," said the Israeli.

Kampass had not said a word to the plainclothesman

seated on his right. He had been introduced to Kampass as *Herr* Stassen who would accompany him as far as Frankfurt. Kampass remembered him as the unidentified man who had accompanied him to the airport in New York. So long ago it was. Did it ever happen? he wondered.

Not even the Jews themselves insisted on manacling him during the previous trips to Jerusalem. But on this, his last trip, Stassen did. It was unnecessary. Shoval was right. They were going to put him up like an animal.

Stassen, thick-chinned, sat posing as though he were profiling in the turret of a Panzer on parade. He watched the escort weave out in front of them on their motorcycles. His face might have been sculpted from stone; a representative of his nation on review. Kampass had seen them all before. They were nothing new for him. He ought to know them. He had been one himself.

Kampass turned to Stassen. "There are some things I have been meaning to ask," he said.

Stassen stared out ahead at the escort, unmindful.

"It's about some decorations I won in the war," Kampass persisted. "I am wondering if they might be replaced. There must be records of them in the regimental history of the *Reich* Division."

Stassen moved his neck as though his collar was too tight. He said nothing.

The black limousine drove on, easily taking the sharp corners of the road, following the escort, and then, suddenly, they were out of the hills, away from the tortuous road. Ahead of them, in the sun, was Jerusalem. They moved along the Jaffa Road now, the traffic directors at the intersections waving them through. They made a left-hand turn as they reached Shlozion Hamalka and drove up a narrow street. The limousine stopped at the entrance to the police station. The escort leaned their machines against the wall and kicked down the stands.

This was it, thought Kampass. They would sign the extradition agreement with Stassen, more photos, and then the long drive to Lod and the flight to Germany; the homecoming. He left in disguise and he was coming back as himself. He was going home.

Stassen got out and held the door open and Kampass emerged into the bright sun, frowning after the Polaroid-tinted shade of the limousine. Stassen gripped him roughly by the arm and guided him up a path to the entrance. When Stassen pulled at his arm, the manacles cut into his wrist. Finally he said, "Take it easy." Stassen yanked.

He could see a small crowd gathered at the door. They lined both sides of the walkway and there were half a dozen uniformed officers holding batons across their chests and facing the crowd. The onlookers were young. Students, perhaps, thought Kampass. They watched him coming up the path. They did not seem angry, only curious. Kampass smiled at them and tried to hold up his manacled hands. It seemed the right thing to do. Stassen yanked his hands down.

Kampass snarled. "Lay it on for them," he said.

"Quiet, you," ordered Stassen.

Kampass called him a name under his breath.

"What's that, you *Lausbube?*" asked Stassen, spinning Kampass about so that he nearly fell.

Stassen and Leinhardt, thought Kampass: two of a kind.

They continued up the path, past the crowd, which muttered as they went by. Then they were mounting the steps to the building, taking them one at a time, Stassen pulling him, jostling, showing off.

The old man blocked the door.

Kampass stopped as though he had walked into an invisible wall.

Zagagi's eyes moved over the crowd. "Don't you care?" he shouted. "Is he no more than a traffic accident that you came here to see?"

Stassen pulled at Kampass' arm. Kampass held up his hands. Stassen knocked them down.

One of the escort brushed past.

"Stay where you are," said Zagagi. He held the Mauser at arm's length with both hands.

"Don't be foolish," said the Israeli guard.

"Foolish. Ha. Ha," said Zagagi.

Kampass looked at him, the old man. He tried to step back. Stassen held him.

"Is he a freak, a side show?" asked Zagagi. The crowd was very quiet. Some were trying to move away. They were afraid of him.

Kampass knew what it was about the old man. He knew him as well as he now knew himself.

The escort officer made a move.

"Stop!" shrilled Zagagi. The officer stopped.

"Don't do anything foolish, old man," said the officer again. "Put it down."

Stassen stood by, eyes wide and glassy with alarm. He waited for someone to do something.

"Well, I have decided for you," said the old man to the crowd. "I, Moses Zagagi, have decided." He walked down a step towards Kampass. The hairs in the center of his beard moved. *"Mörder,"* he said. Then he steadied the pistol, shying away, leaning his head back as though the Mauser might explode into a million pieces. The pistol went off with a sharp *pop*.

Kampass felt as though he had been kicked in the chest. He sat down on the steps, his legs buckling beneath him.

They were on the old man, wrestling the gun away, and the old man was laughing, gesturing obscenely to the crowd. Stassen was hysterical, screaming for an ambulance. Someone unlocked the handcuffs and threw a coat over his shoulders.

It didn't hurt, thought Kampass. It was just numb. It had been much worse in Russia. He wanted to lie down.

They arranged him on the steps so his head was uphill.

"Don't talk," someone said.

Talk, thought Kampass. About what? There was nothing to talk about. Parts of him were beginning to lose feeling. His feet were dead. It was climbing up on him slowly. He watched the fleecy clouds overhead; weird shapes, round, bulbous noses and bloated cheeks. His chest felt heavy inside and something moved as if it were broken there and he knew then he was going to die.

They tried to lift his head. "Leave me alone," said Kampass. He was thinking of the alley and wondering whether his name was still legible where he had scratched it on the wall. That, that seemed very important.

•

"Someone is going to be in trouble," said the duty officer.

They all stood quietly on the steps. The crowd had been dispersed by the motorcycle escort and Stassen was on the walkway, smoking. He looked like a man suddenly deserted; left with no task to perform; a wallflower at once aware of what made him different from the others there.

"I was on duty when that bastard first came in," the duty officer continued, looking at the body. "Walked in here as big as life, he did. I didn't believe him. He said who he was, but there's always a few drifters, bankrupt tourists, that keep coming in and you never know."

None of the escort said anything. They stared at the duty officer.

"Look," he said. "I'm not responsible. Zagagi was talking crazy, yes. But, Christ, an old man like that? I call it an act of God."

"It's not your fault," said one of the escort.

"Well, all right, then," said the duty officer, pacified.

"He stood there with his mouth open and took it," said the escort officer. He removed his crash helmet and wiped at his brow with the back of his hand. "He could have ducked. If he'd moved, we could have done something."

"That's right," said another. "I was near the old man. I would have grabbed him."

Three photographers came out from the building. They moved around on the steps to take pictures.

"Forget that," said the duty officer. He lunged for the arm of the nearest cameraman. "No shots. You'll get your clearance from Shoval."

"Shoval?" asked the photographer. "Who's he?" He was busy getting it down in a notebook.

"Foreign Office," explained the duty officer. "Big stuff." He looked down at the body. One eye was open in a sly wink as if a supremely amusing joke had been played and it was pleased with the result. The duty officer bent down and closed the lid, thumbing it over the cheek. The eyelid would not stay shut. It crept up again. The officer straightened. He said, "Gentlemen, if you don't mind,"—he held his arm out, indicating the door of the building—"we're rather busy. There was another sniping at the Gate this morning. Now, if you want the details on that, come inside."

One of the escort pulled the coat over the corpse's face. "We ought to go over there and clean them out," he said. "In the end we have to pay for them and what do they do, they snipe us."

"Yes," said the duty officer.

"They're different, that's all. They're a different kind of animal."

From where they all stood, they could see across into Jordan. The hills were clear of haze, very clear; they seemed to tower only a few miles away.

ABOUT THE AUTHOR

NATHAN ADAMS was born thirty-two years ago in New York City. He has since lived in Kenya, India, and England. More recently he worked for the *Journal-American* as a reporter and presently is on the editorial staff of the American Heritage Publishing Company. He is currently working on another novel.